Praise for Tom Avitabile's
The Eighth Day

"Frighteningly realistic. Most of Washington really works this way. Homeland Security had better read this one and take corrective action."
– U.S. Ambassador Michael Skol

"Awesome. I could not go to sleep last night because I couldn't put it down!"
– Donna Hanover, WOR Radio 710

"The author weaves a tale that will occasionally take your breath away and then cause you to sigh with relief.... He is a master wordsmith who knows the value of just the right phrase at just the right moment. His timing will keep you on the edge of your chair."
– Bill Twomey, CNG Newspaper Group

"A thriller with some insights into human behavior"
– Mel Robbins, CNBC

"I was fascinated. In fact, I had trouble putting it down one night and went to bed late so I could finish the book to see how it came out!"
– Otis Young, "All About Books," N.E.T. Radio

"A gripping and compelling read."
– *The Sun Daily*

THE HAMMER OF GOD

A NOVEL BY

TOM AVITABILE

THE STORY PLANT

This is a work of fiction. Names, characters, places, and incidents either are the product of the author's imagination or are used fictitiously. Any resemblance to actual events, locales, organizations, or persons living or dead, is entirely coincidental and beyond the intent of either the author or the publisher.

The Story Plant
Studio Digital, CT LLC
PO Box 4331
Stamford, CT 06907

Jacket design by Barbara Aronica Buck

Print ISBN-13: 978-1-61188-151-6
E-book ISBN-13: 978-1-61188-152-3

Visit our website at www.TheStoryPlant.com
Visit the author's website at www.TomAvitabile.com

First Fiction Studio Paperback Printing: April 2012
First Story Plant Paperback Printing: August 2013

Printed in the United States of America

This book is dedicated to all those who find themselves in the crosshairs of terrorism, tyranny and totalitarianism purely because they embrace freedom and cherish liberty. And to those who put themselves in the line of fire to preserve these ideals.

– Book 1 –

THE BUG

Chapter One
Highway to Heaven

The M1 motorway was already a clogged and congested artery in the awakening heart of London this early morning. Amidst the lorries, panel vans, and a host of imported cars, a small Nissan was wedged, nose-to-tail, between two big cement haulers. Inside, its occupants were finally relaxing after a successful night's work. They even had time to stop along the roadside and unfurl their prayer mats and praise Allah on the occasion of the new day. After the three months of planning and intense training, that led up to last night's successful completion, Hassad allowed his team this earned respite. This break tempered his instinct to tell Doueed, in the back seat, to lower the volume and hence the tinny racket coming from the ear buds of the young Yemeni's iPod.

"Are you pleased with our performance?" Amil asked Hassad, who was driving.

"Very smooth, very professional, all of your time in Afghanistan was good training."

"I am glad you are pleased: maybe you'll recommend us to another mission. I like the feeling of success." Amil said.

Hassad let slip a smile but then turned his head with a look of annoyance at Doueed, who didn't catch his stern eye, as he was bobbing with his head to the beat and staring out at the hideous facades of the council flats and other bad English architecture passing by his rear window. "We started a drip; Allah's will be done, it will become an ocean."

Amil, flushed with satisfaction, commented no further because Hassad, their leader, was the only one of them with field experience and so his compliment was like a graduation to him and the rest of this team.

When the "ocean" was amassed, it would be a tsunami more effective and more devastating than any other to have befallen the pompous, arrogant American bastards. An ordained act of retribution for their defying and defiling the kingdom of Allah. From this triggering point forward, they would have to do nothing. The system would ensure the extermination of at least 10 million, maybe 100 million, of the soulless Infidels.

Hassad focused on the glow of the morning sun rising, inhaled and then said, "It is a divine irony..."

Amil turned with amazement because Hassad never spoke without first having been prompted.

The leader continued, "The people of the West love their systems; they place their trust in numbers, science, and manmade laws. Soon they would be humbled and learn that a man should only place his trust in Allah." He looked to Doueed in the rear view mirror, "Doueed! Turn that thing down!" He barked trying to penetrate the headphones, then continued in the somber voice of an Imam at a funeral, "Only the Koran speaks for God, through the laws of Muhammad himself. Solely through Islam lay the one path to God and the glory of his kingdom. All other roads are destined to destruction at the hands of Allah."

Those in the car nodded in reverence and deep belief. Hassad knew the hand of God had guided them this night, even when, as in this case, Allah was surely working through the unworthy hands of Hassad Baracus.

Now that their mission was complete, all that remained was for Hassad and his team to wait a few days, and then, one by one, innocently leave Britain headed for various "friendly" regimes. In two weeks time, they would all meet in the Sudan, secure in the knowledge that no one in the world would be any the wiser about their part in the mission. Their safe house, the London home of a true believer, proved to be the perfect base for their operation. Their host, not knowing their actual mission, believed them to be students on a spiritual quest with the local Sheik from a Knightsbridge mosque.

In total, the plan was perfection. Allah be praised!

Then it happened. There was a break in the traffic and the vehicles all picked up speed. Doueed put the ear buds back in and turned it up. Rounding a bend, with the morning sun obliterating the windscreen, Hassad went to turn to admonish the youth again about the racket, when he caught a glimpse of a brake light and reacted quickly – and just in time – as the truck ahead had hit its air brakes and lurched to a stop. His fast reaction narrowly avoided wedging the nose of the Nissan under the rear of the truck's carriage. Unfortunately, the truck driver behind him wasn't as quick. The rule of maximum gross weight being what it is, the one-ton Nissan collapsed from the impact of the 30-ton cement truck. The jolt shattered the windscreen and side windows as the car's frame buckled from the front and rear as if in a giant vise. Hassad was bludgeoned by the air bag exploding out of the center of the steering wheel as the engine compartment accordioned into a flattened hulk. Amil, next to him, was knocked unconscious by a similar concussive blast from the passenger bag. Sarim and Doueed in the back were crushed by the flattening of the Nissan's rear under the wheels of the huge truck. The pressure of the back seat folding in on them, made them explosively vomit blood and parts of their intestines, which sprayed all over the front seat and its occupants.

The two truck drivers ran to the car crushed between their vehicles. Quickly surmising that the two in the back were dead, they felt the necks of the two in the front seat. The driver was dead but the passenger was still breathing. The trucker held the passenger's face into the airbag until he too stopped breathing. The other one reached into the front seat and removed the map of Liverpool and the thermos bottle from between the seats. He climbed up the back of the mixer and threw the thermos into the aggregate mix, sealing in cement its deadly viral residue forever. They then feigned panic. Flagging down anyone to help.

Traffic was at a standstill for more than two hours.

∞§∞

In Liverpool that morning, the plant opened promptly at 8:00 a.m. Production was fully underway as it had been for most of the year. The big pharmaceutical contract had given new life to the factory and most of the local workforce. Bryan Jennings, the plant manager, expected a routine day. His calendar showed a morning visit by the Ministry of Health's inspectors. Same as every week for the last 20 weeks of production. Jennings was proud of his line: 100 days of two-shift, full-run production, and not so much as ten minutes lost. That was because he ran a tight and clean ship. He instituted work rules that called for the periodic maintenance and sterilizing of the line at half-shift intervals. He doubled the number of quality control samplings and created a worker incentive program to keep things running smoothly and efficiently.

It was around 11 a.m. when the inspectors arrived. He led them right to the QC lab. Midway to the clean room, inspector 537 asked, "May we sample right from the line this time?"

That request threw Bryan a bit. For the last twenty weeks, the inspectors were satisfied that his quality control lab held more than adequate daily samplings for them to test. Although couched as a request, Bryan knew that it was actually an order. To maintain decorum, he acquiesced, holding himself back from inquiring about the change of procedure. Bryan knew the inspectors were not bound by law to offer him an explanation or a reason. In fact, they had been very reasonable in not springing any snap inspections or undercover investigations on him thus far. He watched from his office overlooking the floor as the line was stopped, while the inspectors withdrew and sealed samples of the serum from three points along the manufacturing process.

When they finished, a claxon sounded. The next 100 bottles would have to be trashed as a precaution against any variation in the process that came from restarting the line. Bryan didn't give a moment's thought to the waste. He did, however, continue to wonder about the change of pattern of the inspectors. Later that day, as he was compiling his daily report, Bryan mentioned this anomaly. But he was confident of his workers, machines, and systems, so the mention was merely a footnote.

∞§∞

At the morgue, the London police were baffled that no relatives came forward to claim the four deceased Middle Eastern men from the wreck the day before. A check of their papers indicated that one DOA was Egyptian and another Saudi. The two men riding in the back were both Yemeni. The Knightsbridge address that one of them had on him was the only available information about their local whereabouts. Immigration confirmed that they gave the same address on their entry forms when they disembarked their various aircraft.

At around six p.m., the owner of the house at that address returned to find a car from Scotland Yard idling by the curb. All Mustafa Nasser could tell the authorities was that the four men lived in the apartment downstairs for two months and were religious students. A search of the apartment led to nothing with which to notify next of kin. It was decided that the entire matter would be turned over to the Office of the Foreign Secretary. The two drivers of the cement trucks did not have their status questioned and so it was never discovered that the company they drove for was connected through circuitous routes of finance to Bin Laden Construction.

Those reviewing the case decided it was nothing more than a most unfortunate accident. And so it was entered into the official coroner's records and police files. Sealed in that file, destined never to be opened again, was any hope of the authorities divining the men's true reason for being in Liverpool that night.

CHAPTER TWO
PHANTOM DOWN

Edicts from the office of the Surgeon General of the United States tend to cause havoc or calm in a medical community comprising doctors, nurses, and hospitals, as well as major multi-national corporations, governmental industrial policymakers, and a wide variety of others with financial and social interests. "Take nothing lightly" was the oath that supplanted the Hippocratic Oath for the doctor who became Surgeon General. So it was with more than mild interest that Judith Pearson, the current occupant of the office, read the final report from the "guessers." They were advocating a major focus on a strain of *catalysis barracylium* as the epicenter of this year's flu vaccines. Every year the flu virus metamorphoses into strains different from the year before. Using worldwide data ranging from random blood testing to the mortality rate of sparrows in Asia, the "guessers" guess which strain will take the lead in this year's round of epidemiology. Impressively, the prognosticators at the Center for Disease Control in Atlanta had a good track record of nailing the ever-changing bugs.

Judith initialed the document and put it in her outbox and then went on to review a report on new techniques for laparoscopic surgery. It would be a day of reading and catching up on "the pile." The only other thing on her calendar was dinner tonight with the President's science advisor, William Hiccock.

∞§∞

A few blocks away at the White House, Bill Hiccock's day was filled with committee meetings and one-on-ones with various members of the scientific community, each auditioning some new innovation, discipline, or discovery for Bill's (and, by extension, the President's) blessing. Bill used to look forward to high-level discussions and theoretical postulates like these. But ever since he became the sharp end of the scientific stick for the government, he could no longer enjoy the pure science of it. The "political science" of it had contaminated the game. Now he needed to identify the underlying agenda of the presenter. Bill could only set science policy and fund internal administration policies. He couldn't muster a dime for a third-party test tube without Congressional funding. This was where the politics really came in. There were only three men of science in the entire body, two MDs, long out of practice, and a former civil engineer. Most of the rest were lawyers. As far as Bill knew, none of them was ever elected for spending money on "Big Science." That meant that even a cure for cancer would have to undergo the political proctoscope.

A welcome interruption was the call from his ex-wife and current girlfriend (not to mention head of psychology at George Washington University), Janice Hiccock.

"Don't forget we have dinner with the Pearsons at eight."

"No problem. It's a regular day, so I should be home by seven or so. Should I pick up anything?"

"No. I have everything... maybe some white wine. We only have the two bottles left from last month."

"Got it. See ya later...love you."

"Love you too..."

As Bill hung up the phone, his aide Cheryl entered his office and announced it was time for his next meeting, handing him the briefing folder. He started to leave his office, then abruptly returned to his desk and jotted "Pinot Grigio" on his desk calendar.

There was a noise in the outer corridor, but Bill barely paid attention to it – until his national assets monitor went off. He never did learn all of the code words, but the CRT that listed each member of the administration indicated that Phantom (the President's Secret Service name) had switched from a green "OK" to a red "down." Bill barely had time to register this before a Secret Service agent entered his room flashing his ID.

"Sir, I am Agent Somers; you need to come with me right now."

"What's the..."

"Now, sir." The agent put a vise-like grip on Hiccock's arm and led him down the hall to the elevator. To Hiccock's surprise, the elevator went down.

"Now can you tell me what's going on?"

"We're in lockdown, sir. You hold an NCA ranking and need to be made nuclear safe."

The words "nuclear safe" didn't have as much of a chilling effect on Hiccock's spine as he would have imagined. His first thought was whether he told Janice that he loved her at the end of their phone call. The elevator landed and opened to an antiseptic hallway. There, another agent waited with his hand on an earpiece. Agent Somers handed Bill over.

"Follow me," the new agent said. He turned and walked to the end of the hall. "May I see your ID, sir?"

Bill fished it out of his wallet. The agent inspected the green dot added to his card after President Mitchell and he had an adventure aboard the *USS Princeton*. The man then checked the photo against Bill's face in the most non-personable way Bill had ever seen.

"Look in here with your right eye, sir. Focus on the red spot in the center and hold it there till it beeps."

Bill knew the device was scanning his retina. The agent then spoke into his sleeve-mounted microphone. "Sitch Room entrance; Quarterback confirmed."

Bill had never heard his Secret Service code name spoken aloud before. There was a mechanical sound and the door before them unlatched. Behind it was a marine with his hand on the butt of an M-4 in a quick-draw holster. The agent held up Bill's ID to the "gyrine" who used his own retinas to scan Bill's features and make the low-tech decision that Bill was not a duplicitous foreign national or some such dime novel bullshit. The little portico they stood in opened onto the world's most dangerous conference room, located in the Situation Room in the basement of the White House.

A woman he had not met before greeted Bill, introducing herself as Assistant National Security Advisor Reese. "Mr. Hiccock, sit here please."

There were two other men in the room, the Secretaries of Treasury and Homeland Security. Bill looked at the seat at the head of the table. The desk plaque read, POTUS. The current designee of that seat, the President of the United States, had survived a historical Congressional challenge in the aftermath of an election scandal that Bill had revealed. But James Mitchell's luck never failed him as a fighter pilot during Desert Storm and it didn't fail him in the trenches of possible impeachment. The main witness in defense of Mitchell was Professor Robert Parnes, the architect of the Internet process that had millions of Americans unintentionally vote for Mitchell. He testified that at no time was Mitchell or his campaign aware of or in any way involved in the process. At the same time, the American public considered Mitchell the heroic leader who stopped the worst wave of terrorist attacks that had ever beset the country. There wasn't a drop of public sentiment looking for his head on a pole. Congress, not being deaf to this public adulation, quickly mopped up the proceedings after Parnes' admissions. The country then went back to its business and Mitchell went back to work.

The door opened again and the Secretaries of Defense and State entered to the same scrutiny that Bill received, despite their internationally known visages. In front of Bill was a booklet entitled "Crisis Team Management." He noticed it had been updated a week earlier and below the date read, "#26 William Hiccock." The number related to his ordinal ranking in the echelon of succession to the President in terms of the National Command Authority. Despite the constitutional order of succession for actually being President, the Cold War architects of Mutually Assured Destruction decided to mix up the deck a little by allowing the creation of the NCA, peopled at the pleasure of the President. Technically, the Chief Executive could appoint any U.S.-born citizen, from the Vice President to a dogcatcher in Duluth to the order of succession to "the button." Therefore, if the twenty-five people on the list ahead of Bill were to meet their maker as nuked crispy critters, the decision and authority to launch a nuclear war or retaliation would fall to him. Billy Hiccock, the kid from the Bronx, who could throw a football well enough to win a Heisman at Stanford and throw numbers around well enough to earn a Doctor of Scientific Methodology from M.I.T. and become the President's trusted science advisor, was now in line to destroy the world. Wouldn't mom be proud! The awesome powers of that responsibility made the number twenty-six seem as daunting as if the number were two.

Within five minutes, there were fourteen key NCA designees in the room in addition to staff and technicians. Bill knew that six other NCA assets were linked to the room from various "safe locations." The Vice President called in from his ultimate nuclear-safe perch, Air Force 2, at 35,000 feet above Indianapolis.

The Chief of Staff entered and took his seat in the chair reserved for the President. He quickly scanned a clipboard, nodded, and then removed his glasses.

"First let me tell you that this is a drill. The President is fine and in no danger. Second, our response time is up from the last National Emergency Simulation Exercise. We beat our old mark by a minute and a half with eighteen NCA members secured within four minutes of the emergency action message transmission. For those of you who have been through this a couple times, thank you, and you can return to your duties. For Mr. Hiccock, Mr. Rassing, and Mrs. Chulk, I am going to ask you to stay and let the team familiarize you with what happens when we crash the White House like this."

Hiccock breathed easy. The world was safe for now. No attack/counterattack scenarios to wipe out all life as we know it. Just a few more procedures for him to learn and, no doubt, a few more nightmares to have. He spent the next forty-five minutes learning about SIOP, Pave Paws, authenticator codes, and other stuff most people thought went away with the Cold War.

∞§∞

Meanwhile, Surgeon General Judy Pearson was studying a report titled *The Treatment of Infant Pancreatic Cancer through Genetically Engineered Cell Remanufacture* when her deputy barged into her office.

"What's up, Bob?"

"Bad news, boss."

When her deputy finished giving her the details, Pearson's immediate instinct was to call the White House. Instead, her eyes fell on her calendar and her impending dinner. She decided she'd prepare for dinner early.

"Bob, get me a copy of H.R. 7631 – stat!"

∞§∞

It was no ordinary jar of cold cream. The Princess Briana label insured that only the faces of the most well-to-do women would ever feel its deep-cleansing emollients tingle as it beautified, moisturized, and rejuvenated their already too-well-pampered skin.

Chang Su admired the work of her team. They were specially chosen to make this jar by the commissar of the village who was also the head of the factory. It was an honor to serve the PRC in this fashion. Normally she would copy lesser brands and then the factory would run thousands of cases. In this case, though, her instructions were to make only twenty-four of these. They were perfect replicas of the actual jar in every way except that they were 1/32nd of an inch smaller than the original because they were made from a different material. The label was easier to resize but the unique jar required three attempts to get just right. Capitalism not being embraced in China, she never calculated the cost per unit benefit of such an intense effort to derive so few jars. The intended customer however, was glad to pay as much for two dozen jars as others paid for a whole truckload of the knockoffs that had become the stock in trade of the new Chinese economy. The amber colored jars were packed for shipment and tomorrow would be driven by truck four hundred miles to the provincial capital where they would then be sent by airplane to Beijing.

Another job well done.

CHAPTER THREE
COMPOUNDS AND ELEMENTS

For Bill, dinner that night was pleasant but uneventful. How can a mere dinner compete with a call to the Situation Room to possibly save or end the world? Their guests were the Surgeon General, Judy Pearson, and her husband, Rod, a thoracic genius and head of surgery at George Washington University Hospital. Janice had recently joined the staff there, so to Bill's way of thinking, this was a four-point connect with Judy and Bill working for the current President and Janice and Rod working in a hospital named after the first.

After dinner, Bill found Rod in the living room, pursuing the artifacts in the "shrine:" what Janice and he called the wall of built-in bookcases that held the mementos of Bill's illustrious college football career.

"I saw that game!"

Bill looked to see what Rod was talking about. He was looking at a game ball and a picture of his team. "I got knocked out in the first half, sat out two quarters until the team doc pronounced that I only had my bell rung, no concussion."

"Yeah, and you came back with a vengeance. Two touchdown passes in the last four minutes!"

Three, Bill corrected in his head but let it go, "I had a great line taking the hits for me. I guess my having been knocked out of the game earlier brought out their paternal instincts to protect me."

Rod swooned as he turned to Bill's Heisman Trophy. "How great must it be to have one of these?"

"I was offered two million for it by some oil tycoon," Bill said matter-of-factly as he got "the look" from Janice, who was chatting up Judy on the sectional. "I guess they were all out of them on E-bay," Bill added.

"How can you put a price on something like this," Rod said, marveling at the trophy even more.

"You know, if you like it that much, you can borrow it and put it over the fireplace."

Out of the corner of his eye Bill saw "the look" again. He knew it was because Janice wanted them over by the new couch. Mostly because she liked the way, from the new seating area, the living room windows looked out upon the sun setting on the lake at this time of day.

"Judy, would never let me do that, unless you can convince her somehow that it's Chinese modern."

That little man-to-man admission made Bill wonder if a surgeon being married to the Surgeon General caused a problem. Could Judy pull rank and order her husband around? And was he duty bound to follow her directives? *Clean the windows, drive my mother to the store, book a trip to Hawaii.* Nah, no surgeon ever got henpecked.

"Bill, will you get the cognac and the glasses from the cabinet?" came the order from Bill's "general."

As Bill poured the cognac into the decanter, Judy couldn't help but comment, "Janice, I have to know, did you use a decorator? I love the way this room just flows. That chair is perfect, and situating this area to take full advantage of this breathtaking view... all of it, really comfortable, yet beautifully done."

Janice was beaming and gave the slightest of looks to Bill when Judy mentioned "her view." "I am so glad you like it. I pretty much just start with some ideas that I get from magazines and then add a few touches."

After several minutes discussing home decorating, remodeling and Chinese modern motif, Judy opened a new conversation. "There could be a shortage of flu vaccine this season."

"How could something like that happen?"

"How all bad things happen, Bill – politics."

"I think I am going to enjoy this," Janice said swirling the contents of the decanter.

"There won't be a final opinion until Monday," Judy continued, "but preliminary reports indicate that our British supplier may have been sending us contaminated batches."

"How is that even possible?"

"Could be shoddy adherence to quality control."

"Or sabotage." Rod added.

Bill glanced over at Rod. "Why would you say that?"

"I know that company; they took over a plant in Liverpool that had some problems in the past, but they revamped the management, kicked out the dead wood, and were doing well for almost a year. This could have been the work of some disgruntled employee they cut when they took over."

Judy shook her head in frustration. "In any event, these production issues could render half of our vaccines useless."

"Half?" Bill said.

"It will take six months to test all known shipments of this vaccine. That will freeze half our inventory and put us well past this year's flu season."

"And how does England play into keeping America healthy?"

"Better living through geo-politics. It seems we needed to send more trade to England, so a whole handful of stuff that the U.S. made was suddenly outsourced to the U.K."

"For England's support for the war in Iraq, I bet?" Janice said.

"That didn't hurt, but this policy can be traced back to the 90's. Anyway, if the British supply is tainted, then millions of Americans will be unprotected this year. I had some preliminary projections run and it could mean 25,000 more deaths in the high-risk groups."

Bill shook his head. "I still can't believe we don't make enough vaccines here."

"We used to make enough, but over-regulation and pork barrel Congressional hooey left the U.S. high and dry and the drug companies became reluctant to do risky cost-plus contracts with the government without protection from litigation."

"Add to that Congress, being full of lawyers and 'wanna-be' lawyers, launching liability insurance into orbit for any company that still wanted to produce drugs in this country," injected Janice who had felt the sting of prohibitive malpractice rates in her own profession.

"How long would it take to retool another source?" Hiccock asked.

"Retooling is what Detroit does," Rod said. "It takes the Motor City seven years to change a design. The drug industry isn't even close to that. It takes twenty years to bring a new drug to market." Rod finished his Pinot Grigio, got up, and walked over to the dry bar. "Can I refresh yours, Bill?"

"No thanks; I'm good." He looked back to Judy. "I'm missing something. We already have the drug. We just need to replicate it."

Judy's eyebrows arched and then she set the hook. "That's where you can help."

"Me?"

"Get the President to fast-track the Prescription Medications Emergency act."

"I've never even heard of it."

"I left a copy of H.R. 7631 out in the foyer. It should make for a good bedtime story."

Bill sat and let the last swallow of cognac dissolve in his mouth. "Was I just set up?"

"Aw Bill, would a friend do that?"

∞§∞

Thud. Five pounds of legislation, addendums, and amendments makes a considerable sound when heaved onto a nightstand at 1:30 a.m. Bill's miscalculation in throw weight startled Janice out of a deep sleep.

"What's going on…? Why are you still up?"

"Next time friends are coming over with homework let's remember not to serve wine, or serve them dinner either. In fact, let's never have them over again."

"Sounds like you have a real page-turner of a bill there."

"Who writes this stuff?"

"Every prescription drug company in the world, or their lobbyists. Now go to sleep; that's enough civics class for one night. I am expecting a slammer of a headache tomorrow and I want to be well rested for it." Janice reached across him and up to the lamp on the nightstand. Her breast smothered his face as she strained for the switch. She uncoiled back to her side, fluffing her pillow, and trying to get back to sleep.

Bill started thinking. A few years back, that would have been enough provocation to initiate some serious lovemaking. Why not now?

Why not *now?*

He snuggled over, found her, and ended any concern about a headache.

∞§∞

"Seventy-two hours. That still leaves a twelve-hour margin of safety."

"And the thermal element itself?"

"Time released and not unlike the basic structure of heated shave cream."

"No chance of detection?"

"Our Chinese friends and their Pyrex glass copies will insulate the contents."

"Then we are ready?"

"Yes; we just need to place the active strains in all twenty-four jars."

"Keep me informed when the shipment is ready?"

"Yes, Sheik."

∞§∞

The next morning, Bill put out a Point of Information bulletin over his SCIAD network. The network was one of his inventions. In much the same way national security depended on the free and open exchange of data, ideas, and suppositions between agencies, so did a strong scientific defense. He had seen first hand the impact of the first big-science attack on America and it wasn't pretty. It took a long time even to determine that America was being attacked and people paid for that with their lives. A network like SCIAD might have made a dramatic difference.

The name was a double-entendre of sorts; SCIAD was the shorthand for his White House role, but like all scientists, Hiccock acronymed it out: <u>S</u>cientific <u>C</u>ommunity <u>I</u>nvolved in <u>A</u>merica's <u>D</u>efense. Because it was his pet project, and because very few in Congress or the Administration understood the first thing about it, he was able to make up all the ground rules. Bill was proud of SCIAD's layered architecture, which guided the flow of ideas. The real trick that kept SCIAD from denigrating into nothing more than an Intranet version of the Internet was its structure. It was all too simple for any jackass to publish anything on the web, without provenance, peer review, or proper methodology. Add to that the wonders of PhotoShop and other graphic programs, and any "whack job" can make their junk science look as good as real science.

The SCIAD network had built-in gatekeeping and content filtering, with verification and authentication.

In Bill's on-line scientific community, there were two levels - rings, actually. The closely held ring consisted of members Bill had code-named "Element." Members of the second, farther out (in more ways than one) ring were classified as "Compounds." Hiccock's SCIAD handle was Nucleus, although everyone knew it was Bill.

There were ninety-two members of SCIAD's Element ring. They were FBI vetted and cleared to see top-secret SCIAD traffic at its most raw and unedited state. Their primary job was that of gatekeeper to Nucleus. Two Element members had to concur on a thesis, proof, or speculation before it was transmitted to Nucleus. Bill then had the option to send it back to the entire Element ring for comment.

There were now nearly three hundred Compound members on the network, individuals who didn't have the squeaky clean, flag-waving backgrounds or citizenship to pass National Security scrutiny but had unbelievable minds nonetheless. What America desperately needed in scientific defense was mental horsepower and the Compounds provided it. They were privy only to redacted information. None of which would compromise Nat Sec, but it would get their mental engines going. As with the Element ring, in the event a Compound member came up with any significant thinking, that member also had to be vetted by at least two Element members before dissemination to Nucleus and then out to the entire Element level. As a further hedge bet, Bill then had it all fly back out to the outer ring once again, as redacted information about this new item. This then allowed all 300 Compounds to kick it around before shooting it back inside to the Element ring again. This looping of data and vetting by at least two Element class members kept down the wild, off-the-charts speculation that could clog a system.

Yet, because Bill made his bones on "wild ass speculation" in The Eighth Day affair, he didn't want it stifled completely.

On the technical side, this data ring was grand slam and whiz bang with the latest interconnectivity protocol, layers of protection, and some stuff private industry would kill for, like real-time link-up to supercomputers, big fat pipes to download hi-def, and 3D video and images in real-time, satellite imagery, and real-time geologic, thermologic, and electronic signature analysis. All of these tools and tech marvels sprang forth as the illegitimate love child of Bill's shotgun wedding of a former felon in computer crimes – a character who liked to be called Kronos – and the best computer guy the government had. These two *techno sapiens*, left to their own crazy devices and aided by some off-budget funding, built him a ring system that would have been the envy of any hacker, programmer, or tech mogul on the planet...if they knew about it. Of course, no one did. The whole technical side was invisible. Stealth digits, flying around the Internet as a sort of "digital aerosol" sprayed across the web, seemingly never to be condensed again, except by the 392, retinal-scan-protected condenser/expanders out there.

Hiccock's ex-wife Janice was an Element level member but he waived her $50K yearly honorarium fee paid to the members, to avoid raising eyebrows. His old schoolyard chum and ex-FBI agent, Joey Palumbo, handled interfacing with his former agency on the vetting process of members and was in charge of ring security for Bill. Even though Joey was a crucial part of Bill's success in the last science attack, the Bureau had its ways. Joey had spoken above his grade to the then-Director of the FBI – in front of the President's Chief of Staff, no less. His agency career ended at that moment. Bill dragged him kicking and screaming back into Washington, specifically for SCIAD.

Then there was one that got away. Bill would have wanted this person to run the whole thing, even over himself, but that was never going to happen. Rear Admiral Parks was a crusty octogenarian with a mind that beat out the most sophisticated evil science ever stumbled upon. *Hell, forget about getting her in the ring system. I couldn't even get her to hit the power switch on a computer.*

It was a great loss to the country, but she'd paid her dues and won her right to privacy a million fold. Still, Hiccock knew she'd have torn up the rings like a teenager doing donuts in a K-Mart parking lot.

> To: all E and C ring members:
> From: n
> Looking for possible exploitation opportunities by enemies, foreign and domestic, of potential flu vaccine shortage. Focus not limited to vulnerabilities or soft targets, but to any and all ramifications that could be leveraged against us. Timeframe is loose. No specific threats or intel to support above, just pure spec.

∞§∞

The little scientific notation letters were a favorite among the scientific elite, so Bill used them at every opportunity. He allowed the red line of the retinal scanner, which was identical to all the others on the ring, to interrogate his iris one more time in response to his hitting the return key to send the message. This was a double way of ensuring that even if a person walked away from a hooked-up computer, no actions, downloading, uploading, or opening a file could occur without the ring system knowing that the cleared person was initiating the action. "Action Approved: Nucleus" popped onto the screen and then it went blank. The computer in front of Bill had no idea it had just handled ring traffic. The ring was an engine that treated any computer like a dumb terminal. All interaction and work done on the ring was accessed and processed within the ring. No cookies, saved copies, or backups to any local drives or servers. As far as the PC on his desk was concerned the last three minutes and fourteen seconds that he spent on the ring never happened.

Realizing he had two minutes until a staff meeting, Bill picked up the new legislation that spent the night on his bedside table and walked out, smiling with a little more pep in his step because of the way he'd spent the rest of his night.

At the meeting, he re-tasked his White House team to get all the pros and cons on the fast-tracked legislation ready for a position paper to the President in three days. Cheryl had stitched in an addendum to this morning's agenda titled "Crisis Management."

"Cheryl, what's this last item?"

"Yesterday you disappeared. In the event of a real emergency you need to appoint an order of succession so we can still function and be of service if the President or whoever, needs Sci during the crisis."

"Good point. Great point! I'll work on a short list and we'll kick it around tomorrow." Turning to the others, he said, "Anything else? Good, then on with your day people."

As he was leaving the room, Cheryl came over and gave him the look that meant *wait until the others leave.* Even though the room was now empty, she spoke in low tones.

"Mr. Hiccock, I hope you don't mind me bringing this up, but I have lived through a couple of White House crashes before and I thought..."

"Cheryl, I meant what I said. It's a great point you made and I thank you for bringing it up."

"Actually, I was hoping you'd make me your second."

This is why he liked having Cheryl as his assistant. She saw things from the helicopter and very often from the ground up at the same time. "I'll have to check if you would be eligible."

"I reviewed the guidelines. I qualify and section seven specifies it's totally your call."

"Well at least you're not pressuring me."

"During a crisis, if you become President it will just be about running things and making sure information flows. We are not going to be entering into new science areas. I know the machinery and where and when to kick it."

"Again, all good points. Let me think it over."

"Okay fine."

"Wait. What if I don't choose you?"

"Then I'll know you had a good reason and I'll accept it."

She got up and left. Bill felt uncomfortable but didn't know why.

A little bell went off in his head and he redirected his attention to the phone on his desk. He hit the auto dial, "Hi Hon, listen I was thinking about the Indian place on K Street tonight."

"Oh Bill, I don't think I am up for it. I've been dragging all morning. What do you say we just stay in tonight and hang low?"

"Sure, Babe. Are you feeling okay?"

"Yeah, probably just... I dunno; I am not really up for anything."

"Good enough. I should be home by seven. Love you."

"Love you too."

CHAPTER FOUR
DEADLY LIAISONS

Alzir El Benhan was pleased. The handoff of his Chinese package, from the Sudanese government courier, traveling under diplomatic immunity, went flawlessly at the cabstand of JFK's International Arrivals Terminal Four. Both men acted out agreeing to "share" the same cab to New York. Although the courier went on to New York, he dropped El-Benhan off at one of the low-end motels on the access road to the airport.

The clerk at the motel outside JFK greedily accepted his cash advance payment for a block of twenty-four rooms this Saturday, three days hence. In his attaché case were twenty-two domestic round-trip tickets. One to each town in which the National Football League played that weekend along with a few other well-chosen towns, most of them with subways. The delivery of the jars shipped from Beijing to Africa and then to him was the last piece needed for Saturday's meeting. Between Sunday afternoon and the morning rush hour the next day, their work – Allah's work – would be done.

∞§∞

"Feeling any better?" Bill said, kissing Janice on the forehead as she burrowed into the corner arm of the couch with her feet up on the hassock.

"Yeah, a little. How was your day?"

"Better than yours, except Cheryl blindsided me with something and I don't know how I am going to handle it."

"She wants a raise?"

"No, she wants my job."

"Did you tell her you aren't finished with it yet?"

"Not exactly that, no. Want me to make you some tea?"

"Ooooh yeah, that would be perfect."

"Back in a nanosecond."

As Bill filled the teapot from the plastic spring water jug, Janice appeared at the kitchen door. "Bill, what are we doing?"

"Well, water boils at 212 degrees Fahrenheit or 100 degrees Celsius, so I am about to attempt to achieve that phenomenon."

"I think you know that wasn't what I was asking. I mean what are *we* doing *here*, living together like kids again."

Bill placed the pot on the burner and maxed the knob. When the gas caught, he backed off the setting, silencing the clicking of the spark generator. He knew more about the workings of the stove than about the workings of the woman who obviously wanted to have a very serious discussion with him. "Let's go back inside."

They settled on the couch. Bill stroked Janice's hair with his outstretched arm. She caught his hand and ran it past her cheek before kissing it. Then she nestled it in the crook of her neck with the gentle urge for him to rub her there.

"What's on your mind, Babe?" Bill said as he did what she urged.

"I'm not sure where this is going. Are we going to get married again or just live together? I don't know why, but right now the answer seems very important to me."

Bill rubbed Janice's neck harder. "Janice, when we found each other again, it was a miracle. Maybe the first time around for us wasn't the best because I wasn't ready, wasn't aware of what a true relationship with someone meant. I didn't bring any tools with me to fix any of the little things that you need to fix to keep two people together."

He stopped rubbing and turned toward her. "But now, thanks to you, I feel I am ready to try again. If you'll have me, again."

Janice tilted her head. "Bill, are you proposing?"

"Here wait; let me make it official." He slid off the couch, got down on one knee, grabbed her hand, kissed it, and said, "Janice, I lost you once. I never want to lose you again. I love you. I love you more than I love myself and I need to be with you every day. Janice, if you'll have me again, will you marry me, again?"

"Oh, Bill," she hugged him so hard that she slid from the couch and joined him on the floor. He held her tight and he felt her begin to cry. He continued to hold her with his eyes closed until her breathing settled.

A few minutes later, she spoke softly, "When we were almost killed, looking into your eyes gave me courage. It gave me the strength to come through that horrible time. I knew then how much I loved you and that I always had. Yes, yes, let's get married – sooner rather than later."

They kissed and rolled on the floor. Bill was on top when he broke off the kiss, smoothed her hair, and looked into Janice's eyes. "We are going to make this a wonderful life. Just you and me." They kissed again.

The teapot attempted to disturb the moment. They let it boil.

∞§∞

For no particular reason, Bill's eyes sprung open at 4:30 a.m., an hour before the alarm was set to go off. He rolled over and saw Janice in a restless sleep. He put his hand on her shoulder and that seemed to calm her somewhat. He kept his hand on her for a moment, thinking about how their lives had changed last night. Then he rose from bed and made his way into the den.

Might as well get a jump on the day, he thought, hitting the startup key on his secure home computer and then going into the kitchen to make coffee. When he returned, he checked his inbox, finding the usual array of mail and memos. He spent some time answering and redirecting some of it, then decided to look in on SCIAD, using his home-based retinal scan device. His inquiry of the previous day created a torrent of activity. Three, however, came with Element priority. According to his own rules, he'd open those.

The first response was a thoughtful dissertation on nefarious forces masking a biological attack under the haze of an influenza outbreak caused by the lack of vaccine. The gist of the piece was that public health authorities would have been slow to ferret out the biological attack agent from the thousands who would fall victim in the normal course of time. In biological attacks, time is the enemy. Contaminants and agents must be identified, then quarantined, and then eradicated. The longer it took to realize an attack was taking place, the bigger the attack got. He bookmarked this message and used the comment tool to highlight "time is the enemy" in yellow. He'd go back to his one later.

The second message dealt with the need to harden the notification network of first responders. Here the emphasis was on preventing outside forces from affecting or skewing our biologic reporting system, blinding us from the severity of the outbreak and having the same effect as giving a natural virus more time to spread throughout the population. Bill decided to have that one redacted and released back to the outer compound rings for further comment.

The last position paper was a bone chiller. It was a short list of known viral strains, both natural and synthetic, that could wreak havoc in a poorly inoculated population. Lots of nasty little bugs nestled in labs and in arms factories all over the world. They were all deadly but, thank God, all very delicate. Some would die in direct sunlight. Others had no tolerance for temperature swings. Some hated smog while rain rendered a few strains impotent. The fragile nature of most of these viruses eliminated their possible use as weapons. But a few were robust enough to scare the bejesus out of anti-biological response teams.

One particularly nasty little bugger was HCD Complex 33, a synthetic strain that needed to be incubated right up until its time of release. The heat of the human body was incubation enough, but the Complex 33 had to get into the body from a warm source to begin with and that wasn't that easy. Sunlight killed it. UV actually. So you couldn't just release it in a warm climate. However, once it was inside a person, it spread by the simple act of breathing. Then the next victim's internal heat incubated it for the next migration through the new host's breathing patterns.

Bill read the blurb again to make sure he understood that in order to start the chain of infection you'd have had to set it inside a body from an incubated environment intentionally. Then he put the message at the top of the list. He wanted everyone's thoughts on this. Pronto.

He was about to call up some position papers by the NIH when the sound of retching made him fly back to the bedroom. He saw Janice in their bathroom bent over the bowl throwing up. At a time like this, a man makes a choice, one that will either dog him or herald him for decades to come. Bill chose wisely. He pulled back Janice's hair, placed a gentle hand on her upper back, and was ready with a damp washcloth when she was able to stand again. He then guided her by the shoulders back to bed and sat alongside her.

"You okay?"

"I don't know what happened."

"You were pretty restless all night."

"I can't imagine what got into me."

"Probably some bug or twenty-four-hour thing."

He spoke reassuringly, but inside, Bill's silent alarm went off. *This is how it would happen.* Thousands of Americans dismissing the first sign of an attack as a bug or bad sushi. He got another washcloth, wet it down, and laid it on Janice's brow.

"Rest. I'll call in for you."

"Just give me a minute or two, I'll be okay."

A half-hour later, Janice was ready to get dressed and start her day. She headed off to work, but only after Bill made her promise to see a doctor later.

∞§∞

At 7:30 a.m. from his office phone, Bill called Judy, America's "MD #1." By 8:00, she was in his conference room.

"What's the gestation period of the kind of influenza we are going to get hit with this season?"

"Thirty-six to forty-eight hours from the time of infection, depending on the antibodies and general health of the exposed."

"Ever hear of HD Complex 33?"

"Whoa. Yes. Very nasty, a super-strain on steroids. Helped along by synthetic technology. And unfortunately that genie is out of the bottle. We couldn't stop the propagation of the synthesis process because it was Chinese-Soviet research initially. When the Soviet Union went down the papers got out."

"So why isn't this more of a concern? I mean, I just learned of it." Hiccock asked as he tapped the printed out email in front of him.

"The only good thing is it is very unstable outside the host and not easily transported. Can I ask why you brought it up?"

"What would the gestation period of Complex 33 be?"

"Again it's supercharged; maybe twenty minutes."

"So how long would it take before our public health system was alerted to any spikes in influenza with a normal virus?"

"I know you are going to tell me why you are asking me, but three to four days is the generally accepted timeframe for confirmation of a major event."

"Roughly twice the gestation time. So if we were hit with Complex 33, the confirmation time would be forty minutes?"

"I see where you're going, but let me call in the boys at CDC. They have some epidemiological data sprays on stuff like this." She picked up the phone and dialed. "You know, if you think this agent is in play, you are duty bound by law to inform my office."

"I assure you all of this is just speculation, a big what-if."

She nodded to the computer. "Is this an exercise in your SCIAD group?"

"Yep. Just egghead stuff. For now."

"Let's hope it stays that way." She drew her attention toward the phone. "Hello George, Judy. Can you flashnet over to Mr. Hiccock's office the first three tiers of the EP study you ran for me last week? Oh and George one more thing, does Complex 33 have a dormant quotient? Uh hum. I see. Okay, get back to me fast."

She hung up the phone. "You better hope it stays an exercise, Bill. Complex 33 has a dormant quotient."

"Which means?"

"It can lie dormant inside the host for up to seventy-two hours before any signs occur. Yet unlike natural viral structures, it remains infectious while it's napping."

"So that means we have a stealth weapon, a biological time bomb, which spreads silently before going off."

Judy nodded solemnly. "That makes us blind to an attack for the first three days at least. Then hundreds of thousands of cases start overloading the system."

Bill shook his head at the concept. "Infectious diseases were so much more fun when we left them to nature."

"How real is this exercise, Bill?"

"I swear it's just that."

∞§∞

Angela D'Martino adjusted her brand new plunge demi-bra so the neckline of her new sweater showed just the right amount of cleavage. She made a face like she suddenly had fangs to check that the Revlon Killer Red lipstick was not smudged all over her new caps. $12,000 dollars worth of dental work, free! That was just one of the benefits of boinking her Jewish dentist. Here was a man who noticed a woman and all the little things she did. Her husband, the "schmoe," never noticed anything about her anymore. Including her frequent nights out with the 'girls.'

Angela checked her watch as she grabbed the car keys. Harvey was going to meet her at 8:30 at "the place." As she opened her front door, she called out to the blob on the couch. "I left sausage and peppers in the Tupperware. Just heat it up for a minute in the microwave. Didja hear me? The sausage and peppers!"

"Yeah, microwave, right," was the rumble from the living room. He was in for the night; Saturday night no less.

As Angela drove down the Van Wyck Expressway, she felt excited, young even, feeling the warm flush of impending sex. It would go just like the other times. She'd wait in the motel parking lot inside her car, wearing her sunglasses in spite of the night. He'd pull up, go in, get the room key, and then come out and escort her inside.

Harvey Edelstein, DDS was a good lover and didn't mind the oral thing. Her husband, on the other hand, thought it was beneath his manhood to please a woman that way. His loss.

She arrived at the Starlight Motor Inn at 8:25. Even had she not been lost in her sweaty reverie, she would have never noticed the dark sedan that entered the lot with her, parked, and killed its lights.

A few minutes later, Harvey's BMW pulled in. He parked next to her, and came round and gave her a peck on the cheek through her driver's side window.

"Be right back. Oooo, you smell good," DDS Edelstein said. It was that kind of comment – noticing the little things – that made her want to fuck his brains out.

∞§∞

"Short stay as usual?" the night manager behind the bulletproof glass asked the face he'd seen a few times in the last month or so.

"Yes. Something on the ground floor, around back."

"No can do, chief. Got a big block of rooms signed out. All I got left is 108 out front to the left." The manager was telling a half-truth as he slid the registration card under the glass with a pen. Dr. Edelstein signed as Josh Cohen, after a schmuck he hated in college, He used this alias whenever he didn't want anyone to know his real name. He laid $45 in cash into the little tray slot below the bulletproof glass and didn't ask for a receipt.

∞§∞

From the sedan, Wallace watched the doctor – whose picture he'd shown to the clown behind the front desk along with a new crisp $100 dollar bill – collect his girlfriend and go to room 108. Wallace made the deal sweeter for the guy at the desk by also booking that room for the entire night for $129. That meant the clerk could keep the short stay fee for the doc's three hours of humping. Having the room from 4:00 until noon the next day, Wallace was able to wire it up and could retrieve his valuable equipment in no rush after they left. He'd also get some semen samples, hair, and whatever else might be of use to his client.

If Wallace had not been so focused watching the video feeds on his laptop, he would have noticed the unusual number of men going into room 107.

One thing about Angela, she has a great rack, Wallace thought as he watched her peel off her top as the doctor threw her down on the bed. It was amazing. He'd done this kind of surveillance hundreds of times and *everybody* started on the bedspread. Some never got to the sheets at all. The sick thing was that the bedspread was never changed in these joints. So this doctor, who probably uses a mask when he drills teeth not to catch aids or some shit, is slamming his genitals all over a bedspread that's got more spunk, junk, and crud on it than a toilet seat at the Port Authority. That alone should be reason enough for his client, the doctor's wife, to be granted her divorce, her kids, the house and every penny this dentist fuck had.

As Wallace focused on his LCD screens and Angela's magnificent breasts rocking as she got pounded, he missed a man entering the room next door with a large case of cold cream.

When the main event was over, the two lay in silence. Wallace's equipment started picking up sounds from the next room, some kind of chanting or prayer. He turned up the gain on his microphone. *Yes, it was some kind of chant or prayer*...BRUMP... BRUMP... BRUMP. Suddenly the sound was interrupted by a thumping noise, which at this level of audio gain obliterated the sound with every thump. Then he heard a very distorted, "Angela! You fucking whore," as the sound ripped into Wallace's headphones. The three shots that followed almost punctured his eardrums before he could get the phones off. What he couldn't get off was his eyes from his LCD screen – and one seething, snarling, angry motherfucker firing a .38 and blowing the top half of Angela's head clear off before pumping two into the doctor. The blood spray and brain matter redecorated the sleazy room in an instant. All of it was caught in glorious digital color, in two angles, with stereophonic 48K sound.

Alzir El Benhan uttered a curse in the middle of his interrupted prayer. The 24 other men in the room on the floor in prostate looked up to see his right shoulder bleeding and the hole in the thin sheet rock wall of room 107. They had heard the shots next door but thought it was only a loud, American TV program. The 24 jars sat in the center of the room and next to them syringes. Holding his shoulder, Alzir groaned, "Take the jars! Leave now!" Then he momentarily blacked out.

∞§∞

"Starlight Motel, North Conduit, shots fired, two people dead. Gunman still inside." As he spoke with the 911 dispatcher, Wallace kept his eyes trained on the door to room 108. Then he realized he had his HD200X high def video camera in his bag. He got it out and pointed it at the door. He never saw Angela's husband before, who the shooter almost certainly was. The two cameras in the room were trained on the bed and the gunman was not near it. Wallace figured that when the man left the room, he'd get a shot of him on the HD. The cops could use it as evidence. Then he decided to narrate the tape. "9:10 p.m. Starlight Motor Lounge, thirty seconds after shoots fired,

Wallace Barnes, New York State licensed investigator, on an assignment for Mrs. ... What's this?" The zoom range of the mini HD actually afforded a close-up of both 107 and 108. Although the shooter hadn't emerged from 108, men started piling out of 107. "Three...four...five... six... seven...eight. These guys are all coming out of the next door."

The first NYPD unit bottomed out hitting the bump in the motel's driveway at high speed, creating a shower of sparks from its undercarriage. The New York cops quickly assumed that the men fleeing 107 were the perpetrators and winged out the doors of their cars, training their guns on them, and shouting, "Police FREEZE!"

The men were startled and Wallace could see the hesitation in their motion. "*Was a drug deal going down next door?*"

"Put your hands up! Drop to your knees! NOW!"

Inside room 107, the men who were left tried to reason out their next steps. "We should make a run for it. Some of us will get through and that will be enough to at least inflict some casualty."

"We should infect ourselves right here, then try to escape."

"We should kill the cops and proceed with the plan immediately."

Then Alzir spoke. "You must proceed. You must not fail. You can still get away, but go now."

In excruciating pain, Alzir pointed to the suitcase under the bed. One of the men dragged it out, opened it, and found ten, older MAC 10s and a hundred loaded mags. The men quickly grabbed the outdated yet still deadly arms. Those who had trained in Afghanistan treated the weapons correctly; the four who had not trained with Al Qaeda watched and tried to emulate what the others did. Fifteen seconds later, all clips were in, safeties off, and extra clips stuffed in belts and pockets. Then two men broke the glass in the window to the room and began shooting at the cop car as two others went through the doorway.

"Holy shit," Wallace said as World War III exploded in his camera's eyepiece.

The two cops recoiled behind the patrol car's doors as the fusillade of bullets ripped the sheet metal to shreds. One officer was hit in the foot and sprang back across the front seat in agony. The other reached the radio and frantically yelled, "10-13, 10-13, 10-13!"

The men kept coming through the door as the two in the window laid down cover fire. The cop dropped the radio mic and took the shotgun from the dashboard mount. He waited for a lull and pumped two blasts at two guys trying to make it across the lot. They went down like bags of bricks. The guns and something else they were carrying crashed to the ground. The staccato sound of return fire from the machine guns made him retreat back to the rear of the car. More men were leaving the room. The cop took a deep breath, turned, squeezed the trigger, and clipped one the instant he appeared between two dark cars.

More units started pulling up. One blue-and-white unit got totally shot up before the officers ever knew what hit them. The other cops, seeing this, held back to a looser perimeter. A responding sergeant quickly accessed the scene and used his portable radio. "113 Baker portable to Central K. Alert all units, heavy weapons at scene. Multiple perpetrators trying to flee. Request ESU. Get air units up."

Meanwhile, back in room 108, the scene of the original crime, Sal D'Martino sat in an armchair looking at the dead bodies of his wife and her lover, the small war out the window all but non-existent to him. He raised the gun to his temple.

Wallace was so scared and yet still videotaping the battle before him that he didn't notice the flash on the monitor screen of his remote cameras as they, still in record mode, captured the muzzle flash as Sal went to meet his wife.

The NYPD had kicked the shootings at the Starlight Motel up the food chain of crimes to Major Event. Every cop in the borough of Queens was now heading for the shoddy inn on North Conduit. Emergency Services Unit en-route hearing the reports on heavy weapons called for "Big Bertha," the N.Y.P.D.'s heavy weapons truck. Many units set up roadblocks at one-mile intervals from the motel. Their orders: "Shut down everything trying to get in or out." Because the motel was very near JFK Airport, NYPD alerted Port Authority and they went into full prevent-defense. Ten PA cars rolled across runways and taxiways to become a virtual rolling border, guarding fortress JFK. When they rolled up to the perimeter fence, they immediately caught two men trying to scale the wire. One PA cop was injured as the bad guys decided to shoot it out. Twenty cops in cars with shotguns easily outgunned two guys with machine pistols with no cover to hide behind other than a chain-linked fence. Two others were spotted approaching the fence and ran off when the spotlights of the cop cars shone on them.

Aviation was waiting for tower clearance to swoop down on the area, but JFK landed dozens of planes an hour and the tower had to halt all landings so that a helicopter wouldn't foul up the intake manifold of a jumbo jet with 300 or more souls on it.

The PA cops saw enough of the intention of these men to assume JFK was their target. They ordered a ground freeze and declared the airport in lockdown.

That action triggered the Joint Terrorist Task Force, which brought ten more federal agencies into the mix. JFK being a major potential terrorism target, every conceivable asset that the combined agencies could muster was already conveniently pre-stationed there. That meant that every state and federal anti-crime, terrorism, biological, nuclear, chemical, conventional, and support unit was a five-minute roll from the Starlight Motel.

Blue-helmeted members of the Hercules Anti-Terrorism Squad, in all their body armor, started advancing towards the motel. Regular patrol units held ground and laid down support fire as the heavy-weapons guys swarmed in to neutralize the threat. There were six men left in the room. One was Alzir who was bleeding and handing fresh clips to the two men firing from the window. That left three to try to escape. Each tucked the glass jars inside their shirts, waited until the next volley of fire, then bolted out the door. They were immediately cut down, literally at the knees, from four heavy weapons cops who had snuck around to each side of the room. Unlike the movies, these guys didn't have to yell "Freeze" and thereby give the bad guy a shot at making their kids orphans. They aimed low and took out their legs, "Perpetrator Shot Running" was the police terminology.

A sergeant tossed a flash bang into the windows like a Ranger tossing a grenade into a pillbox on Omaha Beach on D-Day. The Kilgore/Schermuly Stun Grenade quieted the room in an instant. Four more body-armored cops hit the room as the four outside secured the weapons from the ones who got clipped trying to run. In the two minutes and twenty-two seconds the heavy weapons squad was on the scene the situation had been stabilized.

Wallace had gotten all of it on tape. As the surviving bad guys were being dragged to an interrogation area set up in a command van in the street, Wallace emerged from his car and went over to the heavy weapons unit commander.

"Commander, I'm Wallace Barnes. I was on the job thirty years out of the 42 in South Bronx. I was on a P.I. stakeout when this went down. I got video of the two homicides next door, and, as far as I know, that perp is still in the room."

"Two homicides! What room?"

"108."

The commander spoke immediately into his portable. "Be advised all units, armed gunman in room 108. Repeat. Armed gunman in room 108. Two deceased persons and gunman still in room. Approach with caution, and advise."

Immediately, a path was cleared at an angle, which would cover the line of fire to and from room 108.

At the exact second of the transmission, a white shield, anti-crime cop, still shaking from the first heavy weapons shootout in his six-year career noticed and approached a jar lying on the parking lot asphalt next to one of the downed bad guys. He had one of the forensic team members snap a photo of it to record its position next to the body. He was reaching for it with his surgical gloved hand when the "take cover" order squawked across his radio. For the split second his hand hovered over it, he could swear it was giving off heat. He sought cover, now keeping his eyes on the window next to the blown out ones of the shoot out room.

Two heavily armed cops then scampered around the side of the building like before, only this time they also carried a fiber optic camera. They slid the slim end of the plastic lens under the door and, from a safe distance, manipulated the flexible cable to scan the room. Wallace heard their radio report.

"We show two down by gunshot on the bed and one down by the door. Total three down by gunshot. No others in sight but we can't see into the bathroom. Advise."

The commander looked at Wallace. "Three's all there was. I got it all on tape – video and audio. I think it's safe for them to enter, Sir."

"Green team, proceed with caution and secure that bathroom."

The men kicked in the door.

Within ten seconds, the commander's radio crackled.

"Secured."

He turned to the private dick. "Video and audio you say?"

On cue, a Chevy Suburban with flashing red, blue, and white strobes lurched to a halt near the command van. Wallace thought it was going to be more SWAT guys. He was shocked when a blonde woman in black blazer and pants emerged from the passenger side. She walked up to the Commander and spoke in the manner of a superior officer.

"What do we got, Commander?"

"All bad guys engaged in the firefight down or secured. Possible secondary, unrelated, triple shooting next door. Unknown number of perpetrators on the run."

"I can help with that," Wallace said.

"Who are you? How can you help?" the no bullshit woman asked, ordered, and demanded in one smooth command voice.

"I am NYPD retired; I was on a P.I. when this all went down. I have video of every guy who escaped and surveillance inside the adjoining room killings."

The woman turned to the Commander. "You know this man?"

"He gave us correct intel on the second room."

"Retired at what grade?"

"Detective 2nd grade after fifteen years in patrol."

"That's doing it the hard way detective." She extended her hand, "FBI Special Agent Brooke Burell, Lead Liaison Officer, Joint Terrorist Task Force. We need to see that tape five minutes ago, Detective."

Fifteen seconds later, they were all huddled around the little screen of his HD camera as he fast-forwarded and rewound the tape so Brooke could take a head count.

"I make it twenty-one through the door, which was the only way out, plus the three in the room. Means we started with twenty-four. Port Authority killed two, we got twelve piled up here, plus three in the bus. That leaves nine at large. Ben, APB all units. Seven suspects in motel shooting still at large, AED."

Ben ran off to the communications van, while Wallace figured out AED must be fed speak for, "armed and extremely dangerous."

An agent ran up. "Boss, the motel manager says these guys were having a meeting here. Twenty-four rooms booked in advance, cash. We're finding plane tickets, cash, prayer rugs, and Korans."

"Someone else look at the tape and check the numbers," Brooke said. She turned to Wallace. "Thank you. We'll get you a receipt for that tape."

She turned and was heading off to the van when Wallace called out, "You know what? Now it makes sense!"

Brooke turned in her tracks. "What does?"

CHAPTER FIVE
LIVE FROM NEW YORK, IT'S...

Saturday night used to be date night. Now, the only date the Hiccocks looked forward to on a Saturday night was a date with the pillow after the week's 7:30 a.m. staff meetings. So when his secure phone rang at 10:30, Bill's sleepy voice answered.

Homeland Security was on the other end. "Mr. Hiccock, I have a high priority message for you from the Secretary."

"Go ahead."

Bill heard clicking sounds and then the connection hit.

"Bill, Brad Grayson, Deputy Secretary DHS. We have a situation in New York that could be – repeat *could be* – a bio-terrorism event. You are directed to monitor the situation through your White House SOP. Sir, do you concur that you have been duly notified?"

"Yes, but one question – who is running the operation on the ground in New York?"

"That would be S. A. Brooke Burell, JTTF."

"I know her, she's good."

"Sir, if there are no other questions, do you concur that you have been duly notified?"

"Yes, William Hiccock has been duly notified."

"Thank you and good night, sir." The operator then switched off his recorder and dialed the next person on his Status 2 Alert List.

Bill redialed.

"Good Evening, White House Switchboard."

"Good Evening, I am Bill Hiccock; please authenticate my identity." A tone sounded and Bill repeated his name into the voice print recognition system. Then an automated voice said, "Acquired and authenticated, William Hiccock Science Advisor to the President."

"Yes, Mr. Hiccock?"

"Switch me to signals."

"Signals, what can we do for you, Sir?"

"I need to patch into the New York JTTF commander on the scene."

"Roger, standby," said the army master sergeant who ran the signals department at the White House, the super-interconnect of the U.S. government. A President could talk to a soldier in the foxhole with this network.

∞§∞

Special Agent in Charge Brooke Burrell was dealing with the ever-changing facts in the crime/terrorism/bioterrorism/fugitive drama into which she had been catapulted. Her secure agency cell phone rang.

"Burell, go."

"White House Signals Branch. I have..."

"I don't have time to talk to the White House right now..."

"Brooke, it's Bill Hiccock on the line."

"Okay, White House, I got the call."

The sergeant dropped out leaving a secure connection between the two participants.

"Bill, a local P.I. stumbled on a terrorist plot to infect some bio-weapon on U.S. soil. Very detailed plan, lots of target cities."

"How far did they get?"

"We have seven still at large. We have nineteen on tape but it will be a few hours 'til the tape is processed into our heads-up alert systems.

"Do you have a communications van there?"

"Yes."

"Still got the tape?"

"Just about to fly it back to Manhattan H.Q. by chopper."

"Do me a favor," Bill said as he punched his cell phone. "Hold on for thirty seconds."

"Thirty seconds, you got, Mr. Hiccock."

∞§∞

"Kronos, get up. Get up now and go to your SCIAD terminal on the double."

"Wha…?"

"Kronos, wake the fuck up!" As Bill yelled, Janice stirred.

"Okay, okay geez, where's the fire?" came the disgruntled voice on the other end.

"In New York. I need the Joint Terrorist Task Force on the SCIAD net now."

"They can't."

"Can you set up a backdoor to SCIAD for about thirty seconds from now?"

"Sure, Hitch, no big whoop. I can create a one-time challenge and passkey to my super FTP."

"Just do it."

As he typed on his end, Kronos couldn't believe what he was being asked to do. "You're gonna give all our stuff to the fucking feds?"

"Relax, brainboy. We're the fucking feds, too. How long?"

"C'mon Hitch; I just woke up."

"How long?"

"Sixty seconds… I'm booting up now. Geez."

Bill smirked and changed phones. "Brooke, get the tape and the camera to the communications van. I have my guy making a password to my SCIAD net. We can use it to process the tape in three minutes max."

Brooke entered the van and placed the camera and tape in front of her comm tech.

"What's this?" the tech asked.

"You'll get instructions."

"From who?"

Brooke spoke into her cell. "Bill, who's gonna tell my tech what?"

"My guy Kronos will be on the line in a few seconds."

Brooke jutted the cell phone at the tech. "Can you capture this call?"

"Sure. What's your number?"

In a few seconds the patch was complete and over the speaker they all heard, "Kronos here. Who am I talking to?"

"Rich Hest, JTTF com officer."

"I'm Kronos. You got HTML?"

"Yes."

"512K Bandwidth?"

"1 meg."

"I'm going to multiplex that to 30 meg," Kronos said.

"Whoa, how you going to do that?"

"Magicians oath. If I told you I'd have to make you disappear."

"Okay, I'll just do what you tell me."

"Cool. X,F,T,P, back slash, back slash, sciad, forward slash, admin."

"Forward slash admin. Got it.

"Here's the answer to the challenge. Charlie, Siera, Tango, Romeo, Papa Siera."

The tech typed simultaneously as he listened. "Papa, Siera. I'm in."

"What are we uploading?" Kronos asked.

"I got a HD camera here."

"Firewire?"

"Shit, no cable," the tech said looking around.

"I'm on it," Brooke said as she bolted from the van. Once outside she yelled to Wallace. "We need all the wires!"

Wallace reached into his car, grabbing the whole bag and ran back meeting her halfway.

∞§∞

Janice took the lull in the action to ask, "What's going on?"

"Kronos is rewiring my network and pulling off another miracle."

"Oh, that."

∞§∞

Brooke opened the bag and the tech found a cord that had a small plug at one end and larger one at the other. He put the small end in the camera and the other in an Core i7 - iMac that was in the van. "Okay I'm hooked up."

Kronos came back on the line. "I just set up, back slash, back slash, tape. Upload to that."

"Okay, I pressed play; it's on its way."

"Bill, where's this going?" Kronos asked.

"FBI labs in New York and Washington, TSA, DHS and Face Recognition Systems in Roanoke."

"I better send them all this Ultra HD video codec as well, so they won't waste time. They never got video like this before."

None of this was lost on Brooke's tech in the van. "Whoa, real-time HiDEF full-bandwidth upload? Who runs this thing?"

"Need to know only, Rich. Erase and forget it when this is over, understood?"

"Yes, Sir, Ma'am."

Kronos had the backdoor shut and SCIAD secure thirty seconds after the tape finished uploading.

Bill asked the tech to hand the phone back to Brooke. "Brooke, what happened up there?"

"Looks like these guys had cold cream jars filled with a bio agent of some kind that had its own heat source."

One of the cops entered with the empty case they found in the shootout room.

"Could be a viral strain, one that needs to incubate right up to the point of release. Are we contained?"

"A few jars got shot up, some were smashed, and one was opened by a cop." Brooke noted the stamp "24 count" on the side of the cardboard. "It looks like there were twenty-four of them."

"Brooke, lockdown immediately! The risk of secondary contamination is too high."

"I already ordered a secure perimeter. I have Bio-response on the way. Any idea what we could be dealing with here?"

"There's no way to know for sure, but we were just war gaming an attack with HCD Complex 33. It's a synthetic strain of influenza. We figured with the vaccine shortage we might be vulnerable."

"So this could be nothing more than the flu?"

"A fast acting, potentially deadly form, but not if you catch it early. I'll notify NIH. Make sure your bio guys know it might be viral."

Brooke was writing as she repeated the name over the phone, "H… C… D… Com… Plex… 33, got it. I'll alert them. Thanks."

∞§∞

Bill dialed another number. "Judy, Bill. Sorry to bother you this late."

Judy was in her den with CNN on in the background. The events in New York were starting to make the cable news. "Bill, I know all about it. I am the one who had DHS call you as soon as I got the call."

"Is there any flu vaccine for Complex 33, if that's what this is?"

"Vaccine is a preventative. Once the cardio-pulmonary is infected you have to treat it with intense medication, face masks and gloves, and lots of soap and water to wash hands with."

"That at least sounds manageable."

"Only if it's C-33 and only if we catch it within the first hours. The chances of which, so far, seem good if all the first responders have been quarantined."

"Some of the jars are still unaccounted for. Can you work up some numbers if a few of those get away?"

"I'll get the epis working on it. Maybe it won't get to that."

"From your mouth…."

"Amen, Bill." Then she called the chief of staff at the CDC's National Center for Infectious Diseases to muster the epis of the Epidemiological Analysis Team and get them cracking on the impact report.

After Bill hung up, he mentally created a checklist to make sure he had done and was doing everything he could. Satisfied, he slouched back under the covers, pecked Janice on the cheek, and tried to sleep. But the singing was keeping him awake.

Singing?

"What are you doing?"

"What do you mean?"

"You're humming."

"Am I?"

"Yes. You am."

"Maybe I'm happy."

Bill pondered this for a few seconds. "Okay, why?"

Janice rolled over and faced him. "You know the other morning when I got sick and you said to see a doctor?"

"Yeah."

"Remember I said I didn't know what got into me?"

"Yeah."

"Well it was you. You got into me. And now..."

"Oh God, baby! Are you saying you're...?"

"Um hmm. Yes, we are!"

"Whoa. So you're happy?"

"Yes. Are you?"

"Yeah, yeah! I'm happy. Wow!"

"I know, wow."

"How... when..."

"The how we covered. The when was probably two months ago."

Bill beamed. "Wait till my folks find out."

"My mom's going to go nuts."

Bill's head was spinning. What a turnaround from just minutes ago. "Janice, I love you.

"Oh Billy, I love you so much." They hugged tighter than Bill ever remembered and for longer than they ever seemed to hold each other before.

CHAPTER SIX
PROTOCOL

Thanks to Bill's SCIAD network, the images of the at-large terrorists were sharp and clear with no degradation. The Federal Face Recognition system got them swiftly. Private Eye Wallace's excellent-quality surveillance camera and the lucky position of a good light source right outside the room made the 1/60-of-a-second field grabs, sharp enough even before processing to trigger seventeen face recognition ID match-ups from the nineteen Middle Eastern men who went through the door that night. Of the two faces that remained unknown, one was among the seven still at large. The other unknown face was one of the deceased. The seven photos were distributed to the TSA, all local authorities, the State Department, the Department of Homeland Security, DIA, FBI and the NSA. Many in those agencies were stunned at the high quality of the images, prodding more than one to ask if this was a drill because in the real world images never started, transmitted, or remained this clean.

Two more bioterrorists were captured at Logan airport the next day. Officials quarantined the terminal and everyone involved received prophylactic doses to inhibit HCD Complex 33. Luckily, the spread of the virus was severely curtailed since the two terrorists took a New York City taxi to Boston. It turned out that the cab driver was a member of the Atlantic Avenue Mosque community, a group that still had a hazy connection with Al Qaeda.

If the plan that was uncovered had been carried out in just the NFL towns, and the stadiums that the men were scheduled to visit, it could have meant twenty-five million deaths in the high-risk groups of elderly, those with heart conditions, and pregnant women. In total, the jihadist effort could have killed forty million Americans. It would have been the greatest public health emergency ever in the history of the world. At this point, the risk had been reduced dramatically, but the five remaining at-large terrorists posed a lethal risk to more than ten million people.

Armed with the picture of the four known men and the one unknown man, law enforcement officials swarmed into Muslim communities from coast to coast. There was a terrific outcry from all the usual sources. These cries of stereotyping and prejudice towards one specific cultural group was strangely not as loud among smart-thinking Muslims in those communities who realized that an infected bioterrorist hiding in their midst would infect Muslims and non-Muslims with non-stereotyping, non-discriminatory accuracy. Two known terrorists were found hiding in those communities. Because one of these proved to be infected, intense medical teams also swept into these Muslim communities curtailing their infectious breathing of Complex-33. Untold thousands of innocent Muslim-American men, women, and children were saved.

∞§∞

It was impressive; this was a prayer mat of the same weaver as his father had, all those many years ago. That alone was the sole comfort he now had at the Manhattan Correctional Facility. Unable to merge into the general population, his confinement couldn't be deemed solitary because there was a constant stream of nurses, doctors, and psychiatrists, as well as guards. An imam came once a week – a prayer session attended by a translator and a member of the American security community. These visits were also recorded for later scrutiny. He was not allowed a lawyer because he was being "detained;" he had not been arrested.

Then she came to his room one day. His danger sense went immediately up. She was either a young girl from a college course doing research or a she-devil, sent to seduce him away from Allah and the cause.

"Aliz Berniham. I am special agent Brooke Burrell, the F.B.I. agent who took you into custody when you were wounded at the motel."

Upon the term, "F.B.I.," Sheik Aliz Berniham focused on a crack near the sink in his one room "cell" and tried to let the remembered sound of midday prayers fill his ears in an anemic attempt to drown out her words in his head. But his mind swirled; Allah's plan, which he had been so close to carrying out, with its two years of training and planning, had been thwarted by a woman. A woman who, from the looks of it, didn't even bleed yet. What had he done to displease Allah, to be rebuked like this? *A woman!*

Then a smile creased his face ever so slightly. If the Americans were this desperate, conscripting a mere woman to combat jihad, then surely victory was a matter of when, not if. His attention eventually tuned into the voice of the woman speaking at him.

"... it's up to you. In our system you have been designated an enemy combatant. Therefore, we can hold you indefinitely. Now, the manner of your incarceration can be good or not so good. It can be here or in a nicer place, eventually with an outdoor garden, maybe contact with certain other inmates."

She was good, this one, well briefed about his garden at home, his sole expression of art, and the many satisfying hours he spent gardening. It was a remnant of the British influences of his youth when they occupied his country, dividing his homeland up like a holiday goose at the dinner table. His father, through his connections with the British Empire, secured free passage for his mother, his brother, and him to relocate in Hungary.

His father died soon after their arrival in that new country. He and his brother strayed from the religious teachings into the ways of science. They were both naturals at it, with each achieving academic honors and degrees in various disciplines.

“Okay, so here’s what I want to know: how did you adulterate the vaccine? How did you get operational ability in the U.S.?” The agent slid a pad across the plain wood table. He disregarded it, instead he remained focused on the wall, calculating the stress forces that combined and created the horizontal crack in the plaster.

“This is the only way for you to get some semblance of normality for the rest of your living days, Sheik.”

She was showing some small amount of respect to his position. Still, he remained focused on the fracture. He shifted in his seat.

“Aren’t you going about this all wrong?” he finally said, recognizing her against his better instincts.

“I am not going to insult your intelligence and befriend you then use that friendship to weasel information out of you,” Brooke stated flatly. She finally got eye contact from him for her gambit. “You will never get out of here, unless you tell me what I want to know. That is an iron-clad fact, sir.”

The Sheik smiled. He knew he wouldn’t be here long.

∞§∞

It reminded Bill of P.S. 21, the little, red brick front part. The original school building to which, in 1957, the modern extension was attached. The basement of that 1900’s elementary school was the same as the basement here in the White House, right down to the moisture-controlling gray sealant paint.

It was uncomfortable for Bill to have a gun in the White House. He held it dead at his side so no one would notice it and take a shot at him, especially no one in this room – the target range beneath the portico of the West Wing. Brent returned after signing out the ammo.

"The last time I fired a gun was up at my uncle's cabin." Hiccock said.

"Handgun?"

"No, mostly .22s rifles."

"I bet there wasn't a safe Coke bottle or old toy within a mile."

"Bathroom tiles! Uncle Jack was a plumber. They shattered like you hit 'em with a bazooka."

"Was Jack former military?"

"Hunter. He actually hunted for his winter meals. Mostly venison."

Brent reached down and took the gun from Hiccock's hand. He threw off the safety, pulled back the slide, and popped the clip. "My little rule is approach every gun as loaded and every time for the first time."

"Yeah, you look more cautious than me."

"Every firearm accident happens because overconfidence makes you get sloppy. Every gun is loaded, even the one you just put down." He placed the unloaded gun on the cleaning table next to his own identical automatic then intentionally picked up his. "Until you know that this time it isn't." He hit the slide hard and ejected the live round from the twin gun.

It was a bit of obvious sleight-of-hand, but it made the point to Hiccock. "Got it."

"So since you just want to be proficient, we'll start on the basics."

And so Hiccock's Introduction to Firearms 101 course started with Brent Moscowitz, the Secret Service agent from Queens. This was all happening because Bill confided to the agent, who was assigned to protect him, that he didn't want to be seen as a weenie by the men and women of the various law enforcement agencies over which he now held sway.

∞§∞

By the time Bill got to his office that Monday there were just two bioterrorists left at large: one known, one unknown. It seemed that America got lucky this time. But there were a million more bugs out there and millions more fanatics willing to infect themselves as bioterrorists in a slow-motion version of suicide bombing.

The news that Janice was pregnant made that normally worrisome prospect utterly terrifying to Bill now. *Is that what impending fatherhood does to a person: magnify all the sharp edges and pointy things in the world?* he pondered as he signed on to his SCIAD net. The top three messages were about Edward Ensiling, a scientist found dead in Vienna. He was a member of many teams that brought about a good deal of innovation and discovery. As the science advisor to the President, Bill sent a memo to the Office of Protocol for the appropriate response or letter to be issued from the President. The office would first run an FBI and CIA background check, because Ensiling was a foreign national, Hungarian, if Bill remembered correctly.

In the afternoon, Bill came back from a meeting to find an older staffer awaiting him in his office.

"Mr. Hiccock, Dave Dwyer from the Office of Protocol. Nice to meet you." "Nice to meet you too, Mr. Dwyer. What can I do for you?"

"You alerted this office to the demise of one Professor Ensiling and suggested a presidential commendation or letter of sympathy. Your request has been denied."

"Really? Why?"

"It seems during the '60s, the good professor made some enemies within the Air Force and NASA. Those letters in his file are a red flag against any presidential recognition. I am sure you understand."

"Certainly, although I am amazed. He was a top scientific mind of the last century. But if it's red flagged it's red flagged. Thank you for coming over to tell me personally."

"No problem, really. I actually wanted to meet you."

"Me?"

"Yes. I followed your college career and, well, let's just say it's a pleasure to meet you, Mr. Hiccock."

"It's Bill, please, and the pleasure's all mine, Dave."

"Your two-minute shootouts, well, they were the most exciting thing in college ball. Still, to this day."

"Well, thanks, Dave. But you know I had an excellent offensive line. I could have washed my socks, trimmed my nails, and still had time to throw."

"Well, I'll be going. Again, a thrill to meet you."

"Have a good day," Bill said as Dwyer left.

Twenty minutes later, Bill was sitting at his desk, deep in analysis of how to defend against the next bio-terror plot. As he sat, he absentmindedly spun and caught a football in one hand, something that he first perfected on the sidelines, as a backup quarterback his sophomore year at Cardinal Spellman High School in the Bronx. Using his thumb to pivot the ball in his palm, at regular intervals he would swoop his 3x-size hand over the top and catch the ball in a perfect fingertips-on-the-laces grip. Eight out of ten times, he got it without looking. So inured was his muscle memory and acuity at finding the laces that he actually was able to focus his mind on something else, while performing this mindless feat.

Ray Reynolds, the President's chief of staff stood in the doorway hypnotically watching Bill perform this one-handed trick. Eventually, he knocked on the jamb. "Got a minute, Bill?"

Bill caught the ball mid-twirl and placed it back on the wooden stand on the credenza behind his desk.

Ray sat down in the chair across from him. "Bill, the boss was very pleased with the way you moved things along up in New York."

"We got lucky because Kronos didn't get lucky, so he was home Saturday night to wire the patch up."

"All the same, it's your team. We've got bio-med crash units in the two Muslim communities where we found two of the infected men. So far it's contained, but we are losing people. Almost 3,000 innocent folks are dead because they were first to get infected by the bastards hiding in their neighborhoods. They were already dying long before we got to them."

"But those 3,000 could have in turn exposed 90,000. Both communities could have been wiped out," Bill said.

"Of course, those 90,000 could have infected millions before this thing burnt out," Ray said closing the briefing folder on his lap. "Again, you don't wire up the fast patch thing and we don't get facial recognition on these animals. Then untold millions would be dead or dying now, Bill."

"The cop didn't make it..." Bill said without moving his head or eyes.

"Which cop?"

"At the motel. An NYPD cop found a jar cracked open on the asphalt. As far as we can tell, he didn't touch it, but he inhaled a full dose. He was quarantined but slipped away yesterday."

"I hope those sons of bitches, rot in hell for bringing that shit to America."

"Nationally, the Center for Disease Control says we are talking 26,000 additional deaths this flu season. And that's with 21 of them caught or killed before they could infect anyone." Bill had just read that report a few minutes earlier.

"Even so, I'd say we dodged a bullet."

Both men uncharacteristically sat in silence, each dwelling on what could have been.

"Well, I better be getting back to my office." Ray got up and looked at the game ball behind Bill's desk and noticed what was written on it in white paint. "Stanford 27, Penn State 3? Bill, I watched you on three consecutive New Year's Days win all kinds of bowls. What was so special about this mid-season snorer?"

"That was the best game of my life, Ray."

The quizzical look on Ray's face begged for more clarity.

"That was the first game that Janice came to. I got in trouble talking to her on the sidelines during the game, but I didn't care. Right in the middle of the third quarter, I knew she was the one, and that I loved her."

"So that solves a mystery that's bugged me for a while."

"What's that?"

"How, with all the awards trophies and souvenirs you've collected in your football career, the only trace in this office that you even threw a pass was this one game ball. I though scientists were supposed to be cold and unsentimental."

"Only the ones who never meet Janice, Ray."

"Touché, my friend." And with that he was off.

Bill picked up the phone. He scribbled something on a pad as he dialed home. "Janice, let's stay in tonight. I don't know. Just hang a little... maybe get to bed early. Yes and get to sleep late... you got it!"

Bill smiled to himself as he hung up the phone. He checked his calendar and called out to the outer office. "Cheryl, can I have the summary for my eleven o'clock?"

Cheryl came in with the summary and said, "I have a Mr. Remo on the phone?"

"Remo? From where?"

"He says he's an old friend."

Bill's mind whirled. "Peter Remo? Yeah, I'd say so. Okay, put him through."

Cheryl went outside and a few seconds later Bill picked up. "Peter, how the hell are you, man?"

"Hey, Bill; thanks for taking my call."

"Don't be silly. How ya been, buddy?"

"I've been okay, but something's come up and I need to sit down with you."

"This doesn't sound too good."

"I wish it were good, but Bill, I'm scared, and I need help."

"You got it. Where and when?"

"Not in your office. Can you meet me in twenty minutes, at the Lincoln Memorial?"

"Little dramatic, Pete, ain't it?"

"Bill, please."

"Okay, twenty minutes."

Bill hung up the phone and called to Cheryl. She wasn't fond of the "scream intercom," and her expression showed it.

"Cancel the rest of my morning and my two o'clock."

"Huh?"

"There's nothing cabinet level and you can cover the eleven and two o'clock for me if you want."

"Oh, okay. Where will you be?"

"On my cell."

"No, where? The Secret Service is going to want to know."

"The Lincoln Memorial."

"Why?"

"Dramatic interlude."

Cheryl shrugged. "Fine, don't tell me."

"Now you're getting it."

– Book II –
THE BOX

Chapter One
History Repeats

It was the best knockwurst in the neighborhood. In fact, his little stand was a six-sided, umbrella faceted jewel in the gastronomic crown of Hungary. Claude's traditional preparation in his humble kitchen in Kivorst held the secret. He stewed the meat in three kinds of sauerkraut from earlier the previous afternoon. Each of the krauts brought out the individual flavor of the beef, pork, and veal that was knockwurst. He also added a dash of molasses, apple vinegar, and wine to the pot to compliment each. As was happening more and more, a businessman from the area was proudly buying lunch for a visiting client. He was spouting praise for Claude claiming, as many others had, that the knockwurst was just like his mother's. The anticipation on the faces of those who knew what awaited them, with many actually rubbing their hands together like children expecting a treat, made Claude proud. And he had little to be proud of since the war.

There was a time when he owned one of the best restaurants in Budapest. It involved thirty-three years of toiling everyday, getting up before the chickens, and going to sleep after the cows, but he loved it. Those were truly the good old days. His whole family worked in the restaurant, which kept them close and caring for each other. It provided a good life for all, obviously there was always enough to eat, and his sister, Mary, even met a doctor. It wasn't too bad a life.

Then the Nazis came, the dream ended, the nightmare began. Now, he was the only one left. His wife, mother, father, sons, daughters, aunts, uncles, all shipped off to the camps, never to be seen or heard from again. He had a different fate because of his cooking skills. The Germans found Claude, emaciated and near death, when hunger forced him to leave his hiding spot in the root cellar of the restaurant. The Nazis had taken over the place to be an officer's mess. He didn't get as far as the front door when they caught him. A sniveling coward of a Nazi captain, left behind to secure the phone system of Budapest, ordered him carried off to the street to be shot. However, when the captain overheard Claude protesting that this was his restaurant, he ordered his men to halt.

"Can you cook?" the captain asked.

"Yes... I was... the... chef," Claude said, coughing.

The Nazi turned his head as he ordered, "Take him to my house, clean him up, and see if he can boil water."

Claude became the captain's personal cook. It was barely survival, but again where there was food there was life. Claude stayed alive by feeding the fat Nazi officer like he was the Archduke. While the Hungarian people starved under Nazi occupation, "the Pig" always had fine butchered meats and fresh vegetables for Claude to prepare every day. Many times Claude thought of adding a dash of lye to the soup or iodine to the sauce, but that would only kill Hans, the lowly private who served as the pig's credenza, tasting everything before the swine ate.

During one of the final days of the war, when the battles outside the city were looming closer and closer, Claude and all the servants and workers who had evaded death by becoming slaves to these "Aryan Supermen" were rounded up and hastily put up against a wall to be killed. Claude heard the bolt action from the rifles of the SS troops as they aimed their weapons. A once proud people were about to be robbed of the only thing they had left, their lives.

Claude flinched as the shooting started. He waited a seeming eternity for what would surely be the searing pain of hot bullets puncturing his body, but it never came. He crouched low covering his head. From somewhere deep inside him he drummed up the courage to look behind him. All the SS men were sprawled over the ground, steam vapor emanating from the bullet holes in their crisp, black uniforms as the heat of their blood hit the cold winter's air. Beyond them were the mud-stained, olive drab uniforms of American soldiers, their guns smoldering as a few of them continued firing sporadic bursts and single shots at SS men still alive or trying to escape. At that moment, Claude started to believe in God once again, a belief he had abandoned in the face of all the evidence to the contrary that the Nazis brought with them into Hungary.

At war's end, he set up the street cart and reasoned that if he just made enough money to survive the winters, then he was living the life of a king. Accordingly, he only prepared so much meat every day and, when it was gone, he was off. He'd go home, simmer tomorrow's pot, then read, walk, or watch the children play.

So it was, that on this fine autumn day, the two businessmen were dabbing sauerkraut juice from their smiling mouths when he heard it. Although his mind didn't recognize it at first, his body reacted. He slammed down the lids on his cart, dropped the serving fork, and started running, as fast as his old legs could carry him.

"Claude! Where are you going? My friend wants more of your fine knockwurst! What is that noise?"

Like a low hanging fog, rolling in from around the corner, a rumbling growl swept over the cobblestones. Then came a metallic clanking sound, then the barrel and finally the tracks of a Soviet TU-24 attack tank. Hundreds of Soviet infantry troops swarmed behind the tank. The two businessmen, who were only thirteen when the Germans left Budapest, started running as well.

It was the beginning of the Communist siege of Hungary in 1956.

∞§∞

"Tony, enough with the clanging, it's no use. You're just waking everybody up."

"That cheap, tightwad, son-of-a-bitch of a landlord, I'll clang him with a wrench!" Clank, clank, clank was the sound Tony's crescent wrench made as he rapped the radiator in his fifth floor walk-up tenement apartment. "Send up more steam fer Christ sakes, ya bastard!" Tony, the burly truck driver, yelled at the pipes as if the landlord was nestled warm in his apartment on the first floor, with his ear frying on a steam pipe listening in delight to the freezing cold agony of his tenants on this bone-chilling winter night.

"I'm going to check on Peter," Anna Remo said as she went into the other room and found her little two-year-old son curled up and shivering in his brown snowsuit and mittens. She plucked the child from the crib and felt under the blanket for his bottle. It had been warm milk when she put him to bed, but it was now partially frozen. She brought the little boy into their bed and held him close to her body for warmth under the covers.

Tony came back to bed swearing he was going to kill that wop of a landlord. Although he was Italian, Tony Remo selectively used the term whenever anybody, whose name ended in a vowel, acted like a criminal. As he lay there, a faint whistle started and grew progressively more sibilant. It was the air valve on the steam radiator; the whistling would stop when the unit was hot. It took twenty minutes but the warm silence commenced. Tony had won tonight's war with the pipes. *Maybe the old wop was listening.* For Tony and his family, that was life in the Northeast Bronx in 1956.

∞§∞

Suddenly, it was the horror of 1939 all over again. Hungarians were being arrested and others were being beaten into submission. Like then, many congregated secretly in the basements and tunnels trying to find a way out. Tonight seven men – seven scientists, who escaped the Nazis by luck, were huddled in the basement of a church awaiting their savior. He was a freedom fighter during the last war and had made a name for himself. He was fearless, striking the enemy silently and then disappearing. Now that the heel of the Soviet boot was on top of them, Hungarians only whispered the legends about him.

The group of men had only the warm clothes on their backs and one small suitcase each. The Monsignor who ran the church was a member of the newly formed Underground Railroad that sprung up as the Russians took more and more prisoners. Not just laborers, but also the intelligentsia. Those people whose fertile minds alone posed a threat to the great irrationalism of the Soviet State. The aim of the apparatchik was a "re-education" campaign to convert these Hungarian national treasures into right-thinking communists. The last lesson, if all else failed, was a bullet to the brain.

"Where is he?" Dr. Brodenchy asked.

"He cannot very well take the tram, Doctor," the Monsignor said. "He must make his way through alleys and back roads. They know his face."

Brodenchy's hand was shaking. Not in anticipation of the dangers that lay ahead, but in concern for his father and sisters who he would be leaving behind. Surely, the Russians would treat his father, an Imam, with the respect due a member of the clergy. Still, the worry mounted, but he could not get past the army, back to his hometown. He was caught here when the Russians came. *They will be all right. They will be all right.*

There were two knocks, then three, then one at the storm cellar door to the church's basement – the prearranged signal for Kasiko Halman, the one who would shepherd them from the red menace. The men were surprised when they saw him. He was smaller and dirtier than his legend and the Kalashnikov machine gun that was slung around his torso, was held there by a frayed rope.

"How many?" Kasiko asked curtly.

"Seven."

He spun and turned to the Priest. "You said six."

"Err, it's my fault," Dr. Brodenchy said, stepping forward. "My brother was caught staying with us when the tanks came.... I promised our father."

Kasiko walked up to Dr. Brodenchy, his cold stare frosting the doctor's graying temples.

It was as if Kasiko peered into his soul, "You. You are Muslim?"

"Yes." He tried not to flinch, doing the best an academician could in the face of this hired killer.

Kasiko continued his stare. Suddenly the doctor realized there was a new calculus at work here. He could almost hear Kasiko deciding if risking his life for a Muslim was worth it. The fear of being left behind welled up inside the older brother. His mouth went dry and swallowing was hard. He stuttered and mumbled, "My broth... brother was away in school but suddenly he came...."

"Fine." Kasiko's contemplative mood seemed to switch off like an electric light. "All of you give me all your money!"

"What? Why?" a tall member of the group asked.

"You can stay," was Kasiko's icy response that stabbed at the stunned scientist, who instantly became very compliant.

In single file, they exited the cellar of the church. A small relief to the Brodenchy brothers, who wouldn't want to be caught dead in a crusader's church. Under cover of a moonless night, they made their way through dangerous countryside that had been friendly and serene only a week before. To a man, they wore the same kind of sensible shoe, an Oxford style appropriate for the halls of science and academia but ill suited for the terrain they now traversed.

They had only walked twenty minutes from the church when a small Soviet patrol crossed their path. Kasiko didn't hesitate or delay. He opened fire and killed all three Soviets before they knew what hit them. The seven gentle scientists were horrified as he then took out a knife and stabbed each one in the heart without wasting precious ammunition.

Kasiko felt their looks. He went over to one of the Cossacks and pulled a radio from his dead hands. "With this he would have had half the Russian Army here looking to skin you alive. It's my job to keep you safe and get you out of here. That is the only thing you should judge of me. I am going. If you are behind me, then you will be free. If not, it's your life."

The brothers Brodenchy were stunned but the younger observed to himself, "Strength, decisiveness, no mercy is the key to survival." The young scientist-in-training had just learned a lesson he would never forget.

Kasiko's plan was to travel by night on the back roads and forests that the Russians did not yet control; the group would then rest at two farms over two nights before finally crossing into the Alps on the third night by railcar. Kasiko's uncle, a railroad foreman, had pre-arranged their meeting at a watering station.

Kasiko had little discussion with the men entrusted to him; he didn't want to be distracted. Every sense he had was tuned to danger. He could almost smell the Soviets on the wind if they were close.

Kasiko's arms waved downward in big sweeping arcs as the seven men behind him silently lowered themselves to hug the ground. After a minute, the freedom fighter came to the center of them and whispered, "There are Hungarian Home Guards up over that ridge. Wait here."

As he scampered off in silence, the last thing the men saw was Kasiko reach inside his jacket. They could only imagine what type of terrible knife he was about to dispatch the Home Guard with. Each avoided the other's stare, no doubt feeling guilty that their presence meant the death of more men. A minute passed and they saw Kasiko waving them on from the top of the rise. No one wanted to go first. They all feared the gore and blood surely awaiting their eyes. One more emphatic wave from Kasiko got them moving. As they reached the rise, the first to go over looked back in shock to the six straggling behind. Soon those six came across the same scene.

Kasiko was dolling out bread and wine from the guard shack to the scientists with the help of the Home Guards. Each man took a bottle and two loaves of bread. When the guard shack was well behind them, Dr. Ensiling asked, "Were those men partisans?"

"No, Doctor, just open to being bribed. What did you think I needed your money for?" Kasiko moved up front to his lead position.

Dr. Ensiling breathed his first deep breath that evening. *Maybe he wasn't such a bad sort, this Kasiko.*

The rest of their journey was blessedly uneventful until they reached the watering station. They had arrived three hours ahead of the meeting time. Kasiko's uncle had seven workers ready to disembark the train so that the six men and Kasiko could assume their places and sleeping bunks for the two-day train ride through northern Europe. Unexpectedly, Soviet troops had descended on the railroad siding. The reason became apparent as the men watched the tracks from a berm two kilometers off. A Russian armament train with troops, tanks, trucks, and even folded-wing airplanes stopped to fill its water tanks at the tower.

"We wait for the freight train," was all Kasiko said to his charges.

Four hours later, the anemic whistle of the northbound freight echoed through the valley. Kasiko led his men to within fifty meters of the track. To his eyes and nose, there were no Soviets near. The old train rumbled into the yard area. His uncle was hanging off the end carriage of the train waving a lantern, signaling the engineer. Kasiko approached him cautiously.

"Uncle, are we still going to Antwerp?"

"Yes, my nephew. The train is a little behind schedule, but we are. Do you have your packages?"

Kasiko whistled and waved his scientists onboard. As they entered the crew van at the rear of the train his uncle said, "Kas, you said six. I count seven. I only have cover for seven including you."

"I know. There was a change of plans. I'll stay behind."

"You can't. Those soldiers you shot are all the news. They are looking for you, my nephew. They have searched this train twice. That's why we are delayed."

"I'll take my chances."

"No, I will," Dr. Brodenchy said. "I am the one who forced you to bring my brother. I am responsible and I will stay."

Kasiko took in the scientist. "Your brother, is he a scientist?"

"Yes. He just graduated as a physicist. He was visiting..."

"I know; he was home from school...he is as good as all of you. It is I who am expendable here."

Brodenchy was intrigued. The last thing he expected from this coarse and gruff freedom fighter was chivalry.

"Now, now, nephew," Kasiko's uncle said, "no one has to be sacrificed. I've got an idea."

∞§∞

The train started with a slam, then jolted and started chugging down the track with some very odd, soft-handed, white-skinned, and manicured crewmen. Meanwhile, some very well dressed railroad workers waited in new-found overcoats and suits for the railroad employees' bus to take them back across country to their freight yard. Kasiko tried out his hidden place in an upper berth in this old sleeper car that was now the crew's rolling home.

Two days later, and without incident, the train arrived in Switzerland.

CHAPTER TWO
LIGHTS AND SWITCHES

Six years later, in 1962, young Peter Remo came home from P.S. 21 with a note from his second grade teacher:

> Your son Peter is expected to have a project for the science fair this Monday.

When Tony got home, Anna showed the boy's father the note. The next night Tony came home with a grape box and a bag. After dinner, young Peter watched as his father went to the closet and got the hammer. Using his foot and the claw of the hammer, he pried the box apart. The sides of the box were 5/8" clear pine and had a label across the face. He took one of these sturdy ends and flipped it label-down. He put the wood on his knee and looked at his son. "Ever hear about the cobbler who worked on his knee?"

Peter watched as his dad nailed little things onto the board in his lap, and then fitted a battery and a small light bulb to it. When he finished, he said, "C'mere." Tony opened his arm above his knee, which Peter knew meant, "Hop on."

The board was on the table as Tony told his son what it was. "This is the battree, this is the light bulb, this is the switch. When you trowe the switch, the juice goes from the battree, through the switch to light the bulb. Here, it's your science project, take it to school tomorrow."

With that, Peter walked away marveling at the invention in his hands. He spent all night in his darkened room closing and opening the knife switch and lighting the bulb. Eventually he found his way under his covers and now had an illuminated tent. The simple working circuit was mesmerizing to the little boy. So much, in fact, that it completely rewired his brain.

CHAPTER THREE
GIFTS LARGE AND SMALL

Many Hungarian immigrants settled in Jackson Heights in Queens. So it was no surprise that one day, when a big box from Budapest arrived at Kasiko's apartment, the kids and neighbors all crowded into his place. It had been a year since he had arrived in the United States after traipsing around Europe. He was thankful that he was able to get his mother out of Hungary and she was now with him in the apartment. He opened the crate and couldn't believe his eyes. Coffees, cakes, condiments, clothes, jewelry, and one very special box. "The gifts of a grateful nation," the card read. Kasiko was a true Hungarian hero. Even if Hungary was behind the Iron Curtain, his countrymen made him know he was in their hearts. When the crowd left the apartment, Kasiko opened the special box. In it was a scribed egg on a beautiful gold-spun stand. It was of the deepest blue color and the etching on it was like a fine lace masterwork. He proudly placed it on the mantle.

∞§∞

In 1968, the United States was in the midst of volcanic upheaval. Anti-establishment lava flowed from college campuses down the main streets of cities big and small, igniting passions and inflaming politics. To be young then was to be in a perpetual state of rebellion. In a previous generation's movie, the sheriff of a town invaded by young Marlon Brando's motorcycle gang asked the brooding teen what his group was rebelling against. Brando's answer, though uttered in an earlier decade, summed up the social/political movement of the '60s: "I dunno, what do you got?" In the latter part of that decade, that sentiment was now, literally, on drugs. Whatever could be revolted against was. Whatever could be protested became a *cause celebre*. Sex, drugs, and rock 'n roll made it all sweeter. Revolution hung in the air like marijuana smoke.

All of the '60s dissonance, clamor, awakenings, and infamous moments were mere background noise to Peter. He was so focused on his current project that his friends on the block hardy ever saw him. No stickball, no ringolevio, no hot beans, no king queen, no box ball, none of the street games. Not even two-hand-touch football. The reason for Peter's self-imposed exile went back to the great blackout of '67 when he quickly concocted several of the devices his father made for him for the second grade science fair and placed them at the landings of the stairs in the pitch-dark tenement. Those little lights stopped many tenants from taking a tumble down the marble steps while the electricity was out. So grateful were the neighbors that they started giving him wires, phones, radios, even televisions to tinker with. This sudden windfall of electronic parts started Peter on his greatest project ever. At fourteen, he was going to build a computer.

The estimated amount of money the computer would cost was a small fortune for a boy his age: almost $35. There was no way that kind of money was going to come from an allowance of fifty cents a week. Undeterred by the financial challenge, he started to improvise. He read up on all manner of early computer science and found out about the new transistor that was rapidly replacing tubes in electronics. He started to make his own basic building blocks of computers from old salvaged parts and a discarded knock hockey set he found in the lot. The Masonite playing surface became the material he drilled to make circuit boards. He copied wiring diagrams from a

1960 article by Ronald Benray in *Electronics Illustrated* on making a digital computer. It showed the basic schematic for the "E-J Flip Flop."

Then he discovered "radio row" in lower Manhattan. It was in the old Port Authority Trans Hudson terminal, later shortened to PATH. Many old Jewish and Italian merchants who started to specialize in electronic junk had little stands and stalls there. They would buy/sell/trade their wares. It was the trade part, however, that enabled Peter to build his computer. He would find an old TV set in the lot that someone had thrown out. For a fifteen-cent token, he dragged the TV onto the IRT and schlepped the thing all the way downtown, then up the stairs and to the feet of one of the guys on Vesey Street. Often he'd walk away with a few 2N554 PNP power transistors or some 1N34 diodes. All precious gems in the collection that would become his DEMIAC 256.

A race with the clock started when he learned that all the old guys down on radio row – his friends Sol, Manny, Vinny, and Izzy – were on their last days. The entire Hudson Tubes Terminal was going to be knocked down to make way for some big old thing called the World's Trading Center or something like that. Peter had to hurry to find, drag, and swap as many electronics carcasses as possible to have enough parts to finish his computer.

∞§∞

The seven scientists that Kasiko had gotten out of Hungary went on to find places to do their work. Some with governments, some with private industry. All in all, things were going well. Hardly a day went by that Dr. Brodenchy didn't say a silent thank you for his luck. Many times, he thought of Kasiko and his surprise when they had reached Switzerland and Kasiko handed them back all the money he had taken minus the amount to bribe the officials and to feed them. Not a *forint* for himself. Just as often, he thought of his father and three sisters. They were all killed by the Russians. His father and two sisters were shot trying to "escape" to a mosque on a Friday. His other sister, Afifah, was raped then shot. If not for Kasiko leading them out of Hungary, he and his brother, all that were left, would have suffered a similar fate.

Dr. Brodenchy was thinking just this as he awaited a car to pick him up from the Idlewild Airfield in New York. He was on his way to a meeting at the United Nations. He had heard that Kasiko had settled in New York and if there was time, he intended to look him up.

∞§∞

Demiac 256 soon became a rare thing in the world. It was actually one of the first digital electronic computers not made by IBM, Honeywell, Control Data, or Burroughs, the big four computer mainframe makers of that day. Peter had taken the initial simple design and created a true operating environment by adding a tape drive utilizing sequential access. It involved a Craig portable reel-to-reel tape recorder, (thank you Mr. Cantor in apartment 3B) that he modified with a second "address" track. Added to that were some relays and stepping solenoids (thank you Mr. Catugno in 6A) from which he created an electro-mechanical operating system. He also added a card reader, which he built from other scrap parts and a wire scrub brush (thanks Mom, when you weren't looking). Being influenced by James Bond movies and "The Man from U.N.C.L.E." TV series, Peter built all his units inside attaché cases (thank you Pat from Palumbo's Music on Gunhill Road).

Once it was all hooked up and working, Peter took the CPU he built in the attaché case with him and jumped on the downtown IRT. The outside of the case had a huge "1" in the computer-styled numbers of the day with the word PREMO underneath it. Each attaché case that made up Demiac 256 had a huge number on the side of the case, like his favorite show, "Thunderbirds Are Go," in "*marrionation,*" where each of the amazing vehicles the marionettes used to save the world each week had big numbers on them. The Premo was his signature contraction made from his first initial and his last name.

Peter planned to show the guys down on Vesey Street his project. But when he got there, the wrecker's ball had started taking whacks and big chunks out of the Hudson Tubes terminal. Those guys, and an era, were gone. He started walking north, for what seemed like hours. Eventually, he found himself at Grand Central Station. From here, he could take the subway home. But he had another idea. The Union Carbide building was around the corner on Park Avenue. They were the company that sponsored the science fairs. Maybe a little advance publicity would be good for this, his mother of all science fair projects.

The lobby was daunting. It was so huge. The elevators only went to certain floors and a directory took up an entire wall. He scanned it and his eyes locked on "Computer Dept. NYRCC. 47th floor."

He found the 35 – 50 bank of elevators and got on. The only elevator he had ever been on was the one in his cousin's house in the "projects" that moved slow but still beat walking up the six floors of the subsidized housing complex. His stomach reacted as if he were on the Dragoncoaster at Rye Beach Playland as the elevator sped straight up. It was his first time in a Manhattan skyscraper. When the doors opened, he walked around a little and then saw a door that said, "Authorized Personnel Only." So, of course, he walked right in.

He walked up an incline to a raised floor. There were computers humming, buzzing, and blinking everywhere.

Dozens of big red tape drives and big rectangular cabinets with flashing lights and colored knobs crammed the entire 50th floor. Inside this computer room, the air was crisp and cold. It smelled sharp and acrid. There was the whirring and an occasional swooshing sound as tape drives rewound and their power windows opened. He was taking all this in when a hand came down on his shoulder.

"How did you get in here?"

Peter looked up and saw the scowling face and grim demeanor of a man in a blue shirt and yellow tie.

"You can't be here, kid. I'll walk you out."

Thinking quick, Peter said, "Er… I built a computer."

"That's nice, son. Aren't you supposed to be in school?"

"No, really. I have it right here in this case."

That stopped the man. "Show me."

"Can I put this down over there?" Peter pointed to a return table off the CPU of the IBM mainframe that was currently one of the twenty computers operating at Union Carbide's New York Regional Computing Center. The man who collared him, Ed Cortez, was a director. Peter plopped down the attaché case and popped the latches. As he opened it, he saw Mr. Cortez' eyes widen and jaw drop. Whose wouldn't? There before him in a nineteen-inch wide by eleven-inch deep attaché was an impressive array of light bulbs, switches, red-and-black binding posts, jeweled power lights, and a big telephone dial. Peter hit the power button and then the reset button. The light bulbs, which were randomly lit across two rows, all reset to the lower row. He then dialed a ten, and as the dial turned, the lights jumped and flashed in a special order that only a computer scientist would recognize. The number he dialed in was transformed into on-off-on-off, or the number "10" in binary code.

Peter further ingratiated himself to Mr. Cortez by pointing out that the bank of register lights in the attaché case – 1,2,4,8,16,32,64,128 – was the same as the register monitor on the IBM SYSTEMS 360 – 65 CPU main panel. In short, he just equated his thirty-five dollar science project with the six-million dollar machine that was one of the biggest operating anywhere in the world.

Soon, many C.E.s, programmers, and operators were gathered around the pimply-faced kid with the suitcase computer. So much so, that in time the big blue machine went unattended and that brought out Ed Ryan, Chief of NYRCC. Although Ryan started out hard-assed, soon the little kid and his science project had the same "Gee Whiz" effect on him. To many of these computer engineers – among America's business computing elite – this was the son they wish they had. And like good stepfathers, they showered him with gifts. Manuals, schematics, power supplies, and coveted circuit boards – with the gold contacts still on them! Sol and the boys at Vesey Street would have given him the whole store for one of these, just for the gold. This new paternal group offered him a summer job, but more than he could ever imagine was about to come.

∞§∞

Meanwhile, at the UN meeting, Dr. Brodenchy was about to walk out of the room. He was sure that the Undersecretary General of the U.N. for Economic and Social Affairs must have been drinking. Otherwise, he was insane. Either way Brodenchy didn't want any part of it.

Sensing the impossible position he was in, the undersecretary took the chance of his career. "What if I show you proof?"

That stopped Brodenchy. Now this bureaucrat was either pulling a prank or had misinterpreted something as "proof" of the outlandish claims he just made. His intellectual interest piqued, Brodenchy acceded.

"May I ask you to wait here while I make the necessary preparations?" the undersecretary said.

"Certainly," Brodenchy said. He took a seat in the outer office. His mind raced with the implications to mankind if what he had just heard was true. Why had he never heard anything about this before? Furthermore, if it were a fact, why did they want him involved?

"Doctor, the Secretary will see us now."

"The Secretary?" Brodenchy asked.

"The Secretary General of the United Nations, U Thant."

A chill went through Brodenchy. U Thant was a world-respected figure. If he was buying into this nonsense, maybe there was something...

CHAPTER FOUR
FOLLOWING YOUR NOSE

Peter had hit the mother lode. It was like taking candy from big babies. All he had to do was violate the sanctity of some computer room and within minutes he had them right in the palm of his hand. Peter was now firmly committed to his goal of actually building an older IBM 1401 computer from all the parts they threw at him. He'd have to talk his uncle Joe into giving him space in his garage. A 1401, even just the boards, was a big machine, too big for the three-room apartment in the two family house he, his parents, and brother now lived in.

Peter remembered the pinch in his nose that the computer room caused. It became the basis of his plan of attack. He'd go into a midtown skyscraper, press all the buttons on the elevator and at every floor, sniff the air. The clue Peter was sniffing for was the smell of acetate. It was the base layer of the Minnesota Mining and Manufacturing's magnetic tape that was unceasingly run at high speed past the heads on the big computer tape drives of the day. The odor was unmistakable, a little like vinegar, and a little like old galoshes. 3M used it because when they broke, acetate based tapes broke clean with no stretching, meaning they could be repaired by a simple splice of tape with no loss of data.

In the Pan Am building, Peter sniffed his way to two IBM 360 – 40s in one room. He walked off with a power supply compliments of an enamored computer engineer. At Lever House (IBM 360 –30) he got manuals and two register motherboards. Even at just a plain white building on 51st and Park, he smelled out an IBM 360-30 at a brokerage house and got to make up punch cards with his name on them. He had the idea to type in the alphabet and numbers 0-9 and get the whole alphanumeric card code right there in his hands. The largess from his little forays into corporate America was filling up his room in the Bronx – he'd better talk to Uncle Joe soon!

∞§∞

Brodenchy left the U.N. in a daze and checked in to a room at the Waldorf. He ordered room service and sat trying to figure out how to accomplish the outrageous mission he had just accepted. He had agreed to chair a committee that at this point had no one on it. The conundrum he faced was that someone had to be on the committee before he could tell that person what the committee was about. His fear was that once he told anyone, he would probably not want to be on it, or worse, suggest Brodenchy stop drinking. It didn't take any part of his prodigious brain to figure out that this was not going to be easy. He needed some event or convincer to attract some of the greatest minds in the world onto his panel. That panel would then advise the world on something it would never believe. The more he thought about it, the more he doubted his own sanity.

Before room service arrived, he reached out to three of the men who he had escaped Hungary with. They would at least give him a straight answer as to whether he was sane or not. Maybe even help him sign up committee members. After a quiet dinner and some very good port, compliments of the U.N., he settled down to a restful night's sleep.

∞§∞

Peter decided it was time to see what RCA could contribute to his cause. Although their computers weren't as commonplace in 1968 as the big four, they still made them and they had parts. Peter walked towards the big tall letters RCA, seventy stories up from 6th Avenue in Manhattan. This was a huge building. People were taking guided tours of the lobby. It smelled of steam heat and plaster. As he approached the bank of elevators, Peter met his greatest challenge ever: elevator men. These weren't automated elevators with push buttons; the elevator operators were people who could stop him cold. What to do?

The building directory was a study in itself. Peter spent twenty minutes looking for the right listing. Then he found it.

"Accounting on the 10th floor," Peter said to the uniformed elevator operator. Other people were already on and others followed, each calling out their floor. Peter was tall for his age but he prayed no one took a real good look at him, at least not until he was on the computer floor. Then he'd have them, once again, mesmerized by the computer.

This elevator only served the first ten floors of the building. At three, a few people got off, and one got on and said, "Five please."

At four, someone said, "Thank you, Charlie."

At five, the doors opened and there it was: the pinching in his nose. He made the instant decision to get off there. As the people left the elevator area, he stayed behind. He walked a little in each direction like a hound dog on a scent. He went left. He found himself walking down long corridors of offices. When the hallway made a sharp right, he followed it. The rug on the floor became a hard vinyl floor. The walls were now blue-ish. The hallways became shorter and made more turns as he kept going. Having turned a corner, he came across a huge glass window behind which was the biggest tape drive he'd ever seen in his life. The tape that it used was wider than the 1/2" tape IBM used, even wider than the 3/4" Honeywell used. He stood in awe with his face up against the glass. There were no vacuum columns, which acted like shock absorbers to fast jerky moves of the tape. *That must mean this machine doesn't have sequential address.*

Two things happened simultaneously. The first was that he noticed a black-and-white monitor on the drive. On it was Dean Martin. It was a surreal experience for Peter. Being in an Italian-American family there were two things you did without question – you went to church every Sunday at ten in the morning and you watched "The Dean Martin Show" every Thursday night at ten. Peter knew the show well enough to know that the guy standing next to Dino was Frank Gorshin, who played the Riddler on "Batman." It was then Peter knew he was looking into a time machine. Frank Gorshin was going to be the guest star on this Thursday night's show and here he was watching them at 11:30 in the morning on Tuesday. Wow!

Then the other thing happened. A hand came down on his shoulder. Accompanied by, "What are you doing here?" in a foreign accent.

Peter did a slow pan and to his relief saw that the arm was in a white shirt and not a uniform. Doing the fastest thinking of his life he said, "I am here to sell you something."

"You are?"

"Yes. You see, I built a computer and, in it, I use a sequential access tape drive. And I figured you could use it to put all your news stories on and then you can play them back in any order you want to... here at NBC."

For a moment, the man took in the kid holding the attaché case. "We don't need that."

"Oh." Peter feigned disappointment and was ready to exit quickly with a line like, "Well, Sorry to bother you, bye," when the man surprised him.

"Come on; I'll show you."

∞§∞

Brodenchy met his fellow political refugees at the Thames Coffee shop on 44th Street, just east of Madison Ave. Hellerman, who was always a sickly sort back in Europe, looked good and healthy. He was now a consultant for Fairchild Corporation working on missile guidance packages. To the degree that he could, Brodenchy explained the unexplainable to his compatriot. Hellerman agreed to lend his name, sight unseen, if Brodenchy thought it was legitimate enough. Brodenchy thanked him for the proxy and they discussed the issue of security. It was Hellerman's feeling that if the committee was going to be dealing with top-secret matters, it should have a core of security to protect not only its findings but also its members. Only one name came up, only one person they had both trusted and would trust again with their lives. Kasiko Halman. Like Brodenchy, Hellerman had heard he was working in New York. He had an idea where.

∞§∞

There were three radio studios all behind glass. Peter and the man entered the one on the far end. He saw rows of tape recorders and racks of equipment. There was a huge console with big knobs and meters. Two huge record turntables and more tape machines book-ended a man working the controls, but that wasn't what caught Peter's attention and had him riveted. Behind two panes of tilted glass, wearing an open collared, white, short-sleeved shirt, looking down at a piece of paper in his hands through thick glasses, was Chet Huntley! The NBC microphone poised by the bridge of his nose wasn't necessary for Peter to know that he was the anchorman for NBC. Well, *half* the anchorman. The other guy was David

Brinkley. But here he was twenty feet away from Peter. The man operating the big console pointed his finger at Huntley as a light went on that read ON-AIR over the doorway and then Peter heard the famous voice.

"This is NBC Monitor News on the Hour. I'm Chet Huntley reporting."

"Wow!" was all Peter could muster.

His host, not phased one iota by all this, said, "So you see we put every story on these carts." The man held up a grey plastic Fidel-a-Pac cartridge that looked just like an eight-track tape. Only this one had a clear top and you could see the tape spooling around in a loop inside.

Peter caught on quickly. "Oh, so that's actually Random Access. Much better than Sequential Access."

There was a pause and Peter figured "the tour" was over.

"You hungry?" the man said.

"Me? Sure!"

"Okay, come back to my office for a second then we'll go up to the commissary and grab a bite."

Peter tried hard to remain cool, but the Commissary was the place that Johnny Carson made jokes about almost every night. Now Peter was going to have lunch there. First, he saw Chet Huntley, now he was going to have lunch with Johnny Carson! This was turning into one incredible day. He stole one last peek at Chet behind the glass as they left.

It was about to get even better.

It was a short walk down the hall to the place where the man worked. Peter noticed the room number 523 and another big glass window. In this room, there was no radio equipment, though. Instead, the room had rows of Teletype machines all noisily clattering and ka-chunking away.

The man who was taking him to lunch pointed at a chair next to the only desk at the front of the room. "Sit here for a minute; I'll be right back."

One thing struck Peter right away – some of the people working in this room were his age or a little older. *Odd*, he thought.

All of a sudden, red lights started flashing and the machines started ringing. A boy not much older than Peter went to one of the blue machines and tore off some paper. He then thrust it into Peter's face and said, "Quick, take this to Hourlies." Then he went off into the other room.

Peter, keying off the urgency of the boy's voice, ran out into the hall but immediately stopped because he had no idea where he was going. Then his brain kicked in. "*This is NBC Monitor News on the Hour. I'm Chet Huntley reporting*" played back in his head. Hourlies? He took a shot and went back the way they came. He went through the glass door to the studio where he saw Chet Huntley. A bald-headed man was sitting at the desk reading a script, following along as Chet was broadcasting. Peter handed him the piece of paper. The man scanned it quickly and said, "Great! Bring me the 'first lead.'"

Peter went back out into the hall, retraced his steps once again to 523, and found the blue machine that he thought he saw the kid tear the paper from. There before him, typing out at thirty-five characters per minute was: "1-s-t-L-D." *First lead.*

Peter started to read:

> UPI - Mexico City, Mexico. A Boeing 737 with 87 aboard crashed on takeoff from Mexico City Airport. All on board are presumed dead. The Aero Mexico airliner struggled...

"What are you doing?" asked the man who was taking him to lunch.

"I'm waiting for the first lead?"

Just then, the desk assistant who handed him the paper realized that Peter wasn't who he thought he was and that Peter didn't work there. Panic registered. "Where did you bring that paper?"

Peter answered to the man instead, "Glass doors, down the hall, bald-headed guy."

The man barked, "Sit!"

So Peter sat, terrified that he did something awful. The commotion in the room started to wane in about five minutes. The last time Peter was this close to coming to tears was when he was eleven and his father got pissed off at him for blowing up the old Dumont TV. He was sure they were going to call his parents. Forget about whatever he just did wrong, he was also cutting class, so there was no way he wasn't going to get in big trouble for this. His life passed before his eyes twice, because he as only 14! Then the man came back and sat down at the desk next to Peter.

"First off, I'm docking him a day's pay," he said, pointing to the kid who started all this.

"And I am paying you. Would you like to work here?"

"Me? I'm..."

"Look, you showed a good sense for news and you showed me you're a pretty smart kid. Do you want to work here?"

"Sure. If it's okay."

"It's okay; what's your name, kid?"

"Peter, Peter Remo, sir."

"Good. Welcome to the NBC News, Peter. I'm Kasiko Halman."

∞§∞

"Hold it! Wait, Peter..." The Washington Monument appeared gray under a cloud's shadow, while the reflecting pool and the mall were in brilliant sunlight, but that wasn't the reason for Bill's squint, "So far this is a nice story and all, ...WWII, Hungarians, Science Fair and what have you, but honestly, you expect me to believe that NBC hired you at fourteen!" Hiccock said to his old friend from the Bronx (who he hadn't seen in twenty-five years) as they sat on the steps of the Lincoln Memorial. "I couldn't get a paper route with the *New York Post* until I was sixteen and had working papers."

"Yeah well, kid, my folks didn't believe me either. But you were only four then, and the world was a different place back in '68. Nepotism was alive and well in those days. The entire cadre of desk assistants – in print they'd call 'em copy boys – was a dumping ground for the kids of RCA and NBC Senior Executive VPs. From summer jobs to after school work, it was like day care or day camp."

"Your pop was a truck driver. You weren't 'anybody's' kid."

"And I got let go three times for not belonging to anybody. But I got hired back four times."

"How?"

"I was good and I had a little secret I shared with the news managers."

"Job security?"

"In our room was one of the first Xerox machines, a 3600. It was massive and had stuff we take for granted today: document feeder, 20-copy sorter, up to 999 copies. Had a Nixie tube readout."

"Ahhh, Nixie tubes... please stick to the story." Bill checked his watch.

"Anyway, do you know why it took so long to invent copy machines? Because they had to invent copier repairmen first. 'Cause you couldn't run one of those suckers for more than a few hours before they broke down. I only worked Saturday and Sunday nights cause of school, but I made seventy-five dollars for the weekend. I was paid through newsroom dinner vouchers. Every week I was somebody's dinner."

"Wow. Seventy-five a week back in '68. That must-a been good!"

"My dad broke his ass on the stone truck for one-seventy-five a week! So anyway, one Sunday night the news manager has a report to get out and the Xerox is down. He's about to retype the whole fifteen pages on Rexograph masters when I say, 'I think I can fix it.'

"'You think you can fix the Xerox machine?' he says.

"'I might have to shut the lights in the newsroom for a while.'

"So then he says, 'Peter, I'll give everybody flashlights to work with if you can fix it.'

"I started by defeating all the cabinet door sensors with paper clips. The problem was the tray that you pulled out to free jammed paper came all the way off the runners and the ball bearings went everywhere. So I shimmed up the tray using shaved down pencils. I got that sucker right in line but had to run the machine wide open cause of all these sticks and tape and paper clips hanging out of it."

"I bet NBC news was never the same after this," Hiccock said.

"Billy, you had to see it. At one point this big arcing light was swooping across the entire newsroom with each page being copied. I had to shut the lights because it was an electro-photostatic process. The inside of the machine was like a dark room, so when it was open the room had to be dark, but I had it running and humming. At the last minute, the news manager came in and asked for the last page of the report back. I remember I used to have to print it on NBC stationary that had hundreds of little interlocking NBC logos on it. He gave me back the last page and I collated it into the thirty copies of the fifteen-page report. Then I went about my job distributing it to the inner-office list. I did that every Sunday as the last thing I did before I went home. This way the VPs had it on Monday first thing when they got in."

"So that's how you stayed employed?"

"No. It's how I got fired. Actually, on that last page? He rewrote the end to say, 'This entire report wouldn't be possible without the ingenuity and determination of desk assistant Peter Remo.'"

"Nice touch." Bill said.

"Actually, not really. When the head weenie in personnel read that about me, he checked his list and found that I was nobody's kid and fired me the next day. A week later, I was hired back."

"Great story Peter, but what the hell's that got to do with why you called me?"

"What happens then is Professor Brodenchy sets up his committee and gets Kasiko to be the Sergeant of Arms. Around the holidays a year or so after I started working there, Kasiko invites me to his home for a little Christmas Dinner..."

CHAPTER FIVE
ROLL OF QUARTERS

Joey Palumbo didn't like off the record meetings. They ran against his Quantico cut, by-the-book, grain. His reluctance to meet with Agent Burrell, "out of the house," was hard to hide as she approached the bench in the park located at the beginning of Madison Avenue in Manhattan.

"Thanks for coming, Mr. Palumbo."

It still stung that he'd lost the SAC salutation ahead of his name. "No problem, Special Agent Burrell."

"Brooke, please."

"Brooke. So what's on your mind?"

"Aliz Berniham."

"Nice job processing him. That was a career-making collar if there ever was one."

"NYPD SWAT did the hard cheese. Your guy Hiccock's magic network zipped the I.D.s in record time. I just mopped up."

"Still, it goes on your dance card."

"I've been dancing with the good Sheik, and I got a bad feeling."

"Did you report this?"

"I don't report feelings because, being FFBI, they still don't rise to the same level of male intuition. "

"So then unofficially give me the Female FBI intuition."

"Something big is in play... I don't know what... I just know that this creep knows that another shoe is going to drop and drop big."

"How or what can SCIAD do to help you?"

"I didn't want to meet with you because of SCIAD, sir."

That surprised Joey.

"I wanted to talk with you because you were a good agent. How can I stop whatever this is that I think is going on?"

"He's been in 'iso,' right?"

"From the moment he came conscious, it's been FBI only."

"So he couldn't have any current info."

"Exactly, so this must be a long range plan."

"Like 9-11!" Joey said.

"That's my fear."

"But, Brooke, you stopped him and his plot, which at the end of the day could have killed 80 to 100 million Americans. That isn't chopped liver. That was a big shoe, too! Maybe the one and only, not a pair."

"See, that's part of my… Okay, let's say you were him, the mastermind of the biggest bio-plot ever, and it failed like it did. You would think that was it; the big wad had just got shot. Wouldn't you be defeated, introspective, hell, angry! Yet …"

"Your other shoe feeling?"

"See why I didn't want to send this up the chain?"

"It could just be him in denial?"

"He's too cool. Too smart."

"Yeah, we forget that despite the popular opinion, most of these terrorists are college-educated, most with degrees, and all middle-to-upper class."

"This guy talks like he has two degrees in science, but we can't track him back further than 15 years."

"Can you work him?"

"Not in this environment. The director is yielding to public pressure, so the Sheik has had uninterrupted sleep at night, in climate control comfort, without any discomfort caused by his detainment. He is allowed to pray five times a day and he has weekly, monitored visits with a holy man."

"So you have no interrogation leverage?"

"None. That's why I have been flat out straight with him on how his life can get even better."

"Get better? What's the death toll estimate at, right now? 26,000 additional deaths?" Joey curtailed his instinct to slam down on the park bench with his fist.

"Around that number. Thousands needlessly killed just because this asshole decides to infect America."

"And because those deaths are statistically within the range of possible deaths from influenza, a really bad influenza, there isn't the same hatred of this bag of excrement that there would be if he poisoned the water supply of a small town, or blew up 80 airliners to reach 26,000 dead." Joey was getting less objective and more agitated as he focused on the kid glove, politically correct, religiously sensitive handling of this mass murdering scumbag.

"So he gets the royal treatment, while his 'comrades in alms' don't think twice about cutting off Daniel Pearl's head. Makes me wanna go in there and introduce him to flesh-eating bacteria. Slow, flesh-eating bacteria."

In a way, she stole Joey's thunder and rage, and he took on the role of objective mentor. He looked at the woman agent, who appeared not much older than a teenager, and as American as apple pie. *'Corn Flake!'* That's what the guys in the Bronx would call a person from Iowa or the midwest, a corn flake. Then he remembered this one had frosted a terrorist in a parking lot in New Jersey on the way to foiling a chemical attack on the New York area that would have brought unimaginable death. This was one tough corn flake and if her sixth sense was tingling, there was probably something to it.

"Whoa. Agent Burrell, we're the good guys remember?"

"He just..."

Then Joey saw a flash of something he missed before, subtle and quickly dissolved, but there nonetheless. "There's something else, isn't there?"

As she looked at him, Joey could see the two opposing forces waging battle in her head. The deep breath she then took was the surrender flag of one side. "He scares the bejesus out of me, sir."

"You are in fear for your safety?"

"Not just me, although yes, me too, but he thinks... no, strike that, he knows, he's getting out. He doesn't have to play ball with me or give up any info. He just has to wait it out because one day he won't be there."

"He's manacled, right?"

"24/7 and anchored at night and at meals."

"Ten bucks!"

"What?"

"Go to the bank; get a roll of quarters..." What Joey then described was in no agent's field manual ever printed by the FBI.

CHAPTER SIX
MAKIN' COPIES

In late December 1968, twenty-five people attended the traditional Christmas dinner in Kasiko's apartment in Jackson Heights. Peter noticed a shelf above the fireplace where there were more than 40 finely etched and brilliantly colored eggs. All beautifully displayed on gold stands. Of the people there, many of the men were scientists. Peter actually recognized many of them from TV shows on Channel 13 and the Sunday morning shows that featured scientists who talked about everything Sputnik, Gemini, Teflon, and beyond. The men were very engaging; most spoke with thick foreign accents, but Peter was able to have deep discussions with most of them. They spoke of things that Peter had never heard of, Global Warming, Nanotechnology, Large Scale Integration, Cold Fusion, and Supercomputing. None of which at the time could be read about or was even mentioned in *Scientific American*. When Peter left, he felt he had met some really smart guys. What he didn't know was they had all agreed later, in a small impromptu meeting, that they had met a really smart kid. So Kasiko got their permission to bring the kid into the fold. His first assignment would come Saturday night.

Before "Saturday Night Live" began its reign, NBC Studios at 30 Rockefeller Plaza was deader than a doornail on a Saturday night. In fact, aside from master control and a few videotape guys, the news was the only department with even half a staff. After the torrent of activity getting the "Weekend Huntley Brinkley Report" on the air at 6:30 (it aired off tape in New York at 7:00 p.m.) things settled down to a constant drip of non-events.

Every 30 minutes or so, Peter, often working alone on weekends, would make the rounds in the room and spike copy. Spiking was the process of distributing the five impact copies of teletype paper from each newswire machine to the various on-air talent, producers, writers, or directors whose names were above spikes running all the way around the room. During the day the spikes were cleaned every 15 minutes or so. But on weekends, only the news manager, domestic and international film desks, and a few local writers across the hall doing the "11th Hour New York" local news came to gather their copy. So once every thirty minutes was all it took to do a fine job keeping up with the slow moving stories.

Peter was surprised when Kasiko came through the door. With the exception of the Christmas party the other night, he had actually not seen him, in or out of the office for months, because during the school year, Peter only worked weekends.

Kasiko didn't waste time with small talk. "Peter, you know some of the people at the party were very impressed with you. They agreed to ask you to join them as my assistant."

"You mean the scientists?"

"Yes, they are doing some important work for the United Nations and I handle the security for the committee."

"What's the committee?"

"First you have to sign this and swear not to divulge the work that you may be called upon to do."

"Sign what?"

"This it's a non-disclosure agreement."

Peter read the paper, then signed and dated it.

Kasiko knew this was more for effect since Peter was way under the age of consent, but he felt it would make the desired impression. "The first thing I need you to do is tonight, when no one is around, make five copies of this." Kasiko handed Peter an envelope and dangled a key on a chain. "Here's the key to my desk. Leave the copies in the bottom drawer and put the key under my phone."

"Sure." Peter held up the envelope. "What is this?"

"It's just something we need five copies of, no questions asked. Can you do that?"

"Yes of course, tonight, later."

"Thank you, and welcome to the committee."

Kasiko took the envelope back, put it in the lower desk drawer, locked the desk, and handed Peter the key, adding, "Remember, when no one else is around." Then he left.

The 11 o'clock net feed was the only story tonight. Other than that it was an unusually slow news night. That meant the 8-to-12 shift would be leaving early. The 12-to-8 shift would be light. Peter was working a double again so that he could make $37.50 a shift, times two, in one night during school months. That was a ton of money for a 14-year-old in the late '60s.

By 11:30 p.m., Peter was the only one in the whole newsroom. The manager, domestic film desk, and exec producer of local news were down in Hurleys, the watering hole located on the 6th Avenue and 49th Street corner of the RCA building. So popular was Hurleys with the hard drinking men of journalism, that a special yellow phone was connected from under the manager's desk to a phone in the table's booth. In case of any emergency, Peter's orders were clear: ring up the yellow phone. The execs had an elevator operator standing by and could teeter into the newsroom within 40 seconds of Peter's call.

When the news manager left at 20 after 11, Peter checked on the "nightman" and saw he was in an office typing. The coast was now clear; this was the time. He unlocked the desk and retrieved the gray envelope with the blue interlocking NBC logo. Inside was an oak tag file folder, which contained something called a galley proof. It was pages of a book. It looked to Peter as if someone opened a book and placed it down flat on a Xerox, so that both adjoining pages could be read across. Peter took half the pages and set them in the document feeder. He then set the digital nixie tube display by turning a knob beneath each number. He turned the right-most knob five clicks until the number above read "005." Maybe because he felt like a secret agent just then, he then turned it two more times just to see the 007 in thin, red gaseous numbers. Then, for some reason he didn't understand, he set the display to 010 and pushed the sort button and then the start button. Papers started slotting into the 10 sort bins as the machine clunked and ca-chunked along. When the first half of the original had passed through, he tapped down and smoothed the last half and placed it in the feeder. Soon he had 10 copies of something called, *Harmonic Epsilon*. He put the five copies and the original in the big envelope Kasiko brought. It was a tight fit but he got them in. He placed them in the desk drawer, locked it, and pocketed the key.

The other five he put in a similar gray NBC envelope and spent the next hour trying to figure out what to do with it. First, he put it on a shelf behind the Rexograph machine. Ten minutes later, nervous that it would be found, he moved it to below the Reuters machine. Twenty minutes later, he moved it behind the Xerox machine. He had never felt this guilty or self-conscious before. He moved the envelope five more times before he finally decided to hide it in the men's room under the sink. At 7:55 the 8 a.m. shift was in and Peter signed out. He went to the men's room, retrieved the stuffed envelope, and slid it under his winter coat. He headed for the elevators feeling as though he'd robbed a bank. Only when he was safely aboard the uptown Lexington Ave. local did he abandon his usual place in the front car looking out the front window of the train and risk peeking into the envelope.

Harmonic Epsilon
by
Blake C. Lathie

1968 Auckland, New Zealand.
Printed in Hong Kong.

He turned to the first page.

> I have never been abducted by aliens, nor have I ever chatted in Venusian with a green skinned, extra terrestrial; in fact, I've never even seen a flying saucer! That's not what this book is about. This book is a call to anyone reading it to refute or reinforce the evidence I have stumbled upon which supports the existence of UFOs. I have taken these mathematical formulas as far as I can with my rudimentary knowledge of math; maybe someone out there with access to the new, large calculating machines can further the work or, again, refute it.

That sent a chill down Peter's spine. It was an ominous opening for not only the book but for the next chapter of Peter's life. He flipped through the pages and saw lots of mathematical formulas. There were charts, maps, and tables. Normally after a double shift Saturday night, Peter got off the train on Gunhill Road and went straight to the 9 a.m. Sunday mass at Immaculate Conception. On this day, he went right home and started reading. He read about the Bermuda Triangle, Easter Island, the Lines of Nasscar, Vortexes, and the Grid. The Grid was the principle argument in the book. Somehow, the Grid was inexorably linked to other physical phenomena of the Earth. The Grid's effect on man was considerable but unknown to the world. In fact, except for the postulates presented in the book in his hand, the Grid didn't exist. The geometry and power of the Grid was a discovery awaiting revelation, until this book put it together.

There was little in this book that Peter had ever heard before. Even the math was strange. It was centered on a number system based on 2.73 or Epsilon. Some of the equations were navigational; others dealt in something called harmonics that he hadn't a clue about. At 2 p.m., his phone rang.

"Peter, it's Kasiko. You didn't leave the key under the phone."

"Aw, shit! Damn it! I'm sorry. I did lock the drawers, right?"

"Yes, you did that."

"Mr. K, I'm so sorry. Do you want me to run in there right now and bring you the key?"

"No Peter, I have another key. Bring your key by my house tonight. A few members from the committee are meeting around 7 p.m."

Peter hung up the phone with relief. He'd screwed up, but now he got a second chance to meet with some of the men on the committee.

He put on the TV to see if there was a Giants game on. The black-and-white set was tuned to Channel 13 and a show called "The Open Mind" was on. He adjusted the rabbit ear antenna on the top of the Sears-Roebuck TV. Lewis Rukeyser was interviewing Dr. Ensiling and they were talking about whether or not nuclear power would ever be safe enough to deliver the promise it once held. Ensiling maintained that it was safe in the American design of double-walled reactors, but that the rest of the world didn't have that technology and therefore as other countries became nuclear dependent the danger level would rise as less-safe reactors went into operation. He then almost casually threw in the point that, of course, the problem of nuclear waste is still to be adequately resolved, but in 10 years maybe they'll have figured it out.

When the program was over, Peter was blown away. *Wow. I know that guy.* There was a Sinbad movie on Channel 2's "Picture for a Sunday Afternoon." He watched Sinbad in badly dubbed English fight a two-headed dragon and save a princess. He'd gotten dressed and, at the insistence of his father, he went to 4 o'clock mass. Then he took two trains and a bus to arrive at Kasiko's house at seven sharp.

Peter handed the key to Kasiko as soon as he entered. As he said hello to everyone, he couldn't get his eyes off Ensiling. It was sudden hero worship, as if Y.A. Tittle, the New York Giants quarterback, was in the room. Peter said nothing but listened intently to every word that flew around the table. They were speaking Hungarian politics and the politics of Europe as a whole. As dinner was served, one of the men asked Peter his thoughts on the SALT agreement. He felt a momentary wave of panic welling up inside him, and then he remembered that Ensiling had mentioned SALT in the show. He quickly rifled through the main points as he remembered them. "Well, I don't know too much about it, but the problem is the two-headed serpent that nuclear power is. One head is the peaceful use, which is inherently dangerous, except for the United States reactors. But if we gave the world our design, then they'll be that much closer to making high-quality atomic fuel for bombs." And there in one succinct sentence was the summation of Peter's day of watching TV. The only thing he'd left out was the Brylcreem commercial.

"My, what a colorful analogy," another scientist named Brodenchy said. "A doubled-headed serpent; how insightful."

"Peter, you are correct. But are you suggesting we limit the proliferation of nuclear energy?"

"Well... no. We could operate it for all the other countries then we can make sure it's only used for peaceful means."

"Peter, there are so many geo-political problems with that solution that I can't even start."

"Oh." Peter was a little deflated.

Ensiling noticed his embarrassment. "Now you can't blame Peter for his America-centric view of the world. He is, after all, the only American at this table."

Peter smiled and felt that Prof. Ensiling was a nice guy because he was speaking up for him.

At one point, someone asked for mustard and Kasiko warned, "Only take a little; it's very hot, you know."

"Yeah, a little dab will do ya," Peter said making it a clean sweep for Sunday afternoon TV.

After dinner, they retired to the living room. There, the talk turned to the committee. Most of it was procedural: when to plan future meetings, creating subcommittees, and the timing of interim reports. Eventually, the subject got to the book.

"Have the reports from Egypt come in yet?"

"No, we hope to have them by early next week."

"Kasiko, do you have the document?"

"Yes. Thanks to Peter I have a copy for each of you on the Harmonic Sub committee." He then doled out the books that Peter had copied. He returned the original to Prof. Ensiling. Thank you for bringing this to us."

"I was never so nervous in all my life going through customs."

Peter resisted the urge to add, *I know what you mean, shheez*! lest he reveal his skullduggery.

CHAPTER SEVEN
BLUE-EYED DEVIL

When Alizir had finished his morning prayers, he rattled his chain, the signal he had trained his captors to understand meant, "Bring me my food." These Infidels were fools, He had braced himself for the worst after the stories of Abu Ghraib and Guantanamo Bay. He thought they would surely torture him. But yesterday, he sent back his lunch because his meat was undercooked. They weren't guards; they were servants. This wasn't a country to be feared; it was a nation of men whose fathers abdicated their roles in teaching a man to pray and fight and die for a cause. Probably in deference to their wives, who were not intended by Allah to raise sons. They were half-men. He had fought the half-men of Russia as a Mujahedeen in the eighties. He volunteered in retribution for his father and sisters being brutally killed in his younger years. Lives extinguished for being nothing more than devoted Muslims; praise Allah, that he was able to save his younger brother. He and the Afghans with which he trained defeated the great Russian Army and sent them home to their weeping mothers to be breastfed once more. It was during those days he met the wealthy son of an Arab billionaire who traded a flamboyant life as a playboy in New York and Paris for the bone-chilling sanctuary of deep caves. Since those days, Osama had left his mark and, had the virus plan been executed, his name, Alizir, too would be blessed with the adoration of all those who fought the great Satan.

"Put it on the table." The Sheik said, to the servant delivering his meal. His back was to the door. He turned when he didn't hear the tray sliding onto the table.

It was her again.

"Good morning, Shiek," was all she said as she walked over to the chain that was locked to the hoop on the floor. She tugged on the chain and gestured for him to give her some slack.

"You are releasing me?"

Without saying a word, she produced another lock and by threading it through the links, shortened the chain by about five feet.

"Sit down!"

He almost sat, but then remembered that this wasn't a man or even an American half-man. This was only a woman.

"Are you going to sit?" She gestured to the chair.

He didn't respond.

The impact between his shoulder blades made him lose his breath and he found himself dazed and confused on the floor. She was now standing in front of him, swinging a sock with a heavy weight in the end. He immediately scrambled to his feet and rushed at her, forgetting the newly shortened chain. It snagged him back just as he reached her.

"I used to do this with the neighbor's dog. I knew how long his leash was and he just snarled and barked but couldn't bite me."

Brooke was lying; it was actually her dog that was tormented this way by her neighbor's unbalanced son. But never let the facts get in the way of a threat. She smashed the sock onto the table, the energy and force made the Sheik wince.

"I'm not going to lie to you, Sheik. You scare the living daylights out of me. You have become a star in my nightmares." Wham! She hit the table again. "My daddy taught me to face my fears, look them right in the eye, and see that they are nothing and only had the fear I gave them."

She looked the Sheik in the eye and didn't blink. It was he who eventually turned away.

"How did you achieve operational ability in America?"

He didn't respond.

"Two, three, four." Wham! She hit him so hard in the shoulder he was knocked to the floor on one knee.

"Hmmm didn't leave a mark? Oh, we're going to do this all day! And it will just be our little secret."

He looked up at the girl. He noticed she was dressed differently. Not in the boxy man-suit of the female agent needing to conform to look like a man. She was in what the west called warm-up clothes. Tight fitting.

She saw his eyes on her chest. She had the AC turned up so that the room was cold.

She is a sadist. She is getting a thrill out of this.

Brooke's chat with Aliz lasted about 40 minutes. As she left, she said to him, "You are so full of shit, you must have to flush twice."

An hour after Brooke had her special "breakfast" with the Sheik, one of his guards came into the room.

The Sheik quickly complained, "That woman has tortured me!"

"I wish she'd torture me."

"She hit me!"

"Aw... come on. That little girl? Nice try." Counting the towels, he left.

Twenty minutes later, a man in a suit, whom he had not seen before, entered with the bitch who hit him.

"Shiek Aliz Berniham, I am Robert Fusco of the Inspector General's Office. You have leveled charges against agent Burrell. I am here to take your statement to determine if any disciplinary action should be enforced. Do you understand English?"

"Yes. Of course I do."

"Show me where she allegedly hit you."

"My arm, my back, my shoulders, my legs..."

When Robert looked, he saw no signs of trauma or impact. He turned to Agent Burrell. “Did you strike this man?”

“No, sir.”

“Did you threaten him in anyway?”

The little bitch now in a skirt and jacket looked like a librarian and incapable of swatting a fly as she answered with a look of wonderment. “That is against procedure, sir. I will not expose my prisoner to any treatment not in compliance with the director’s guidelines, sir.”

The inspector gave both of them a final review and then left the room. Brooke looked at Aliz without a trace of the anger or rage she had previously shown him.

She is a two-headed beast, he thought.

She left.

CHAPTER EIGHT
WOWING THEM IN JACKSON HEIGHTS

"What's the book about?" Peter asked, Feigning ignorance to hide the fact that he'd read it just before coming to Kasiko's Sunday night dinner.

"Only Professor Ensiling has read it. We are all looking forward to studying it," Brodenchy said as he took another ladle of creamed onions.

"Basically it's a mathematical postulate asserting the teraphysics involved with maneuvering and navigating an interplanetary craft in the Earth's atmosphere," Ensiling said.

"Interesting term, Professor – 'teraphysics,'" Brodenchy noted.

"Yes. It is the physics of Earth from a perspective outside of Earth's domain."

"How does one achieve that point of view?" the younger Brodenchy asked.

"The beginning of 'teraphysics' is best visualized by the following construct: coming from outside the solar system, Earth is the third planet from the sun. Therefore three was a logical divisor. So why not divide the Earth into not 24 but 27 hours per day. Twenty-seven being three to the third power also added parabolics to the mix. The author bought an ordinary globe of Earth and circumscribed 27-hour meridians on it. He almost had it, but there was no point of origin with which to anchor the new grid. Then he placed the crosshairs of an intersection over a point in Auckland, New Zealand where a flying saucer was rumored to cause a tremendous explosion. Everything then snapped into place. All previous UFO sightings were now along lines of the new grid. Not only longitudinally but latitudinally as well. His big discovery was that major grid intersections fell on places like Giza, where the great pyramids were. The Bermuda triangle was at the intersection of three lines. The Exeter Vermont sightings from the '50s were right down the major line on America's East Coast." Ensiling paused to tamp down the tobacco in his pipe.

Brodenchy filled the pause with an observation of his own. "But Professor, now that Lathie had divided the Earth into 27 longitudinal meridians, then navigationally, the math also has to change, correct?"

"Exactly. Using 27 meant new smaller degrees, minutes, and seconds of arc and, along with them, shorter new hours, new minutes, new seconds. Suddenly a whole new world of co-incidence appeared. He started converting everything into the new math. Natural phenomena, manmade events, even celestial events.

Doctor Adam Borda spoke up. "Yes, I researched a fellow; his name was Frank Edwards and he wrote a book in 1957 tantalizingly called, *Flying Saucers: Serious Business*. In that book, Edwards reported on a suspected crash in a place called Roswell, New Mexico of three flying saucers in 1947. He claimed his source on the details of the crash was an ex-Air Force investigator who gave the dimensions of three round craft as 99, 66, and 33 feet respectively."

Ensiling picked up the tale from what was in the smuggled book. "Yes, Adam, and this struck Lathie as a detail that could be crucial. He converted those measurements into new feet and then factored in a constant of .2640, which had been showing up more and more in the math of his grid work. The resulting new measurements had proven to have a harmonic relationship with his worldwide grid. At the time, he didn't know what that meant, but it was a startling discovery with a scientific probability of a million-to-one against random numbers getting the same result.

"Why did the book have to be smuggled in?" Peter asked.

"As far as we know, that galley was the only remaining copy of this book," Kasiko said.

"Yes. The printing company in Hong Kong had an unfortunate fire and the manuscript and all the copies of the first printing are gone. The folder I brought in is the only surviving copy of the text."

"It is one of the first books ever banned by the United States?" another said.

"Can't the author write it over again?" Peter asked.

"He died in a plane crash," Ensiling said. "He was a commercial pilot and crashed in his private plane on a beautiful day with no weather problems, Peter. There are now only six copies of this book in the world."

Eleven thought Peter, but his face remained like stone.

"How do you know the book is legitimate?" another man of science asked.

"Ahh, that is our task, gentlemen."

Kasiko noticed Peter's furrowed brow and faraway look, "What's on your mind, Peter?"

"I was wondering; did the harmonics prove the grid, or did its harmony to the grid prove the saucers' existence?"

"That's very good, Peter; hold that thought." Ensiling left and returned with a big lawyers' briefcase. Out of it, he pulled a giant red loose-leaf book. Embossed in gold leaf on the front was the seal of the United Nations.

Chapter Nine
THERE BUT FOR THE SAKE OF JANICE

Somebody's cell phone rang and Peter jumped nervously, turning in the direction of the sound. The paranoia being infectious, Bill also was startled, but looked and saw nothing but tourists and a Boy Scout troop visiting the Memorial.

The interruption gave Hiccock a chance to get a word in edgewise. "Peter, is this professor, in the Queens apartment back in 1968, the one who smuggled in the book… Is he the same Professor Ensiling that just died?"

"Yes. That's why I am here, telling you this story. He didn't die – he was murdered."

"Whoa. You know this for sure?"

"He was old, but he was in good shape. They got him."

"Who got him?"

"That I can't tell you."

"Can't or won't tell me."

Peter stole a nervous glance away from Bill. "Four out of the five remaining committee members are dead. All within a half a year. Actuarially, those are lottery ticket odds. Bill, something is going on. I need you to help me."

"Help you? What this got to do with you?"

"I think I might be next."

"Why? You aren't a professor, are you?" Bill realized there was a lot about "Peter Robot" he didn't know. In fact, all Billy remembered about Peter before this meeting on the steps was that he had built a robot in sixth grade (hence his schoolyard nickname) and won all kinds of science fairs with a computer he built. He had faded into the haze of Bill's Bronx memories until Cheryl said his name this morning.

Today a guy like Peter would set off alarm bells in every quarter of society, but back in the '60s and '70s people were still considered innocent until proven perverted. So it was, that, the mentally-advanced Peter was socially-retarded; outcast from his age group in the first known case of a nerd-ectomy in the U.S.A. Although jocks and cool guys shunned him, Peter actually had no need for them as well. On any given Friday or Saturday night he was content soldering and inventing in his room. But there was one group to which Peter Remo was the coolest guy, mostly because he was older – his younger brother Johnny's friends, like Bill. These younger guys were enthralled by his stories and science wizardry. In addition, because he was older, he could take the rap for one of Johnny's group and, for example, claim that the pack of Parliaments that hit the floor were his, or maybe give you a swig of beer. And if you hung with Peter, the bully guys, who were maybe a year older than you, were 'a-scared' of him.

So it was that Tommy Mush, Joey Plum, Billy Hic, Larry Soch, and B.O. all related to Peter as if he were also in the seventh grade.

The neighborhood was close knit. Everyone knew everyone and each parent was the parent of every kid as they played in the courtyard or on the sidewalks. Therefore, every parent knew Peter, his good nature, and his brains. In a word no one would ever use today, Peter was "harmless."

In many ways, Peter was Bill's entry point into the wonders of science. Bill spent many hours on the stoop of the apartment house with tape, wood, motors, batteries and buzzers building "electro-cities," actually electric busy boxes that rang, beeped, lit up, spun, and blinked. At first, done under Peter's careful guidance, they soon became a canvas upon which Bill would create newer and more complex circuits and combinations, at times surprising Peter with his ingenuity. Yet, Peter always had the next challenge, such as challenging him to make two lights alternate every time the buzzer rang. That one took Bill a week to figure out, but when he finally got it, the praise he got from Peter was like his winning the Nobel Prize in Science.

After Bill reached high school, he only saw Peter around the neighborhood from time to time. Their age difference guaranteed they never traveled in the same social circle. In his teens, Bill was the geekiest guy in the "football" crowd, but the older Peter spent his formative years as a true mainline geek – no sports, no girls, no nothing other than science. Upon reflection, Bill realized that was how he could have been described today if he hadn't let Janice finally get through to him.

Today on the steps of the Memorial, the look in Peter's eyes was hard for Bill to decode. It could either be the deep-set hollowness of a man in mortal fear or the warning signs of insane indifference to reality of the delusional. This was more Janice's area than his. He'd discuss this with her tonight.

"Bill, Professor Ensiling and I kept in touch after the committee was disbanded by Kurt Waldheim. Ensiling was working on super-conductivity and I was asked to join his team as a 'theorizer.'"

"A what? I've two degrees in the sciences and I have never heard of a theorizer."

"He liked my opinion on things that many felt were already settled as science or proven as fiction."

"I know a little something about outside the box thinking myself, Pete."

"Like, I told the engineers once about relative absolute zero."

"Wait – you can't have a relative absolute anything." Bill then relaxed. After all, this was Peter the Great, as Billy the Kid had called him. He was the great science whiz who fed into Bill's hunger for science and answers. So Hiccock once again became what he had been on the stoop of the apartment house, now the stoop of the Lincoln Memorial... an apt pupil.

"See, that's where I came in. I theorized that at around -273 degrees Celsius the temperature coefficients of likely super-conducting materials aren't linear but are skewed by the specific gravity and mass of the sample being tested. Therefore..."

"Therefore, their molecular stasis points don't necessarily follow the degree intervals."

"Exactly. Believe it or not, those scientists would never consider that and whole reams of data was discarded as being junk or polluted."

"So are you saying super-conducting got the Professor killed?"

Peter paused before speaking again. "Bill, did you ever hear of the Jesus Factor?"

"What is it, some bible-thumping fad?"

"No. But if you've never heard of it, and you're the one in the White House, then I am really fucked out on a limb."

"What are you talking about?"

Peter looked at Bill. Twice he started to form a sentence and then stopped. "I did some preliminary work for the professor on instantaneous values of Epsilon H33," he said at last. "He told me to destroy my notes and then they killed...." Peter pulled up short.

"What?" Bill's interest was thoroughly piqued.

"Nothing, Bill. I don't think we should talk any longer."

"Why?"

"I should go."

"Peter, you are starting to weird me out here?"

"Thanks for the time, kid. I'll see ya round." With that, Peter trudged down the steps of the Memorial.

CHAPTER TEN
SCHIZOID

There were 14 messages on Bill's personal cell phone as he glanced at it sitting in the back seat of his government supplied Town Car. His government cell would have rung, or Bill's driver, Secret Service Agent Brent Moskowitz, would have been beeped to retrieve him from the steps of the Lincoln Memorial if anything of national consequence had occurred. He scanned the messages quickly and decided to ring back Janice.

"Hey, Bill. How's your day going?"

"I got to tell ya, a really weird thing happened. I met up with an old friend... acquaintance...from the neighborhood and the guy goes on and on and tells me a story that sounds like a science fiction author wrote it. Then, for no reason, he suddenly runs away!"

"Schizophrenia?"

"Maybe, but it was more like he suddenly didn't trust me."

"What triggered this?"

"I dunno, one minute we're talking... he's talking, I'm listening, then he asks me a question. Then he freaks."

"What was the question?"

"He asked me if I ever heard of the Jesus Factor."

"You mean 'W W J D?'"

"What's that?"

"What would Jesus do?"

"Oh right. No, I don't think they call that the Jesus Factor. Besides, I asked him if it was a religious thing. That's when he freaked.

"Maybe he's in a fundamentalist cult. And you were suddenly an outsider."

"Maybe, but he's a real science nut. Religion has to have faith. I don't see him as a holy roller."

"Then back to my initial instinct: schizophrenia."

"You're probably right. What a waste of time. Anyway, how's your day going?"

"I got the board to approve my program."

"Aw, honey that's great! Congratulations."

"You have no idea what I'm talking about do you?"

Bill cringed. "Sure, the program thing. It's great news."

"Nice try, buster. I'll fill you in tonight. Gotta run; love ya."

"Love you too babe. Later."

As the car found it's way back to the White House, Bill's head was reeling with all that he had absorbed from his three-hour "*lunch in 1968*" with Peter.

Cheryl intercepted him as he approached his office. "You have staff at four and I need you to review the agenda for next week's nanotechnology summit. You also need to..."

Bill was not intending to say the next thing he said, but something inside him compelled him to utter, "Cheryl, get Susan Clark, the Ambassador to the U.N., on the phone. Then get me a research person. Maybe that new kid, Harry."

"Horace. I'll take him off of filing. When do you want to see him?"

"From before I asked you." He handed her his cell phone. "Go through my messages and cull and delegate them out, unless one of them needs me."

"Got it."

Once behind his desk, Bill went through his red-lined folder. Cheryl put all the documents that needed immediate attention or signatures in a recycled manila folder with the words, "Operation Quarterback" on the front, a memento from a previous adventure through which

Cheryl had started working for Bill. The load was light and in three minutes, the folder was wedged between the tape dispenser and the stapler; the parking spot that told Cheryl that Bill had reviewed the contents. In that time, Horace came in. Bill gave him the name of Peter's flying saucer book and many of the other details of the whacked out story Remo told him.

His next call was to Joey Palumbo.

"Got a minute?"

"Sure; what's up, Bill?" the former FBI agent said.

"Can you look into the death of a scientist by the name of Ensiling? I'll have Cheryl get all the info I have over to you."

"What are you looking for?"

"Probably nothing. Hey, you remember Pete Remo?"

"Yeah, the only guy who was more of a square than you! Geez, I haven't heard that name in years."

"Me neither, till this morning when I met with him. He started out asking me to look into this professor's demise."

"How did it end up?"

"Weird... unsettling."

"Bill, the guy Peter was always a weirdo."

"Yeah, I know, Joe, but he was socially weird. His science and his brain were working on all eight cylinders."

"Maybe he's self-medicating."

"Yeah... I thought of that. But even though his story was out there, it was very cogent."

"You tell a lie enough..."

"...and you eventually start believing it. Maybe that's it, but check into this just to make sure, will ya?"

"Once again, what are we looking for?"

"Just see if his death was kosher or not."

"Where did he die?"

"Vienna, last week."

"I'll reach out through Interpol and a few other sources."

"Thanks, Joey. Get back to me as soon as you know anything."

Bill hung up the phone and wondered if he had just done the right thing. Peter was probably nuts. Who knew what he did since the days in the Bronx? Drugs, religion, alcohol, indoctrination into a cult, a million things could have scrambled his eggs in the past 20 years. Still, Ensiling was red flagged by the government, and that was bothering him. On the other hand, the UFO nonsense was finished business. Bill was at the top of the government technology Christmas tree and nothing ever went close to extraterrestrial anything. It was purely the stuff of conspiracy nuts and Trekkies. Yet, if the U.N. was... Well, he only had Peter's say-so on the U.N., the U.N. Ambassador would tell him. *Enough! I got work to do.*

∞§∞

"What the devil?" was all the Sheik could say as the music startled him awake. Then the lights went on.

She was there again, in her red warm-up clothes. Swinging the sock.

"Hello, Sheiky. I am going to show you how much I don't like little weasels who run to the teacher and cry about every little thing."

She's insane, he thought as a plan emerged in his mind.

"Come over here, dog."

He remained in his bed.

"Come here now or it will be worse if I have to come to you." She took two steps towards the bed.

He did not move.

"Hey, dipshit!" The sock knocked over a chair.

She stepped closer. "I am talking to you!"

He didn't respond. *Good a little closer.*

"You are only making this harder on yourself, asshole." She came to within two feet of the bed.

He sprang up, intent on grabbing her and falling on her and calling for the guards. He was stopped halfway by the chain.

"Jerk. I shortened it while you were sleeping. Now you are going to wish you had come to me when I asked you..."

She now administered the blows to his body with the sock in the leg of a pair of panty hose. This gave her more striking distance to stay out of reach of his flailing arms. At one point, he grabbed the sock and cradled it to stop the beatings. Wham! A second one beat him in the back, causing him to uncoil and release the first while gasping for breath.

Then he heard her leave. He lay there shuddering.

The next day was Friday. The Imam came to his cell with a guard and a translator who had a tape recorder.

He ran towards the holy man, causing the guard to intercede. He minded his distance and pleaded in Arabic, "Imam, they are torturing me."

"Imam, they are torturing me!" was the translator's immediate echo.

The blue-eyed devil appeared at the door in her business suit and walked in. "Gooooood morning, Sheik. Good morning, Imam. Frank."

The Sheik became instantly self-conscious and averted eye contact with Brooke.

"My son, are you saying these men..."

"No not the men..." He felt her eyes on him. "The food! It is lousy and as good as torture."

"I will speak to the director of this prison and see if they can arrange for a proper meal. Are you ready to start?" the man of religion said as he opened the Koran.

CHAPTER ELEVEN
SERVING TWO MASTERS

State Department Diplomatic Security, or "DS," was a consolation prize for Jamal El Azam. He tried for the ATF, FBI, and Secret Service, but his college GPA index being 3.2 and his one little brush with the law closed those doors. It was patently unfair for his record to still carry the police report stemming from when, as a 17-year old, he and two friends were jumped by some lunkheads who blamed anyone with a middle-eastern look or name for the first attack on the World Trade Center in 1993. He was released and ultimately found innocent of all charges. But the red flag remained. If his Grade Point Average was 3.7 or above, it would have been overlooked, but things being as they were gave any federal administrator an excuse to say no.

The State Department, however, under Madeline Albright and the Clinton Administration, wanted to put the best face on America's image to the world, so they sought out ethnic types for the Foreign Service. Jamal's fluency in both Eastern and Western Arabic languages also helped in his chances of being assigned to Ambassador's Protection Service in Egypt. Since his posting with diplomatic security, however, he had not advanced as he should have, being passed over three times for promotion within the DS. True, he had some attendance and lateness issues, but no more than would have been overlooked had he been promoted on schedule.

Deep down inside, however, Jamal knew it was because of her. She distracted and delayed him all the time. But he was in love and decided that she came first.

His mother would curse him if she knew of Salinda. She was a descendant of a nomadic tribe that was also the tribe of Libya's former dictator, Mohamar Kadaffi. She was beautiful, her body was perfection itself, and, with it, she made him feel like no other woman had ever made him feel. They took up together, but kept a low profile among the embassy's circle of influence. Jamal had two residences. One near the embassy for appearances and the other across town in a very Egyptian neighborhood where no Americans or Brits would dare go.

It was there that he brushed up against the Brotherhood. Salinda had brought him to a meeting. They spoke of the true call of Islam. They led him to the Prophet's own words. At first, because of the fraternizing aspect of his relationship, he made no contact report, as any FSO at his grade was duty-bound to make. Later, the reason was not as benign as covering up a sexual affair. Jamal had acclimated to and then wholly embraced the notion that the only hope for mankind was through the words of the Koran. That America, his America, was imposing its Judeo-Christian ethic of freedom on the children of Allah. Forcing freedom on Muslims was, in a sense, blasphemy, equal to forcing an Arab to take communion from a priest. This enlightenment came to Jamal from many parts of the Koran but the one that still resonated within him was Qur'an 33:36 *"It is not fitting for a Muslim man or woman to have any choice in their affairs when a matter has been decided for them by Allah and His Messenger. They have no option. If anyone disobeys Allah and His Messenger, he is indeed on a wrong Path."*

What he was about to do, what needed to be done, he did for the Brotherhood and on a deeper level, to honor his love for Salinda.

"The Ambassador is moving," his radio crackled, breaking this stream of thought.

He keyed his mic. “Front gate, all clear.” Jamal’s post this morning was at the front gate. He barely took notice of the two white vans parked on each side of the street adjacent to the embassy’s gate. As the Cadillac limo pulled through the gate, on time as Jamal had indicated, twelve men each emerged from both vans with weapons and one with a video camera. They immediately opened fire. There was a lead car and a chase car, each with three security officers inside. The lead car was pummeled by Kalashnikov fire and two of the three men inside managed to get out and return fire. Jamal watched and did nothing as two assailants came around and fired on the men from behind, eliminating them. The limo and chase car were under a hail of bullets. An RPG hit the chase car and it exploded, flipping over on its side. A former Mujahedeen ran up to it and sprayed the car and its inhabitants with three full clips of ammunition. The limo’s bulletproof windshield eventually caved in from the unrelenting torrent of lead coming from ten automatic weapons. The instant it was breeched, the driver and the bodyguard disappeared in a blood red plume. The Ambassador was inside the “cage,” a reinforced armored compartment behind the driver’s seat. This survival space could take a dead hit from a mortar round and keep its occupant alive.

Jamal walked over to the smoking limo as five of the assailants approached it. One tried the door on the far side. Frustrated he then fired his weapon into the lock. The door would not give. Five guards from the embassy were running down the driveway firing as they approached. Jamal hitched his head in their direction and six other men started laying down a curtain of lead that decimated the reinforcements coming to the Ambassador’s aid. Jamal reached into his pocket and simply removed a duplicate set of keys. He pressed the remote and, with a click, the door of the Ambassador’s compartment was unlocked. The diplomat was unceremoniously shoved into the back of one of the vans. Jamal rode with him and was the last person the Ambassador, the embodiment of American foreign policy, saw as one of the men jabbed him with a needle that would knock him out for an hour or so. The two vans then sped off in opposite directions leaving 13 security officers, all co-workers and associates of Jamal, dead or seriously wounded.

The men in the truck shouted, "Allah Akbar." God is great.

∞§∞

At 7:30, Bill entered his office. The big news of the day was a videotape of a captured U.S. Ambassador kneeling before an Islamo-fascist flag as a hooded man held a gun to his head. In a halting, clouded voice, the armed man spouted a string of invectives against the country his captive represented. Obvious to anyone, except the anti-American crowd watching on Al Jazeera, was the fact that he was drugged, beaten, and under some duress. The Americans were threatened with the usual time limit to stop doing something that this group thought violated the sanctity of their beliefs, or the Ambassador would be beheaded. Unfortunately, everyone in the world except the "true believers" and the family and loved ones of the captive, were already bored with this brutal, theatrical bloodletting.

Like millions of Americans, Bill placed the horror of the man's plight in a corner of his mind and made way for the challenges of the day. Today that meant three staff-level meetings and a presentation to the Department of Transportation on the impact magneto-electric hover technology for high-speed trains would have on the environment and U.S. energy supplies. *Real exciting stuff... but at least someone wasn't holding an AK-47 to his soon-to-be-severed head.*

Bill remembered that, in his or her country of assignment, an ambassador outranks any other American official, resident, or visiting government types, even outranking the Secretary of State or Chairman of the Joint Chiefs, everyone, except the President himself. *Move on,* Bill commanded the little committee meeting of all the voices in his head.

Joey Palumbo knocked on the doorjamb. "Cheryl wasn't at her desk, so I invited myself in."

"No problem. How are you today?"

"Good," Joey said as he flopped into the chair opposite Bill's desk.

"Any idea how they got the Ambassador?"

"I hear there's a security tape that shows it was an inside job."

"Some local worker?"

"No, one of ours."

"No shit!"

"That's the only way to grab an ambassador without a full company of marines."

"A double agent?"

"Fucking traitor. Must have masterminded the whole thing."

"Et tu brute."

"Et tu-xactly. Listen, I ran the Ensiling thing. All my sources are coming up natural causes – and these guys are good! You've got the Viennese Prefect of Police, Interpol, and a guy I know who's working private security for an oil company over there. They all agree – no funny business."

"Thanks Joey. It sounded weird when he told me, but I guess Peter's got an overactive imagination."

"Anything else I can do for you, buddy?"

"Yes, I have a meeting at three. Can you tell me how you would go about derailing a mag lev train?"

"Very cautiously, since I don't have the sligthest friggin' idea what a 'mag lev' is!"

Bill tossed a thin, stapled stack of papers over his desk to Joey. "Take a minute to read that. Magnetic levitation is going to be the next big thing in trains. I want you to tell me if there are any more security risks than there are with conventional trains."

"First off, ask your dad, he's the choo-choo engineer. And second, why don't you put this up on the rings and see what you get back?"

"I was just about to when you walked in, so you get to have a head start."

∞§∞

Jamal knew the number. "Station Chief now…"

"There is no station chief here," the voice on the other end said. "Who is calling?"

"Listen, this is Jamal. Don't waste my time and give me the CIA station chief this instant." He looked up at his men smiling. "Technically there are no CIA officers in Egypt."

The other end connected with a beep sequence that meant the call was being recorded. "Rumson. Who is this?"

"Earl, this is Jamal. The Islamic Brotherhood has captured an enemy of Islam and he will be tried and executed in accordance with Muslim law."

"You are illegally detaining the personal representative of the President of the United States of America and that is an act of war. You must release him immediately." The "*not the CIA Station Chief*s" tone was stern and unwavering.

"You are wasting your breath, my time, and his few remaining minutes."

"What do you want, Jamal?"

"A trade: the Ambassador for Sheik Alzir El Benhan."

"Who?"

"You're wasting time." Jamal closed the cell phone, dropped it to the floor, and stamped it into pieces.

∞§∞

"Who?" President Mitchell was having a bad day already. Now his Secretary of State, Charles Pickering, was playing "Name that Terrorist" with him.

"He was the mastermind behind the influenza attack. We have him in a maximum security prison in Indiana."

"We don't negotiate with terrorists."

"This is trading."

"Are you saying there's a difference?"

"Yes. It's one for one. And it's back channel, not trading out in the open."

"The world already knows Greely has been abducted. When he suddenly pops up, Chuck, they're gonna know!"

"We can generate some heat in Turtle Bay and make it look like the kidnappers unilaterally acceded to the will of the United Nations. Only we'll know it's one for one."

"Yeah, and about that, it's only one for one if you don't count the dozen or so who were killed to kidnap the ambassador and you don't count the 26,000 estimated flu deaths this 'Sheik' caused," the President said sharply, then added, "And how is he a Sheik, all of the sudden?"

"Ambassador Greeley is an outstanding American who fought for this country in uniform, gave of his personal wealth to myriad charities as a civilian, and serves his country in a class one post to this day as *Ambassador A.E. & P.* Your personal representative. We have to consider this opportunity to save his life as a serious matter."

"Serious matter? Ah hell, Chuck!"

"Sorry, wrong choice of words. Of course, you are serious. I meant that this terrorist offer is serious."

"Look, if we do this 'trade' then every Ambassador Extraordinary & Plenipotentiary who works for you, for me, becomes the coin of the realm to every fanatic with a grudge against the U.S. or General Motors for that matter. You know that."

"The alternative is to show the world we can't get our ambassador back."

"How long do we have?"

"Maybe 24 to 36 hours. Then they'll either kill him, contact us, or, worse, send out an Al Jazeera video."

Mitchell turned to his Chief-of-Staff, Ray Reynolds. "I want to know if I have any military options. Press the Egyptians hard on where they are holding him. Get me any international law – hell, even diplomatic protocol – that we can have Susan wave at the Security Council up in New York. And for God's sake hold this tight."

"I agree," Pickering said. "We must consider this 'close hold.' The press would have a field day."

"Screw the press. I don't want his wife, Stella, to raise any false hopes of a trade until, and if, it becomes the new policy of the United States."

With that, the men left the room. Mitchell looked out the window into the Rose Garden. He knew that any effort through the U.N. was futile; international law didn't cover this unless the U.S. was going to accuse Egypt of being complicit. Besides, his own administration's Middle East initiatives would preclude strong-arming a friend in the Security Council. At best, a public display of condemnation was a publicity stunt that could possibly have misdirection value if U.S. forces had to go in. Mitchell also knew committing U.S. forces, to invade a sovereign nation – an ally – was risky business. On the other hand, to let an ambassador die, only to protest it to the world afterwards, seemed like a damn bad use of a good man's life. Yet, to save him by any means of negotiated release meant to hang an open season hunting tag on any official of the U.S. Government. For a moment, Mitchell had a terrible thought: *Why couldn't they have just killed him.* He actually shook his head to erase that insane, cold-hearted notion.

His personal assistant entered quietly and said softly, "Mr. President, the Speaker of the House is here for your 10:15 meeting." Like so many other Americans that morning, Mitchell had to relegate any further thought of the ambassador's dilemma to a far recess of his mind so that the rest of his brain could work on the matter's of the Nation's business.

∞§∞

The Hiccocks started their Saturday twice. They awoke at 8:30, each thinking what the other was thinking, then acting upon it, so neither left the bed. At 9:10 they both collapsed into a deep sleep until 10:20, when Janice rolled over and opened her eyes.

"Bill, it's 10:20."

Bill spoke into the pillow. "Errrrmp."

She patted him on his butt until he lifted his head. "Good morning, almost afternoon."

They showered, dressed, and went to a local diner for breakfast.

"No matter what, we are just looking," Bill said. "We are not buying anything."

"Exactly. We're going to see our options then sleep on it."

"We have lots of time. We don't have to rush into anything."

"Exactly."

It was a beautiful, sun-shiny, day. They drove for 45 minutes to a store out on the highway that Cheryl's sister had recommended.

Forty minutes later, Bill was ruing the fact that they didn't take the old wagon. Tied to the top of the Caddy was the big box holding the crib. Jutting out from the tied-down open trunk was the stroller box and the back seat was crammed with little blankets, pillows, and stuffed animals. With over 300 I.Q. points between them, the one thing they did that was smart in 'Babies R Us,' was not commit to any gender specific color scheme or wallpaper.

"Didn't we say we were just looking?" Bill said, as he drove no faster than 40 miles per hour, lest the wind shear lift the crib's box into somebody's front grill.

The nursery wasn't ready yet. It wasn't even a nursery, and it still had to be divested of the books, junk, and old exercise equipment that lived there. Bill put the crib, stroller, and other stuff in the garage. He then began tinkering with a lamp he started rewiring last winter.

"I made you a sandwich," Janice called out from the kitchen.

"Just a minute." Bill snaked the new cord through the body of the lamp and out the top. He left enough hanging out to be able to work with when he would wire the new socket to it, later, after lunch.

The TV was on in the kitchen and CNN was all over the ambassador story with graphics and serious music calling it "Summit with Death?" They had silhouetted the grainy image of Greeley from the terrorists tape and it now flew back over the graphics of a masked terrorist as thunderous theme music played. Being CNN, there was a panel of talking heads who didn't beat the living shit out of the one "Intellectual" who espoused that the taking of the ambassador was "justifiable" due to America's continuing suppression of the Arab sentiments in the world. Instead, they simply went to commercial. Bill just shook his head.

"Did you know him?" Janice asked.

"Greeley? No, never met him, although I hear he was... is, a good man."

"The news is now saying his ambassadorial appointment was a political payoff for campaign contributions."

"Well, ain't that a scoop! They are only about a hundred years late on catching on to that dirty little secret. But that's the soft posts like Canada or Portugal, where some political appointee can't screw it up too bad. Egypt is prime time, Class one. Those only get career Foreign Service Officers. The press is just looking for any way to slam Mitchell because he isn't one of them."

"Because he isn't a newsman?"

"No, because he's neither Fox news "Right," or CNN "Left," and they both hate that neutrality, like he was selling the secret formula of Coca Cola to the Russians.

"So what do you think is going to happen?" Janice asked as she poured Bill and herself more iced tea.

"Thanks. This is just a guess, but I'd say there's a delta force or SEAL strike team warming up the coffee right about now waiting for someone to drop a dime on where the man is being held."

"What about Egyptian sovereignty?"

"That's covered under 'Posse comi - fuck 'em.'"

It took a second for Janice to realize that Bill had just bastardized 'Posse Comitatus.'

Bill added, "If they get a 20 on this guy, our guys will go in first, snatch him back, then spin it as a joint U.S./Egyptian intelligence op or some kind of bullshit so that the Egyptians save face."

"Okay, so now I feel better."

∞§∞

Bill was in the middle of going through a box of stuff in order to throw most of it out and put what was left in a smaller box from which, if he continued the process, he could whittle down the contents of the ten boxes that were taking up valuable baby space in the garage down to one. He was going through old checks and photographs when he heard a familiar voice.

"You *are* human! You actually do normal stuff!"

"Joey, I don't believe it. I just found this in the box."

Bill handed Palumbo an old photograph: a picture of the two of them and some other guys standing in front of a pipe held up by two braced two-by-fours.

"Hey, the high bar, Muzzi, Johnny 'No', Soccio, Mush, B.O. Look at the mop of hair on your head!"

"Look how skinny we were." Hiccock laughed as he tossed the picture back in the keeper box. "What brings you round this way on a Saturday?"

"Something is bugging me and I thought I'd run it by you."

"Wanna beer?"

"Nah."

"Okay, then shoot."

"You remember Brooke Burrell out of the New York Bureau office?"

"Sure do. She was point on the whole virus thing and the poison gas tank plot in New York. Solid agent."

"One of the best. She and I had a talk, off the record. A lot of it was just agent-to-agent, you know? 'How do I do this, how should I handle that?' But she said one thing that...Have you heard the latest out of Egypt?"

"That they took Greely to set El Benham free? Yeah."

"She had an inkling that Alzir knew he wasn't going to be in custody long."

"Have they ever done this before?" Bill asked as he decided to throw out a desk calendar from 1999.

"Not one for one like this, and if they have it's usually a low-level or convenient grab. A local police chief or U.S. military captive. But it's always reactive, almost improvised by them. This has pre-meditated all over it."

"And you're telling me this because?"

"Brooke had a sense about this guy knowing he was going to be sprung, and now she's right."

Bill looked at him in a way that said, "So?"

"This is a big play. They wouldn't do this kinda thing if we caught Al Qaeda number 1. This Alzir guy is deeply connected to something else, something bigger."

"Bigger than potentially infecting and killing fifty million Americans? I don't think I want to know what that could be."

"I want you, as a deputy director of the FBI, to authorize a guy who I have been following for a while. He's Dr. Robert Fusco, a psych-ops guy who's got some methods and practices that might give Brooke and us an edge."

"I am only dep director for stuff under my area."

"This guy is under your area and, besides, the funding can't go on any record, so I need you to bury it in your SCIAD budget."

"Okay, now you're scaring me. Is this one of your wild-assed ideas?"

"Who was it who taught me to think outside the box?"

Joey positioned it perfectly to create the maelstrom in Bill's head. It raged there for a minute then he simply said, "You really think this is going to pay off?"

"It's got a good shot."

Bill responded in the affirmative by giving Joey the Boulevard Blades gesture of a fist with the thumb jutting out between the index and pointer fingers. Not that they knew it, but it was an actual gesture from the ancient Neapolitan society, meaning "to protect."

∞§∞

At 4:00 p.m. in the Situation Room beneath the White House, President Mitchell was being pushed to make a decision between two diametrically opposed evils.

The Secretary of State was uncharacteristically lobbying hard to save the life of the man who worked for him. "Mister President, the ambassador is a prime asset of the United States. He is worth every effort to retrieve."

"Chuck, we can't negotiate with terrorists. You'll be setting a precedent that will have every American overseas being kidnapped round the clock," the Chief of Staff needlessly reminded him. "The only option is military, if we get that lucky. Otherwise, the ambassador is now a combatant and prisoner of war."

The Secretary of State turned to Mitchell. "Mr. President, how can you sacrifice his life like this?"

"Look, Charles, this ambassador makes over $200,000 dollars a year plus all expenses paid. There are dog faced G.I.s, who are just as valuable to me as he is, who die in shit-holes all over the world and their families barely live at poverty level. So they are both soldiers and, unfortunately, he is as expendable as they are. Chuck, what's really going on with you? You know the damn policy as well as anyone, yet you continue to lobby for a trade that isn't going to happen?" The President's agitation was evident in the way he threw down his pencil.

"I pushed Greely into this post, sir. He wanted out and I personally strong-armed him to take another tour. He is a close personal friend of Saudi Prince Ramalli; they were roommates at Choate. I needed him in that post as part of my mid-east initiative."

"God damn it, Charles, then get your head out of your ass. We send people to dangerous places and into jeopardy all the time. It may be a first for you, but, trust me, the bad news is you have to live with it."

CHAPTER TWELVE
FINAL GAMBIT

Brooke took a deep breath as her hand rested on the latch to the Sheik's cell. She hoped this would be the last time she'd have to do this. She hated it. But it was working. The last time, he wet himself as she approached. She wanted to let up on him a little because of it, but that would signal that she was weak. She had double-checked and made sure that she wasn't hitting him in the same spots. That could result in real injury and cause internal bleeding. She wanted him healthy.

Her hand pushed the door open. "What do you know about this?"

She held up the front page of the *N.Y. Post*. On it was a frame grab from the Al Jazeera video showing the ambassador blindfolded, the jihad flag and AK 47's around him, as a knife was near his throat.

"Hey, shit for brains, what do you know about this?"

"Nothing," the Sheik said as he retreated to the corner.

"Oh yeah? Well they want us to release you in trade for him."

"I know nothing of this. Except that Allah's will be served. If it is his way that I will be saved, then so be it." He half closed his eyes in a now rare, cocky gesture.

It was too much for Brooke. For the first time, she wanted to wallop him in the jaw with the sock sending him reeling backwards and out cold.

Instead, she grabbed her gun, turned, and fired at the men coming through the door. They returned fire, sending her spinning back and crumbling onto the floor, lifeless. The Sheik heard more gunshots in the hallway and the sound of men yelling and groaning filled the room. A man in a ski mask grabbed and held down Aliz as another jabbed a needle into his arm. The last thing he saw was Brooke crumpled on the floor.

∞§∞

The Sheik awoke with a light shining brightly in his eyes. He was on his knees; his hands were tied behind his back. There were other people in the room. He turned and behind him was a banner with the words, "But One Answer." There were two tall torches on each side. Two hooded men stood with M4 carbines across their chests. Everyone around him was hooded and in ski masks. One grabbed his face and turned it toward the light again. As the Sheik's eyes adjusted, he saw that the light was atop a camera. He was being videotaped.

Someone held his head back and a bayonet was drawn across his throat without cutting the skin. A man unfurled a scroll and read from it.

"You are no longer a prisoner of the United States nor subject to its protection. The Scared Brotherhood of the Shores of Tripoli, in accordance with the traditions set forth by our founders, has captured and taken custody of you and has declared you as a Practical Prisoner of War. You are hereby sentenced to endure the same life, conditions, and final status as the one that has been kidnapped in trade for your life. Those who have murdered, kidnapped, and extorted so that you might be set free are now warned; your fate and that of Ambassador Greely's are now inexorably one"

Aliz squeezed his eyes at what seemed the conclusion of the speech. Surely that was when they'd cut his throat. He started praying to Allah aloud.

It made for dramatic video. But instead of the knife separating his head from his torso, the man continued speaking.

"To the abductors of our Sacred Ambassador Extraordinary & Plenipotentiary, his Excellency, Wallace Greely: every hardship, every discomfort, every trauma, and, ultimately, the fate of our ambassador, will be inflicted upon, and suffered by your Sheik. Therefore, the Sheik's destiny and the ambassador's are one, and in your hands."

The man released the grip on the Sheik's head. The light went out and he was quickly dragged out of the room and thrown onto a cot in a small dark room.

∞§∞

Back in the makeshift studio, the ski masks and hoods came off. Brooke's smile matched others in the room. They went up to their mentor, Dr. Robert Fusco of the Psy-Ops division of the new FBI. He critiqued their performances.

"Bob, the guy with the knife in the videos we referenced, always stays close to the captive. You veered away."

"Got it." Bob nodded.

"Brooke, you still have a trace of perfume. That could've sent a false signal and compromised the whole ploy."

"Won't happen again, sir."

"Chet, a little more passion when you speak of the Brotherhood. Zealots whip up their emotions, almost to rapture, a torrent of devotion to the cause. They are almost overcome with their own sense of self-importance. Let it flow more in your voice!"

"Thank you, sir."

"I love the banner," the doctor said.

"It was Brooke's idea," Bob noted.

"It's from Thomas Jefferson's speech to Congress in 1801 when he sent our naval armada on its first-ever mission of war across the seas to fight the Muslim Pirates.

He told Congress their demands for money and their call to jihad had left America with '*but one answer*.'"

"To sail over to Tripoli and kill them all, sir!" Chet said.

"Nice touch, Brooke."

"It's a shame no one will ever see it, sir."

"Well, if this works, it will have all been worth it. Ready for the next stage?"

"Yes, sir. Achmed is already in position. Poor schlub, worked out for eight hours, didn't shower, and cracked an egg into his hair. He smells and looks awful."

∞§∞

The Sheik stirred and rolled over on the cot. He came awake and quickly scanned his surroundings. It was dark but not pitch. He was chained to his bed. His mouth was dry and his back ached from the springs in the cot. He lifted his head and saw a shape in the corner of the room. It was a man, naked to his briefs, a manacle around his ankle. He was not moving.

"Are you dead?" the Sheik asked the lump on the floor. There was no response. He lay back down.

The door opened. Two men in masks entered. One held a bowl of hummus with an ant crawling on top of it. "We have learned that your brothers, the scum who are holding his Excellency, are feeding him one bowl of this crap a day. So here's yours. Choke on it, you son of a bitch." He threw the bowl down on the cot.

"Who are you?" The Sheik hazarded to ask.

"We have been fighting your kind since America was born. We'll show the American government that they can't fight you guys like you were criminals – that the only way to beat you is to kill you, eliminate the infestation of our culture by your kind. We are not afraid to die to keep America pure of Islamic zealots like you."

"You killed the FBI girl?"

"Many more than her in busting you out. In war, some die. They were going to make sure you lived a long comfortable life. The idiots. Then your people took our ambassador. That is as insulting as it gets. So we took you. Now what happens to him happens to you. What he eats you eat. When they beat him, we beat you."

"You will kill me?"

"Why? Is that what your guys will do to the ambassador?"

"I don't know."

"You know your kind. If you have any information that will save him, it will also save you. Can you get that into your 7th century head, raghead?" He pushed two fingers into the Sheik's temple with enough force to turn his head. It was the perfect glimpse of concealed rage and hatred he had rehearsed with Doctor Fusco.

"Who is that?" the Sheik said, gesturing toward the body on the floor.

"He is about to be beheaded. Unfortunately your friends in Afghanistan are just about to behead a captured marine. When that happens, we'll mail his head to the Mosque in Istanbul. I think the word will start getting out that we hate you motherfuckers as much as you hate us." He made a fist and pumped it in an aborted attempt to smash in the Sheik's face, but he stopped himself, then leaned in. "I almost hope they torture the ambassador because I am going to enjoy ripping out the nerves running down your legs and arms with a long nose pliers."

They left. Aliz started to tremble. He tried to control it, but could only do so for a few seconds before it became even worse. He grabbed the food and scooped it into his mouth with a shaking hand as his mind raced. Should he tell them of his brother? Of the plans they often spoke of if either was ever caught? Would his brother release the ambassador now that he was abducted and would suffer the same fate? Would his brother even see the video from the Infidels?

The lump on the floor moved.

Without a word, the lump prostrated himself and started morning prayers using a newspaper instead of a proper prayer mat. The Sheik didn't interrupt, but quietly prayed along, offering it up to Allah as the best he could do while being chained to the cot.

When prayers were over, he spoke to the man who looked like he'd been there a long time, "What is your name?"

"Achmed; you?"

"Aliz. Why are you here?"

"Because I am Muslim. Because I believed that in this country you are free to worship."

"Who are these men?"

"They are not government, of that I am sure."

"How long have you been here?"

"Two weeks, three… I have lost count."

"Do you know what they are doing?"

"Yes. They are holding me hostage because a marine is being held hostage in Afghanistan. Why are you here?"

"They are holding me because an ambassador was taken in Egypt."

"That's good. Good that these American bastards cannot just go anywhere in the world they want. They have to pay the price. Do you know where their precious ambassador is? Don't tell me, but do you know?"

"Do you know where the marine is?"

"Ambar Province, I think," Achmed whispered as to not be overheard.

"Then tell them. They may let you go."

"Never. I would sooner die then help these pigs. What did you do?"

"I got shot."

"Come on; what did you do?"

"I was in a motel room and a bullet came through the wall."

"The bust at JFK! I heard of this. You, you are the Sheik? Oh, it is an honor to meet you, a real honor. Forgive my appearance but...

"No need. They beat you?"

"Yes, they say because the marine was beaten, but how would they know? They couldn't know, could they, Sheik?"

Aliz sat there thinking of his own predicament. *Do they know or are they just ruthless thugs?*

"Sheik, I am scared. They are out to kill me. I'm scared."

"If you die, you will die as Martyr. Do not be scared. Don't let them get the satisfaction of scaring you."

"I only fear dying before I see them crushed."

"It will happen; Allah be praised."

"It will, Sheik? How? How will they suffer?"

"It will be by..." Suddenly the Sheik realized the room could be monitored. He scanned around.

In the control room, Brooke and Fusco saw his change of demeanor and decided it was time for stage three. Brooke nodded to two men already donning their ski masks.

"What, Sheik? How will these American bastards be driven to hell?" Achmed's body language became that of student at the master's feet.

The Sheik stayed mum, looking for any sign of a monitoring device. Then the door opened and two men entered and went straight to Achmed.

"Bad news scumbag. Your buddies just beheaded the corporal. Smile, will ya, 'cause we hope your mother is watching when we send this to Al Jazeera."

Achmed started to scamper back and resist. Then his eyes caught the Sheik's. Achmed suddenly cooled and defiantly exclaimed, "You sons of pigs can't take me down."

They unshackled him and dragged him out of the room, slamming the door just as a bright light went on. The Sheik strained to hear. A man was reading a death sentence. He heard Achmed's low steady prayers. The man was now saying that real justice would be carried out for the injustice of the captors of Marine Corporal Lyndon Banks. Then he yelled, "Burn in hell!" The next sound was a peaking of Achmed's prayer followed by a gurgling scream more and more muffled. The Shiek closed his eyes.

Out in the room, Chet finished pouring the water into Achmed's throat as he gave a final gurgling gasp then spit up into a pillow to muffle his coughs as he ran from the room. Chet then pretended he was holding his victim's head by the hair.

"This will be the fate of all who believe that America has lost its way, and that we don't also celebrate death." He took a hammer and started battering a watermelon. The sound that came through the door was unmistakable.

The Sheik imagined them smashing the severed head with a hammer live onto the videotape. He turned and vomited onto the floor.

Chet stood up as Bob punctured the top of a plastic pouch of pig blood. He then squirted the blood onto Bob's body in the manner consistent with that of a severed, carotid artery. For extra measure, he hit Chet's hands twice and one nice spray pattern across his ski mask. Then he bloodied the end of the hammer and placed a patch of skin from pigs' feet on it. The crowning touch was the lock of Achmed's hair, which was glued onto pigskin. The result was a very convincing piece of scalp that any Apache warrior would have proudly waved in victory.

The door opened and the man wielding a hammer, covered in blood, entered. The Sheik watched him with great caution as he approached.

"You killed him?"

"Nah, Sheik. Your fellow ragheads killed him when they decapitated our marine. They did this! This death is on their hands, not ours." His yelling became more intense. "You want to fuck with us.... We'll fuck you right up the ass."

He raised the hammer and started in towards the Sheik, who put up his hands in a defensive manner.

But another man from the room grabbed the hammer. "No, not that way, we need to kill him on camera or he is wasted."

Slowly, the crazed one released his grip on the bloody hammer. He kicked the cot and left.

Aliz's temporary savior leaned over and spoke softly. "Pray to your Allah that they don't hurt a hair on the head of his Excellency, the Ambassador." Then he left as well.

The Sheik's heart rate and nerves combined to make him shake again. This was a new breed of American, outlaws against their own laws and government, yet seemingly more protective of an American ethic, than those laws or the government.

∞§∞

When Chet entered the control room, Brooke went to high-five him, but he demurred holding up his pig-blood-stained hands. "You didn't just take up space minoring in theater at Princeton," she said, patting his non-bloodied back.

"Yes, very good, Chet. Reminiscent of a young, raw, Brando."

"Really?"

"No. But good enough to sell the Sheik."

"Achmed, what can I say? You sold the whole scenario. The proof of your performance is that you had him almost ready to spill, but he got conscious of his surroundings."

"Talk about Academy Award, Achmed, you rock!" Chet said, punching him collegially on the shoulder.

The smile on Achmed's face flattened out when Brooke added, "And now that showtime's over, Ach, please wash that smell out of your hair." She said this laughing as she handed him a wet towel.

"Great preparation, Achmed. He would have seen through any theatrical attempt to make you look like you've been held prisoner for a while," Fusco said, giving the thumbs up to one of the best of the new breed of Muslim F.B.I. agents.

Rubbing a towel into his caked and matted hair, Achmed said, "He's very smart, sir, like an engineer or scientist – his manner of speech and his demeanor."

"Well, thanks to all of you, we've given him a paradigm shift that will take his preconceived defenses out of the equation."

They looked at the monitor to see the Sheik shuddering in a fetal position on his cot.

"We'll move to stage four soon," Dr, Fusco said.

∞§∞

The Sheik was hustled from his bed into the other room. He was forced to his knees, hogtied, and blindfolded.

"What's going on?"

"Bad news, Sheik. Your asshole buddies killed the ambassador and now we are going to show them that they took him for nothing."

The Sheik felt the heat of the TV light on his face and started saying his prayers under his breath. Then suddenly all hell broke lose. Gunshots rang out and he was knocked to the floor. After the yelling ceased, he was stood up and the blindfold lifted as they swept him out of the room. He briefly saw one of them in the mask down with blood pouring from his head and two more crumpled in the corner by a fallen camera.

Out in the hall, a man in an FBI windbreaker grabbed him and said, "Do you want to live?" The man shook him roughly. "Do you want to live?"

"Yes... yes..." Aliz said in exhausted rasps.

"Then tell us your network. Where did you base your operation out of? Tell us, or we will shoot you right now as if you were killed by the Brotherhood."

The Sheik spoke without thought. "Philadelphia. The Al Alaxa safe house..."

"Good, good choice Aliz. You will live. Now tell us more."

∞§∞

Based on the information supplied by Sheik Alzir El Benhan, the FBI monitored and unraveled the Al Alaxa support network. First observing and learning the depth of its tentacles, then in one fell swoop, arresting and detaining 143 known operatives. That haul became a secondary treasure trove of other contacts that led to other networks. All this made Brooke's star shine brighter than any other agent. The little show Dr. Fusco's Psy-Ops division put on for the benefit of the Sheik garnered more funding and personnel for itself. The agents chipped in and had a phony Oscar done up and engraved with the name Chet Ballard. It stated, "Best Actor in a Crime Drama."

∞§∞

Happy to be back in an American prison with its culturally correct food menus and proper prayer mats, Alzir's last iota of self-dignity arose from the fact that he remained true to the sacred oath they made to each other as they ran for their lives through the Hungarian forests. Alzir never betrayed his brother and never revealed the existence or location of "the key."

CHAPTER THIRTEEN
INTO THE BREACH
(GHOSTS OF THE DESSERT)

The Redrock Delta team was on strip alert at Prince Sultan AFB in Saudi Arabia. 20 operators, 4 pilots, 2 crew chiefs were at "Jump Ready 1." The support personnel, mobile air conditioning units, and food trucks would not go on the rescue mission, should the call come. But while they were on the tarmac under the boiling sun, it made the men's lives easier.

Every man on the team was capable of not only finishing but also winning a triathlon with 40 pounds of field equipment strapped to his frame. Every one was an expert-marksman who shoots rounds everyday. All had medic, explosive, munitions, and communications training. In short, one of these guys, by himself, was a wrecking crew of enormous proportions. Twenty of them were an unstoppable force. Yet they were helpless without knowing the location of the ambassador. The Deltas were as forward deployed as they could be without starting a small war. All except for two of them.

Master Sergeant Bridgestone and Sergeant Ross were haggling in Farsi with the street merchant over some bags of rice and flour. Both had acquired impeccable accents and their weather beaten, sun-browned, sandstorm-cracked skin left little doubt to any Arab that they were from the desert. As Bridgestone relentlessly kept dismissing the quality of the man's goods in an attempt to lower the price, Ross kept his eye on the door of the small building across the way. The haggling stopped when he saw her enter the front door. Bridgestone, as "reluctantly" as he could play it, handed over a few coins and took possession of the bags. They were off in a second and headed toward the building. Ross was prepared to jimmy the front door with the bar he had under his traditional robe, but to his surprise, the door was open. They both ascended the squeaky stairs, taking in the smell of evening meals being prepared and the occasional voice or cry of a child reverberating off the walls of the hallway. With only a look between them, they pulled their Sig Sauers out and Ross crouched low as Bridgestone went in high through the door of the apartment in the back.

They caught her in the bathroom. She quickly scrambled, not to cover up out of any sense of privacy or humility, but to reach for a gun she had resting on the edge of the bathtub. Bridgestone got there first and pulled her wrist up hard, forcing her to rise. Ross covered her mouth to muffle any screams. They carried her off to the bed and placed her over the side, her head to the floor and her body bent at the waist. From that position, she would have to fall to the floor before she could do anything else. Ross replaced his hand with a gag made from a torn sheet that Bridge handed him. They tied her arms behind her back. She struggled but to no avail against men who were three times her weight.

Ross put his foot on the back of her neck. In Farsi he said, "Where is your boyfriend? Where is Jamal holding the ambassador?"

She struggled but didn't speak. He stepped on her finger and applied pressure until he heard her catch her breath.

"Salinda, please. You will not be able to endure what we are prepared to do to you if you don't tell us where that dog of a man of yours is holding the ambassador."

Both Ross and Bridgestone were under operational orders to play the role of disaffected Muslim moderates looking to ward off confrontation with the U.S. If Salinda did survive this "interrogation," she would only be able to report to her cell members that some other Arabs roughed her up. Of course, that would be right before her terrorist friends killed her for suspicion of betraying them anyway.

Ross tried to convey this dead-end logic to her. "Salinda, you are now tarnished. Even if you don't tell us anything, none of your people will believe that you didn't tell us something, especially when they see how horribly disfigured we are going to make your face. They will kill you as an insect, without thinking. After all, you are only a woman."

In fact, Ross was thinking exactly the opposite. This woman was tougher than most men, but he and Bridgestone were prepared to kill her. She was deemed an enemy combatant by the NCA. And when the National Command Authority speaks, non-coms like them are paid to listen. Neither of them had any identification on them, and no one would be able to make a connection between them and the USA. They were totally on their own. If caught, they could at best be declared mercenaries. They were truly ghosts.

Bridgestone forced Salinda's head right so she could see her right hand as Ross placed his foot over her ear so she couldn't look away. He then produced a pair of pliers and grabbed her middle fingernail with it. He gave it a tug as he tried to convince her to talk.

"We can do this twenty times if you stay conscious, Salinda. Then we can wait and start snipping off bits of each finger for a few hours. Oh, and look, here's some adrenaline." He produced a syringe. "A shot of this and even the pain of having your genitals removed with a hacksaw wouldn't knock you out."

She made her first human sound, muffled as it was through the now saliva-soaked gag.

"By Allah's will, you are going to talk. You are going to talk, now or later. You are going to talk, all in one piece, or in pieces. But, Salinda, you will talk."

Her middle finger nail pulled back and tore off with ease. She stiffened and gurgled through the sheet.

"This could take a long time, Fasol," Bridgestone said to Ross.

∞§∞

At 19:00 hours, the chopper's radio squawked. "Target Alpha located. GPS downloading. Mission is a go. Repeat. Go."

The twenty men scrambled into the helicopters as the big hoses that kept the turbines going from the support truck on the apron were disengaged. Within 30 seconds of the alert message, *Foxtrot Alpha* and *Foxtrot Bravo*, the mission code name identifiers for the teams of MH60s and AH64-D Apache Longbows, were wheels up and out.

"Delta force en route, sir," the Chairman of the Joint Chiefs informed the President.

"Good. May God protect them and any innocents on the ground."

"Very charitable of you, sir."

Mitchell watched a map in the Situation Room as a triangle blip denoted the progress of the two foxtrot copters as they invaded the sovereignty of Egypt.

"Notify the Egyptian ambassador. Tell him we are invading his airspace. Note time and date and then sequester him till this op is over." The President repeated those words the way his National Security Advisor had suggested 10 minutes earlier after the Egyptian ambassador was seated in the Roosevelt room supposedly awaiting an audience with the President.

"Yes, sir." Charles Pickering said, picking up his phone to carry out the President's orders. He didn't like it; the Egyptian ambassador was an official guest of this country. Stopping him from contacting his homeland was a grievous act of non-diplomacy. Still, for the safety and security of the mission underway, there could not be a chance of leaks on the Egyptian side. In fact, at the end of the day, however it came out, the Egyptians would be glad they were not responsible for any mission compromises. They then could register formal complaints at the U.N. and save face with the Arab street.

∞§∞

Bridgestone and Ross had made a bad decision. They should have left Salinda dead or dying in her room, along with just enough evidence to point anyone in the direction of the desert. But as hard-assed as they were, she was still a woman, albeit one who had plotted against the United States and seduced one of our Diplomatic Security officers over to the other side. So now, here they were, driving an old Datsun with her in the back seat covered in a sheet, unconscious and stinking from the vomiting caused by the intense pain of losing her right pinky. They cauterized her hand and she was alive. They even took the pinky with them in a Styrofoam cup with ice from the fridge. It was a small percentage play, but if their harebrained scheme worked, she could be in Kuwait City in two hours and there they might be able to reattach it. The fingernails would probably grow back.

They were heading towards the safe house with her; first to check and make sure she was telling the truth and, more importantly, to "light it up" for the laser range finders on the Cobra Attack helicopters. Bridgestone rationalized his decision not to terminate her by reasoning that having her alive would prove valuable if somehow she managed to lie through all the pain they had inflicted on her and lead them down an erroneous path. Time would tell.

On board the copter, real-time satellite images were coming out of its printer. The squad commanders on each chopper had identical printouts and were working a Telestrator, the same kind of device used on NFL football broadcasts to draw diagrams over the footage of the game. The difference was that they were drawing attack plans over satellite imagery of the 300-yard square patch of Egypt where, according to Bridgestone and Ross' fresh intel, the ambassador was being held. The two inbound forces were talking over an encrypted satellite link while simultaneously, eight thousand miles away, in a secure room at the Pentagon, other combat controllers and commanders were doing play-by-play and color.

The target area was the abandoned Maghra oil refinery on the northwest edge of the desert. Many of its buildings and pipes were sandblasted down to flat smooth surfaces through years of neglect, leaving it to face the brunt of sandstorms and drifts. Satellite infrared reconnaissance had identified warm bodies out at 100 meters from the main complex. These were perimeter guards ready to alert the terrorists about any threat. Surely, they had radios or cell phones. There were a few heat-generating spots in the main complex warding off the cold desert night. *Foxtrot Alpha's* FLIR spotted a vehicle moving towards the complex about three miles off. They made note of it. If it became a factor, they would kill it with a Hellfire missile that the armament officer had assigned to the target by laying the cursor over it and locking it into his targeting computer. Unless the vehicle went underground or found cover, which was doubtful in this terrain, the Forward-Looking Infrared Radar and computer would keep track of it and warn him if it closed to within 500 meters, the effective range of any shoulder-fired missile at the low altitude they were flying.

In the Datsun, Ross grabbed the laser and pulled himself halfway outside the passenger window. Using it like a pen, he laser-lit the roof of the Datsun drawing a rough triangle symbol. It only took 30 seconds for the armaments officer to register the symbol as the friendly sign used by his squad members.

"Captain, I've got Ross and Bridgestone. Traveling towards target one in a vehicle two-and-a-half miles out."

"Good. We'll extract them with us."

∞§∞

At 1000 meters out *Foxtrot Bravo* launched a drone that was mounted on hard points between the struts. It glided down 100 feet from the copter; its silent drive engine then kicked in and it sped ahead of the copter. On board the copter, Specialist First Class Neumann flew the drone from a joystick and monitor display. When he got to within 200 yards of the refinery, he engaged the EMP switch. Immediately, all radio, cellular, and any other electromagnetic radiation was blocked from an area about the size of a 300-yard umbrella directly below the silently hovering drone. It was the same kind of electromagnetic pulse type jamming device that was used when senators or VIPs visited war zones where improvised explosive devices could be remotely detonated by cellular or radio control. The Presidential detail also carried this type of device to stop would be assassins from getting real-time telemetry or data on the President's exact whereabouts. Now the group holding the ambassador in the refinery was blind and their forward scouts were unable to signal them.

The Apache Longbows went down to the deck and switched on NOE. Utilizing the Nap of the Earth, terrain-hugging software, the pilots became passengers as the computer-guided copter cruised over sand dunes and gullies at 90 knots at 25 feet. Using infrared, the co-pilot turned on his "see and shoot" helmet array. A M230

Chain Gun on a gimbaled mount under the nose of the helicopter now copied every move of his head. The heads-up display on his visor was in infrared mode. He just lined up his reticule by moving his head and trained the gun in on whatever he had in his sights. A red button to the right of the center of his collective control was the trigger. If he held the button down, he could fire 300 rounds per minute. Tapping the button released a 50-round fusillade of flesh/metal tearing 30 mm slugs, which he now did five times as he walked the fire in on the four life forms revealed on his ever-changing horizon. All of the bullets en route created a temporary curtain of white hot lines trailing towards the target.

To the doomed lookouts at the forward post, there was only the sudden percussion of 250 heavy white-hot bullets slamming into and shredding them and everything around them. They never heard or saw the black copters approach.

On the co-pilots HUD, all he now saw were cooling pieces of bodies and glowing hot holes where the bullets either lay embedded cooling in the night air or starting small fires where they met something material. What a few seconds earlier were four distinct heat signatures, was now a mess of green dots and clumps.

"Target neutralized," crackling over the pilots headset, was the only epitaph the dead men, who they were now zooming over, would ever get. *Foxtrot Alpha* flared up at 100-feet and held off at 50-yards, its co-pilot picking off random targets in the compound, while *Foxtrot Bravo* went in for a strut jump. Hovering four feet from the ground as the men piled out 50 yards from the main building 20 seconds later, *Foxtrot Bravo* was 12 feet off the roof as five repel lines sprang out from each side. A door gunner training his counterbalanced 7.62 mm minigun down onto the roof to clip anybody trying to stop the deployment.

∞§∞

"Eight kills, 35 seconds into breach, and no sign of counterattack," the Captain manning the console reported to the room in the Pentagon. He was watching an array of monitors that showed him every feed of video and GPS data. He had seen the action of the gunners much the same as they had through their HUDs.

"Good, then the bastards don't even know they are under attack. This might just work," Pickering said.

∞§∞

As if that comment was heard a third of the way around the world, an explosion rocked the building and blinded most of the heat-sensitive night scopes.

"What the hell was that?" the squad commander yelled into his helmet-mounted tactical radio mike.

"Jonesy tripped a booby trap wire, but he felt it. There was a delay and he was able to get to cover. No one hurt."

"All units, go, go, go!"

Their presence no longer a secret, the men were turned loose to enter, interdict, and neutralize the enemy with all due haste. They moved with lightning speed. Three-shot bursts from their MP-5s crumpled startled terrorists who didn't have the benefit of night vision goggles. Each trooper had memorized the face of the two high value targets believed to be in this complex – the ambassador and Jamal. One they wanted to save, the other they wanted to boil in oil, but were under orders to retrieve for his intelligence value.

The great unknown here was the number of bad guys in the center of the building. The metal roof and pipes made it impossible for the infrared to get an accurate reading. They could be facing one hundred armed men or two night janitors wielding mops. The fighting became intense as they neared the center of the complex. It turned out that some of the terrorists were in fact equipped with night vision goggles. Two squad members were being pinned down in a hallway from a night-vision-capable gun at the far end of the hall. One motioned to the other and, on the count of three, they flipped up their night vision sets and threw a flare into the hall. As soon as it lit off, they were up and firing, guided by the same intense light that was blinding the goggled terrorists. It only gave them a one-second advantage, but when you are the best of the best of the United States military and qualified to brag about it every month, one second can be the enemy's life expectancy – which it proved to be.

Two operators were equipped with infrared scopes/vision assist. That meant they could literally see through walls. They saw the outlines of two armed men lying in wait behind an overturned desk. Seeing no one else, like a hostage, they simply chucked a grenade into the room. The blast flattened the desk against the wall along with the two men. Overall, the resistance was sporadic with no real counteroffensive. By neutralizing their lookouts, the captors weren't expecting a raid and they certainly weren't alerted before the choppers hit.

A flash-bang grenade went off down the hall and three troops ran to it. They were into the room before the sound stopped echoing off the walls. Tied to a chair, his ears bleeding and rolling his head side to side to ward off the pain, was the ambassador. Jamal and two others were writhing on the floor in the immediate aftershock of the blast. Two troops put themselves in front of the ambassador, shielding him with their bodies, their guns trained outward. Another operator put a round each into the heads of the other two men in the room. Jamal was wire-tied and brought to his feet.

The troopers started to assemble in the room. Fifteen of them surrounded the ambassador and Jamal and started leading them out of the building. Two operators were down. Luckily, Kevlar vests protected their vitals, but both suffered leg wounds.

Not taking chances, the 15 stopped at an obvious ambush point before the exit of the building, lobbing five grenades into the area as they all took cover. Grunts and moans accompanied the explosions. Two scouts went ahead to clear the way. A few shots rang out, all U.S. weapons, as the scouts made sure no one was playing possum.

Foxtrot Alpha circled and secured the area as half the team boarded *Foxtrot Bravo*. Then *Alpha* landed as *Bravo* kept guard. That's when the Datsun approached the LZ. Instinctively, the men boarding the copter trained their guns on the vehicle.

"They're friendlies!" the squad commander shouted. "Hold your fire!"

Everybody laughed when Ross and Bridgestone came out of the car.

"Shit, Ross, we almost blew your fucking heads off!" an operator yelled.

"Bullshit. You couldn't hit the broad side of a bull stopped to fuck a cow."

"What's that?" the squad commander asked as Bridgestone and Ross carried the wrapped body from the back seat towards the copter.

"Salinda. I didn't want to dispatch her in case we still needed info."

"What are we supposed to do with her now?"

"Could make Jamal more talkative if he sees she's at risk."

"Okay. Get her on board and let's get the hell out of Dodge."

They clamored aboard the craft as it lifted off.

As soon as they were on board they unwrapped the sheet revealing Salinda, Jamal saw her. He was shocked, but his situational awareness clicked in. He looked to his right and saw the open door of the chopper. He bolted up, jumped on Salinda, and grabbed her in his wire-tied hands, rolling with her out of the open door. Their bodies fell more than 200 feet and broke on a rocky ledge below.

"Ah, shit!" a disgusted Ross said as he tossed the severed pinky out of the same door.

∞§∞

"They got him."

A small smattering of applause broke out around the Sitch Room following the Captain's announcement.

"Casualties?" the President said quieting the room.

"Two leg wounds, non-life threatening."

"Thank God. Enemy killed?"

"Sir, give us some time to debrief first," the Chairman of the Joints Chiefs said. "It will all be in a report in the morning."

"Thank you all. Good work. Hank, I think those men earned some shiny hardware tonight."

"Roger that, sir."

∞§∞

After-action jitters were a phenomenon that most battle-hardened commanders had seen. The adrenaline rush of combat and intense mental alertness often had residual effects once the nervous system calmed down. So Jonesy vomiting into his helmet was to be expected. He took some ribbing for it, but not from three of the men who were also looking a little green around the gills. Within two minutes, four troopers upchucked their guts into their Kevlars and were lying on the floor of the chopper.

Realizing that something else had to be going on here, the commander keyed his tactical radio. "Oasis this is *Foxtrot Alpha*, inbound. Possible chemical or bio contamination. Men nauseous and vomiting. Request bio-hazard and antibiotics."

The Squad commander then checked all of his men on the copter. He heard *Foxtrot Bravo* report three men vomiting on it. He broke out the antibiotics and ordered all of his men to dose themselves. Retracing their movements, he tried to figure out what these men had been exposed to.

∞§∞

Hiccock's phone rang. "William, get on SCIAD now!" the voice on the other end said.

Hiccock scanned his eye and opened the network from his desktop. The voice on the phone was Quan Li, a research scientist out of Cal Tech on assignment in Diego Garcia. He was stationed at a listening station for Pave Paw West, a launch detection satellite in geo-synchronous orbit over the Indian Ocean. He was an Element member of SCIAD because he had led the way on critical mass research in heavy water reactors and held the highest clearance.

To: n
From: #E: Li
Re: Huge spike in Egyptian desert.
17:32 GMT Sensor readings of > 10.5 and < 14.2 rads/meter recorded from source at 34 lat 134 long....

That's all Hiccock had to read. He printed the document, picked up the phone, and pressed "POTUS." But the President of the United States was not behind his desk. The switchboard picked up.

"Yes, Doctor Hiccock."

"Chief of Staff, please."

"Hold on."

"Reynolds."

"Ray, it's Bill. I got something hot here and I need to inform the president."

"Come down."

Bill was out the door grabbing the printout on the way. He ran to the elevator and agents surrounded him.

"I need to get to the boss and Ray immediately."

Two agents went onto the elevator with him and spoke to the agent on station near the President. Receiving an affirmative, they stepped out of the way when the elevator opened in the basement.

"We are at the end of a top secret mission here, Bill. Where's the fire?" Reynolds asked.

"Sir, in the desert of Egypt about 135 miles west of Cairo."

"General, Ray, I am clearing Hiccock for this operation," the President said. "Ray, brief him."

When Ray finished filling in Bill, Bill got to tell him what he knew.

The President was shocked, "Are you sure?"

"Li is not a reckless man. And I think, in short order, other sources will start chiming in. Meanwhile, General, can you verify that these coordinates are the same as your target?" Hiccock handed the printout to the Chairman.

"What do we do?" the President asked.

"Turn the copters around." Hiccock said. "You have to get someone in there to control the situation."

"But they are not prepared for this!" the General protested.

"Sir, with all due respect, those men have already been exposed. They are the only ones who can get there now and report back."

"You're saying they are already dead," the General said.

"Some, not all, may be badly irradiated. But they might even be able to stop this thing from getting out of hand."

"Do it!" the President said.

"Captain, order Foxtrots Alpha and Bravo back to target alpha!" the Chairman ordered.

"They'll need refueling to get back, sir," the Captain said.

"Dispatch refueling ships and get me the Sultan Air Base commander on the double!" the Chairman ordered.

The President turned to Hiccock, "I hope you are wrong, Bill."

"I hope you are right, Sir."

CHAPTER FOURTEEN
BACK TO THE BREACH

"Do what?" the squad commander yelled back over the interphone to the pilot who had received his orders and was already turning back. "Don't they know that we have sick men here? And besides, that LZ is going to be crawling by now. What are we supposed to do if we engage bad guys?"

Here's what never happens – some field grade commander in the thick of it gets a secure call from the Commander-in-Chief. So both squad chiefs were shocked to hear over their tac radios, "Gentlemen this is the President. I am joined here by the Chairman of the Joint Chiefs. What I am about to ask you to do is not easy for me. That's why I had to have you hear it directly from me. During your raid, a large amount of radiation was released from the facility you stormed. This was significant and unprecedented. My staff tells me that many of you may already show symptoms of radiation poisoning. Here's the tough part: we don't know what could cause this. But trust me; there are no comforting answers to the question. You are the only force within hours of the target. You have to ascertain what the source of the radiation is, then secure the area until reinforcements arrive. I know what I am asking you men to do. All I can tell you is that America, and possibly the entire planet, is depending on you. I know you will not fail us. God speed, men."

∞§∞

The President nodded to the Captain and the communications officer killed the circuit. He remained still, looking at the phone he'd hung up. Finally he spoke.

"Ten minutes ago I was putting them all up for a medal. Now I am sending them to their deaths. Where do we find men like this?"

"Sir, you did the only thing you could do given these extraordinary circumstances," The CJCS said.

"Oh God, I just sent Greely back in as well!" Mitchell shook off the human emotion and went back to being the Commander in Chief. "Okay, I want maximum effort here. Everything we have that can help these guys deal with whatever this nuclear thing could be should be moving 10 seconds ago! Ray, get whoever we need here right now. Bill, take a seat; you started this."

"Yes, sir."

∞§∞

"Rules of engagement are, F-E," the commander said as the MH-60 Black Hawk hurled through the night retracing its earlier route, only this time with all deliberate speed and not concerned about alerting the enemy. The big, stinking, glowing hole in the desert floor had already done that. Although there was no actual rule of engagement designated, Frank/Eddie, the commander's troops knew that "Fuck Everybody" meant the mission at all costs, no other concerns or distractions. He went over to the three equipment lockers lashed to the sides of the cabin. Each had a large letter on its top: N, B, and C. The C was where he had gotten the antibiotic syringes. Now he opened the N. Of the three, he always expected to someday use the Chemical or, even worse, the Biological one. But somehow, the Nuclear locker was just not a concept he could comfortably grasp. Not that that mattered one bit. He and his men had extensive training and their procedures for each were exemplary. Any of them would be an equally effective fighting unit in either an N, B, or C combat environment.

First, he distributed radiation pills and ordered everyone to take a dose and a half. Somebody once described taking a pill for radiation is like taking an aspirin for a head-on car crash. He then pulled out five nuke suits, tape, re-breathers, and a Geiger counter. He left the radiation dosimeter monitor badges in the trunk because he probably had enough residual on him to taint them already. He ordered the guys in the best shape, including Bridgestone and Ross who, because they weren't in the refinery, were among the ones not vomiting – to suit up. The others aided the men and sealed their suits with tape at the sleeves, cuffs, and helmet collar. Each man was also draped with ammo belts and machine guns fitted into their gloved hands.

"Okay boys, this is certainly no fucking drill. We stumbled on something back there and it's hot. You men in the suits will go in, locate, identify, and handle the merchandise. The rest of us will cover and support. Okay, I want a by-the-numbers radio check.

"1, Check, 3, Check, 7, Check...."

∞§∞

"Sir, in going over the tapes of the rescue, one plausible scenario is that the explosion may have been, or have acted like, a radiological device," Hiccock said.

"So it could have been a dirty bomb?" the President asked.

"Yes. Or an explosion near some fissionable material. In either case, it spread a plume. This is what Quan Li and later NORAD picked up as a spike."

"Could there be any good news... as a plausible scenario, that is?"

"The bad news is, sir, that *would* also be the good news. Unless the refinery was really a hospital with an overactive nuclear medicine lab which somehow exploded."

"What are you thinking it could be, Bill?"

"Well sir, I don't think it was a deliberate nuclear placement, because there are no targets of any value whatsoever 150 or so miles from Cairo. So it must have been a storage facility as well as a safe house to hold the ambassador. Whether what was exposed was an actual bomb or stockpile for future weapons, like dirty bombs, or possibly even an atom-bomb-making lab, we'll find out if the Foxtrots get through. And just to rule it out, I checked over my SCIAD net. Geologically, there would be no natural source of radiation in that part of the world."

"So it's all in the hands of the Foxtrots now."

"Yes sir, it is."

∞§∞

"*Foxtrot Bravo* will hold off and set up perimeter from the west since that's the only road in. After we jump, *Alpha* will set up a CAP. Hopefully none of this is on Al Jazeera yet so the numbers of yahoos coming at us should be manageable. Right now, under FE, anything that moves is dead. We have one goal, one mission: find out whatever the nuclear material is, secure it, and, if we can, evacuate it to Desert Tango 1. That's a secure site being set up right now to handle whatever we find. If what we find is leaking, we contain it. If it's moveable, we move it. If it's ticking, we evacuate."

The commander looked around at the faces illuminated by the red lights of the cabin. "So far, before it turned into this cluster fuck, this mission was textbook hostage recovery. Each one of you performed and served in the best traditions of the cavalry. Brinks, that leg good enough for you to handle the mini gun?"

"It's a scratch, sir. I got your back," said the man with a huge bloody bandage running from his knee to his calf.

"Got three bogeys on the road heading towards target alpha," the co-pilot reported.

"Cleared, hot," the pilot said back over the interphone. The gunship shuttered as the mini gun, connected to the co-pilot's central nervous system, burped as it fired several bursts.

"Instant junk yard," was the battle damage assessment from the gunner on the door.

"Got five infrared targets on foot coming in from the east two miles off."

"Not worth detouring for. We'll handle them once we switch to Combat Air Patrol."

∞§∞

"Let the Egyptian ambassador in on this, Charles," the President said. "There is a nightmare happening in his country and he should know it."

"Sir, should we tie in Cairo?"

"Let that be the ambassador's call. Either way, I'll speak to the Egyptian president as soon as possible."

"Ray, shouldn't we let the Russians and the Chinese know," Bill whispered to the Chief of Staff. "If something goes wrong, we need them on the cool side of the equation."

"No whispering in here," the President said. "I need all the opinions I can get."

"Sir, Hiccock was just bringing it up, and I think I agree..."

∞§∞

"Thirty seconds," the pilot announced. The lights were off in the cabin now. The guys in the N-suits were in the middle between the men ready to jump and secure the LZ. The Longbow flared and hovered at two feet. The men stepped off and in an instant set up a defensive perimeter to cover the guys in the plastic suits as they exited. Then, as one, they retraced their original steps back into the building, peeling off one or two of their number as guards as the main body advanced. The chopper was up and doing CAP while *Foxtrot Bravo* unloaded the same way. Then it went off to cover the only road into the compound.

Kicking dead bodies, and being ready to fire if you hear a grunt, is a lifesaving practice at a time like this. This place was so hot that the Geiger counters had to be put on the highest scale in order to get a reading that was mid-scale and not pinned on overload. To determine which direction the source was in, a mid-scale was needed so that when the unit was swept in a circle, the direction straightest towards the radiation would give the highest reading. It was called a hyper-cardioid search pattern. These instruments were now pointing the suits toward the spot where Jonesy tripped the booby trap. A quick inspection showed it was something similar to a Claymore mine, probably taped to the now-blown-away doorway. On the other side of that door, the needles pinned and the Geigers were overloaded even at the highest setting, a .5 RAD scale or about 10,000 times stronger than a chest x-ray. When the trooper flipped up his night vision and turned on his flashlight illuminating the room, a muffled "Holy Mother of God!" came through his plastic facemask.

One of the operators was video capable and his signal was microwaved to the chopper. Then the chopper uplinked it to a defense satellite, which sent it to the Defense Intelligence Agency. They patched in the ops room at the White House as well as the guys in the Pentagon.

As the single light source on top of the camera illuminated the room, the lead trooper narrated, "Sir, we got a shitload of what looks like suitcase nukes. Eight, nine

– they're all over. The blast has definitely breached one or two. I can't believe some idiot raghead placed a Claymore on the wall behind these suckers."

In the chopper, the commander, upon hearing that two nukes were breached, took out his knife and slashed the thick canvas straps that secured the N case to the lightening holes in the frame of the chopper. He dumped the contents on the floor and told the pilot to go back in. Then he keyed his mic to the guys in the refinery. "Sergeant, send two guys out to the LZ and have them bring the N locker to you."

Back in the room, the count was concluded. Twenty-three suitcase nukes, two damaged by blast. When the N trunk arrived, the first damaged bomb was gingerly laid into the case. The N case had minimal nuclear shielding to protect the instruments and monitor within from ambient or slightly elevated radiation. That same shielding would temporarily contain the brunt of the radiation until help arrived. They were about to lower the second damaged case into the locker alongside the first when the one of them had a thought.

"Sir, lets get the other N case in here. These two bad boys may interact if we keep them in a tight shielded case."

"Good thinking, Marks. You may have just saved this godforsaken patch of desert for future generations."

The two helicopters traded positions and the second ship's N case found its way into what the men were now calling the "nursery." Once *Foxtrot Alpha* was up and back in CAP, the pilot decided to deal with the human targets now a half-mile off to the east. He pointed the 9 tons of death and destruction at the five unwise men traveling in the dessert. Then he had a moment of conscience. "I am going to do a magnetometer pass first."

"Jack, we are under FE engagement!" the co-pilot said.

"I know; but what if those are just some camel jockeys down there?"

"And what if they put a shoulder-fired up our exhaust?"

"These guys are walking, not running. I don't want to kill some poor bastard just for taking a walk."

"Okay. How about, we lay down a line of red lead in the sand and see if they change their direction. I'll stay locked on them and if they so much as hiccup, I'll cream 'em." The co-pilot lined up the life forms on his reticule.

"Mini-gun, kick up some sand and let them know we want them to turn around."

"Roger" preceded the shuttering as the chain gun let go.

Through his infrared display, the pilot saw the people run in the other direction. "Okay, good. Let's get our guys out of here."

"Had that gone the other way and they tagged us, you could have been brought up on charges posthumously," the co-pilot said.

"Don't dwell on it," the pilot advised.

∞§∞

"Captain, have that soldier pan back right again, to that table," Hiccock requested as the Captain relayed the request.

"What is that? Tell him to go in closer."

"Looks like my wife's vanity," the Captain blurted out.

"Captain, warn the men. Those jars could contain a lethal dose of a viral flu strain."

Hiccock didn't know it but his voice was now patched directly to the headset of the troopers in the nursery.

"Negative on that. We opened a few. All they contained were these things." The camera walked in to get a close-up of the thing in the soldier's hand. The focus was momentarily soft, then the operator adjusted and the device came into critical focus.

"What do you make of that?" Reynolds asked.

"Sir, I think that's a Thyristor," Hiccock said.

"In a cold cream jar?"

"I've seen terrorists use these jars before. But for bio-agents."

"So what does a Thyristor do and why do they need them?"

"Those old suitcase nukes either aren't armed or the arming mech is past its freshness date. Those Thyristors are the main triggering units to start the fission process."

Then Hiccock had a chilling thought. "Trooper, is there a box that the cold cream came in anywhere in the room?"

The camera jiggled and swept over the floor and up again until it landed on a cardboard box. "Princess Briana – 24 Count."

"Captain, confirm for me the number of suitcase nukes and cold cream jars you have there."

It took a few seconds. "Twenty-three nukes, 23 jars. Confirmed. Can we get out of here, now?"

"General, I'm done as long as they take everything out of that room with them."

"Delta Foxtrots you are go for extraction. Good work and Godspeed."

"What's on your mind, Bill?" The President asked.

"Sir, we may have a loose nuke."

∞§∞

Designated Desert Tango 1, it was a hastily thrown together decontamination and quartermaster camp. The tough desert floor supported the 25 C-130 and C-17 transports that landed here after having been scrambled from Germany, Diego Garcia, and Saudi Arabia. It was the military equivalent of a NEST team. Only this Nuclear Emergency Search Team was looking for serial numbers. The Russians, who for some unfathomable reason thought a nuclear bomb in a suitcase was somehow a good thing, were very cooperative. In fact, a Tupolov 24 airliner landed amongst the U.S. transports with three Russian nukers on board. It took almost a day, but Hiccock's theory proved correct. The serial numbers were consecutive except for one missing one.

As for the troopers who went to hell and back twice, two had succumbed to the effects of radiation and six were critical. Bridgestone and Ross were the luckiest, having missed the initial blast and then wearing nuke suits for the remainder of the mission. The rest would have the specter of an immediate and severe breakout of cancer with them for the rest of their lives. Not to mention a possible inability to procreate. The ambassador was one of those in critical condition due to his age and health. He was termed fifty-fifty for survival. They all would have been toast if it were not for the minimal shielding afforded by the N lockers. A directive went out to The Army to increase the shielding even more for exactly this type of containment scenario reoccurring in the future.

For its part, the Egyptian government cursed the terrorists for bringing nuclear poison onto their soil. But somehow, as with all Arab denouncements of terrorism, there was an unspoken caveat that seemed to imply, "instead of just conventional weapons by which to kill Americans."

CHAPTER FIFTEEN
LOVE THE BOMB

The Administration decided that trying to keep the suitcase nuke a secret only invited conspiracy theories to get in the way of public information and allowed the terrorist to have their "scoop" on Al Jazeera. The Departments of Defense and State held a rare joint press conference to announce that a nuclear device was soon coming to a baggage carousel near you. The world, and the U.S. population, went apeshit. Eventually, when the size of the suitcase was leaked over the Internet, air travelers themselves started detaining and harassing any poor Arab-looking fellow with a large suitcase. The U.S. Department of Transportation rose to meet the new threat level by taking out of line, and doing extensive body searches of, even more little old gray-haired ladies en route to Omaha than before, while managing not to insult any bearded followers of Allah or al-Qaeda. The TV networks responded with night after night of "investigating" which presidential administration was to blame for suitcase nukes.

Overnight, the most popular site on the Internet became www. WhatsMyCEP.com, which allowed visitors to enter their street address and then virtually plant the suitcase bomb anywhere within 100 miles of that location. It told you how much damage you could expect, how much radiation, if you would survive, and if your pets would live to lick your glowing remains. The irony was that the engine for these calculations was hacked from the Department of Defense study done at Purdue University to determine the effects of nuclear detonations on cities and small towns. It calculated the Circular Error Probable of a detonation at various kilo- and mega-tonnage and then, using GPS mapping software and weather models for wind direction, the site determined likely death counts and fallout patterns. Real homey, comfy stuff.

In short, America was scaring itself to death, and doing almost as much damage to the national psyche and commerce as if the other 23 bombs were on the loose.

Then the extreme lunacy hit. Hiccock was reluctantly appearing on a talk show under the agreement that he was to be the only guest on for an entire half-hour segment. With the administration's approval, he went on to separate scientific fact from science fiction. The show was going well until the last commercial break for Bill's segment. That's when a senator who was on the next segment "bullied" his way onto the set just before they were going back on the air.

"Mister Hiccock," Senator Barnes said, "when is the administration going to make public its retaliation policy for when the bomb goes off?"

Hiccock should have gotten up and left right there and then, but the stage manager called out, "Back in 5, 4, 3, 2...." Then threw his finger cue.

"We're back and are joined now by Senator Barnes," host Wolf Blitzer said. "Welcome Senator Barnes. Senator, during the break you were asking the President's science advisor a rather poignant question. Would you mind repeating that for the benefit of our viewers?"

Barnes repeated it exactly as before and Hiccock's brain went into overdrive. To answer this question was to fall into a huge trap. "When the bomb goes off," meant that any positive answer would signal that the administration believed the detonation inevitable. Any negative response meant the President wasn't "going to make public our retaliation policy" and was therefore not being forthright with the public. Bill hated this political crap; it was another good reason why he believed he should never appear in public in any official capacity. As Bill's inner play clock ticked down, he looked the senator in the eye, trying to figure out where he was coming from, but felt politically inept for not even knowing whether this guy was a friend or foe of his boss. *A friend wouldn't ambush us like this* was the last thought he had before he found himself speaking.

"Would the Senator care to further elaborate on his question?"

"Sounds plain enough to me, Mister Hiccock. When is the administration going to make public its retaliation policy for when the bomb goes off?"

"Oh, okay. First off, it's Professor Hiccock. And second, I thought I didn't hear you right the first time because that is the most ill-informed, ill-composed, and ill-conceived question ever asked. It presupposes a whole series of non-factual and fantastical assumptions. It is, to put it simply, a trick question. And I don't do tricks, Senator."

Wolf Blitzer's jaw seemed frozen open. Bill could hear the scratchy sound of the producer hollering at Blitzer from the control room through the little earpiece stuffed into the ear away from camera. The senator looked to Wolf for some cover, but Wolf was distracted by the screaming in his ear.

"Wolf, you need a minute here, buddy?" Hiccock said with the smallest of smirks.

"Senator, would you like to rephrase your question?"

"No, Wolf, let's move on. I and many on my side of the aisle are calling for a simple, clear, declarative statement from the President on a retaliatory policy that would force the nations who sponsor and support terrorism to clean up their own act and stop this heinous crime before it is carried out."

"What are you looking for the President to say, Senator?" Wolf asked.

"That five Arab capitals will be targeted by our ICBMs. That if the suitcase nuke goes off on American soil, the capitals of Syria, Jordon, Iran, Libya, and the Sudan will be wiped from the face of the earth."

"A sweeping proposal. Mister...Professor Hiccock, as a member of the administration, would you care to respond to that?"

"No. But I'd like to respond as a private citizen if I may."

Blitzer was visibly uneasy with the request but acceded without thinking.

Hiccock leaned over towards the windbag senator. "You are out of your ever-loving mind, my friend. Thank God you, nor any of your cohorts on the hill, are the President right now, because that is the dumbest, most counterproductive idea since somebody elected you into office, pal. Do yourself and the government of the people you are sworn to protect and serve a big favor and shut the hell up!"

Hiccock sat back in his chair again. "There; that was me, the private citizen, voicing my personal views. Speaking for the administration again, I have no comment."

The senator recovered quickly from the attack. "You bastard! The American people will not stand idly by while Islamic terrorists detonate a nuclear device on our soil. You and your President may be too weak-kneed to get tough with these Arab thugs, but the American people are sick and tired of these terrorists threatening us and terrorizing us. The American people are demanding and deserve a get-tough policy, not some touchy-feely approach that the Hate America First crowd and academics like you, Pro-fes-sor, embrace."

"Now gentlemen, let's try and keep the tone of this debate..."

Bill leaned forward again. "Senator, first of all, he's not just my President. He's yours too, unless you and your Capitol Hill cronies are also rescinding the constitution in your new order. And secondly, threatening to kill millions of innocent people over the acts of madmen makes us nothing more than madder madmen with bigger bombs. Wolf, this fear mongering serves only cheap politicians who are posturing for votes by perpetuating exactly the kind of fear, rumor, and innuendo I came on your program to address. If there was ever a time in American history to let diplomacy and our State Department make policy, this is it."

"Gentlemen, I am afraid we are out of time. Thank you for this... lively...and... spirited discussion, we'll be back after this..."

"And we are out," the stage manager announced. "Four-minute break."

"You fellas really went at each other...." Blitzer stopped talking when Hiccock tore off his lapel mic, got up, and moved right into the senator's face. The man backed up in his chair, hands gripping the arms, searching the studio for his security people.

Hiccock clamped his finger over the lapel mic clipped to Barnes' blue suit and unloaded. "As for that academic crack, you go to intelligence oversight committee, you get cleared for top secret/need to know, and then you find out what kind of action this 'academic' has been involved in, Senator! Until then, don't ever demean my patriotism again."

Hiccock punctuated those last words with two finger jabs to the shoulder, which were strong enough to make the senator wince and rub the area as Hiccock walked off set.

Blasting through the studio doors, the makeup lady ran to catch up to Bill to give him two paper towels so he could wipe the pancake from his face. At that minute, the show's producer came out of the control room.

"That was great TV! What did you say to him just then? We couldn't hear..."

"Don't worry about what I told him. Worry about what I'm telling you, hard-on. You ever lie to me again or blindside me on the air with another asshole like that, and I will kick the living shit out of you. Do you hear me?" Hiccock took the two makeup smudged towels and stuffed them in the producer's breast pocket, then brushed him aside. "Half-hour exclusive my ass!"

When Hiccock got into his interagency motor pool car, his cell phone rang. It was Margaret Lloyds, White House Press Secretary.

"I think that went well, don't you, Peg?"

∞§∞

Janice was laughing. "So he got the full Bronx treatment? Oh, to have been a fly on the wall."

"Yeah, I guess I kinda got all Gunhill Road on him and the producer. I swear that little producer nerd didn't know whether to shit or go blind."

Bill placed the dish with the half-eaten peanut butter chocolate pie on the cocktail table. "You know, your cravings better include a fat husband."

"Not a problem, but count your blessings. In some species, the male dies after fertilization." As she placed her practically-licked-clean plate next to Bill's, Janice was about to take his uneaten half, but a look from Bill dissuaded her.

"So you're just fattening me up for the kill?"

"More of you to love, Billy." Janice stood. "Well, I'll clean up."

"I'll do it. You sit and contemplate life after fatty dies." Bill took the plates, cups, and forks into the kitchen.

Janice felt around the couch for the TV remote. She turned on the set and found CNN. Bill was on the screen.

They were replaying his exchange with the senator. It was the most played clip of the day and, unless some disaster, political assassination, or sports star scandal occurred, it would probably be the stuff of Sunday morning news shows. In the few short hours that he was home, Bill had already gotten calls from every major paper and news magazine. Now, as she watched the clip of Bill's confrontation with the senator for the third time, something in Janice's mind confronted her. Her body started to morph into something like the fetal position around a throw pillow. She was riveted to the screen as the two men, one of them who she loved and trusted, were engaged in a discussion that was the stuff of nightmares. As a little kid who had grown up during the Cold War, expecting to be atomically bombed into ash shadows at any moment, she had studied, and was familiar with, the feeling of certain doom that was encircling her. Living under the threat of nuclear annihilation made many of her older patients and predecessors create the anti-culture and alternate-culture movements. Sex, drugs, and rock 'n roll were largely the self-medication that the generation before hers had prescribed for a bad case of the nuclear heebie-jeebies.

Although she didn't know the senator, his party affiliation made it a good bet they shared very few common views. But as she listened to his proposal, which her man Bill rightly framed as insane, she felt something deep within her resonate to the radical ultimatum. It was an anger brewing, being stirred up by the senator's declaration that the "Arab Street should no longer be a one-way street," that they can't be constantly whipping up the winds of hatred against America, yet remain immune to the consequences. Her hand was resting on her already protruding belly as she felt a warmness, a comfort, wash over her from the senator's words. This was a disconnect that she had never experienced. Intellectually, there was no question the idea of nuclear retaliation was an unfair, inappropriate response. Yet, emotionally, she wished the senator had won the argument, even over her own man. She turned her own profession inwards and diagnosed herself. Her self-image and long-held beliefs accounted for her instant and magnetic attraction to her husband's level headed, "fair" position. However, a whole other part of her, a new part, wanted to gnarl and roar causing any who would threaten the budding life within her to cower and scamper away.

The result of this self-inspection was Bill returning from the kitchen to a different woman from the one he left a minute ago – something that would not be a singular event in the next five months. He sensed something in the catatonic way Janice locked onto the TV.

"I hope you still think the guy on the left is hunky?"

"I am suddenly sad."

"No hunkiness?"

"Do you realize what happened here?"

"You mean on the show? Yeah, I held my ground against a reactionary, blowhard hawk."

"That's not it. You proved that we are all going to die in a nuclear barbeque."

"I must have missed that part."

"This isn't funny. There couldn't even be a televised discussion of this without you threatening this guy with violence. And I am sure if he had his Second-Amendment-protected-right-to-carry an assault weapon on him, he would have shot you where you sat."

"Okay, so it got a little heated."

"Bill, what chance do we have to survive this thing when even just talking about it went nuclear?"

Janice started sobbing. Bill didn't have any reference for this. Janice was not from the waterworks crowd. He sat down next to her and put his arm around her.

She recoiled slightly. "You've got to stop this thing!"

"Me? Stop what?"

"You gotta make sure this doesn't happen. I waited a long time to have a baby and now there's a chance the world will end!"

"Whoa, whoa, the world isn't going to end."

"Bill, I'm scared. I've never been this scared before."

"Jim Mitchell is a good man, Janice. I'll be there and if anything is going to happen, I'll know. We'll be okay… the three of us."

CHAPTER SIXTEEN
THE HAYSTACK IN THE NEEDLES

The head of Homeland Security reported to the 15 men and 32 assistants crammed into the war room of the White House. "All ports are in lockdown, all border crossings are under manned aircraft and unmanned aerial drone surveillance. The Coast Guard is in full inspect and detect mode. Radiation detectors are at 17 major airports, but that still leaves a gaping hole in our baggage screening. There are airborne radiation detectors on 1400 state and municipal helicopters and all N.E.S.T. units are fully deployed and operational. In addition to the Nuclear Emergency Support Teams, the big cities have just shy of 2,300 handheld and truck-mounted rad detectors between them."

"Okay, we'll work on emergency legislation to beef up airport detectors and increase public information messages. What about if it's already here?" Reynolds said.

Joey Palumbo, the Special Assistant to the President attached to the science office filled in. "The timelines on possible entry of the suitcase device prior to our alert are marginal, meaning we doubt they would have sat on these devices for very long. They have been covertly obtaining them since the break up of the U.S.S.R. It is possible that we, or more correctly the boys of Delta Foxtrot, stumbled upon the Nursery very early in their planning. And at that time, they had only managed to get one unit out of the facility."

Bill was seated to the right of Joey, looking at the faces of the men and women around the room. He was thinking about Janice and the promise he made to her and his child yet to be. Back when he was growing up they called this the unthinkable: the actual use of nuclear weapons between warring factions. The people seated around the table here today were starting to learn how to get their brains around the unthinkable in a directionless effort to stop the unthinkable from becoming the inevitable. The sobering enormity of the task of trying to find the device was demonstrated when somebody, maybe American Tourister for all Bill knew, calculated that there were 700,000,000 suitcases in, and going through, the U.S. at any given moment. Of course, there was no rule in the terrorists' handbook that said a suitcase nuke needed to remain in a suitcase. So very quickly one out of 700 million started to look like good odds against one in "everything bigger than a breadbox."

The Surgeon General was reporting on the strain on the nation's hospitals if there were a detonation in a medium-sized city. Hiccock knew calculations for cities like New York, Chicago, or Los Angeles were useless since four square blocks of those cities could mean 100,000 people killed or wounded and these Russian devices were capable of 100 square blocks of destruction, with partial destruction reaching out to almost two miles. What'sMYCEP.com had gotten those numbers right. Real estate values in most cities were dropping as firms pushed up moving dates or broke leases to flee the possible blast epicenters of 200 cities. All this economic and civil chaos was in full gear and yet there was no credible or actionable intelligence to suggest that terrorists planned to attack a specific city at all. Boulder Dam or any dam would also make a devastating statement. Fort Knox, Kentucky would be a major blow. (On second thought, Bill doubted the terrorists had ever seen the movie "Goldfinger" with its plot to irradiate the American gold supply thus rendering it untouchable for thousands of years.) You could even try to wedge the thing at some geo-critical point in the California mountains and use the energy of the blast to possibly initiate a tremor that could tear open a rift in the San Andreas fault and cleaver all of California into the sea. *Oh wait, that was the plot of Superman: The Movie.* Bill's mood sank as he realized that Hollywood had already written the only how-to book any terrorist ever needed.

"Anything else?" the Head of Homeland Security asked the room.

Bill was tempted to add something but held back. Instead, he leaned over to Joey. "Joe, we need a special team here. You and whoever you think we'll need, have them remain in the room after the others leave."

In five minutes, six people remained around the large table. Bill had convinced the facilities manager of the White House to put the next meeting intended for that room into the Mural room. Bill took out two folders and a fresh pad from his portfolio. He drew a bull's eye target on the yellow-lined paper then split it in two.

"Here's the way I see it. One of two realities; the bomb already here, or on its way here. The new tighter security is going to have to do the job if it's the second possibility and the bomb is on its way. For now, I want to assume the first proposition: that it's already here."

"How do you figure that it could be here already?" one of the men around the table asked.

"The ports are locked down now. But a week ago, maybe 20 percent of containerized freight got scanned."

"Maybe 20," Joey repeated.

Luck is the only way we are going to interdict this thing and scientifically luck is an undefined number, like zero divided by anything, or infinity. The only way to stop this thing without luck is intel. So here's what I am proposing: a two-pronged approach. We hit all the cells and suspected cells hard and mine any data that's retrieved. At the same time, we game it out on a few Crays and get some probable scenarios and start running those down."

"So start gathering data or intel then feed it into a big computer and see where the computer points us?" the head of the Defense Intelligence Agency asked.

"Essentially, yes. This way, if we do it ourselves, we aren't stopping everything else that's going on. This just becomes another tool."

"How do we get raw intel from the various agencies?" Joey asked. "I mean, that's already supposed to be happening through the Director of National Intelligence and the DHS. And so far we haven't gotten enough to feed into an adding machine much less a super computer."

"We'll get alternate sources," Bill said.

"That's a pretty tall order, Mr. Hiccock," Admiral Swank, head of National Security Council noted.

"I think I already have the men for the job." Bill slid the personnel files for Sergeants Bridgestone and Ross across the desk.

"Are these your aces in the hole? Then, my friend, you haven't seen this." The head of the FBI's counter terrorism unit slid back over the table that morning's *New York Times*. The above-the-fold headline read, "Army Rangers Face Torture Charges."

Bill quickly scanned the article. "It doesn't mention them by name."

"We've asked them for restraint in publishing their pictures and kids' schools' addresses. At least until we play out if the charges will stick."

"Play out means there's no doubt they did it, just whether or not you can hang them with it. These guys should get medals! They found the ambassador and, from that, we found the nukes. That's 23 little Hiroshimas canceled and, God willing, 24." Bill shook his head.

"We don't control the press in America, Bill."

"How did this get out anyway?"

Harold Salter, Deputy National Security Advisor, spoke up and filled in the blanks. "Their key was the

Embassy Guard, Jamal's girlfriend. They found out about her and how she apparently conscripted our man over to the terrorist camp. Bridgestone and Ross went into deep cover. They became nomadic tribesmen, stink and all. They tracked her down and used whatever force necessary to get the information in a timely fashion."

"Whatever force necessary sounds vague. What does that really mean?" Hiccock asked.

"They could have killed her or anybody else. They were not connected to us in any way. They were so deep and so disconnected that they could only be considered mercenaries or freelancers if they were ever caught or killed."

"The secretary will disavow any knowledge of your actions," Bill said, interjecting a line from the old TV show, "Mission Impossible." The title seemed very appropriate to the current situation.

"Exactly! B and R managed to get the location of the ambassador after some physical torture."

"How bad?"

"She didn't talk till she lost a finger."

Bill winced.

"Then, for some odd reason, they brought her to the LZ. That was their mistake! It opened them up to crap like this in *the Times*."

"But how did anybody find out?"

"Along the extraction route, her boyfriend and she jumped out of the copter at 200 feet. Some nomads in the area saw it and when they found the bodies, they camel-backed them into the town. Some Arab reporters were there and the rest is in the paper."

"Okay, but how does anybody know it was B&R?"

"They don't. Not by name. But street vendors and some neighbors saw them enter her apartment. They should have killed her in the apartment. That way, at best, they would have been thought of as desert thieves.

Eyewitness accounts of them falling from a clandestine U.S. helicopter, however, allowed the Arab press to connect the dots another way around."

"Has their identity been compromised in the least?" Bill asked.

"We don't know. But the last thing we want is someone to identify them as the two from her apartment. So for now they are still over there but in tight control."

"Not arrested, I hope?"

"They understand that they cannot go beyond the base right now."

"These are my guys. I want them on the team."

"These men tortured this woman," the Judge Advocate said.

"No, we did. All of us. The United States of America did in our name. These guys just got to be the working end of the stick. We need that stick now to help find the bomb before we find a big hole where Times Square used to be."

∞§∞

"Bill, are you sure about this?" President Mitchell asked as he pulled out a piece of White House stationary from the desk made from the planks of the *H.M.S. Resolute*.

"Sir, I am convinced we can have a better chance at interdicting the device with these men on the team."

"They are already on the team. You mean *your* team."

"They are benched right now, sir. I want to get them back in the field doing what they do best."

"You know, even though they don't know who it was, any Arab claims that it was the work of Americans will be enough to get some to scream bloody torture, start quoting Benjamin Franklin," Ray wryly observed.

"Those who give up freedom for security deserve neither," Bill said, repeating the quote. "Well, that's just another reminder of why, despite what 42 percent of Americans think, Ben Franklin was never President. Flowery language withers in the face of real world responsibility and devil's choices."

"I thought it was because he was a Francophile," Ray added.

The President was finishing a note to the Secretary of Defense, ordering him to assign Bridgestone and Ross to Hiccock, when he looked up. "Ray, help me here. Who, or what, am I asking the Secretary to hand these men over to?"

"Good question. Why don't we have them assigned to the NSC here at the White House?"

The President nodded and finished the note. He handed it to Ray, "Get this over to Barney. What are you going to call this idea of yours, Bill?"

"If it weren't so close to the bone, I was thinking Mission Impossible, sir."

"Get a better name and good luck, to you and to all of us."

∞§∞

Along with the President's agreeing to the plan came his directive, which immediately did two things. One was that it established the "QuOG," or Quarterback Operations Group, a new, top-secret cluster to be run out of the West Wing, at the sole discretion of the President, with a 27-million-dollar operating budget. Bill could get more if he needed it, but that was what was lying around in a discretionary fund at the White House that day. This money had already passed through Congress and was held in reserve for the Presidential shopping list of emergency actions or commissions. It was, essentially, anonymous money, and the lack of immediate Congressional oversight was the best way to keep Bill's not-yet-named operation secret and unhindered. The second part of the Presidential order made Bill's Quarterback group the "LFA" on the suitcase nuke investigation. By being designated Lead Federal Agency, Bill was immediately given standing in all the departments under the administration, Justice (FBI), DHS, INS, IRS, TSA and a handful of others, suddenly had a new deputy director. Hiccock's thickened wallet of new ID cards allowed him to have one-way conversations and intel exchanges with these federal agencies without having to explain anything that could expose the true top-secret nature of the QuOG.

When Bill returned to his office, he found Joey was on the phone with Janice. "I know; my wife was sick for nearly eight weeks with Joe Jr. ... Eup, he just came in. Take care lady; see you soon."

Joey handed the phone to Bill, got up, and let him sit behind his own desk.

"Hi babe, how are you feeling?"

"My stomach feels like I'm on a rollercoaster that never stops," Janice said as she pushed a pile of papers to the edge of her desk and laid her head on her arm as she cradled the phone.

"Maybe you should have stayed home today."

"I had these patient summaries that I already put off long enough. But I am just beat. How did your meeting go?"

"It went well. That's all I can say right now. You understand."

"Sure. Oh, Joey was just telling me how his wife used buttermilk to qwell the same Category 5 typhoon that I have going on inside me. Can you stop off..."

"No problem; I'll pick it up on the way home."

"Thanks, Billy. I think I need to go now."

"Feel better."

Bill hung up and looked at Joey. "Thanks for doing that."

"What?"

"Not letting Janice think she's the only woman who's ever been through this."

"Hey, Phyllis had her sister around when Joe Jr. was born, otherwise she would have been even more frazzled."

"Well, I hope Janice can manage without you for the next couple of days."

"Why, where is she going?"

"Not her. You, Kimosabe. You are on the next flight out to Forward Operating Base Delta Tango 1, wherever the hell that is, to personally give B&R their orders with the President's executive decree of immunity for the ambassador affair."

"So they went for this whole cockamamie idea of yours?"

"*Ours*. This cockamamie idea of *ours*, Joey boy. Oh, we need a operational name?"

"How about 'Stork?'"

CHAPTER SEVENTEEN
PHONE CALLS

"Thank God, Francoise, that he died up here in the street," commented Pierre as the ambulance pulled up to the cobblestoned curb on the Saint Germain street. Many of the kitschy jazz and rock clubs went three or four stories below the street. In the past, they both had to lift deadweight up the old stone narrow and sometimes winding staircases. Those were mostly drug overdoses. Occasionally a knife fight or rare gunshot victim. Judging from the trail of blood on the sidewalk, this man had made it to the street. Unfortunately, he was apparently run over by a car as well. At 4:30 in the morning, the driver was probably drunk and didn't stop. The Sûreté would handle the hit and run. Pierre's job would have been to see if this poor soul was still alive and in need of immediate medical attention but his stethoscope remained in the large pocket of his uniform, especially made to hold it. He placed two fingers on the victim's bloodied neck, not to find a pulse, but to check the temperature. The coldness of the body meant he had been lying there for some time.

The cop's intuition of the Inspector who arrived on the scene, that this fellow was killed before the car crushed his skull, was confirmed when Pierre, pointed to the knife wound in the body's chest. That being the case, Pierre and his partner would have to wait until the police collected any evidence. From experience, he knew this would take a while, so he opened his thermos and poured two cups for Françoise and himself.

∞§∞

Bill was entering the White House at 7:32 a.m. As he swiped his I.D., a man was waiting for him at the security post.

"Mr. Hiccock, please come with me."

"Who are you?"

"Mr. Smith, Special Assistant to the President. Please come with me now."

"Smith?"

They headed to the Situation Room. After the usual vetting and scanning, Bill was facing the President and an older man he did not know.

"Mr. President, what can I do for you, sir?"

"Bill, I am really sorry about this."

"Mr. Hiccock, please surrender your White House I.D. and all other federal I.D. you may have on you."

"What?"

"Please Bill; don't make this any harder than it already is," the President said.

Bill fished out the six I.D.s from the various agencies he was temporarily technically in charge of.

"May I ask why?"

"Bill, NSA intercepted you on a phone call. At that time you used a term on a non-secured phone that even the knowledge of is classified."

"Sir, I certainly have the highest clearance," Hiccock said, pointing to the pile of alphabet soup cards that started with FBI and went straight through OHS.

"Bill, only three people are cleared to know this – me, this man, and one other person who I designated. In fact, I really don't know all of the specifics myself. But I know the code words and their intent."

"Okay, so what did I say?"

"How did you come to hear the term, 'Jesus Factor?'" the other man asked.

"Is that what this is about? You'll have to revise your numbers. I got that from an old friend of mine, who learned it from a group of scientists. In fact, I have 10 people working on it now."

"That's incredible," the President said. "You could be shot!"

"Sir, this cat is well out of the bag."

For the next five minutes, Hiccock told the story of the scientists, Peter Remo, and What Would Jesus Do.

When it was over, the President sat dumbfounded. "But he didn't tell you what it was?"

"It didn't get that far. As soon as I said I never heard of it, he freaked... and now I understand why."

"Bill, I want his name and address. We have to contain this. I also want the 10 people you say are working on it."

"Mr. President, please don't make that a direct order, because each of the 10 is very highly cleared on my SCIAD network, which is hyper-encrypted and random encoded. They are scientists and handle all kinds of sensitive material. Besides, most of them don't believe in UFOs."

"Bill, what do UFOs have to do with this?"

"Wait, what? You mean the Jesus Factor isn't about UFOs?"

"No. Is that what your men are doing?"

"Yes. I guess I left that part out of Peter's story. So this isn't your Jesus Factor? This is just a coincidental name?"

The President looked at the man Bill didn't know. "Bill, this was harrowing, to say the least. Look, save yourself more headaches. Forget you ever heard of Jesus Factor and just call this damn thing something else, okay?"

"Yes, sir, of course sir... Er... should I take these back?" Bill asked pointing at the pile of agency I.D.s.

"Certainly," said the President.

Bill left.

"Flying saucers," the President said with disgust.

∞§∞

“Bonjour... Bonjour...” Yardley Haines always greeted the embassy staff with that double-metered greeting. The same way, every day, for the six years he was posted to Paris. Arriving at 7:30 in the morning gave him time to review reports and the overnights from Foggy Bottom. In fact, most of what was his overnight was midday at the State Department. His usual routine of getting the first cup of coffee from the morning brew then settling in behind his desk for at least 30 minutes of precious solitude was immediately shattered by a man who he spied already awaiting him in his office.

“Bonjour... Bonjour... Emily, who is that in my office?”

Emily, a secretary whom he shared with his counterpart, explained, “He’s a policeman. An inspector, I think. He was very insistent. Your computer is off and there are no documents on your desk. All your drawers are locked and I took your calendar out with me. It’s right here.”

“Very good; but what does he want?”

“I think a tourist died last night.”

“So? Was this tourist an FSO?”

“No. He didn’t mention that.”

“Okay, give us five minutes and then buzz me with my next appointment.”

“Sure.”

Approaching his office, Yardley took in the man seated across from his desk. He was around 50, broad-shouldered, balding spot emerging from thinning, once brown, hair. He had a small scar off the left ear in a jagged design, the kind a broken bottle would make. There was a tilt to his shoulders that the fledgling crime novelist within Yardley might ascribe to the weight of his firearm snugged in his shoulder holster. Shoes were worn but well-polished. He wore a wedding ring and had suffered a break of his left pinky. *Why do policemen everywhere insist on those ratty trench coats?*

"Inspector! So sorry to keep you waiting."

"Ah, Mr. Haines; it's Lieutenant. And not to worry; I am actually at the end of my day."

"Night shift! Keeping Parisians safe while they sleep."

"Unfortunately, I am sorry to say, I could not keep one American safe last night."

"Yes, I heard. A tourist, I believe?"

"Seemingly so. Do you know this man?" He handed Haines the driver's license retrieved from the wallet of the American. It was a New York State license with a picture.

"No, no, I can't say I know the man."

"Forgive me, but because you are Embassy staff and a diplomat, I must request more specificity. You cannot say you know him because you are under orders not to say, or you mean you don't know who he is."

Yardley was thrown. *What was this cop getting at?* Maybe he should look again; maybe he should wait until the Chief of Station got in and clear any answer to the local authorities through him. After all, at Yardley's FSO pay grade, he didn't know everything America was doing in France.

"I don't believe I caught your name, Lieutenant."

"Malveau; Tristan Malveau."

"Well, Lieutenant Malveau, I am just a mid-level Foreign Service Officer. The chances of me knowing the dead man only extend to the random possibility of having gone to school with him back in the States. May I ask why you are here? Last year we had more than 30 Americans who died in France and I don't recall the police ever being here once."

"A mere courtesy, monsieur. This was also found on his person." Malveau handed a business card to Haines.

All Yardley saw was the seal of the President of the United States on the card and he was off. "Would you be so kind as to wait here, Lieutenant, while I check into this?"

"Of course."

∞§∞

"The baby is not made out of glass. Although you have to be mindful of certain developmental issues, don't overcompensate. In fact, the more you make the child a part of your life, the better the child's development. That doesn't mean you take a six-month old to the stock car races and then for a steak dinner, but for your sake and the child's, you should try not to change everything all at once. Many parents... Many par... Please make sure all cell phones are off or switched to vibrate please."

"Sorry, excuse me," Hiccock said as he retrieved his ringing cell phone from his pocket under the glaring eyes of Janice. "I'll just take this outside..."

He wedged his way past two other expectant couples in his row and headed for the exit in the back of the room. "Hold on," he whispered into the phone.

Out in the lobby, he went toward the doors of the learning center to get a better signal. "Hello."

"White House switchboard. I have Joseph Palumbo on the line."

"Put him through, operator. Hey Joey, We're auditing a baby catching class. What's up?"

"They let you audit those now? Listen, we just got a call from State. There is a deceased American citizen in Paris and somehow he is connected to you."

"Me? Who is it?"

"Don't know but they want you over there."

"Over where -- Paris?"

"No, the State Department."

"Now?"

"They were very insistent."

"Okay, thanks Joe." Bill hung up and walked back to the room. He hesitated at the door. He hated to bother everybody again, but he was practically ordered to the State Department. He entered and squeezed past the two couples again, then sat beside Janice.

"Honey, I have to go."

"What? Now?"

"I have to get to State. Somebody died in Europe and they want to talk to me."

"That doesn't make any sense..."

"I know." He handed her the keys. "You take the car. I'll catch a cab."

The instructor once again stopped in her dissertation. "Is there something the matter?"

"Uh, I'm sorry. I have to get back to work. So sorry to interrupt."

With that announcement, the other two couples in the row got up and moved out to avoid further butt-facing from Hiccock.

Bill kissed Janice on the cheek. "Love you; see ya at home."

∞§∞

As Bill approached the security post on the C Street entrance of the State Department, he flashed his White House I.D. A man on the other side of the magnetometer greeted him. "Mr. Hiccock, I'm Martin Kelsh, Undersecretary of State for European and Eurasian Affairs. Come this way, please."

Four minutes later, they were in a secure videoconference room. As soon as they walked in, the grainy image on the left of two videoscreens caused Bill to utter, "Oh, no!"

On the other screen, to the right, were Yardley Haines and Frank Randall. Frank was the Station Chief of the Paris Embassy. Once Bill sat in the chair, his own image came up on a smaller monitor below the two big ones.

Frank spoke first. "Mr. Hiccock, do you know this man?"

"Yes, I do."

"Is there anything about him or his purpose here in France that affects the national Security of the United States?"

"Nothing I know of. I mean, I doubt it, but I can't be 100 percent certain. Why are you asking? And how did you know I knew him?"

"We found your card in his personal effects. We have to make sure that we are not dealing with a potential security incident or secret envoy."

"No. He met with me recently, but it was not in any way connected to my job at the White House." As soon as he said it, Bill's mind started to race.

"There was a notation made on the back." Frank turned and addressed an embassy staffer. "Can we put that under the camera?" On the left monitor, large fingers swiped away the license and replaced it with the back of the card. The words "Prof. Ensiling" were scrawled across the width. "Do any of these references mean anything to you?"

"I believe the professor was a friend of his who died recently. That's what he came to see me about."

"We know of this professor. Why was the deceased seeing you about him?"

"Peter Remo was a bit of a conspiracy... lover." Bill couldn't bring himself to use the word "nut" in relation to his dead friend. "I had my department's investigator find out if there was any foul play."

"And what did you find?"

"That the professor died of natural causes."

Even through the video screen, Bill saw the slightest of hints of "really" emanating from Frank Randall's face. It immediately bothered him, but he thought not to go down that road at this time.

"Is there anything else we should know, Mr. Hiccock?"

Bill was about to correct him to his proper bona fide title of Professor Hiccock, but decided it wasn't worth bringing another Ph.D. into the mix. "No, nothing else I can think of."

"Well then, thank you sir. Sorry you lost your friend."

"Thank you. How did he die?"

"That's a little murky right now, but it appears he was murdered."

"Murdered? By who?"

"All we know was that it was at a nightclub. We are waiting for the police to finish their investigation."

"Can you keep my office informed as well? I would appreciate it."

"Of course."

∞§∞

Bill got home and saw the pamphlets on baby care on the kitchen table. He opened the fridge, considered the potato salad, but just grabbed a Dos Equis instead. He screwed off the top and tossed it into the kitchen basket. He took a long draw, then did the lip-smack thing.

Upstairs in the bedroom, Janice was coming out of the bathroom a towel turbaned around her freshly washed hair. "I thought you'd be later."

"No, it was quick. But I got some bad news."

"Oh dear, what?"

"Peter Remo was found dead in Paris last night."

"I'm sorry, Bill. How did it happen?"

"They said he was murdered."

"How horrible."

"It could have been just a fight in a club... or maybe something more. Listen to me, I'm starting to sound like Peter."

Bill started to laugh.

"Your friend is dead; what's so funny?"

"It's not funny; it's ironic. They found my card in his wallet and had to check that he wasn't working for the government. Peter was a conspiracy theorist who spent most of his days trying to prove the government was behind everything bad that ever happened. In the end, he comes under suspicion of working for that same government. You couldn't make this stuff up."

"Well, God rest his soul. You coming to bed?"

"Yeah, I'm beat."

"Did you shut the lights downstairs?"

"Yes, dear."

Two hours later Janice got up to use the bathroom. She found Bill wide awake looking at the ceiling.

"I know why I'm up. Don't tell me it's sympathy peeing for you." She nestled under his arm.

"Peter came to me and I just wrote him off, like he was a nut. Now he's dead. What if I had listened? Maybe something was up with him?"

"How could you have possibly known?"

"He hadn't bothered to reach out to me in decades. Suddenly he does and then gets killed. I just hope I didn't miss something."

"Billy, if he was murdered, it was something that he got involved with that has nothing to do with you."

"He said he was afraid that he was going to be next and it just rolled off my back like he said he thought he was getting a cold. When did I get so cavalier about life?"

"Stop it now. If he had shown you any of the traditional signs of stress or impending doom, your reaction would have been totally different. The fact that he did not broadcast imminent danger to you means he was just positioning or posturing or testing your level of gullibility and was in no real danger that he perceived."

"Is that the behavioral head doctor talking?"

"One of the best in the field, so believe her and get some sleep." Janice kissed him and snuggled in even more.

∞§∞

Rodney had been waiting for this phone call since 2001. He had just missed the previous endeavor. Bad Luck. A flat tire on the way to the airport. Now, another chance. Sitting in the Wal-Mart parking lot in Canoga Park, California, he let his mind fantasize about what this adventure might mean. There was a possibility that recent events in the news could have played a role, but more likely, since he had been out of the loop, it was probably something else. No matter. Whatever it was, it would be what would be.

A tan Escalade pulled up next to his car, very close on the passenger side. As a woman and two kids emerged, one of the kids slammed the door into his car. The driver, obviously the father, called out to his son, "Careful Roshy!" As the wife and kids walked towards the store, the man got out and came around to Rodney's driver-side window. Looking down at the scratch in the rear door, he apologized. "I am sorry, although it's just a scratch really. Here, take my insurance information. Have a good night." And he was off in the direction of the store.

Rodney opened the envelope; in it were directions to a meeting place, two airline tickets, and 10,000 dollars in hundred-dollar bills. For the first time in public and outside his inner prayer room, Ali Rashid, a.k.a. Rodney Albert, dared mutter a phrase under his breath.

"Allah Be Praised!"

CHAPTER EIGHTEEN
UNAUTHORIZED ACCOUNTS

"So, La Grande Fromage, what was the call from France all about?" Joey asked as he popped into Bill's office at 7:25 a.m.

"Hey, if I am the big cheese, where's my coffee?" He tossed the State Department's preliminary report on Peter's death to Joey.

"Sorry, I thought you'd have yours already." Joey scanned the summary. "Wow, that call last night was about Johnny No's big brother, Peter Remo?" Joey plopped in the chair across from Bill's desk. "Poor guy."

Both sat quietly for a moment.

"Hey, you ever think about it?" Joey said, coming out of it.

"About what?"

"About all the guys who are dead now."

"Never thought about it, but now that you mention it...."

"Benny Elmont, rolled his car. Eddy Rissar was smoking in bed. Darlene Freemont got the big C. Danny Boyd got crushed on his construction site...who else?"

"I guess this happens as you get older. It's the odds. Think about it; if you live long enough, everybody you've known would be dead."

"You think its just odds?"

"You don't?"

"I keep raking my mind. Guys like Eddy, Danny, even Peter. Was there something about them, some look or some trait, some harbinger of death?"

"What you really are asking is, 'Whatever it is, do I have it?'"

"You know, you're right."

"I'm going to go to the funeral. You wanna go?"

"I don't know. I hardly ever hung out with the guy past sixth grade and his little stoop sessions on moon shots, nuclear mutants, and perpetual motion." You and him though... with all your egghead crap...he found a real dork in you, pal. I'll just send a mass card."

"Suit yourself."

∞§∞

"Rodney" was entering the address into the navigation system of the car that he was forced to rent from Hertz on his personal credit card. Cash was more of a hassle when it came to renting a car and would have set off many flags. Flags were the enemy at this point. His spoken English was good and his American accent pretty decent, but reading this strange language was another story. It boggled his mind that the Arabic number system got mixed into this hodgepodge of odd characters and punctuation. So rather than trusting the English written instructions, he programmed the destination into the system. He had already, unconsciously, walked around the car checking the tires, a remnant of his last disappointment when a flat tire denied him his place of glory as the 21st hijacker.

His cover for these past years was as an assistant cameraman in Hollywood. He wasn't union but he found enough work to blend into the indie film community. Oddly enough, he enjoyed the work. Many times, the content of these films was that of Satan himself, but his craft, pulling focus and making sure the lens and image path was always clear, gave him satisfaction that was small recompense for not being able to be the openly devout man he had studied to be.

The meeting place was not far off the New Jersey Turnpike, in Jersey City, New Jersey. Seven men assembled in a Store and Lock in the industrial part of town. Due to local blue laws and deference to the religious nature of a Sunday, the storage warehouse was closed to the public.

Upon entering the facility, a bearded man met Rodney and said, "No names. You are number 3." He then put a sticker on Rodney that had the printed words, "Hello, I'm" under which the number 3 was written in black Sharpie. The two other men arrived in the next 10 minutes.

A man who would only ever be known as Number 1 began talking to the assembled men. "We have been chosen to be the hand of Allah. Each one of you has been picked for this honor because you have certain skills and abilities. As we go through the operational plan, each of you will also learn each other's parts so that you may take over in the event of one of us being caught or killed. We will work from six at night until morning prayers. I have turned the basement of this building into a dormitory. You will each have a room. We have a kitchen, bath, and exercise room. When you are not working, you are either praying or exercising. We all need to be in perfect physical shape. Also downstairs is a shooting range. I expect each of you to be proficient with handguns and automatic weapons. We have 20 days."

∞§∞

Port of Newark was a bustling metropolis made of millions of containers loading, unloading, coming, and going to every point in the world. The new on-demand warehouse economy kept the cost of doing business low because merchants no longer needed warehouses and financing to cover goods awaiting shelf space. Now as one item is purchased at a big box store in Wisconsin, another item to replace it is loaded on a container in Taiwan. Containers were the blood cells of this new economy. And the heartbeats of this economy were measured in "turn time." A port's pride and rating were based on the time to turn around one of these containers. So any delay in the processing meant higher costs, higher prices, and, worse, turn time. The pressure was always on not to slow the pace of the economy. Therefore, no containers were scanned until scanning could be done without slowing the journey of a single container. New fast scanners were big, expensive, and less efficient than manual inspection. So the realities of the potential threat succumbed to the actual realities of the marketplace.

That was, until last week, when the papers started talking about a suitcase bomb on its way to America. Now the motto was, "Economy be dammed! Check every container coming in!" In the Port of Newark alone, there were 455,000 empty containers in turnaround, a suspended animation of sorts for these large trailer-truck-sized boxes as they awaited being stuffed, sealed, and sent on to their next port of call. The job of checking the empties was assigned to four customs officers across three shifts. At the rate of inspecting 14 per hour, per eight-hour shift, (because they were stacked and had to be separated by huge ZPMC cranes), 2,240 containers a week – or less than one half of one percent – could be searched manually. Further impacting the odds was the fact that containers are designed to ride piggybacked on trains or trucks to points all over the U.S. and that meant that in addition to the ones here at the Port, there were maybe three million more out there in the economy.

If Bill was right in his supposition, that the bomb was already here, then there was a good chance it came in one of the millions of boxes also already here. That's how U.S. Borders and Customs agent Hector DeNardo suddenly got put on an overtime-rich new schedule of twelve-hour days, six days a week. He didn't mind that one bit. After 38 years in the department, this bump in extra pay would go a long way in calculating his pension. Every extra hour he put in now was two bucks more in his monthly pension check when he was ready to retire to the beach.

∞§∞

Bill never chatted with Bob Henley, the White House Director of Communications before, so his attendance at the meeting was a sure sign Bill's phone call of the previous night hit an exposed nerve. Bill called Margaret, the Press Secretary, when he got the call last night at home informing him that *Time* magazine was going to be running a story on the virus attack and Bill's role in it. Bill followed the protocol and demurred comment pending the decision of the White House Communications Office. Sometime overnight, a mock up of this week's magazine was dropped of at 1600 Pennsylvania Avenue and it sat on the conference table, the 3,500-word story having already been copied and distributed to all in the room for comment on whether they should comment.

Not for publication was Bill's positive opinion of the cover. It was a picture taken in the White House Press Briefing Room maybe during the Bio-Tech initiative briefing, when Bill was standing behind the President with the Presidential Seal on the podium. With Bill being taller and larger, they photographed as the same size, as he was awaiting his turn to comment. The headline on this *Time* magazine read, "Commander and Geek – An Unauthorized Look Behind the Scenes at the Outsmarting of a Terrorist's Plot."

"It's a good picture of you and the boss, Bill," Margaret offered.

"Ya think so?" He took the opportunity to right the cover one more time and feign gauging it. *I don't look as old as Joey does.*

"So then we are agreed. We do not comment, stand by, or endorse the story," Margaret's boss said. Then, flipping through the mag one more time, the man addressed Bill, "Did you actually do half the stuff in here?"

"For national security reasons, I can neither confirm or deny anything about my participation, or lack thereof, in any of these scenarios," Bill said as serious as a heart attack.

"Well, I guess we don't have to worry about you leaking anything to the press today."

CHAPTER NINETEEN
FAVORITE SONS

St. Lucy's Church in the Bronx had a grotto. It was a catacomb-like structure located across from the church. Lots of candles, and a few crypts seemingly chiseled right out of the blue gray stone. It was a dark and somber place. A kid's first impression was that of going through a haunted cave. Later in life, it became a cool place to take a girl and, with the help of a buddy, get her to jump into your arms when he sprang out at the two of you from the shadows. Still later in life, it became a place of solitude and reverence or, as in Bill's case today, a place to light a candle to remember his Irish grandparents who both had their funerals here.

Peter's funeral had been a high mass. One of the guys from the neighborhood, Arnie, who was always an altar boy and hanging around the church when they were growing up, sang the hymns and "Ave Maria" from the balcony. An older, grey-haired woman played the church organ accompanying him. After the service, Arnie came over to Bill and introduced his wife and kids. She was neat and petite and had what used to be called beauty parlor hair. The kids were cute, and all together they made a great family picture for any Christmas card. Bill liked the idea that Arnie turned out well: a family man, all around good guy and citizen. Somehow, it gave him a good feeling about many other things, including his own family-in-progress.

Seeing Peter's parents was hard. When he and Johnny 'No', had sleepovers, Anna Remo made ravioli and meatballs or lasagna or mineste. He loved having dinner at the Remo's. It was Johnny and Pete's mom who gave him his first taste of demitasse, making Bill feel like one of the grown ups. Anna Remo hugged him and spoke through sobs. "Peter talked of you all the time. He would always watch you when you were doing the football. He'd say, 'There's that Billy the Kid.' That's what he called you—Billy the Kid. Then when you went with the President, he would always tell everybody how you and his little brother Johnny were friends. Thank you for coming here for my sons. Peter would be so happy to know you were here."

"He knows, Mrs. Remo. He's up there seeing all of us right now."

"You think so?"

"I know it, Mrs. Remo."

"You're a good boy, William. You always were. How's your mother?"

"She and Dad are fine, living out on Long Island. They do some traveling and Dad's always ready to go fishing."

"You tell her Anna said hello and that she should come around the old neighborhood sometime for coffee."

"I'll tell her, Mrs. Remo."

The funeral procession rolled down Bronxwood Avenue. Bill saw that the White Castle was still going strong, the lumberyard was gone, and Gino's restaurant was now an IHOP. Somebody, probably a Haitian family, took over Paul Manelo's house and now there were baby blue shutters, a large Virgin Mary, and plastic flowers in window boxes. It was pretty, but stuck out like a family in Easter Sunday clothes at Orchard Beach in July. They slowed the procession when they passed Peter's house on Matthews Avenue then down Burke Avenue to White Plains Road; then it made a left onto Gunhill Road and headed to Woodlawn Cemetery.

At the gravesite, Bill was looking out across the cemetery. In the distance was the elevated train running down White Plains Road. That reminded him of the reason

Peter and Bill knew each other. It went back to the day Bill's dad came into school for "what's your father do for a living" day. Many of the dads who showed up were truck drivers like Pete's dad, storeowners, a few cops, firemen, mailmen, Con Ed workers. Eddie's dad was an elevator mechanic. When Peter, a train freak, heard that Bill's dad was a subway engineer, he latched right on. Peter eventually got the senior Hiccock to allow him to "front end" the entire trip from Woodlawn in the Bronx to Utica Avenue in Brooklyn. To Peter, it was as if Bill's dad was Mickey Mantle.

Peter, however, never got to watch the Yankee games, or the Mick, from the tin shed at the end of the 161st street el platform as Joey and Bill did. Most of the guys who worked for the T.A. scheduled the shed for one of their kids on game days. All the engineers and conductors would keep an eye on 'em like surrogate fathers peering from each passing train. The token booth clerk would check on them every half hour or so just for good measure. By the time Billy was old enough to enjoy this perk, Peter was in his room a lot, building stuff and almost burning down the house. In fact, while the other guys were going to Orchard Beach or horseback riding on Pelham Parkway, Peter apparently got a job working at NBC. That was why nobody ever saw him.

Bill's train of thought, triggered by the number 2 train, stopped when Johnny Remo, Peter's brother, and Bill's childhood pal, came over and gave him a big bro-hug and thanked him for coming.

"Billy Hiccock, It's been too long."

"Too long, Johnny, too long."

"We know how busy you are. It really means a lot to us to have someone like you here." He was shorter than Peter, tight-cropped razor haircut in a Frank Sinatra, circa 1970's way. He was a mass of muscle and wore a gold pinky ring. He talked like an ironworker, mainly because he was one.

"Whoa, John, I ain't someone like me," Bill said. "I'm someone like you; we both grew up here, and Peter and you and all the guys know me like nobody else does."

"No Billy, you were smart. Always were, you work with your head, not your back like us stiffs."

"Paycheck's a paycheck, Johnny."

"No. Well, just the same, thank you, and thank you for being there for Peter. He was all excited about seeing you last month."

"John, I got to tell ya, I wasn't much help to him. In fact, there was nothing I could help him with."

"No, hey, Billy, you gave him time. You listened; you did what a friend does. Towards the end, Peter didn't have too many friends, you know what I mean?"

"He was driven to..."

"No, no, he was obsessed. I wouldn't be surprised if that's what killed him," John said turning to the coffin now lowered into the grave.

"Have you found out...well maybe this isn't a good time to talk about this."

"No, Bill you are right, later. You coming to the house after this?"

Bill checked his watch; he had a 4:30 out of LaGuardia back to Reagan. "Sure, I got time."

"No, we'll talk then. I got something I want to show you."

∞§∞

David had been a cop in Haifa before taking on the security detail of the West Bank. His responsibility was for the safety and peace of Palestinians and Jews living side by side. There were flare-ups and occurrences that would be shocking in places of other demographics and geographics, but against the centuries-old rivalries of two peoples positioned in close proximity, these schisms just passed as any other day in this once proud prize of Israeli land. So the reported death of Hamir al-dashabi, a truck driver for an Israeli MRI manufacturer was little more than a footnote in the homicide log for that day.

CHAPTER TWENTY
KEY TO THE CITY

"On behalf of the bank, welcome Mr. Rashani," loan officer, David Wasserman said as he rose and shook the hand of Commercial Bank's newest customer. "And thank you very much for your business."

"I am sure this will be a long and fruitful relationship. We have many movies to make here in America and, hopefully soon, a TV series," Rashani said.

"Good, good, we like to hear that."

"Yes, your state's new tax incentives are a long time coming. Our investors are very happy we are shooting in New York State."

"Our bank lobbied hard to get the Governor and the State Assembly to offer these incentives and, may I just say, Mr. Rashani, you are living proof that these incentives are good for New York. Please don't hesitate to call me personally if there is any further way we can help you." Wasserman stood and earnestly reached out to shake the man's hand.

"Actually, in about three months, I might want to bring some new investors to the city. Perhaps you could be in attendance and show them what a good job you and the bank are doing for us." Rashani emphasized the lie he had just uttered by clasping his free hand over their clenched grip.

"I'd be honored; helping our clients grow is how we grow."

As the impeccably dressed producer of Iran's biggest production company left the bank, Wasserman called his wife.

"Honey, I just signed a 25-million-dollar account with the largest independent producers of film in Iran. Yes, just now! That's going to bring my three-month total to 185 million. They have to give me that V.P. slot now!"

∞§∞

Rashani's next stop after establishing a production bank account was the insurance company. Along the way, he reflected on the brilliance involved with paying a Hollywood agent $50,000 cash just for a favorable introduction to the bank. That agent, nor Mr. Wasserman, could pick the real Rashani out of a line up of him and a Girl Scout troop, let alone care about the color of his money. *Yes, greed is good,* Rashani thought, remembering a line from an American movie that was actually made here in New York.

So far, the creation of American Partners Iranian, L.L.C. had cost about $85,000, a mere grain of sand next to his 25-million-dollar "production budget." With his new API, L.L.C. bank checks, he was able to write the $10,500 dollars necessary to obtain the Producer's Liability package. It was a mixture of many diverse insurance policies that protected the producer from all kinds of calamities that can befall a cinematic production, from rain to bad film stock ruining a shot. He did not purchase E and O insurance however, even though it was discounted with the package. Errors and Omission insurance protected the final movie from all claims. There would be no final movie. In fact, there were only two reasons to have the Producer's Package at all: it had workman's comp, which any good crew person or trade union insisted on before walking onto a working set, and, more importantly, you could get a permit to film on the streets of New York. Even with police escort and protection – all free of charge! You could close a bridge, clear an avenue, wreck cars, and burn down buildings, theatrically of course. As long as you held the insurance naming New York City as loss payee for one million dollars per event, you were instantly a reputable production company. A New York City film permit was truly the key to the city.

∞§∞

"Wanna see what got my brother killed?" John said motioning upstairs in the two family house that the Remos lived in since their sons were three and thirteen. On the way up the stairs was a framed photo of John and other hard hats down at "the pile." It made Bill stop.

"John, you were there?"

"No, not just me – the whole union. We all turned out. There was thousands of metric tons of steel there, had to cut it where it lay. Every time we came across remains, we had to stop. Then there was a ceremony; then we'd start working again. There was 250 tons of human remains compressed into the 10-story pile."

As they went up the stairs, the effort made John cough. *9-11 sickness* Hiccock thought. At the top, under a table, were work boots that looked like they were sitting in pancakes. John bent down and got them. "No, look see, these were brand fucking new, first day look, look here, the souls are melted. That fucking pile was like walking on an oven for 10 days. Brand new fucking pair of steel toes – instant garbage. That was some hell of a place. But we cleaned it up in record time."

"You guys were amazing."

"No, sometimes I think we should-a let it sit there forever, to remind everybody what those fuckers did to us. People, they are forgetting, getting soft, letting down their guard. It's not good, I tell ya."

"The President and me, we'll never forget, John."

"No, you'll keep all those Washington jerks on the trigger, no, I know that."

Bill suddenly remembered why John's nickname growing up was "Johnny 'No'."

"C'mere, let me show you what I brung you up here for."

Bill remembered the hallway, from when they were kids and the bathroom at the end of the hall. How embarrassed he was one night, when, on a sleepover, he walked in on Anna washing her nylons in the sink. She was in a slip, but in those days, even seeing your friend's mom in a slip was a weird and creepy thing. They went into what used to be Peter's room. There, amid the guest bed and older furniture, was a box of stuff. John reached in and pulled out a gray envelope with the old, interlocking blue NBC logo on it. Inside was a brown binder with yellowed pages. John flipped open the binder; it was a photocopy of a book. It looked as if someone had laid it flat on a copy machine.

Bill was frozen. *Just as Peter described. Holy shit he wasn't hallucinating…at least about this part.*

"This is what I figured got Petey killed."

Bill felt as though someone had just showed him the original draft to a Shakespeare play. This was the book Peter told him about on the steps of the Memorial.

"How do you know he was killed over anything more than a bar fight?"

"No, what the fuck was he doing in France? No, he never cared about places like that. I'm telling you, that old man got whacked, then Peter went on his crusade shit and bam now he's dead."

"Old man? You mean Professor Ensiling?"

"Bingo! Dat guy!

"I hear you, John, but Joey Palumbo – you remember Joey – he works with me now."

"No, Palumbo? No shit. Last I heard he was working with the feds."

"Yeah, I kinda screwed that up for him, so now we... anyway, he checked the Ensiling thing out, and he says the fat lady sang natural on this professor guy."

"No, Billy, I don't mean to argue here, but that's bullshit. Peter told me about the threats, the attempts, the time they missed him and the old guy and killed that broad."

"John, I never heard about any woman being shot."

"No, all I'm saying here is that this book, with all this gobbledygook and fucking formulas, got everybody killed. You want it?"

"After a sales job like that? Yeah, sure I want it, John. I'm dying to have somebody come after me, too."

"Then at least you'll know Peter was right? No?"

Bill just looked at his childhood friend's smirking face. "Thanks a lump."

∞§∞

Between what was in Peter's files and Mrs. Remo cajoling him to stay for cake and coffee, Bill just made the 8 o'clock back to D.C. from La Guardia and decided to skip going to the office and had his driver take him directly home. It was 9:30 and the funeral had taken more of a toll on him than he realized. The thought of going home to Janice and splicing into some iota of a normal routine was a comfortable idea.

He rolled out the garbage cans to the front of the driveway and went into the house from the garage entrance into the kitchen. As if he were eight years old, there on the fridge, being held up by magnets shaped like bananas, oranges, watermelon slices, and lemons, was the *Time* magazine cover. Under it was a Post-it note that read, "I always wanted to tramp around with a 'cover boy.' I await you upstairs Mr. Bond."

Bill smiled, opened the fridge, grabbed the orange juice, and was about to take a slug from it, when the door closed and he was looking right at the cover picture of him with the President of the United States. Self-consciously, he got a glass from the cabinet and poured.

Janice was under the covers and her body was radiating heat. He snuggled close and she spoke softly into the pillow. "You look like *you* should be the President in that picture, Billy boy." She reached around and pulled him into her.

Bill kissed her neck. "You're just saying that to have your way with me..."

"I'm going to have my way no matter what I say, Mr. Commander n' Geek." Then she rolled over and made good on her promise.

Forty-five minutes later, she was curling Bill's hair around her finger while he dozed off with his arm over her stomach, his head on her chest. "Did you read it?"

"What?"

"The article; did you get a chance to read it?"

"Yeah, good writing. Like a serialization of a novel."

"Bill, I am concerned."

Now he was up. He rolled over on his back, sat up, and took a swig of the orange juice in the glass. He jutted it to Janice as if to ask, "Want some?"

She shook her head. "The article makes it seems like you single-handedly caught the terrorist mastermind."

"Jan, you know I can't really talk about this..."

"Yes I know. But what if these guys get pissed off at you?"

"Who?"

"The terrorists; what if they come after you, personally? If I were them, and I read that article, I'd want to kill you for ruining my plans."

"Hey, I'm an American, so they'd want to kill me for that alone. I'm in the government, so that's another reason. And I let you speak back to me and go out in public with your face and ankles showing, so they can cut my head off three times before they ever get to 'I ruined their party.'" He dragged his index finger under his chin in a slashing gesture for emphasis.

Janice grabbed the finger, pulled his hand to her lips, and kissed it. "God damn you, I am serious!"

"Okay, sorry. I have Brent."

"He's only a driver."

"A driver with a gun!"

"No, I mean he's only around when you are working." Janice untangled from him and spun around, sitting up and locking her eyes into his. "Get a protection detail. Tell Mitchell I want you to have one. He likes me and I'm sure he doesn't want to see me as a widow."

Bill rolled over, pulled the pillow over his head, and spoke into the muffling mattress. "I was feeling so good five minutes ago. Thanks for the buzz kill, kid."

She pulled the pillow off him and leaned into his face. "I love you. I don't want anything happening to you because of fucking *Time* magazine. Promise me."

"Janice..."

"Bill, promise me you'll talk to Mitchell – tomorrow, or that was your last blow job!"

"You play dirty."

"I like to think of it as, 'below the belt.'"

∞§∞

Rodney left the Lock and Store at 10:30 headed for the New York City Mayor's Office for Motion Picture and Television. His mission today was to secure three film permits for what would ostensibly be the first two days of shooting the New York exteriors for the Iranian/

American co-production of "Byline of Death." He was instructed to get two shooting permits and one rigging prep permit. One was for filming on Park Avenue at 45th street across from the Waldorf Astoria hotel. He was to get the second one for that same day, a build/prep permit for the parking lot at Citi Field in Queens. The baseball team that played there was scheduled to be out of town those days. The second shooting permit was for filming at the Citi Field location the next day, ostensibly to film what was prepped the day before.

Leaving Jersey, he made the big, sweeping turn that screwed down from the elevated roadway of the Route 3/ Tunnel approach to the toll plaza below. All of New York City was backlit by the rising sun from the east out his window. He looked south to the hole in the lower Manhattan skyline.

"No flat tire this time, Allah be praised."

He lowered the prayer tape playing in the AM/FM/CD cassette radio in the car as he neared the Port Authority tollbooths of the Lincoln Tunnel.

∞§∞

"Sonia Hansen," Joey said in Bill's office. "Died in Vienna on Dec third last year. She was shot on the street. No motive, no priors, no killer. It's in the books as open case. Crosschecking Ensiling's travel itinerary, it would put him in Austria on that same day."

"Okay. That could just only mean what we already know – that this woman was killed the same time Ensiling was there. We need to put them together to see if Peter was right. Wait a minute, John said something that seemed to make it like Peter was there too. Can you check with State and see if they come up with a visa from the Viennese, er... Austrians?"

"I am having Interpol check any street surveillance or traffic camera to see who was around the woman at the time she was gunned down. Maybe we'll catch a glimpse of the professor and Peter."

"Also Joey, this is just a hunch, but have them check ATM machines and any hotel cameras where the professor was staying. That might tell us what he was wearing and what to look for."

"Good thought. You sure you don't want my job?"

"Nah, it's easy to think up stuff when that's all you have to do. It's harder to actually do it."

"Duh," Joey said as he left Bill's office.

Bill focused on the pile on his desk. Next on his agenda was to get the legitimacy of Peter's book confirmed or denied. He had Kronos scan it then used a scan-to-text converter to make it all one big word-processing file. He then put it up on the SCIAD network. After a day or two, he expected to hear something back.

With his commitment to "Johnny No" in the works, to investigate the book that got his brother killed, he was now free to focus on the suitcase nuke and how he and his team might possibly prevent any detonation.

Or so he thought.

"Mr. Hiccock, would you come with me into the Oval?"

"Agent Renko, when you put it like that..." Bill stood from his desk and immediately followed him to the Oval Office.

"Ah, Bill, you know Williams, head of the Secret Service Presidential detail?" the President said.

Bill extended his hand. "Sure. How are you, Mr. Williams?"

"Fine, Mr. Hiccock."

"Bill, Williams gets paid to think of this stuff, and today he thinks it would be a good idea if you had some protection."

"Is this about the article?"

"Exactly." Mitchell flipped through the magazine. "It's made you very visible and since you hold NCA ranking, are the head of an investigation, and the lead agency on the loose nuke, you have become a high valued target."

"Well, this will make my wife happy, just last..."

"She will also be afforded a small detail," Williams said. "And we'll need your permission to install some security and communications equipment in your home."

"Well, maybe she won't be *that* happy."

"Bill, don't even think of saying no." Mitchell ordered as President of the United States.

∞§∞

In the Mayor's Office for Film and Television, Rodney filled in the columns on the Citi Field permit. Under "describe shot," he copied the text from scrupulously written notes: "Bita Asayesh, ace reporter, exits news helicopter, into boyfriend's arms. Crane up - End credits." The other permit, for the day before, was to rig the helicopter and set lights. It was to be done by an advance unit of carpenters and riggers. Under props went the notation, "One Helicopter."

∞§∞

It stopped Hiccock dead in his tracks. "Say that again?"

"You had a call on your private number," Cheryl reported. "The caller asked for 'Billy the Kid.' When I said I'd take a message he hung up."

"That's impossible."

"How's it impossible?"

"Because I buried that guy last week. Get me Joey quick."

Bill closed the door to his office, a rare occurrence, and plopped into his chair. *Who else called me that?*

Four minutes later, Joey knocked and entered. "What's up?"

Bill pointed to the single-line phone on the return of his desk. "Can you trace where the last call on that phone came from?"

"Yeah, I guess so."

"Do it. Five minutes ago."

"What happened?"

"Do you remember anyone else who ever called me 'Billy the Kid?'"

"Anybody *else*? I never heard *anybody* call you that!" Joey said as he picked up Bill's office phone. "Signals, please. Yes, Sergeant Anders, I need you to pull the luds on Science Advisor Hiccock's personal line." He held the phone away from his mouth. "Bill, what's the terminal I.D. on the wall socket there?"

Bill bent over to where the phone was jacked to the wall. "WW-143-04." From down there, he saw one of his business cards, which had fallen behind the credenza. He reached over.

"Okay, I'll need a location as soon as you know." Joey hung up and saw Bill pensively flipping the card in his fingers.

"Where do you keep your wallet?"

"I keep it in my pants."

"That's a good practice for a married man... and an American."

"Where do Europeans keep their wallets?"

"I guess you aren't looking for 'pants' as an answer."

"Not if they are wearing jackets!"

"What?"

"You know, it's very continental to have a billfold in the breast pocket of your jacket," Bill said sliding his hand into his inside sport jacket pocket.

"You gotta stop having a quick one at lunch, Billy boy."

"Just find out where the call came from and call France to find out where they found Peter's wallet and my card."

"Oh crap!"

"Exactly."

When Joey left. Bill clicked the address book icon on his desktop, found the number he was looking for, and dialed.

"Johnny, it's Bill Hiccock. How you doing? Listen, I wanted to ask you something. Your brother, Peter; did he live with anyone in Paris? Could ya? Great; let me give you my cell number."

Cheryl came in and waited for Bill to finish.

"It's probably nothing, but I just had a crazy thought. Later, Johnny."

Bill ended the call and looked up.

"Joey called and said '14 Rue de Roosevelt, St Germain.' Isn't that Paris?"

"Yes it is. Get me that CIA guy at our embassy in Paris."

"Does Joey know who the CIA guy you are talking about is?"

"Yes. I'm sorry Cheryl… of course, you wouldn't know who that is. Have Joey call, and request to have surveillance of that address."

"Who are they looking for?"

"A dead guy."

CHAPTER TWENTY-ONE
LEADS

Bridgestone and Ross were active and fanning out from the source of the bombs, the refinery in Egypt. In a widening circle from the Nursery, they were trying to uncover any information about where the bomb was and where it might be headed.

The best lead they had ferreted out yet was a truck driver who they now believed delivered the 24 nukes to the facility two weeks before the raid. They based that belief on information provided by the long trail of broken bones and soiled undergarments of those who needed some persuasion to cooperate with them.

They were sitting in an old Range Rover at a truck stop along the desert road from Syria waiting for the truck driver.

"Ever hear of this guy Hiccock before?" Bridgestone asked.

"No, but he's got enough juice to get us out of jail free. That's all I need to know."

"So we are part of what now?"

"Quarterback ops, or something like that."

"Ah, now I get it."

"Wanna share?" Ross hated when Bridge knew something he didn't.

"Bill Hiccock! Played for Stanford! Now he's like the science guy for Mitchell. He sprang us!"

"Like to meet him someday. Thank him face to face."

"You and I should live so long."

"Is that the truck?"

"Plate number BH7234, roger."

They watched as the truck pulled into the rest stop. The driver, one Jamal al Najime, stepped from his cab carrying his thermos and made a beeline for the restroom. Ten seconds later, Ross climbed into the cab to look for any records or clues to his affiliation. Bridgestone positioned himself outside the truck stop's men's room. Not being listed in the Michelin Guide meant this roadside oasis essentially had holes in the ground for commode facilities and since ventilation was still two centuries off, the odor was very distinct.

When Jamal emerged, Ross watched him walk to the counter, place his thermos on it, and sit. Ross entered and went straight to the men's room. Bridge followed. They checked that they were the only ones in there and spoke English in low tones.

"You take him, Bridge. He's from the south; you'll do better with him."

"What else did you find?"

"He's not real religious. He is on his way to Cairo out of Damascus with a load of televisions in the back. He's got two daughters and one son. He takes pills for high blood pressure. He's had riders in the shotgun seat. I found prescription glasses in the passenger door pocket. He doesn't wear them and I don't see contacts. He's studying up on chicken farming."

"Stay close; I'm going to try and jump a ride with him."

"Got your back, Master Sergeant."

Bridgestone sat next to Jamal and ordered strong coffee. Jamal ordered and ate like a truck driver. Bridgestone started small talk in Arabic.

"Sandstorm's coming this afternoon."

"They always make it sound worse than it is." The driver grunted as he tore off another piece of flatbread.

"Where are you headed?"

"Cairo. Got four hours to make it."

"You have to go pretty fast, and then the storm."

"I've done it in three-and-a-half during worse."

"May Allah guide your trip."

"Thank you and a blessing upon you. Do you drive?"

"I drove before I lost my truck. I'm hoping to get some relief work in Cairo. Trying to make my way there now."

"How are you going?"

"On the charity of others. Allah has seen fit to have gotten me this far."

"Where did you start?"

"Lake Nasser, early yesterday."

"You made good time for someone without a truck."

"Some of the drivers still know me, so I was able to beg a few rides."

The trucker dabbed the bread in oil. "Ever drive Syria?"

"Sudan, Jordan, Sinai, Syria, yes, on many occasions," Bridge said in perfect desert cadence. "Some a little less legal than others, but it's not my place to speak."

"I am afraid it's the only way to make a good living these days."

"Praise Allah. But they do pay like the devil."

That made Jamal laugh. "Shame on you, brother. You are going to need much luck in Cairo. Don't get Allah on your bad side."

"My friend, if I am not already on his list, it is purely an administrative oversight." Bridge stressed the vowels of the last two words in a manner consistent with...

"You are from the desert?"

"Yes, south of Al Kharijah. You are quite astute."

"When you drive as far as me, you get so that you can tell people."

"My father was a herder. I hated it. I started driving at 14, got my own truck at 22, but it seems like I have no head for business."

"No, it's not your head, it's the business. It's madness! Rules, regulations, fuel, and insurance; they have many ways to put you out of business, but never help you stay in business."

"I was talking with someone who knew a Minister, to get a government contract. I thought I would be set for life. But he wanted too much money and I wasn't able to pay for the introduction."

"Camel's asses all. There is a special place in hell for people like that."

"If I can't find another job. I don't know what I'll do." Bridge laid that out there like a big fat softball pitch on a Sunday afternoon.

"You still know this Minister?"

Swing and a hit. "My friend does."

"It might be interesting to speak with him; how much did he want?"

"Ten thousand pounds, then five percent of each load. But you get 100 trips within the Misr, guaranteed a year." Bridge used the local term for Egypt.

"Interesting."

"When I get to Cairo, if I get to Cairo, I can look him up if you are interested."

"Come with me; I have a seat."

"Why, thank you, brother. That is most kind."

The waiter returned with a full thermos for Jamal and a check.

"Here, let me get that, er… the coffee I mean," Bridgestone said sheepishly as he laid down enough coins to only pay for the refill of the thermos.

"There's no need."

"Please, to cover the fuel."

"Okay. What is your name?"

"Mohammad Ali, and please no jokes."

"You must have heard them all."

"Regrettably so."

Ross watched as Bridge climbed onto Jamal's rig. He started up the Rover and tailed them from a safe distance behind.

∞§∞

Bill went into his den and turned on his secure laptop. It took two minutes for it to regain all its ability for SCIAD and would lose it all once again at the end of the session. During the boot-up time, he glanced out the window and saw a Secret Service agent was on post at the end of his driveway. The new 12-foot fence around his humble little home, motion sensors in the hedges, cameras on trees and 16-foot posts, and the gatehouse at the end of his driveway must have made the neighbors wish he'd never moved there. Bill scanned his retina and opened his in-box. It was stuffed with responses on Peter's book. As he started to read, it became clear he needed a meeting with everyone. One response in particular rattled him to his core.

> To: Nucleus
> From: Abramson
>
> The treatise of the book, mathematical proof of UFOs, is compelling but the science is not fluid. Certain jumps in celestial and quantum calculations may invalidate postulates. From a scientific point of view, more research is in order. However, if I may editorialize on a personal observation, in the author's attempt to tie natural and manmade phenomena into the mathematics of the grid, I noticed that each atom bomb and hydrogen bomb test he charted, a relationship between his extraterrestrial math and the success or failure of a nuclear explosion exists. In fact, 107 out of 110 successful blasts were correctly predicted by

> this confluence of the Earth and Sun's "harmonical" relationship. More astounding was that 100% of the non-explosions, or atomic duds, happened when his extraterrestrial math showed the Sun and Earth to be out of harmonic relationship. This extraordinary observation is well outside the laws of chance. I will apply his algorithm to nuclear tests conducted after the printing of this book in 1968, and see if the trend continued. How curious that an amateur investigation into aerial phenomena and the stuff of science fiction might have stumbled over a natural law regulating nuclear warfare.

Bill blurted out the words, "Jesus Factor!" He found the printout of Peter's copy of *Harmonic Epsilon* and read the three chapters entitled, "The Mathematics of the Grid," "The Harmonic and Nuclear Testing," and "Sorry, Mr. de Gaulle." The last chapter recounted the many times the French nuclear tests kept fizzling and how many of those times then-French President Charles de Gaulle had flown to the Mururoa Atoll test site only to be disappointed. Bill then read the paper generated on his SCIAD ring calculating the dates and locations of those tests with the mathematics of the grid and the terra-physics involved.

Damn.

What the author had pleaded for in his book 35 years ago – that someone with access to the "new calculating machines" would run his numbers and pick up where he left off – was all in the report that Bill now held in his hand.

Bill sat motionless for nearly five minutes. His mind replayed the President's serious concern, Peter's running away at the mere mention, scientists stumbling across that which was only held in close confidence by three living men in the world, then disappearing. *Correction* he thought. *Three men in the* free *world.* Did every nation who possessed nukes know that the rules of warfare were subject to solar tides?

He picked up the phone and called Cheryl. He asked her to get the White House travel office started on getting 10 SCIAD members to his office the day after tomorrow at 10 a.m.

∞§∞

Rodney had an instant dislike for the new guy, Number 11, who showed up today. It was the leather jacket. The guy was full of himself and that leather jacket and sunglasses were the height of smugness. Number 11 was the helicopter pilot. Unfortunately, Rodney had to train for two days with him.

∞§∞

Joey waited for Bill's 10:30 meeting to wrap before he went in. Five glum-looking people walked out of his office.

Joey went right in. "No happy campers in that bunch, boy."

"Why is it that they think lawyers beat scientists like rock beats paper? They think because it's a political football that I can just change the science! Science is not negotiable. It's not politically convenient. *It is what it is.*"

"What it is. Right on brother!"

"Shut up!" Bill picked up a red pen and – with extreme prejudice – crossed out the title page of whatever it was they left behind. He then tossed the document into the out basket. "What do you have for me, Joey?"

"Your call the other day could be the walking dead. We are very quietly exhuming the body from Woodlawn. We'll have DNA and fingerprints in a few hours."

"I just hope Signora Remo doesn't get wind of this unless we are sure her son isn't in that grave."

"I got Johnny 'No', as next of kin, to approve the order. He and I agreed it's better not to put his mom through this."

"Do you think Peter gave his jacket to someone or do you think it was lifted?"

"It could have gone down like this: the Sureté has seen neither hide nor hair of a grifter that operated in the clubs in that part of St. Germain for the past two weeks. Word is he crossed a family member of a very connected Frenchman who wanted him hurt bad for ripping off the man's nephew. It's possible Peter had his jacket off in the club, maybe behind a chair, and this guy sees one of the men the uncle sent to break his legs so he quick changes his appearance by grabbing Pete's jacket, then heads upstairs, but the henchmen catch on and get him on the stairway. They break his legs and stab him for good measure. The creep doesn't die fast, manages to make it to the street, but goes cold in the gutter and some poor schmuck on his way to make baguettes before dawn runs over his pumpkin. Splat! No identity other than Pete's papers in the 'borrowed' coat."

"The FBI teach you to talk like that?"

"No, Mr. Garafolo in gym."

"So everyone just accepts that he's Peter because he's got my card and that makes this a case the locals want no part of."

"So they don't do the basics and we just accept the body."

"And poor Anna Remo cries because we tell her she lost her son."

"Yep."

"What a way to run a railroad."

∞§∞

Riding along in the passenger seat of Jamal's truck, Bridge peered into his satchel. The L.E.D. meter of the radiometer, the latest generation of Geiger counter, was kicking above normal. That almost certainly meant this could have been the truck. Bridge decided to take the risk.

"What kind of loads do you usually work?"

"Used to do a lot of furniture – desks, tables, chairs. Lately, a lot of electronics. I have televisions back there now."

"Ever carry any dangerous stuff?"

"Like what?"

"Radioactive material."

"Why would you ask me that?"

Bridge took the Berretta out of his bag and pointed it at Jamal.

"You jackal; are you going to rob me?"

"Pull over. And say nothing."

"You are a dog, you bastard."

"I said shut up and pull over."

Jamal acceded to the gun. He looked at the picture, taped to the dashboard, of his wife and four children.

"Okay, shut it off, hand me the keys, and get out on my side," Bridge said as he opened the door on his side and back stepped down off the cab. He had his gun trained on Jamal. As Jamal slid across from the driver's seat to the passenger seat, he looked at the family photo one last time, then down onto the ground. Bridge tossed the keys back to him, "Now open up the back."

Jamal opened the lock, then pushed the big door up.

Bridge took out the radiometer. With the gun in one hand, he held the device inside the cargo area of the truck. It showed a very high reading.

"I hope you've got health insurance my friend. Your truck is hot. Radioactivity. It makes cancer."

"No, you are wrong! This is a trick."

"A trick, is it?" He then took a knife and slit the front of a TV box. He pulled down the cardboard and, in the dark of the night, the screen glowed from the residual radiation. "These sets are glowing like your insides must be. The headaches and nausea you are having are from the radiation poisoning." Bridge was guessing there, but Jamal suddenly placed his hand on his stomach and stood speechless.

"Jamal, I am not here to rob you. But whoever you worked for has robbed you of your health. Let me help you. All you have to do is tell me who hired you."

"I will be killed."

"You are dying now, my friend."

Ross pulled up behind the truck and came over to Bridge. "Wow, the TV is glowing. That must mean one of the cases was leaking even before the operation." Ross then turned and spoke in Arabic to the driver. "You have been handed a death sentence along with the payment for that shipment."

It didn't take long before Jamal told them the entire story. They then escorted the driver to Desert Tango 1 and made sure he got radiation treatment. His truck and the cargo were decontaminated and searched for any other forensic clues. Bridgestone and Ross then left to follow the new trail.

∞§∞

Joey Palumbo was getting more and more pissed off. His initial information concerning the death of Professor Ensiling was starting to become more and more suspect as he personally dug deeper into the case. Being 7,000 miles away didn't help, but through Bill's SCIAD net, he was able to get high quality video and stills that allowed him to do his own investigation. The big moment came when he received a street camera's image taken just seconds before the kill-shot that ended Sonia Hensen's life. In it, the man standing just beyond the woman on the Denmark street was indeed Professor Ensiling. Although his face was hidden, there was corroborating evidence from his hotel's security camera that caught the professor leaving that morning in a blue coat with one sleeve button missing. Next to the ill-fated woman was the sleeve of a blue coat with a button missing. It was a dead match. It didn't solve anything; it could just mean that the professor was there at that time or lent his coat to someone. Circumstantially, though, in the intervening weeks, no crazed lover of this woman, disgruntled employee, or random nut with a gun surfaced to discredit Peter's claim that the professor, not Sonia Hansen, was the true target. Furthermore, there was nothing in Hansen's background that suggested anyone would want her killed. The bullet was from a standard rifle, the likes of which were plastered all across Europe. As interesting as this was, with the loose nuke floating around out there somewhere, Joe didn't have much time to devote to this, so he made a call to his buddy at Interpol. Ten minutes later, Bill walked into the room, and threw down a worn, yellowed, and out of print, hard-covered copy of *Harmonic Epsilon*.

"What's this?"

"I forgot a whole bunch of stuff, which I am going to brain dump on you right now. I had Horace check into this book when Peter first came to me with this cockamamie story."

"And what did Horace find?"

Bill tapped the old book with his finger. "He ferreted out this book in a used book store. He also found that the author was still alive and that the formulas inside were, as best as he could deduce from the techs he spoke with, bullshit."

"But...?"

"But Peter's original galley, which his brother gave me at his house in the Bronx, is 323 pages long. This book is..." he flipped the dust jacketless book to the end page "303 pages long. I spot-checked some of the pages. Much of the text is the same, but all the formulas in Peter's galley are vastly different from the ones that wound up in this version of the book printed for public consumption. Later today, my SCIAD group is meeting to give their opinions."

"So all that could mean is that Peter's formulas are a different, or an older, kind of the same bullshit!"

"Not likely. My guys would have smelled it and we wouldn't be meeting."

"Okay, that's mildly curious, intellectually. But I'm a cop. What else you got, boy?"

"Peter said the publishing company in Hong Kong was burnt to the ground along with all the books and plates and manuscripts and he had the only surviving copy of the book. Check it. Also, he said he was on a secret committee for the U.N. on UFOs; he called it UNCOMUFO. I called the Ambassador, Susan Clark, but she can't find any record of it. Yet..."

"Yet..." Joey repeated.

Bill handed Joe a letter in a plastic sleeve. "Yet in Peter's shit was this letter signed by Secretary General U. Thant defining the committee's scope. Check it; make sure it's real. And lastly, since he alleges Ensiling was just one of the committee members killed, check the other names mentioned in the letter. See who's living or dead and get them here to the White House... the living ones, that is."

"Slow down Hiccock. Anything else?"

"Yes. Ensiling's file was red-flagged, I found that out when I was trying to arrange for a posthumous Presidential Letter of Recognition for him."

"Is that why Peter first came to you?"

"No. Peter had a suspicion that he was murdered. Anyway, find out why the government pegged Ensiling persona non grata and what for."

"Hey, pal, there's a loose nuke out there. You just gave me a month of homework."

"Here's the topper, copper – one of the names on that letter rang a bell at CIA." Bill affected a bad impersonation of a game show announcer. "And now the next answer on 'Jeopardy:' The country this former member of the committee was last seen in... drum roll... wait for it...."

"Shit...Egypt!" Joey said.

"Actually, I was looking for 'What is Egypt?' but I'll accept it."

"Is he still there?"

"Let's move onto the final question on 'Jeopardy.' Would you like to try 'Famous European Cities' for $800? This city of lights is where two secret investigators, mean mothers, have followed leads to..."

"Paris...er, what is Paris?"

"Astounding," Bill announced.

"Okay, tell me what I've won and it better be half the fucking FBI because we are going to need a lot of shoe leather help."

"That was the other thing I came to tell you. I got you five million dollars to start. Go hire, get, grab, or steal whoever you need. Somehow or other, Peter may have tripped over the suitcase nukes plot without even knowing it. And the committee members may have been sacrificed to keep the identity of one of their members secret, lest he lead us to the nukes."

"Five million can get this puppy moving all right. Hey, who was the embassy guy in Paris?"

"Frank somebody. Frank...Randall! He's the Station Chief."

"Good, then he's CIA. I'll wake him up." Joey grabbed the phone. Hiccock left, already late, for a meeting.

Aside from the President almost firing him over a code name, Bill couldn't remember the last time he was called into the principal's office. But it wasn't so long ago to stop his stomach from producing a few butterflies. The principal this day was Ray Reynolds, the Chief of Staff. Bill and Ray had started out on opposite sides of every issue. But eventually, after Bill had success and more success, he won the trust and respect of Ray and Ray's boss, James Mitchell, the President of the United States. Twice before, the President had given Bill carte blanche to investigate and operate separately and autonomously from the rest of the government. The last time proved to be a good call when it turned out the government itself was the bad guy.

This time the bad guy seemed to genuinely be a foreign entity. Bill knew, however, that all the brownie points he had amassed couldn't avert the "heart to heart" that was on the other end of the call to come to the Chief of Staff's office. Bill knew Reynolds was calling him in because his "Operation Stork" was getting operational fast. In Washington, a town of institutional rivalries, that kind of money, attention, and power attracted more detractors than supporters. Twenty seven million to start up, five million more on a hunch, and unlimited access to the Justice Department had to ruffle feathers inside the corridors of power.

As Bill stood before the principal's desk, Reynolds hung up the phone on a call with the sultan of some emirate. He made a notation in a folder, closed it, placed the folder in his out box, leaned back, and smiled.

"You know, Bill, we've been through a lot together. You've earned everything and every privilege you have right now. I speak for the President when I say that you have saved this country from unspeakable calamities and all Americans are in your debt..."

"Wow, that sounds like a set up for a bigger 'but' than Aunt Esther's."

"Who?"

"Forget it, Lamont. Go on, sorry I interrupted."

"Bill, no one is questioning your judgment, but I have to ask you some questions."

"Sure, Ray, I understand."

"Your new French initiative. How does the death of your friend, which I am sorry to hear about by the way..."

"Thank you."

"How does his death connect to the search for the loose nuke?"

"Ray, you know, I've been so deep into this I didn't see the obvious inference of preferential treatment that I am giving an old acquaintance. That also means you were much nicer about this than you had to be and I thank you for the benefit of the doubt."

"As I said, you earned it."

"Sergeants Bridgestone and Ross are now in Paris after tracing the 24 nukes back through an Iranian connection."

"Iran? Does CIA or State have this?"

"We're sharing what we know..."

"So share with me."

"One of Ensiling's associates, Dr. Brodenchy, whom my friend Peter was close to, popped up in Egypt around the same time as the nukes did. Now's he's believed to be in France. His last posting with the U.N. was with IAEA. After his stint with the International Atomic Energy Association, he went to work for Fallon Technique, a French nuclear reactor company. That job brought him to Iran when the company started advising the Iranians about building their own nuke plant. Somewhere in between, he converted to Islam. He now goes by the name 'Jahim El Benhan.'"

"Wait!" Ray started scanning the file cards posted on the inside of his forehead. "Isn't Alzir El Benhan the bio-terrorist we have in custody for that flu thing up in New York?"

"And getting him released was the reason the ambassador was kidnapped in Egypt. And that all led us to finding the nukes."

"So Jahim and Alzir, are brothers?"

"Hungarian Muslims. The brother adopted his Muslim name first back in the 50's. Dr. Brodenchy converted when his brother and he were reunited in Iran."

"You figure Jahim kidnapped Greeley to get his brother Alzir back?"

"Apparently while he was in the middle of the nuke thing."

"There must have been a stronger reason than blood for Jahim to risk the nuke op just to get his brother back?"

"We'll know when we ask him."

"Bridgestone and Ross?"

"They cut through countries, culture, and bullshit like a laser through butter."

"Thank God they are on our side."

"Allah be praised, man."

"You sold me, Bill. I'll tell the President that you and your team are on to something and you'll report as soon as you can."

"Actually, Ray, I need to see the President right now."

"Why?"

"You are not going to believe me, but you are not cleared for this."

Ray's eyebrows went up. He picked up his phone and asked the President's secretary if the boss was alone.

∞§∞

Ray walked Bill into the Oval and left. Bill waited until the door latched.

"What is it, Bill?"

"Sir, one of my Element members stumbled across the Jesus Factor. The real one this time."

"How do you know?"

Bill stepped onto the shakiest limb of his professional career. "The Jesus Factor says that on certain days you can't have a nuclear war."

"Close enough." The President sat silent for a second then erupted. "Ah for the love of Mike, I told you to drop it."

"Mr. President, we were following the UFO angle and it cross-connected to the suitcase nukes."

"What? Little green men with nuclear suitcases? Are you trying to give me a brain aneurism?"

When Bill finished filling him in, the President had calmed down.

"So we are contained?"

"Yes, sir. The man already works in our nuclear program and has been sworn again to secrecy on this one subject and will be here in two hours."

"Good," the President mumbled with his head down.

Bill bent down trying to reconnect to Mitchell's eyes. "Mr. President, you aren't going to have him shot are you?"

That made him smile. "Ah hell Bill, lets just make him our guest here at the White House until we figure out what to do about this."

"That would be 'White' house arrest."

"Call it what you like, but this is the most dangerous idea on the Earth. I can't risk having someone out there with the power to destroy the world."

"Whoa, now I'm lost, sir."

"Shit; I've said too much."

"What about me?"

"What about you?"

"Sir, I know what he knows. Am I also invited to stay indefinitely?"

The President got up and walked to the window. He clasped his hands behind his back. It made Bill think that if a photographer were there at that moment he would have snapped the defining picture of the Mitchell administration. It was like the famous moment of Kennedy during the Cuban missile crisis, snapped as he pondered at the same window.

The President came around to the front of the desk and sat in the chair alongside Bill's.

"You know what the difference between you and me is?"

"You'll be buried in a Presidential library and I'll be in Woodlawn in the Bronx?"

"Odd thought, but I was going more for, 'Not much,' as a way of stressing what we have in common. We have been through a few close calls together. Me almost getting impeached, the rocket aimed at the nuke plant. Hell, I met your mom and dad."

"I still want to apologize for the whole family album thing."

"Sweet people. Bill, I know I can trust you. But I have to impress upon you how dangerous this is without actually telling you. So please just take my word for it. You don't want to know what Jesus Factor is... ever!"

"Yes, Mr. President, but..."

"But? No one says, 'but,' to the Commander-in-Chief, Bill."

"Sir, if we stumbled on to it, the bad guys may already know it or possibly stumbled onto it themselves. We should let Professor Li continue his work; see where he goes. Maybe by doing that we'll discover how to keep it undiscovered."

∞§∞

Bill was back in the State Department teleconference room with Joey Palumbo by his side. On the monitor in front of them, with the digital read-out "Paris" below it, was Yardley Haines seated next to a very much alive Peter Remo.

"I was talking to the D.J.; he was using those new Planotech Mark 7 power amps and he had them latched up in parallel and…"

"Peter, what happened?"

"Anyway, when I go back to the bar I can't find my seat 'cause I left my jacket on the back."

"With your wallet in the pocket?"

"Yeah. Anyway I freak and start searching all around the club. A guy says he saw someone grab my jacket and head up the stairs. When I get to the top… it was horrible… the cops were there and the guy's head was crushed right into the cobblestones. Then I hear the cop say my name. I turn and realize he's reading my driver's license. For some reason, I didn't speak up. I just wedged through the crowd and went back to the boarding house."

Bill looked to Joey with a nod that said, *just like you said it happened.*

"Did you know the guy who took your coat, Peter?" Joey asked.

"No, Joe. I mean, I wouldn't know, because he looked like a pizza when I saw him. Do you know who he was?"

"He was a grifter named Henri Brochard."

"Nope, never heard of him."

"Peter, why didn't you reach out to your family or someone to tell them you were alive?" Hiccock said.

"Billy, when you didn't know what Jesus…"

"Hold it! Pete, don't say it, just move on…"

"Right... Anyway you freaked me out, Billy Kid, so I wanted to disappear. France was a good place to do it. Bonnie had a place outside Paris, so I headed there."

"Wait, Bonnie from Ocean Parkway?"

"Yeah, she's singing here in France and doing well."

"But we have you living in a boarding house."

"Yeah. Bonnie's living with a guy and they didn't have room. But she had a friend who ran a boarding house."

"He must have been thrilled when Peter Robot showed up," Joey said under his breath gaining a glare from Hiccock.

"Anyway, Bill, the instant I realized they thought the guy in the street was me, I knew I was safe."

"Pete, by order of the Secretary of State, Mr. Haines there will escort you back to the United States and through customs – no questions asked. I want you to come directly to my office. In fact," he turned to Joey with a snide look, "Joey here will meet you at Dulles and personally escort you to the White House."

"Pete, what got you so spooked buddy?" Joey asked.

"I called Kasiko in Queens when I left you. His housekeeper said he died in a car accident."

"Where? We'll check it."

"In New York. But don't bother, Joe. Kasiko didn't drive."

Joey looked at Bill.

CHAPTER TWENTY-TWO
ON THE ROCKS

You wouldn't know it from all the hype, but one of the worst beaches in the world is in the South of France. There, you can literally see the rich and famous from all over Europe and their beautiful, topless women, lying upon and walking over... rocks. Cannes has been the playground for the idle rich and the *nouveau riche* since the Second World War. Lately, it has become the haunt of the film and television illuminati due to the Cannes Film Festival and MIP shows that attract them here twice a year.

"This is so much better than burkas and long black clothes," Ross said looking out from the Croisette onto the array of topless women, some of whom were applying suntan lotion in a way that would temporarily revert any man to the age of 14.

"Wouldn't mind some R&R here when this is over," Bridgestone said as they crossed the palm-lined boulevard, headed for the Negresco.

In decent French, Ross asked the deskman at the front to see the manager. In less than a minute, an impeccably dressed man walked up to them.

Bridgestone held up a photo. The man's eyes widened, then the sergeant said in Farsi, "Your office now!"

Without hesitation, the man led them to his office off the lobby. Bridge put the photo they had taken with a long lens earlier that morning of the manager dropping his kid off at school back in his pocket.

Once inside the office, Bridge continued speaking in Farsi to the man of Iranian decent who had lived in

France for the past 15 years. "You will never see your daughter again if you lie to us. Do you understand?"

A sweat was building on the hairless top of the man's head as he nervously nodded.

"You will never see your entire family again if you tell anyone we were here. Do you understand?"

Again, the man nodded.

Ross held up the only picture they had of Brodenchy, a.k.a. Jahim El Benhan. The man squinted, so Ross pushed it closer. "When was the last time you saw this man?"

"Two, maybe three weeks ago."

"Who was he with?"

"Monsieur Rashani. He is a big client of the hotel."

"What does Rashani do?"

"Cinema; he's a producer."

"Where can we find him?"

"He lives here, in Cannes."

"I thought you said he was a hotel client?"

"Yes, he books the hotel for the festivals… for parties and premieres."

Bridgestone threw a pad on the desk. "His address."

The man looked up the address in his private, locked file box. He didn't trust his personal list of clients to the computer, where others could gain the advantage that having this information would bring. He wrote down the information then, with an unsteady hand, offered it to Ross.

"We found you this morning. We can find you or any member of your family in 20 minutes. Don't betray us. Forget we were ever here and little Shawra will live to see her next birthday."

That these monsters knew the name of his daughter rattled the hotel manager to his core. Again, all he could do was nod. They left. He sat there shaking for a while.

∞§∞

Back in Washington, a file arrived by diplomatic courier. A member of the Israeli secret service, Mousad, acting at Joey's request, and Joey acting from the information B & R obtained from the truck driver Jamal, had asked to be red flagged any police activity that had to do with trucks or transport in Israel and the greater Middle East. Joey read the file with extreme interest and decided to pick up the phone to call his old friend, Hiram.

∞§∞

Ever since the heart-to-heart in the President's office, Bill was focusing on the man's words "Close enough" and "the most dangerous idea." What did that mean? *How could an idea be dangerous?* At 12:30 a.m., with Janice sleeping next to him, he realized his brain was stuck on this. He carefully got out of bed and went down to the den. He switched on the desk lamp and booted up the SCIAD terminal, then went into the kitchen and grabbed an orange. Back at his desk, he spread out a paper towel and was about to rip into the fruit when he noticed something. The desk light had the effect of lighting the orange like a half moon. That got him thinking. Twenty seconds later, he was rummaging through the garage.

He sat back at his desk, put the basketball he retrieved on the blotter, and held up the orange. That was pretty much a good representation of the basketball "sun" to the orange "Earth." He sat there and nothing came to him. He held up the Earth and cast a shadow on the ball. As he moved the orange, watching the shadow cross the larger ball, it hit him. He took a pen and drew, right on his desk blotter, an arc from the lamp. He then rolled the big ball over the arc. The shadow moved across the ball.

There it was: the dangerous part of the Jesus Factor.

∞§∞

Bill left a note on the bathroom mirror telling Janice that he had gone to the office in the middle of the night. Those Secret Service agents were good, he thought. Seeing the lights go on downstairs they got his car warmed up and ready to go.

At the White House entrance, he swiped his I.D., telling the sergeant at the desk to awaken Professor Li and get him to Bill's office. On the way, he stopped by the storage closet and rolled out a white board.

By the time Li got to Bill's office, Bill had already drawn orbits and planets on the board in different colors.

"What's on your mind, Bill?"

"Phil, the Jesus Factor does not define a place on Earth. It's extraterrestrial physics, meaning from a point other than Earth."

Li caught on. "It's a threshold point somewhere in a harmonic relationship to the sun!"

"Exactly. But is not a point – it's a cusp, a distance. And that distance is the same all around the sun, creating a ring in space, a zone where celestial mechanics and nuclear physics nullify each other. Probably some interaction at the atomic level that resonates with the solar system level."

"Both the atom and planetary system are similar with the solar being the macro of the atom."

"Somehow, Blake Lathie unraveled a math system in his book that revealed the harmonics of the two systems."

"The empirical data on the 107 A-bomb tests I have been accumulating can easily be cross-calibrated to solar positioning charts and pretty much define the cusp ring with 107 points."

Bill stopped him. "Li, what must never be known is the following." Bill grabbed his basketball. With a

Sharpie, he drew "USA" on one side and "China/Russia" on the other. He then went up to the board and placed the ball on the red "nuclear cusp" ring. Bill then rotated the ball as he moved it around in an elliptical shape, which approximated the actual orbit of the Earth around the sun. The ball crossed and re-crossed the cusp line four times.

"Holy shit!" Li said.

"Yep. That's the problem and the most dangerous idea on Earth."

∞§∞

The address was on the Lerins Islands, an exclusive community 15 minutes from the hotel. It was like the Beverly Hills of Cannes. The home of Rashani rivaled any mogul's home on Mulholland Drive. There was an electric fence and keypad arrangement. The place was quiet. They rang the bell. A woman, with an Iranian accent answered over the scratchy intercom.

"Two visitors for Mr. Rashani, please," Bridgestone said in Farsi.

"He's not here."

"When will he be back?"

"He's on a Hajj. Not for one more week."

"Okay; we'll call on him then. Thank you."

"All right."

As they walked away, Bridgestone said to Ross, "So if you were him, with all this, would you fly to Madinah commercial or on your own jet?"

"This guy's got to have his own G4."

∞§∞

Bill was in his office going over the speech he was scheduled to make in a few days to the Society of Chemical

Engineers in New York. Cheryl was briefing his Secret Service detail on the itinerary, which was purposely not squelched. The President didn't want to send the message that they were in a bunker mentality, and had been crystal clear when he ordered that all administration public activities not be affected by the loose nuke. Bill was right in the middle of rewriting a sentence about synthetic polymers and the tax incentive for creating them from recycled material when, thankfully, Joey came in smiling.

"Why the shit eatin' grin, Joe?"

"B&R played a hunch that this Rashani guy had his own jet. Bingo! He did. According to the flight plan, he went to Madinah for the Hajj. There's a filed flight plan for his return from Mecca to France next week. But here's the thing – in between, the plane is making a quick trip to New York. How's that figure?"

"That's easy; he either ducked out of the Hajj, came here, picked up some White Castles and got back fast before anybody noticed, or he gave someone a free ride?" Bill said as he closed the folder with the draft of his speech in it.

"Pretty sweet $32,000 trip even without the murder burgers."

"Anyone ask the pilots?"

"Saudi Air Force interviewed the crew. They say it was a friend of Rashani who they were ordered to fly to New York."

"And..."

"No name, and here's why: in addition to be being the biggest producer of film in Iran, Rashani is also, and wow what a surprise this is, the Minister of Film for Iran."

"So he's got DPL disease!"

"And, unfortunately, so does his aircraft."

"So no documentation of who came in?"

"No. I think this is a probably a screw up, because the only record is that it was Rashani."

"Wait. I'm confused. He did come here for belly bombs?"

"Someone says it was Rashani. Even though the pilots say it wasn't him."

"Okay, Mr. FBI, what's your working theory?"

"As far as I can tell, some guy walks into the U.S. off Rashani's plane; some rent-a-cop at private aviation says, 'Welcome Mr. Rashani,' and the passenger says, 'Thank you,' and he is out of there."

"Find that guard and find the new Mr. Rashani."

"That's what B&R are doing. They're two hours out of New York now. They'll talk to the security hack, pick up the trail, and track whoever this was down in a manner that would take us, minimum, a few days, if you know what I mean?"

"You know, too bad I just thought of this, but I wonder if those guys are cleared for domestic work.

"Good point. Find out quick!"

"Let me check with someone," Bill said as he looked down at something Joey had slid across his desk. "What's this?"

"You like it?"

"I don't know… a football?"

"Catchy, don't you think?"

Bill was looking at the familiar blue and yellow seal of the Executive Office of the President of the United States, which was just like the large OSTP one above his desk, but modified with the words "Quarterback Operations Group" in the lower arc that usually read "Office of Science and Technology Policy." Right under the eagle's tail was a little football! "Joey, where did this come from?"

"I had Dara the new kid in communications do it up. She's a whiz with Photoshop."

"First of all, the Office of Protocol is going to have a shit fit if they see this."

"Why?"

"Numb-nuts, it's the government. I'm sure there are no less than 55 people who have sign off on shit like this."

Joey reluctantly retrieved the glossy print-out from Bill's desk. "You know, sometimes you can be a real joy killer."

Bill sighed and took it back from Joey. "Okay, let me look into this, but no promises." He placed it under the speech folder and laughed under his breath. "Football."

∞§∞

Half the 'boiler room' was now full, Dariush thought as he started his shift. A few years back, there were three translators at the Farsi Desk. Now half of the 108 listening stations here in the giant room in West Virginia were staffed 24/7 with more translators coming on line all the time. The output from NSA listening posts of phone, e-mail, military, and commercial traffic in Farsi and other Middle East languages was a booming business. Cable and satellite networks like Al Jazeera and others weren't even covered in this room and probably had four times the numbers of translators and monitors. His review list was set by his supervisor. The loose suitcase nuke had everyone working overtime and tonight would be another 14-hour shift.

The first audio file he opened, earmarked OF#3DF23, was a tap of an optical fiber and from the hexadecimal code, 3DF23. He calculated in his head that it was the 253,731st capture from optical fiber this calendar year. His real knack, aside from languages, was his ability to detangle stuff like hexadecimal code in his head, which is why he was the chief decoder in the Farsi section. He played the file and understood it to be a chirp warble of an encoded data string. He patched it through a digital analyzer and rotated the step knob. At modulo, 13 he got a hit – the output stopped being random and started having repeating, intentional patterns. What followed was a cryptogram of sorts, a grouping of letters that meant something to a key index. What the key was, was the hard part to figure out and this prevented him from identifying the meaning of the data string.

He looked at the arrangement and pattern of the letters and something caught his eye. It was t-y-y-f-q-r-q-b-s. Seemingly meaningless except that if the modulo held for the length of the word, then it was a letter followed by two of the same letters followed by a letter followed by the same letter that was following the next letter, then two other letters. It wasn't a word but the "footprint" of a word, as he liked to think of it. Also, it was probably a word in Farsi that had to be translated to English. But it could also be any language translated into any language, or not a word at all but a number. He called his superior and asked for some Cray time.

∞§∞

The House Oversight Committee on Intelligence is a tough crowd, but they control the purse strings for all the spook houses of the U.S. Therefore, you have to play nice with them if you need something done, like grant unprecedented powers – a.k.a. license to kill – to two grunts in hot pursuit. So it was with cautious trepidation that Ray Reynolds sat beside Hiccock in a top secret, hastily called, closed door meeting of the committee. Being populated by politicians, the members spent a half hour peppering Ray with criticisms of administration policy. Hiccock remained patient and took his cues from Ray. The Chief of Staff knew how the game was played, and Bill wasn't going to start worrying unless he saw sweat on Ray's forehead. Hiccock was under strict orders not to speak unless specifically addressed. If he answered anything, it was not to be a syllable more than the bare minimum.

Things didn't seem to be going well at all, what with the Congressmen lining up to take their punches at Ray and the rest of the administration. At last, the chairman called for a voice vote: there were seven yeas and nine nays. The committee then adjourned.

Hiccock was stunned. "That's it?"

Ray swallowed but kept a poker face. "That's it, Bill."

"They can't..."

"They just did. Let's get back to the House."

"Wait..."

"It's over, Bill. Live to fight another day."

Bill looked at the committee members collecting their stuff and preparing to leave, then at Ray. He then broke the first commandment of his office and spoke aloud.

"Mr. Chairman, Mr. Chairman."

"Bill, don't," Ray snapped as he grabbed his arm.

"Mr. Chairman, right now there is a group of men, terrorists to be sure. They may be here in Washington, New York, or your home state of Iowa. They need no permission from any committee, they are bound by no U.S. law, and they have no constituents. But more importantly, they have no reservations about killing millions of Americans. You have just played into their hands. You have just hog-tied us, while amazingly not encumbering them in the least. We are not talking about probability here. It is a fact that they have a nuclear device and they will, they will, they will... detonate it on American soil. Maybe right in this very building. I implore you: do not let politics as usual or some political hard-on you may be carrying for the President be a death sentence for millions of Americans. To do that would be a gross disservice to those you have sworn to protect."

Ray just put his head in his hands. The committee members all stopped in their tracks for a moment to listen to Bill. They then resumed their shuffling of papers and exiting, as if he said nothing.

"What are they doing? Didn't they hear me?"

"Bill you are such a fucking amateur. All you did was waste their time. The committee is adjourned, meaning they have ceased hearing anything as a body. You spoke to no one."

"No one, huh?" Bill raised his voice again. "Listen, you bastards! You are weak, spineless, and impotent. You are hiding behind procedure. Well, I'm not. Any one of you thinks you are man enough to face me, I'll be right outside, you bunch of hypocritical, ideological wimps. Outside!"

"Will the sergeant of arms remove Mr. Hiccock from the room," was all the chairman said as he leaned into the microphone clutching his folio close to his chest. Two security guards winged Hiccock.

"Okay boys, let's get me out of here," he said to them.

Ray Reynolds was beet red and out the door. In the hall, Hiccock turned to the guards. "Thanks, fellas. Sorry I got upset back there."

As Bill smoothed his ruffled jacket, Congressman Jacob Edelstein, from the committee, approached Bill.

"You got a big mouth, Mr. Hiccock."

"What are you going to do about it?" Bill said getting in his face.

"Try to help."

The response stole all of Bill's bluster. "Oh. Well. Okay then, let's hear it."

"War Powers Act."

"I'm listening."

"Section 214 and 104 are contradictory and could open a crack that allows the President to suspend various legalities. As long as he notifies Congress within two weeks."

"Wait, are you saying?"

"Goodbye, Mr. Hiccock. Not all of us are wimps by the way." And he was off.

∞§∞

"You want me to invoke War Powers?"

"Yes, Mr. President. It's the only way to protect Bridgestone and Ross on domestic soil."

"For only two weeks. Then you rescind the finding and it never leaves this room," Reynolds explained sliding the finding under the President's hands for signature. "The Congressman's idea is a little like a two-cushion shot, but our counsel says there's enough teeth in it or enough ambiguity in the language to fight off any Congressional inquiry."

"Unless they kill a few people and get caught," Mitchell said.

"Forget kill; all they have to do is muss a Muslim's hair in front of a *New York Times* reporter," Ray added.

"Why not bring in FBI and Justice if you are so sure about your intel, Bill?"

"Sir, I am afraid that then we will be talking 'cats out of the bag' in a big way and we'd be mucking up B&R's speed with procedure. But of course, any actionable intelligence will certainly be shared, sir."

"You realize I am giving these two men more power than any citizen or police force ever had on American soil?"

"Sir, these terrorists could achieve what the entire U.S.S.R. couldn't in 50 years of the Cold War. We need to even the playing field, get some advantage over the terrorists. Or at least not be caught dead playing by the rules against guys who aren't."

"Lousy argument, Bill. No bad guys play by the rules, yet we never did anything like this before."

"So why did you just sign it?"

"Because in this case the rules may take us into sudden death overtime. Just tell me you trust these two with the keys to the kingdom, Bill."

"These are my guys, Mr. President."

"Good enough for me, Bill."

CHAPTER TWENTY-THREE
SLEEPING WITH THE BOMB

Janice was sure that somewhere in hell, a man was slow roasting on a turning spit for creating "fashion." It had to be a man because no woman would wish this on her own kind. From the grotesque malformations of their pedal extremities – forcing those appendages into size 8 pointy-toed pumps – to the spectrum of carcinogens absorbed into the brain through the scalp for the sake of keeping up with this year's "in" hair color. So it was, that for Janice, what most women would welcome as a day of beauty, was to her a day of torture and discomfort, although she passed on the dye job because she was pregnant. The necessary small talk and opinions that historically accompanied a gathering of females in these settings was markedly different in tone due to recent events. "Circular Error Probable," a term once only uttered by nuclear scientists, was now bandied about by beauticians and manicurists replacing themes like shopping, families, extensions, dermabrasion, mud wrap, facials, and Botox.

Most amazing was the nuclear gossip. "Did you know a little radiation could clear your complexion?" "If it's a plutonium-based bomb then the residual radiation is more conducive to multiple orgasms?"

Janice shuddered at the way people were making peace with the seemingly inevitable detonation of the suitcase bomb. Every niche market theologian or practitioner of the New Age had creatively woven the nuclear calamity into their spiels, as if they always knew it and had spoke of it for years. And now the cathedrals of the inane, the very essence of talk for talk's sake, the spa/

salon dialogue, was newly polluted with bomb management phraseology.

Janice viewed this phenomenon from a level of global consciousness. Since there was only one bomb, the devastation would localize in one place. Wherever that locale was, once exploded, the rest of the globe had to have a way to categorize, sort, and finally set the event on some mental shelf. On that shelf would also go the remnants of the random terror generated prior to the detonation: namely, that it could have exploded, literally, in anyone's backyard.

During her nail wrap, after her mud pack and facial, she overheard two women scaring one another to death. Most of what they spoke so confidently of was merely parroting the overblown rhetoric of various talk shows. One notion, however, sent a chill up Janice's spine. The idea that, within a twenty-mile radius of a nuclear blast, serious genetic damage and miscarriages could result from the first millionth of a second's worth of exposure to a radioactive wave front. Buildings and other manmade structures being porous to this initial surge or radiological pulse meant there was no place to hide. As Janice's nails were drying, a plan formulated in her mind.

Everyone on her floor was surprised to see Janice on her day off. She went right into her office and called the COO of the hospital. Ten minutes later, she was being driven by her Secret Service agent, Brenda, to an address in Baltimore.

∞§∞

"Peter, after we finish, I want you to meet Kronos," Bill said across the table in the Map Room as Joey sat beside him. "The two of you were separated at birth."

"Billy, thank you for believing me. I thought you were one of those Trilateral Commission guys or one of their puppets."

"Peter, I don't know what you're talking about but I don't want to hear any conspiracy theories from this point forward. Only fact, pal. Now tell me what you think is going on."

"It's a conspiracy."

"Damn it, Pete! I am not fooling around."

"Okay, I'll bite, Pete," Joey said. "What's the conspiracy?"

"Don't encourage him!" Bill protested as he threw down his pencil.

"There is a key code that Ensiling created to detangle an algorithm that deals with the…you know, "

"You can say it in here, Pete."

"The Jesus Factor. He found a warble, a non-linear blip in the cusp. A loophole in the natural law."

"Good God, Pete, this is whacked. Now you're telling me the biggest secret on Earth has an even bigger secret!"

"Bill, you know how science is. Every answer to every question just creates a new set of questions… until you hit the unified field theory. Then you go fishing."

"So you're telling me my dad already figured all this out."

"How is Hank doing?"

"Better than your family. You realize, of course, you're going to have to stay dead a little longer."

"I hear that. And it's better than being dead for real."

"So where's the key code?"

"No one knows. Ensiling never told me. But he obviously didn't tell anyone else either before they killed him."

Joey spoke up. "So why kill Kosmo?"

"Kasiko!"

"Whatever!"

"He was the last official member of the committee, Sergeant of Arms."

"What about you?"

"I was an aide, an assistant."

"A theorizer."

"Right, I told you that."

"So you think you're next?" Joey asked.

"I was two attempts ago, but I eluded them. It was me they were aiming for in Vienna. I was walking next to Ensiling when that woman was shot."

Joey perked up. "They were shooting at you?"

"I stopped when I caught a glimpse of the new 5g Black pad. Europe gets all the cool stuff first. She walked into my bullet."

"Peter, you are just a magnet for all this cloak and dagger conspiracy shit, aren't you?"

"Just spectacularly unlucky there, Billy the Kid."

Bill pressed a button on his phone and then stood up. The others followed. "Cheryl will take you over to Kronos' office in the OEOB. I'll come by later." He grabbed Peter with one arm and gave him a man-hug. "Glad you're not a pizza, buddy."

After Cheryl and Peter left, Bill turned to Joey. "What do you think?"

"I think even a stopped watch is right twice a day.

∞§∞

"Why can't you just call the Veteran's Administration?" the petite blonde, standing in line ahead of Janice, demanded out of frustration as the man behind the counter threw up his hands in response to government bureaucracy. She took a deep breath to quell her frustration and asked, "Is there a manager I can speak to?"

"I'll go get him," the salesclerk said as he went into the back.

The woman turned around to Janice standing behind her. "Do you believe this? My father lost his leg for this country and getting him a new seat for his wheelchair is a federal case."

"It's maddening, I know."

The sales clerk returned, "The manager is just finishing up something and he will be out here in a minute. In the meantime, may I help you, Miss?"

"Yes, I need three X-ray aprons," Janice said.

"Any specific make?"

"No, but good ones. In fact, the best!"

"Sure thing, Miss." The clerk went off to fill the order.

"Are you a radiologist?" The blonde asked.

"Oh, no. They're for me. I'm pregnant."

"Congratulations. When are you due?"

"November."

"Do you know?"

"No. We don't want to know."

The man returned with a flat rolling cart holding three cardboard boxes. "Here you go: three Radshield 1050 Protective Aprons. Will that be on account or cash?"

"I don't have an account. Do you take credit cards?"

"Visa or MasterCard?"

Janice fished her credit card from her wallet.

The blonde noticed her White House ID and name. As the clerk ran Janice's card she asked, "So what are you going to do with these?"

"I'm going to sleep in one, drive my car in one, and have one at my office."

"Why?"

"If the bomb goes off within 20 miles of me, I want to protect my baby from the lethal dose of radiation that will spread in the blink of an eye."

"Wow. I never even thought of that."

"Me either, but nowadays...."

Just then, the manager came out and introduced himself to the blonde who immediatley started in again about her father's wheelchair.

Janice signed her credit card slip, handed it back to the clerk, and asked, "Can someone help me to my car with these?"

"Sure thing, Miss."

∞§∞

Special Air Missions, or SAM, is the President's airline. Whenever anyone important to the government has to get from point A to B in record time, SAM is called. Run by the Air Force, its fleet ranges from Air Force One (actually any plane the President is on, but most notably one of two Blue and White 747s that becomes the very image of American prestige and power on every Presidential trip), down to little Gulfstream jets with the stars and stripes on the rear of the fuselage. One of those little "skeeters" was parked on the runway, engines idling, awaiting Hiccock when his car pulled up to the ramp at Andrews A.F.B. He walked from the car up the four steps and into the super posh cabin. An Air Force sergeant advised him to fasten his belt; they would be wheels up in 45 seconds. Before the belt went click, the door had been sealed, the chocks removed, and the military version of a corporate jet was rolling down the taxiway, priority number one for takeoff. The pilot, Air Force Major Henry Stemmis, accelerated through the turn onto the runway and in less than half the distance of a regular airliner. The small jet was eating sky in an almost vertical trajectory.

Stemmis greeted his one and only passenger over the P.A. system. "Welcome aboard SAM 611, Professor Hiccock. Direct service to New York's La Guardia Airport. Our flight time this evening will be 38 minutes. We have landing priority with New York ATC and should be on the ramp three minutes after wheels down. Once we hit our cruise altitude of 41,000 feet, I'll shut off the seat belt sign and the sergeant will be happy to serve you. I'll come back on when we start our approach. Thank you for flying Special Air Missions even though, we realize, you didn't have a choice."

The g-force Bill experienced was considerable. Maybe he shouldn't have insisted on a fast trip. Maybe he should have said, "Just get me there sometime in the next few hours." However, time was critical. Bridgestone and Ross were in New York tracking down the next lead on the trail of the nukes. Bill carried with him some operational orders and background material in a briefcase on flammable paper. Any attempt to fool with the case would cause the insides to combust into ash. Once read and memorized, B&R would flash-burn them to keep Operation Stork as tight as tight could be.

Joey, or someone else from Hiccock's newly formed QuOG, could have made this delivery, but Bill wanted to look into their eyes and know who they were. He had gone out on the biggest political, judicial, and law enforcement limb you could find to give them carte blanche on American soil..

At mid-flight, the Major came back into the cabin. "Professor Hiccock?"

"Yes, Major."

"Excuse me, but I am not very good at this.... My son, he plays varsity for Roanoke High. QB. He's got some scouts looking at him right now. Anyway, I know that if I didn't get an autograph from you, he'd stop easing off on his old man when we shoot hoops in the driveway."

Bill laughed. "Sympathy from the offspring? That's gotta smart?"

"Wanna feel your age? Have kids."

"Thanks, I am."

"No kidding. First one?"

"Better late than…"

"Best move you ever made, and I've seen you make some great moves slipping out of the pocket."

"Yeah, but what do I do when he starts letting up on his old man out of respect for the old geezer?"

"Make peace with it now, my friend. Actually, start praying for it now, so then, when it happens, it'll be the answer to your prayers. That way it won't gall you so much then."

"Oh God, what if *she* starts easing up on me."

"Daughters? Then I would suggest considering heavy drinking. Never had a girl, but I hear horror stories."

"What was that old song? 'When you're the father of boys you worry…'"

"'When you're the father of daughters…you pray!'"

"Yeah, that's it." Bill took out one of his White House cards. "What's your son's name?"

"Hank, Hank Stemmis."

"Junior?"

"Yes, but we don't go there." The Major watched as Bill jotted down his son's name. "You know, out of all the big wigs and notables I've flown over the years, this is the first time I've ever asked for something like this."

Bill wrote, "Hank, always trust your front line. Take your time. See the whole field. Aim for the numbers." Then he signed it neatly and legibly. "Major, what's your address?"

"My address? Why?"

"I can't give you this right now. Hush-hush mission and all. But when I get back, I'll have it mailed to you."

∞§∞

Idling on the La Guardia tarmac was a New York State Police helicopter, wet and wild and ready to zip Hiccock into Manhattan. From the cabin, Bill looked down at the cluster of buildings huddled in the middle of Manhattan Island. Below 34th Street, the skyline receded, owing to the fact that the bedrock under that part of the island couldn't support the weight of skyscrapers the way the midtown area could.

At the 34th Street heliport, a Secret Service war wagon and two N.Y.P.D. chase cars had their lights flashing. Hiccock walked from the copter to the wagon and they were off.

Inside was Secret Service Agent Henry Barnes. "Welcome to New York, Mr. Hiccock. We will be going right into the Federal Depository. There we'll switch to my personal vehicle and meet up with Tom and Jerry quietly in the park."

Made sense, Hiccock thought. Secret Service was part of Treasury; they ran the Fed Dep in Lower Manhattan. The switch was necessary not to bring attention and flashing lights to B&R, who the Secret Service codenamed Tom and Jerry. They didn't even know who these guys were.

It turned out agent Barnes' personal car was a tricked-out Scion TC. It made Bill look at the agent one more time. Without the suit, dark glasses, service weapon, and earpiece, he was probably just a 28 year-old kid. "Nice ride."

"Thanks. I customized it on the web, picked it up two weeks later. Listen to this." He punched the satellite radio; it was like thunder and lightning. Heavy bass filled the car and the dashboard lights pulsed. Suddenly Bill was in a disco, a very loud disco. After a few seconds, Barnes turned down the music, probably out of deference to the blood that was surely trickling from Bill's ears.

"Cool. Does it go slower when you are draining all that power?"

"Fuel injection."

"*Very* cool." Bill never felt so old.

∞§∞

The Soldiers and Sailors monument down at Battery Park was an open space with 12-inch walls of granite, which meant no clear shot for a would-be assassin. Two agents had watched the area for two hours prior to Bill's arrival. There was a police boat 200 yards off the lower Manhattan seawall just in case somebody was snooping with a speedboat or raft. In all, 23 agents, police officers, and sailors were making sure this Washington VIP could visit this sight, and pray or look up his father's name or whatever he was doing, undisturbed.

Barnes talked into his sleeve mic. "Quarterback has arrived!"

Bill couldn't hear the "all clear" that followed, but Barnes got out and came around, opening the door for him.

The two walked through the park under the watchful eyes of the other agents. Bill then separated from Barnes, went to one of the walls, and looked at the names. On the first wall facing the water, next to the name Ross, Charles E. Fireman 2C Maryland, was a Post-it note. It read, "The Fort. Come alone."

Bill was momentarily thrown. What was this, a hostage situation? He steeled himself. *These are my guys. They are just being super-cautious.*

He yelled over to Barnes. "Stay here; don't follow."

Adjacent to the monument about a half-mile away was Castle Clinton, actually a fort during the War of 1812, now a national monument. Clinton was a big name in New York history even before Bill and Hill. DeWitt Clinton was the first governor of the state. As he walked past a giant eagle statue, Bill saw that the castle was still open and U.S. Park Service officers in their Smokey the Bear hats were standing guard.

He entered the castle and was immediately flanked by two men.

"Professor?"

"Bill."

"Bill, Sergeants Bridgestone and Ross at your service," Bridge said.

They brought him to a dark place, out of the view of a security camera. "How are you guys doing?"

"This is a cakewalk for us, sir," Ross said. "We are usually in some godforsaken shithole eating things you'd usually step on. Last night we actually had a beer and corned beef down here."

"New York, a city of anonymity."

"Sorry for the spy crap sir, but whoever is running your security here might be popping some pictures. We don't take much to being photographed."

"I totally understand."

"We both want to thank you for going to bat for us; we owe you."

"You got it all wrong," Bill said. "We owe you. You guys get to do the dirty work so the rest of us can keep our hands clean. Here are your orders and background, 50 thousand in cash to get around with, and a few different I.D's. There is also a digital camera and laminator so you can pop your own photos for ID. Also in there is a secure phone directly to me."

"Who outfitted this?"

"My best friend and a former FBI agent now working for me. You met him at Desert Tango 1."

"Palumbo! Yeah, good man. No bullshit."

"There's a lot of good men and women on this, guys. You two are 'on-point' for all of them. You have two weeks, if the bomb doesn't go off before then. After that, you will have no Presidential coverage and your mission will be called off. Any questions?"

"No. Any communications from us will include the code word 'bling.'"

"Bling?"

"We overheard some kid say it. It has no connection to us, so nobody could ever infer it."

"Not if you're eating bugs it doesn't. Be safe, you guys. And good luck – for you and all of us."

"God bless America, sir," Bridgestone said.

"God bless and keep her," Ross added.

Bill was once again thrown. Then clarity washed over him. *Of course; these are the men who risk their lives for something greater than themselves, for their country. It isn't just a phrase to them. It is their creed.* "God bless America, men."

They disappeared into the dark recesses of the castle's dimly lit exhibits as Hiccock made for the door.

The ride home was just as quick and uneventful. He was home by 9:30 and rolling out the garbage cans to the end of the driveway for tomorrow morning's pickup. On the kitchen table was a casserole with a note that read, *I'm beat. Microwave this. See you in bed.*

In the den, Bill sat on his Barcalounger and shoveled in Chicken ala King ala Janice while watching ESPN. He thought of B&R and their corned beef feast last night. Then he thought of all the men and women stationed all over the world, some chowing down on MREs, others eating without their families or loved ones near. All doing what B&R was doing, believing in something greater than themselves and willing to suffer hardship and, if necessary, die for it. It made Bill wonder if he was worthy of being in a position over such people. Not that he didn't do his part. On his right hand was the scar from the propellant burns he got aboard the Aegis cruiser when he stopped a nuclear-tipped rocket from launching on a Southern California nuclear plant. That was all top secret, the only public trace being the leathery patch of skin on the back of his hand. Even though he was currently serving his country, it was a cushy D.C. posting.

He rinsed the plates and slid them into the dishwasher, then headed up to the bedroom.

He padded lightly into the room not to disturb Janice. He slipped off his watch, put it on the nightstand, checked the alarm, and rolled over to give his wife a peck on the cheek. His right hand came down on something hard when it was expecting a soft protruding belly to rub gently along with the kiss.

"What the hell?"

Janice shifted and awoke. "Hi, baby."

"What is this?" Bill rapped on her midsection with his knuckles.

"I bought it today. It's to keep our baby safe from radiation."

"Huh? Are you drunk?"

"No, I am certainly not drunk. I heard about the pulse of intense radiation that could reach out from an A-bomb detonation. Even if you are far away, the radioactive spike can create miscarriages or genealogic damage."

"Where did you get this from?"

"I heard it today."

"Where?"

"That doesn't matter. The point is I don't want to take any chances."

Bill had to force his face back from his "are you screwy" expression to something more rational and non-judgmental. "Darling, what is this thing?"

"It's an x-ray apron, I bought three."

"Three?"

"Home, car, office. Since we don't know when or where the bomb will explode."

"*If*. We also don't know *if* it is going off."

"Isn't that what you're supposed to be doing?"

"*That's* what I forgot today. It was bugging me all day."

"No need for sarcasm." Janice kissed him and resumed her nuclear-safe position.

Bill reached up and shut the light. He lay there looking at the moonlight coming through the window. His own wife had succumbed to the public paranoia over this nuke. Janice was a smart woman. Intellectually, she had to know that she was acting irrational. Yet she was pregnant and her protective instincts were in full force, a force apparently even stronger than her intellect. Nature was an amazing thing. He set his mind that tomorrow he'd check on the radioactive pulse and see if there was anything to it. His last thought before he slipped under the haze of REM was the realization that nature was working on him as well.

∞§∞

The next morning, Bill got to his desk at 7:25. At 7:26, Press Secretary Margaret Lloyds entered and ruined his day. She threw the early bird edition of the *Washington Post* down on his desk.

"What's the matter, Marg..." was as far as Bill got when he saw the subhead, under the headline, WHITE HOUSE PLANNING FOR D.C. NUKE. In smaller type below was the line, "Wife of Science Advisor dons lead-lined fashion." The article went on to be the first-hand account of a woman who witnessed Janice buying x-ray aprons and Janice's logic that the bomb was going off within 20 miles of the White House.

Bill picked up the phone and hit the *Home* button. It was busy. He tried again. Busy. He then hit *Jan Cell*. She answered.

"Bill, the phones haven't stopped ringing. ABC, NBC, they all want to interview me. I am so sorry. The woman who was in the store with me must have been a reporter."

"Ya think? Listen; sit tight. Don't answer the phone. Margaret's here and I'm sure she'll have some ideas of how to handle this."

"Okay. Sorry this happened, Bill."

"It's okay; don't worry."

Bill hung up and said to Margaret, "I'm worried."

"So it's true? Oh, dear God, this isn't going to be pretty, Bill."

"Look, she's expecting and it's scary out there right now."

"It's scary for everybody and they look to the White House for assurance. A story like this means we are running scared as well."

∞§∞

Dariush's hunch played out and the Cray found 17 words in 149 languages that fit the footprint. As he scanned the list, an English word popped out at him: Roosevelt. Another word in Eastern Arabic that the Cray spit out from the data string was "maghra."

∞§∞

It was an unusual and hastily called meeting: a "by invitation only" press briefing in Margaret's office. Five reporters, three from TV and two from print, were in attendance. The subject was lead-lined underwear.

"Is your wife privy to intelligence that points to the intended target for the nukes being the White House?"

"Neither my wife nor myself are privy to any information or speculation that the White House, or Washington for that matter, is a target."

"Why did your wife buy these aprons?"

"All I can say is that she reasoned and decided to do this on her own and for her own reasons. As you know, my wife is pregnant with our first child. She is acting in a manner prescribed by instinct, nature, and evolution. But not by any connection to me, the government, or this administration."

"How far along is she?"

"Seven months."

"Do you know if it's a boy or a girl?"

"No; we decided to be surprised."

"Is Mrs. Hiccock protecting her…your baby from the suitcase nuke due to anything you might have said to her?"

"Again, I have no information to share with her on that topic."

"I mean, about radiation in general."

"I never discussed it with my wife. As far as I know, she overheard other women discussing it."

"Women here at the White House?"

"No, at a beauty salon."

"Professor Hiccock, your wife is a doctor, an educated woman. Are you asking us to believe that she did this because of gossip and not some top-secret report on the intentions of the terrorists?"

"I don't know where you are going with that, but I am going to guess. Yes, my wife is a very accomplished and intelligent person. She is actually also a professor. She does hold a White House ID, but she does not hold any security clearance at the present time…"

The room erupted. Bill put up his hands. "Hold it. Before you ask, she did have a clearance at one time but it was on a project totally unrelated and predating any of this suitcase nuke affair."

"Why does she have White House access?"

“She is pretty much in private practice now, but still acts as consultant to the administration from time to time.”

“What is the nature…?”

“Thank you folks; that will be all,” Margaret said, and began to usher everyone out. Once the room was empty, she said, “I don’t know why everyone, including me, says you can’t handle the media. You did very well right now.”

“Thanks. Wow, what a bunch of lunkheads.”

“What do you mean?”

“I answered the same question five times. Aren’t they listening?”

“Yes, they are. They were hoping that you weren’t and that you would slip up when the question came at you in a different way. But you stuck to the script and gave them no wiggle room. It was good.”

“So does this end it?”

“Hopefully it will get only one more cycle of airplay and then fade.”

“I hope so. Janice is really upset by all this.”

“Look, I don’t blame her. Hell, if I were pregnant, I’d build a house out of lead these days. It’s just your position here at the White House that….”

“Yeah, I know; I got it. Thank you. I’m going back to my office. Let me know if you need anything else from me.”

“You and Janice should take some time off. Maybe go to a lake house or the beach?”

“Lead aprons and all, I suppose.”

∞§∞

Bill had shaken off “Apron-gate” and an hour later was back at his desk focusing on his speech and three other briefing papers he was falling behind on. There is an almost imperceptible swoosh of air, and an energy wave that pours through any open door when the President, on the move, walks by any West Wing office. Most political appointees used it as an early warning system of sorts to kind of perk up and look busy. Bill however, slinked down a little deeper in his chair hoping that the entourage of aides, Secret Service, cabinet officers, congressmen, senators or who ever else was constantly around the leader of the free world whenever he left the Oval, would pass by without the Boss noticing the husband of the "apron lady." His heart dropped when he heard the most famous voice in American politics say, "Bill, got a minute?"

Bill immediately stood as the President left the parade in the hall, and shut the door.

Oh Boy here it comes, Bill thought, stiffening as if a 300-pound defensive lineman had locked onto him in the pocket. "Of course, Sir."

"During the campaign, my wife was quoted as having said she wasn't fond of pennies; they cluttered up her purse so she always said 'keep the change' or she put them in the little 'take a penny, give a penny' thing...."

Bill listened as intently as he could. The moment hung. The president just looked off four years in the past. Bill finally figured he was finished and started to say, "Sounds innocuous enough a statement..."

"We were campaigning in Illinois, Bill!"

Okay this is a pop quiz, Bill thought, *Illinois... pennies.... Got it!* "Oooo, not such a kiss to the land of Lincoln was it?"

"Exactly, Bill. So don't let this thing with Janice rattle you too much. Remember, the words of the divorced poet: 'For better or worse is a blessing and a curse.' You may not quote me."

"What happens in my office, stays..."

The president interrupted. "What's this?"

For the second time today the blood rushed from Bill's face. There, in the President's hand, was Joey's stupid counterfeit seal of the QuOG. Trying to read the expression of the man who stood down the Russians in the geopolitical poker bluff of all time over the sovereignty of the Georgian State was futile. The only sound Bill heard was the sound of the blood rushing through his ears.

"You know...I like it!" the President said as he put it back down on the desk. The he turned and snorted, "Football," and walked out of Bill's office, leaving the door open.

The giant sigh of relief that escaped from Bill's lungs had a quick, sharp stop as he realized that Joey would never let him live this down.

CHAPTER TWENTY-FOUR
CIVIL RIGHTS AND WRONGS

It was a field day for the press. An Al Qaeda operative was caught in Karachi, Pakistan with, of all things, a New York subway map in his possession. Immediately, the NYPD and other agencies went into prevent-defense. "Random Bag Searches" became the *phrase du jour* as subway stops became checkpoints. What followed was the expected torrent of outcries from every religious, racial, and civil liberties group. Instant polarization occurred between the conservative, if-you-have-nothing-to-hide-then-you-have-nothing-to-fear crowd and the liberal, how-am-I-going-to-smoke-some-weed-at-work-now group.

It all went away after a news cycle...until Thursday. That was when Ali Rashid, a.k.a. Rodney Albert, having not read the papers, tried to take the number 1 train from 50th Street to 34th Street/ Penn Station to take New Jersey Transit back to the Store and Lock. His senses tingled as he saw the two officers going through the bags of a blonde woman right ahead of the turnstile. It momentarily froze him. A New York City subway station has a constant wave of people coming and going. Therefore, someone stopped in his tracks creates eddies as scores of people start swirling around that person like water around a rock in a stream. The effect created a highlighted human circle around Rodney. Officer Levant Harris took immediate notice. His eyes met Rodney's for the briefest of seconds then Rodney averted, turned, and climbed back up the stairs onto 7th Avenue.

"I'll be right back, Phil," Levant said to his partner as his hand rested on his standard issue Glock 9mm, steadying it in its holster as he took the stairs two at a time against the flow of entering commuters. On the street, he saw Rodney walking fast downtown. He weaved his way through the throngs of lunchtime workers, visitors, and street vendors. At 48th Street, for the first time, Rodney hazarded a look behind him. Levant startled him by being right there.

"Sir, would you step over to your right."

"Why? Why you bother me? I not doing nothing."

Note to anyone visiting New York during a heightened terror alert: do not, repeat, do not under any circumstances disobey a direct order from a member of law enforcement. This especially includes any lip…especially lip in broken Arabic-English. Just ask Rodney.

Before he knew what hit him, Rodney's face was up against the brick wall of an office building, his arm twisted behind his back, his legs kicked apart, and his wrist smarting from the cuffs that crashed down on them. He was hearing but not understanding what the policeman was saying to him. "…silent, you have the right to an attorney…"

Midtown South was the cop house for that part of Manhattan. David Ginsberg, a proud member of the ACLU, was always poking around there looking for his "issue," a tort or malfeasance of the law that would catapult him to the stratosphere of the great civil libertarians, the best known of which he shared a name with, if unfortunately not the blood. He felt as though he'd hit the lotto when Levant manhandled Rodney up to the sergeant's desk for booking.

Within two hours, David had a court order releasing Rodney from a sympathetic judge, who just happened to once be his law professor at Columbia. One Police Plaza had made a political decision not to fight the judge's order. The commissioner, the Mayor, the New York Visitors Bureau didn't want to have a major brouhaha over the new subway searches unless this guy Rodney was caught with a weapon, a bomb, or Bin Laden's baby picture in his wallet.

Levant punched his locker so hard he dented it when he heard the news that his bosses let his collar go. "They want us out there to find the bad guys. These creeps don't wear it on their sleeve. It's in the eyes, man, and I am telling you this guy was bad." He told his sergeant, who then reminded Levant that he was a good cop with 27 years in, and that going up against the bosses was a surefire way to patrol Far Rockaway on foot in the winter.

The various papers and news outlets ate lunch and dinner on the story. Rodney had been referred to as an "immigrant" in the stories, which used as their angles that this was a case of racial and religious profiling. The far-left crowd started making allusions to Hitler's storm troopers, Pol Pot's ethnic cleansing, and the lynching parties in the south.

Finally, not being able to take it anymore, the commissioner went on one of the Sunday morning shows and made only two points. One was that the NYPD never released the ethnicity or religious affiliation of the alleged immigrant. That could only have come from the lawyer or the press. The second was that the arresting officer was black. He then gave a look that might have confused the rest of the country but every New Yorker knew meant *so shove your racial profiling charge up your ass.*

This sideshow aside, the big story nobody got was that the only concrete lead, the only tangible connection to the biggest assault and mass murder ever to be planned against any country, was allowed to walk out of police custody. It was a great feather in the cap of David Ginsberg.

∞§∞

Bill entered the Situation Room. Only Reynolds was there.

"What's up, Ray?"

"NSA intercepted encoded traffic from a suspected terrorist cell node. They have not been able to decode the entire message, but two words are setting off alarms and I wanted you to know."

"Thank you."

"Roosevelt and Maghra."

"Isn't Maghra the name of the oil refinery where we found the nukes?" Ray was starting to catch on.

"Exactly."

"Holy shit."

"Double-xactly."

"What's the brain trust think?"

"Well, there's a Roosevelt Island in New York City."

"Sure. I got a buddy who lives on it, along with a lot of U.N. personnel."

"Well, a nuke on the island would take out the U.N. buildings as well as most of the East Side." Hiccock said as he opened his I-pad to a list. "There's Roosevelt Raceway, Roosevelt Field Shopping Center, the Roosevelt Hotel in midtown."

"There's a Roosevelt Hotel in Paris, too. In fact, there are hundreds of places named Roosevelt, including dozens of schools and the Roosevelt Room upstairs."

"You know, Ray, Bridgestone and Ross are in New York, *from* Paris. I feel pretty strongly that if they are here, Paris, Long Island, or even upstairs isn't going to be the target. Roosevelt Island, right smack dab in the center of the East River. That sounds like a reasonable target."

∞§∞

At the Store and Lock, Number 1 knew of the difficulties Number 3 had encountered in the subway. According to plan, he knew Number 3 was now hiding out in a Jersey City mosque where the blind Sheik had once presided and presently was little more than a meeting hall for devout Muslims to pray and discuss the Koran and all the other aspects of the religion of peace and love. Those good, law abiding Muslim-Americans had no idea that below the building was a safe house, initially built to house the conspirators of the first World Trade Center bombings back in the early nineties. This chamber was so well hidden that the federal agents who swept the building in late '93 never discovered it. Therefore, the place where the enemy had already looked offered the best place to hide Number 3.

Number 1 thought of having Number 3 killed because he was now a loose end and could compromise the entire operation. Rodney's job was practically done. All that remained was the actual location managing of the prep day and that could be handled by Number 5. Number 1's only hesitation came from the fact that Number 3 also had a backup role on the helicopter should Number 8 be injured or killed. There was not enough time left to train someone else. He'd have to think about this and pray to Allah for wisdom.

Soon it came to him, a plan so perfect that it was surely the idea of God himself, delivered to him and his mission as a sign of invincibility.

∞§∞

Rousting a federal judge at 4 a.m. is never a good idea, but Brooke Burrell was under orders to execute with all due haste, and that doesn't mean wait till the judge has had her coffee. Now, with search warrant in hand, she waited at the ramp at Butler Aviation as the little G5 government jet rolled to a squealing stop. The stairs uncoiled from the doorway before the plane lurched to a halt. Joey Palumbo and Peter Remo jogged down the steps and right to her.

"Agent Burrell, Peter Remo," Joey said over the noise of the plane's engine winding down.

"Good to meet you, Mr. Remo," Brooke said, her hair whipping her face.

Peter's mouth was literally open. He knew they were meeting an F.B.I. agent, but he never considered that a woman would greet them. Especially this blonde in the dark blue blazer with sunglasses and either a killer of a great body or a form fitting bulletproof vest. They drove in a small fast motorcade to Jackson Heights.

Peter hadn't been to Kasiko's apartment since his last visit in '98. Everything looked the same in the still meticulously-cared-for apartment, now in the care of a part-time housekeeper hired by Kasiko's nephew. For a second, Peter dwelled on the long dining room table where he, at the age of fourteen, sat with some of the greatest minds in the world prognosticating scientific theories that today are accepted and well-known fact. "Look for a lawyer's briefcase," Peter said, snapping out of it. "He always kept stuff in one of those."

"Got it," Brooke said, coming into the living room from the bedroom. They dumped the contents on the couch. A quick examination revealed nothing but legal papers, leases, deeds, citizenship documents, and the like. No key code.

A knock on the door announced the local N.Y.P.D. forensic team. Now the dismantling of the apartment would begin in earnest. As they filtered in, Joey and Brooke asserted their control of the scene and issued orders on what to look for.

Peter finally drummed up enough courage. "Er... Excuse me, Agent Burrell?"

"Yes, Mr. Remo?"

"Can I ask you a professional question?"

"Shoot."

"Do you wear a bulletproof vest?"

"I do."

"Oh, okay. Thanks."

"When I am on a case or stakeout. But not now."

"Oh... Oh well then, I understand."

"Mr. Remo?"

"Yes?"

"They're real. Can you get over that? 'Cause I did long time ago," Brooke said walking away from Peter.

"I hadn't noticed, but good for you, detective..."

"Agent!" She corrected not even looking at him.

Feeling 10 years old, Peter tried to make himself invisible. He gravitated over to the mantle above the fireplace. Thirty brilliantly bejeweled eggs on spun gold stands adorned the entire width. In a further attempt to avoid making eye contact with the gorgeous agent, he focused on the minutiae of the artisan craftsmanship. He picked one egg up in his hand and rotated it. The work was exacting and delicate. The blue one caught his eye next. It was heavier than the other was.

The crashing sound turned Brooke around. When she saw the smashed egg on the floor, she looked up to Peter. "That's about 20 grand in intentional damages that I am going to have to spend a few hours filling out a report on."

Peter bent down and pulled a key from the wreckage. "You can't make a nuclear omelet without breaking an egg."

Joey approached them. "A safe deposit key." He grabbed it and checked it out. "It's foreign... could be Swiss."

"I thought you said we were looking for a key *code*?" Brooke said.

"Key code, Key to code, or Key where code is. All within the error of Hungarian translation in broken English.

Joey turned to Brooke. "Have them finish up here by the numbers. We have either found it or found where Kasiko kept his darkest secrets."

On the ride back to the copter, Brooke was in the back seat next to Peter. Joey was riding shotgun as another agent drove. Peter looked upset about something.

"What is it, Mr. Remo?" Brooke asked.

"Call me Peter, please. It's just that these guys must be monsters. Kasiko was a hero and no pushover. Even at 80 years old. He was really nice to me, and how Brodenchy – or whatever he is calling himself now days – could have him killed is mind-boggling. Kasiko saved his life and his brother's life. Protected them in Europe and their committee here in America. What kind of animal can turn like that on a friend and protector?"

"Unfortunately, Peter, sometimes religious fervor or dogma can allow a person license to do the most heinous things in the name of their cause," Brooke said trailing off in self-conscious censorships over the few "un-lady-like" things she had done to protect her country and its citizens.

"If this key leads to the code, you will have gotten even with the killers big time, Pete." Joey added.

A silence came over the car after that. Peter eventually broke it when he leaned over and said in low tones to Brooke, "Sorry about before. You know, the vest thing. I didn't mean any offense by it."

"No offense taken, Peter."

Brooke looked out the window and added with a smile, "Boob man."

CHAPTER TWENTY-FIVE
THE BIG STICK

Seaman First Class Orville Hayes was weary and bleary-eyed. He had stayed up all night studying for his petty officer exam. Still, he reported for duty as starboard fantail lookout at dawn. As he scanned the horizon for anything that wasn't wet or blue, he swore that as soon as his watch was over he'd hit the bunk and catch some heavy 'z' instead of attending the steel beach picnic the crew had planned for tonight.

At first, he panned right over it...then he swept back. He rolled through the focus of his Nikon binocs and, when the image was sharp, he saw that there was something out there. He flipped down his polarizing sunglasses and saw the bouncing bow of a zodiac type boat. No, wait, two zodiac boats heading right at the "Big Stick" right out of the wash of the rising sun reflecting off the inky blue waters of the Persian Gulf. He pressed his chest-mounted, sound-powered microphone and reported to the captain of the watch.

"Sir, this is starboard fantail. I have two bogeys, surface craft, incoming direct vector. I make them to be zodiac type, sir."

"Roger that, starboard."

A claxon horn sounded, and the P.A. system called for "Force Protection." This was a call to stations just shy of battle stations, in which the known threat was not a heavy displacement surface or submerged ship or an airborne intruder like a plane or missile.

Immediately, the radio shack started hailing a warning on all frequencies and in many Gulf languages. "*Craft approaching U.S. warship. Turn away or you will be fired upon. Repeat: turn away or you will be fired upon.*" Ten guns up and down the side of the "Big Stick" took a bead on the incoming boats. The mostly-rubber crafts were essentially impervious to sonar or surface radar scan. So Orville used the low-tech triangulator and read the distance as 700 yards out. He started broadcasting the distance in 50-yard intervals.

Out of the corner of his eye the U.S.S. *Donald Cook,* a guided missile destroyer, was making full-steam to intercept and shield the "Big Stick" in a potentially self-sacrificial gesture, but Orville's time/distance calculations told him they'd never beat the fast, low-slung zodiacs. At 600 yards out, the order was given to fire one across their bow. The auto-loading five-inch gun on the Cook punched out a round that flew like a line drive and exploded in the water 100 yards ahead of the two on-rushing craft. It did not deter them or cause them pause.

"Sir, bogeys are not veering away."

"All starboard guns: train on incoming boats and await my order to fire."

The Officer of the Watch turned to the captain of the ship, Commander Wes Halbrook, who had just made it to the bridge. "No response to hailing; they have not changed course and are heading straight in."

"Weapons loose, Captain. Boatswain, make sure we are running tape."

"Roger that, Commander."

"All guns, weapons are free. Fire at 500 yards."

All there was to do now was watch and hope that maybe these guys would turn away. But they didn't.

Orville winced as Cook's five-inch gun and the 20 mm PHALANX Gatling gun auto-cannon, amidships, opened up as the ocean 496 yards away went up into a wall of blue water, white steam, and orange flame. Then something happened that scared the crap out of him and the better part of the 5,500 men and women who were the crew of "the Big Stick," U.S.S. *Theodore Roosevelt*. A siren and an automated P.A. announcement tore across the ship and flight deck.

"Nuclear Radiation Detected. Take appropriate measures. Nuclear Radiation Detected. Take appropriate measures."

Instantly, sprinkler heads started washing down the flight deck and superstructure of the ship. Everyone scrambled to get inside. Orville slid down the railings outside the ladder rungs like a trapeze artist and scurried onto the deck, closing and sealing the hatch behind him.

∞§∞

Bill's government phone went off as he was leaving his office.

It was Li. "I just got another spike."

Bill grabbed a pencil as he swung back around his desk. "What's the location?"

"Persian Gulf."

"What country?"

"No, in the Gulf. In the middle."

"Do you know what it was?"

"No, just a radiation event. Not small, but not megatonnage either."

"Like a suitcase nuke?"

"Possibly."

"Thanks. Keep me updated."

Bill ran out of the office and barged into a meeting of Ray's. "Li called with another spike" was all he had to say to get Ray's full attention.

"My God, where?"

∞§∞

Six minutes later, Hiccock, Reynolds, and the President were being briefed by the Secretary of the Navy.

"The Nimitz Class carrier, *Theodore Roosevelt*, CVN 71, went to Force Protection level at 0600 zulu and hailed two zodiac-type craft from nearing. After a warning shot was fired and the boats failed to alter course, the main batteries opened up. Both boats were immediately sunk. At that instant, the nuclear alarms tripped and the boat went into nuclear-safe lockdown."

"Are the men all right?" the President asked.

"All who were on the deck are going through standard de-con, right now. Time will tell."

"Mr. Secretary, was there a secondary explosion?" Hiccock asked.

"I don't have that detail yet."

"Bill, what are you thinking?"

"Sir, our intercept said, *Roosevelt*. I certainly never thought of the aircraft carrier, *Teddy Roosevelt*."

"Intercept?" the SECNAV asked.

"NSA found two words in a message. One was the name of the safe house where the suitcase nukes were stored and the other was Roosevelt. I am sorry I didn't think of the ship, Mr. Secretary."

"Doesn't matter, Mr. Hiccock. The 'Big Stick' was already on war watch. They couldn't have been more prepared if you had a telegram with the exact date and time. But I see now why you asked about the secondary detonation." The Secretary turned to the President as he gestured to the phone. "May I?"

"Of course."

As the SECNAV got the commander of the *TR* on the phone, Hiccock thought about the fact that everything could be over. The loose suitcase nuke could now be at the bottom of the sea. It had to be or the commander of the ship wouldn't answer the phone because he, his

97,000-ton warship, and its whole Carrier Strike Group, would be vaporized.

"Go ahead, Commander Halbrook, I have you on speaker with the President, the COS and Sci Ad."

"As far as we can tell there was no nuclear detonation. There was, however, a nuclear event."

"This is Hiccock. The boats went down to direct hits, commander?"

"Yes. In all, 10 shells were fired along with two 'sea whiz' systems on manual."

"This is the President. Any idea who attacked you?"

"No sir. They disappeared in a blue-white flash, sir."

"Good shooting, commander." The president actually pumped his fist as the ex-combat fighter pilot in him responded to the neutralized threat.

"Sir, we train hard for this type of thing. I've got a cool, effective crew here, sir."

"Commander, it's Hiccock again. You did say CWIS, didn't you?"

"Yes, two of our Phalanx systems open up in addition to the five-inchers."

"Is that important, Bill?"

"Could be, sir. Those systems fire depleted uranium bullets. Commander, could the sea whiz have accounted for tripping the nuclear alarms?"

"Highly doubtful, Mr. Hiccock. One, they are truly depleted and two, our sensors are calibrated to take our own reactor and weapons like that out of the equation."

"Commander, do you think you sunk a boat with a suitcase nuke on board?" Ray asked, summing up the whole reason for this call.

"Indeterminate, sir. Something set off the sensors and I guess a breached or destroyed suitcase nuke would let out a spike like that. I *can* tell you that the area remains hot and we are tracking a line of radiation down to the ocean floor."

"How deep is the water there, Commander?"

"Pretty deep, sir. At least three miles."

"So we couldn't recover it even if we could get close enough to the radiation," the President guessed.

"Yes sir. I am afraid whatever it is, is going to be down there for good."

The President looked around the room. "Anything else?" When no one answered, he said, "Again, job well done, commander. My commendation and gratitude to you and your crew."

"Thank you, sir. I know the crew will be honored."

The SECNAV ended the call and said, "Wes is a rock-steady commander, sir. It's no surprise the *TR* has numerous battle E's for....

Then the intercom interrupted. "Mr. President, the National Security Advisor would like to join you."

"Send him in, Doris."

The NSA walked in and grabbed the remote to one of the five TVs in the Oval Office. He was getting numbers from his cell phone. "564. Got it!"

He punched 5-6-4 into the remote and on channel 564 was a feed from Al Jazeera. A ski-masked man sat reading a statement. Just then, another man from the State Department entered the office as interpreter and started translating immediately, "... praise unto him. The good and righteous forces of the brotherhood have on this day cut off the head of the great serpent in our holy waters. We have, in one act of justice, vaporized the mighty fleet of the Infidels. We have melted their ships and sent their sailors to an agonizing death. This is the power of the true, the righteous, the believers. And this is the fate of the Infidel. Allah be praised."

On the screen, the whole thing started again. First, there was music then some hokey graphics of an old A-bomb test, scratches and all, superimposed over a picture of an American aircraft carrier. Then to the spokesperson in the mask who said, "Brothers of the great battle, we come to you tonight with joyous hearts and the goodness of praise onto him... The good and righteous...."

"That's enough; we get the gist," the President said.

"Obviously, they pre-recorded that and don't know their mission failed yet," Bill observed.

"Thank God," the NSA said.

"It certainly supports the fact that the attack was with the loose nuke," Ray said. "Melting ships, vaporized fleet."

"It makes sense to me," the SECNAV said. "The *TR* all by herself is one of the most powerful entities on earth. She is definitely a crown jewel of America's foreign policy and, as such, a big prize to bag. Taking out an entire American Carrier Strike Group with the nuke would have been a grand play and one the world wouldn't soon forget."

"Also, she is purely a military target," Reynolds added, "so world recrimination would be less than if they nuked, lets say, New York or L.A. where millions of civilians would die. It kind of makes sense politically."

"When did these guys ever start making sense?" Hiccock wondered aloud. He started coming to the realization that he had been wrong about a detonation on U.S. soil. It bothered him; it shouldn't, but it did nonetheless.

The looped message played one more time then it was abruptly cut off mid-sentence and a slide in Arabic went up.

"I think they just found out they celebrated a bit prematurely."

∞§∞

The story on the attempted nuclear attack on the *TR* broke and broke big. The Defense Department's immediate release of the video from the carrier that showed the attempts to hail and warn the approaching boats, the warning shot, and the inevitable explosions made for great TV. The sound of the nuke alert siren was clipped off the official release version. Also priceless was the almost pitiful way the terrorist spokesperson was bragging about the success of the attack and its abrupt removal from the airwaves.

Along with a giant sigh of national relief, blustering political posers invaded the cable and on-air news channels rewriting recent history. Most of them now clearly pointed out their skepticism over a terrorist actually detonating the suitcase nuke in a major city, declaring that they had an inkling that all these guys really wanted to do was attack a military target.

Then, in a wave of nationwide Alzheimer's, everyone chastened President Mitchell for allowing America to think that its cities were ever in peril, when surely his experts and daily security briefings must have been telling him about the intended attack on the carrier.

Two final cultural nails were put into the coffin of the loose nuke nightmare. The first was that the website, MyCEP.com, went from four million hits a day, down to forty-four. Then came a "Saturday Night Live" parody of the Al Jazeera "Melted Ships" video. In this version, the masked terrorist spokesperson kept having premature orgasms as he tried to follow the script. It ended with a shot of 72 virgins, some bored, some sleeping, and some playing solitaire up in Heaven.

The audience response was the convulsive laughter born out of the deep terror shared just a few days earlier.

∞§∞

"I think it's a great idea. You and my mom can plan my kid's life. All I'll have to do is show up and pay for everything." Bill was being sarcastic – big mistake with a pregnant woman.

"Hey, I pay for just as much around here as you. And she's your mother! God knows how she survived you."

"Cool your jets, lady. I was kidding. Although I do think you and my mom getting some time together is a good idea. Besides, my dad loves you."

"He's so sweet to me. So it's set then for next Thursday."

"Yes, only we'll stay in a hotel. Somewhere midtown."

"They're not going to like that."

"Their apartment in Commack is too small for us and the Secret Service detail and it's too much work for all of us to go upstate to the cabin. Besides, you'll lose Dad to the fish up there."

"They'd never let you splurge for a hotel room for them."

"First off, we'll fib a little and tell them Uncle Sam is paying for it. And second, since we have tickets to take them to the play Wednesday, then dinner after, where we will tell them we are going to get remarried, it makes sense for them not to go all the way back to Long Island late at night. I'll call her after we eat."

"What do you want for dinner?" Janice asked glad for a change of subject.

"Whatever. Don't go to any trouble."

"No trouble. Do you want pasta, meat, chicken, what?"

"Well, maybe if you could make that chicken dish with the sun dried tomatoes and the wine sauce… and maybe a little ziti with pesto on the side. Oh, and those cheesy croutons in a Caesar salad. Or with the blue cheese dressing if it's too much trouble to make Caesar. Oh, and maybe you could steam some asparagus with that hollandaise sauce from the pouch?"

"From the pouch?"

"Hey, I don't want you to go to too much trouble."

"You don't want me to go to too much trouble... but a little is okay?"

"Hey, you asked!"

"Go sit down, dreamboat, and the kitchen staff will have dinner ready in about an hour."

"You sure it's no trouble?"

"Ahhh, shut up, already."

Bill went into his study. Now that the nuke was absent and accounted for, much of America got back to living a normal life. For the Hiccocks, that meant making plans to go up to New York. Bill had a speaking engagement up there and he needed to decommission Bridgestone and Ross, officially, face to face.

CHAPTER TWENTY-SIX
RENDEZVOUS WITH THE DEVIL

When word came of the death of the Palestinian truck driver, it matched an account from B & R that their truck driver, Jamal, had dropped off what he thought were plumbing supplies at another truck in the desert driven by a Palestinian. Pictures of the dead man were confirmed as the driver to whom the "hot load" was transferred, by Jamal, who was now very grateful and talkative in return for American radiation therapy. Joey placed the report in the normal pile with a note reading "Possible route of Roosevelt Bomb" (which is what they were calling the exploded suitcase nuke now).

∞§∞

Ann climbed the steps of the Bedford Street subway stop. As she exited into the Williamsburg, Brooklyn night, past the chained bicycles, the pizza shops, and Polish restaurants, it took all of her will not to turn around to get back on the L train and back to Mark's place. But she steeled herself and quickened her pace, as if the mere act of aggressively walking would change her resolve when she faced Gary. He would try to deny it, of course, but enough of her friends saw him with that tramp. She had to confront him or she could never look herself in the mirror again.

She met Gary at a Truth for 9/11 rally. Gary was fearless as he stood yelling at the top of his lungs "Bush knew! Cheney too! 9/11 was an inside job." She remembered how he faced down a group of steelworkers who objected to his exercising his right to free speech by trying to muzzle him just because he was the lone, courageous voice crying out during the moments of silence and the ringing of the bells at the 9/11 ceremonies at Ground Zero.

Ann had seen the Internet videos and she was enamored with the likes of Sean Penn and Rosie O'Donnell who had the guts to say that fire couldn't melt steel and reveal the truth that a missile hit the Pentagon, not a plane. Overall, she came to learn from Gary that the attack on the towers was planned to be a "New Pearl Harbor" by the neocons, who were mostly Jews, like Irving Kristol, Paul Wolfowitz, and Richard Armitage and who had been planning for war against Islam well before their propped up puppet, George Bush, stole an election and took power. She was disgusted over how they used the peaceful followers of the religion of Islam and activist Muslims as scapegoats, all the while denying them fundamental freedoms such as Habeas Corpus. With all these wrongs to right, things between Gary and Ann were great. Protesting by day and making out by night. But as soon as the protests became passé, Gary started to become less attentive, less involved...with her.

As she turned the corner of Bedford Avenue, walking closer to her confrontation with Gary, Ann steeled herself with the knowledge that Professor Keller... 'Mark' was right. She *was* a human being, no less than any other, and entitled to her rights and dignity. In the last weeks, Mark had helped her realize that she possessed an inner strength and beauty that was undeniable to anyone who got to know her. *"Our relationship no longer feeds my emotional, spiritual, and essential self."* Those were the words she chose. A closing argument designed to utterly defeat any objection or sense of guilt Gary might try to lay on her. Well, she didn't as much choose the words as Mark suggested them. But true to his teachings, she took ownership of their power and now they were her mantra. Like profess...Mark said, "These are the only words you'll ever need to say to anyone, Treasure Ann." Although she discouraged others from using it, Ann liked when Mark called her by her whole name. He found it on her NYU enrollment form, and he asked if, when they were alone, he could call her by it. Of course he would never use it in public or when he called on her in his lecture hall, which she attended three times a week. He was older, charming, and so smart. He shone even brighter in her eyes when he spoke inspiringly of the nobility of the struggle of the Muslims against the forces of Judeo-Christian capitalism and its imperialist colonization. How Muslims were an entire culture left behind by history. In fact, things really got started between she and Mark when he invited her to listen to a radical Imam in a basement on Atlantic Avenue. She had to watch through a basement window because the men also prayed on mats prior to the speech and women weren't allowed. But on the way home, she knew he was all she had ever hoped for.

On the other hand, Gary, when he learned Ann's entire first name, simply decided to call her Pleasure. That worked for a time, especially in the beginning of their relationship. They would sneak around looking for places to kiss and grope. Occasionally, they'd find a closet or empty room and they would go at it, usually ending with her on her knees and him with his hands behind her head. At first, he would always wrap his arms around her and hold her for a moment afterwards, always kissing her on her cheek instead of on her lips afterwards; nothing like the deeper way he would kiss her before she had "Pleasured" him. She wondered if he had an aversion to his own....

She banished the thought from her mind when she saw the steps to the six-story tenement walk up on North 6th where she and Gary had shared an apartment since they were freshmen. Well, it was Gary's place originally and she kind of moved in. As her feet scraped the gritty, steep steps, her thoughts returned to how, after a while,

Gary didn't even bother to hug her afterwards. He'd just neaten up and say something about being "late." Then a quick peck on the cheek and he was gone.

As she turned the key in the front door of the vestibule, she made note to take her peace sign off the ring before she threw the keys back at him. Once inside, she stopped at the bottom of the stairs and took a deep breath.

The fact that Treasure Ann Hunnicut was a victim, was old news. Now she was one of the walking wounded as well. Shunning her Mormon roots at 17, and armed with a 1584 SAT score and a scholarship, she fled to New York City and NYU. Her open heart and naiveté became a beacon to the predators that inhabit this city of anonymity. Falling in with the young crowd around 8th street and the surrounding coffee shops, she learned of the social ills and political realities that she had been shielded from in her pristine Utah environment. She shortened her name to Ann to better fit in without having to be "the Mormon girl." She soon started to become overwhelmed by the tremendous amount of information on the arrogances and prejudices the United States of America was inflicting on the rest of the world. It was then that she met Gary, an NYU student, who, even though his grades were nowhere near Ann's, immediately set himself up as her mentor. Within a week, he had the 5'8 blonde with a healthy body and soft, endearing eyes, under his spell. She became his following of one. He mostly kept her in check by his never letting her feel as though she totally satisfied him. That kept her trying anything and everything to gain his approval.

Subservience was her pattern with men, whether they were in her family, her community, the men she met socially, or when she was working as a waitress one summer. She was emotionally damaged and her esteem was inexorably tied to the nearest male figure. Gary perfected his advantage by getting her to be his sexual convenience.

Besides, blowjobs were what passed as "making out" these days. It was almost expected that the oral gratuity was part of the new courting ritual. On Astor Place, it was referred to as "pulling a Lewinsky" and eventually shortened to, "Getting a Lewy." Of course, among the 20-somethings, only the Poly-Sci students had a clue what that ancient reference alluded to. The ultimate level of casual oral sex reached its pinnacle with the buy-in from young women, on something relegated as harmless, called "Rainbowing." A young girl would "register" a unique shade of lipstick and transfer that shade indelibly onto a male's member as a way to prove to his friends that he got a specific girl to do him, and also as a way a girl could mark her territory to warn off other "sluts."

In all, it was the greatest scam ever perpetrated on young women. This new ethic was in many cases supported by their very mothers, who were operating under the same male oppression in their lives. This new rule about the oldest male urge benefitted from, and was taking cover under, the new cultural mores that if "*there is no penetration then there is no sex.*" What a great time to be a young horny man; what a terrible time to be a young "disposable" girl.

As she entered the apartment, the smell of pot hung heavy in the air; that substance having also played a huge role in her transition to becoming one of the "cool" people. Then she heard a moan – a female moan. Impulsively, she stormed into the bedroom, *her* bedroom. There was Gary getting a Lewy from the Tramp! He was so wasted, he didn't even hear her gasp. But the Tramp did. She just turned and, without missing a stroke, looked right into Ann's eyes as she was consuming Ann's boyfriend.

Treasure Ann opened her mouth and was surprised that not a sound came out. Eventually, she just turned and left the apartment. On the Bedford subway platform, she stood stunned. There was the rumble of the approaching Manhattan-bound L train, the sound swallowed her up, and her head pounded. She took two steps closer to the yellow grip mat that edged the last two feet between the platform and tracks. Maybe it was the residual of the contact high, but her head spun as the lights of the approaching train splashed along the grimy tiled wall of the station. She felt her body go limp and herself falling; the little voice inside of her didn't object; she was okay with the idea of ending it all. As her body was collapsing, a woman screamed.

∞§∞

Number 1 was taking a roundabout way back to the Store & Lock. He had just met with two members of the Brooklyn cell who had formulated and stood by to execute the plan, which would have been his way out of the country. But now that the bomb had disappeared from the American authorities' watch lists, he would never have to use the carefully prepared escape route that these men created, as the Americans would say, "just in case." He had thought of killing them, so that they would not become a possible hole or loose end threat to his perfect plan. Instead, he invited them into the main plot. They were devout and committed and at least they could be useful even as just added gun power more than as soldiers, in the second diversion. He instructed them to report to a safe house in Trenton. There they would be watched for three days. If they didn't draw any attention or surveillance teams, then they would be brought to the Store & Lock of which they had no clue existed.

This being the third subway he randomly boarded, he looked around the station to make sure no face or clothing piece was familiar and to check if anyone was paying any attention to him at all. He was watching the train pulling in when a scream turned his head in time to see the young girl beside him falling in front of the braking train.

He instinctively reached out and pulled her to safety just as the cab of the train swept by the exact place where her head had been a split second before. She collapsed in his arms. Not wanting to draw any attention to himself, he walked her up the stairs to the open air.

They sat in a Starbucks as she sipped on a Chai Tea while he only had bottled water. He could see she was really young, not past 20. He could also see she was troubled.

"Where are your parents?" Number 1 asked.

"Utah. I left home without their approval." She self-consciously cleaned up the table around her cup.

"Do you have anyone in New York?"

"I did until about a half hour ago."

"So you would have killed yourself over a mere boy?"

"I wasn't trying to kill myself. I was just dizzy, woozy."

"As you wish."

The woman started to tremble and then broke out in tears. Number 1 offered her his napkin. She dabbed her eyes and then stammered, "I...I want to thank you for, for...saving my life." Then she cried again.

"Well, I have to go," Number 1 said.

"Wait; I owe you so much."

"You owe me nothing."

"No, you saved me."

"I really must go."

"What's your name?"

Number 1 was stymied; he thought quick, "Mahmoud."

"Are you a Muslim?"

"Yes."

"I take Muslim history as part of my Middle Eastern Studies degree," she said brightening up.

"I am happy for you. Now I must go."

"But wait, where do you live?"

"New Jersey. I hope you feel better. Now I must go."

As she objected, he walked out. She sat there for moment and then bolted out the door.

CHAPTER TWENTY-SEVEN
KEEPS ON TICKING

Halliburton 602 suitcase: $339 dollars.

Radioactive waste from the nuclear medicine department of NYU hospital: $5,000 bribe to a Palestine-born custodial assistant.

A willing suicide bomber to create a secondary diversionary tactic to avert attention from the main plot: priceless.

Number 1 was amazed at how America's shameless advertising was infiltrating his mind. More astounding was that he found any humor at all in this sacred work.

As for Number 3, Rodney, now alone in the safe house, he finally knew his destiny as Allah had willed. The lead container in the package on the table, which held the four ounces of barium with its 70 rads of deadly instant cancer causing, super-carcinogenic radiation bursting to get out, was the key piece. The rest of the small package he was delivering was C-4 plastic explosive provided by the Syrian Army, or someone in it.

The way Number 1 explained it to him, the lead shielding had to be breached prior to detonation to make the most effective dispersal of this dirty bomb. Since it was Allah's will that, in his earlier role in the attack, Rodney would die when the suitcase bomb was given life, he was prepared for death and looked forward to his reward in the afterlife. The gestation period of cancer being weeks longer than his life expectancy – which was one hour after he exposed the deadly metal to the air – meant he could handle with impunity this massive dose of radioactivity for such a short interval. That interval being the time between detonating the dirty bomb and being vaporized by the suitcase nuke along with a million or more New Yorkers and, more importantly, the financial center of the world.

Rodney, who from this point forward thought of himself only as Rashid, checked the NJ Transit schedule for the train he would take into Pennsylvania Station, then looked at his watch. It was a Tag Heuer. He chided himself for not thinking of this sooner, but his brother would have liked to have had this watch. He should have left it to him and used a cheap Timex instead, but it never occurred to him until now that the watch was going to melt.

As he left, Number 1 knew he had just added another dimension of trickery to his expansive and ingenious plot. Rodney's unfortunate run-in with the police offered him a second opportunity to add deception and confound the enemy. The first diversion so meticulously planned and trained for would still be executed as well, in no small part because of the *fatwah* against its primary target.

∞§∞

Adjunct Professor Mark Keller was frustrated. Treasure Ann had moved in with him and he made sure to be careful to avoid any appearance of impropriety or favoritism as she was still taking his Middle Eastern Studies class. He even gave her above average grades for work she didn't have to hand in. This is why it hit him so hard that she was suddenly enamored with some stranger who "interceded" while she was dizzy on the subway. After a lackluster session of sex, in which he felt she wasn't trying, he confronted her.

"What's the matter, Treasure Ann?"

"What do you mean? Nothing is the matter."

"Come on; you are just going through the motions here."

"I've got a lot on my mind."

"What could you possibly have on your mind?"

"Don't be condescending."

"No, really! Your school or grades can't be a problem. I mean you are fucking your teacher…or at least going through the motions."

"Look, don't think I am not grateful for you taking me in after Gary was such a jerk."

"Grateful? I am supporting you, feeding you, clothing you! I deserve more than just grateful!"

"You know what? I can't believe you said that! How dare you throw that in my face! *You* asked *me* to move in. In fact, you instigated my leaving Gary. 'Our relationship no longer feeds my emotional, spiritual, and essential self.'"

"You needed clarity and…"

"You needed to control me." She walked away.

He stood there and stewed for a moment, then came at her with both guns blazing. "You seem to have issues. Maybe you should talk to a therapist."

"Oooo you know what? Suddenly, I have clarity!" She put her fingertips to her temples as if she were suddenly a seer, "Let me see if this *resonates* with you: if I don't swoon when you fuck me, then it's me who needs therapy?" For the first time in her life, Ann was angry. Angry at a male! Not guilty, not sorry, not blaming herself but real, true anger!

"Listen, you little cunt, I'm risking my job for you everyday."

"Little what? I am so out of here."

"Good. I am going out; don't be here when I get back."

He slammed the door. Off to One Police Plaza to protest the harassing of Ali Rashid, the innocent immigrant arrested for not cowering to a cop.

Ann plopped down on the bed. She could not believe what had just happened. Immediately she realized that she was about to be homeless and penniless. The small stipend she received from the scholarship didn't go far in New York. Falling back on her parents was not a pleasant thought. For a minute, she thought about apologizing to Mark and maybe making it up to him by doing that thing he wanted to do with the exchange student from Morocco who had confessed to him her love of three-ways. Maybe if she did that, he wouldn't kick her out. But those thoughts lasted for only a few seconds more and were replaced by a new plan, one which she had fantasized about, especially after doing a little snooping. Her mood changed in a second and she got up and went to the bathroom to douche Mark out of her body and out of her life.

∞§∞

"Peter, it's over. I wish I could be there when your mother finds out you're not dead. Hug her for me, too."

"Billy, you were the smartest kid on the block, and now I owe you big time."

"Nonsense, man. You made me understand science and math in a way none of my teachers could ever do. Peter, I am the National Science Advisor today because you took the time to challenge a little kid to do more. Hell, I have used that as part of my National Science Teachers Initiative. It's really just what you taught me and how you taught me."

"Really? Pretty good then for a guy who never graduated college."

"Anytime you want a degree, just let me know. Shit, I'd sponsor your doctorate!"

"Trying to make me legit?"

"Perish the thought. But you should keep in touch with Kronos; he's so plugged in he short circuits when he showers."

"I'll see."

"Pete, it's none of my business but have you given any thought to what you are going to do next? I mean, that doesn't involve black helicopters and listening devices?"

"You know, now that I am alive again, I might try to see if that FBI girl back up in New York goes for older men."

"Something tells me you'd be safer investigating who shot Kennedy. But hey, go for it. Just remember she is one stalwart piece of crime-fighting apparatus. Don't ever get on her bad side."

"I think she likes me."

"Pride goeth before the fall, man."

"Thanks, Billy the Kid."

"Anytime, Peter Robot."

∞§∞

Ever since the ACLU complained that the radiological surveillance of mosques was unconstitutional, federal authorities backed off the many search teams that aimed sensors at the various, logical places where radical Islamic fundamentalists would seek cover amid the other law-abiding American Muslims. So when Rodney/Rashid, hiding out in the basement safe room of the building adjacent to the mosque, opened the case in a nervous act to assure himself that all was right with the package, the radioactive blip passed unnoticed in all directions and out into space to blend in with the background radiation emanating from this part of the Milky Way.

∞§∞

Number 12 was on perimeter patrol around the Store & Lock. He was armed with nothing more than a cell phone. It was all he needed if someone were serveilling them or sneaking about. He'd just place a call and the men inside would come out and neutralize the threat. On his east-west pass across the front, he saw the outline of someone looking through the glass doors of the facility. He saw this person pressing the buttons of the electric lock. He decided not to call this in. Instead, he simply walked up behind her and said, "What is it you want?"

Ann jumped. "Oh, you startled me. I'm looking for Mahmoud?"

"There is no Mahmoud here and it's closed. You go away now." The threat in his voice would have been obvious to anyone else, but Ann persisted.

"Well, I happen to know that Mahmoud lives here. I followed him here."

"You followed him here!"

Number 12 punched the keypad and the door buzzed and unlocked. Unceremoniously he grabbed Ann by the arm and manhandled her inside.

"Hey, let go of me..."

"Silence!"

"Where are you taking me?"

"I said, silence." He slapped her hard.

∞§∞

Number 1 was reviewing the back up plan with Number 4 and 9 when he turned in the direction of the commotion coming through the door. He was shocked to see the girl from the train being dragged by Number 12 into the room.

"Mahmoud! It's me, Ann. Tell this guy to let go of me."

Number 1 closed his eyes, and washed his hand over his face. "Sit her here in the chair."

"Who is Mahmoud?" Number 12 asked.

"That is not your concern, Number 12. Just leave her here and get back to your post." He turned to Numbers 4 and 9. "We will finish this later. Go to the kitchen."

Ann watched the men leave. She looked at Mahmoud. He was just as she remembered. "I am so glad I found you. I wanted to get to know you better. Maybe even work with you."

"How did you find me?"

"I kinda followed you that night. I saw you come here. I waited all night but you didn't come out 'til morning. The man at the deli down the street told me you live here. It's pretty cool living in a storage place. Do you have an apartment here?"

Number 1 just stared.

Ann felt her cheek. "That man hit me. Why would he hit me?"

"Did you tell anyone you were coming here?"

"What? No, who would I tell?"

"Please, Ann, this is very important. You told no one?"

"No, no one. Wait? You are worried, aren't you?"

Number 1 crouched down to her seated level. "Now what would worry me?"

"I am so into your cause. I know how hard it's been, how unfair you and your entire nationality have suffered."

"Is there anyone who is expecting you back?"

Ann saw an opening to appeal to the man. "No, no one. I am free as a bird. No one to report to and no one to go home to."

"Surely, someone will miss you."

"Why Mahmood, are you expecting me to spend the night? I mean, it's okay with me."

"Why are you here? Why did you follow me?"

"I left Mark. He's a monster. I want to join you. I want you to teach me about the great struggle. I want to learn from you."

"I run a storage warehouse. There is nothing to learn."

"You must be suffering from prejudice, hate, and social injustice."

"Where do you get such ideas?"

"I studied Islam along with all the oppressed religions: Buddhism, Hindu..."

"Enough; wait here."

Number 1 left the room. His men were waiting in the kitchen. He scanned their faces, faces awash in confusion and worry. He knew what they were thinking. That he somehow had seduced this girl, brought her here, and, in doing so, risked the entire operation. Number 3 was looking at him in the way an undertaker looks at a body he is about to bury. He remembered a lesson from his earlier life. "Strength, decisiveness, no mercy is the key to survival." He took a knife from the counter and, without a word, left the room.

On the way back to where he left the girl, he thought of his mother who died when he was young, and of his sisters who were killed by Russians, the youngest and prettiest, Maya, raped repeatedly and savagely, then shot in the head. All done by Infidels, Infidels who disrespect Allah, who deny his supreme reign over all the affairs of men. Infidels who are no better than dogs, to be kicked and slaughtered before they attack.

He stopped outside the door. Up until now, Jihad had been a cause, a way of life. Although he was the key to what would soon be a massive amount of death and destruction, he would never live to appreciate it (or worse, regret it). The few instances of killings from when he trained with the Mujahedeen were matters of death at long range, roadside bombing Russian tanks and troop carriers. This would be his first up-close elimination of the enemy. He gritted his teeth. He would not falter, not fail. He entered the room.

Ann rose. "Mahmood. Are you angry that I came here?"

Without a word, he approached her. She dropped to her knees and started to unzip his fly and open his belt.

His thoughts caught him off guard. *I am a sixty-five-year-old man. What is this Infidel whore expecting?* As she took him, he felt a flushing over his entire body. The girl had skill. He found himself responding, pushing himself deeper. She responded, accommodating him and bringing pleasure. The hand that held the knife relaxed. His back arched and he experienced the first orgasm since he was a young man in Budapest with the butcher's young daughter. He shuddered and she moaned. But Ann didn't relent. He had to pull away because of the sensitivity. She went to follow, but he held his hand out to stop her. She obeyed and began to stand.

She didn't see the knife as she went to hold him and rest her head on his shoulder. The sharp shooting pain in her stomach followed the punch that forced the breath out of her. Then searing pain as Number 1 pulled the knife up through her sternum, cutting her open like a filleted fish. She fell away with an expression of fear and seeming disappointment. In a few seconds, she stopped breathing. He stood there, looking at her, zipping his fly. *It had to be done.* She would have threatened the whole operation.

He returned to the kitchen and threw the bloody knife down on the counter. "Clean it up" was all he said. He left the kitchen now filled with the new respect he had gained from among those he would lead into death.

The next night, Number 5 waited until the deli was empty and entered the store. He approached the Pakistani immigrant who scrapped together enough money to purchase the store from the old Jewish couple who ran it since the '30s. Number 5 grabbed a newspaper and threw a dollar on the counter, "Did a girl come here asking about the Store & Lock?"

"Um yes, a few days ago. She was asking about that other guy."

Number 5 looked around and, seeing no one near, raised a street-silenced .22 gun and shot the owner once in the forehead. The owner crumpled behind the counter. Number 5 then banged on the register and pulled all the cash out of the opened drawer. On the way out, he turned the "open" sign to "closed" and walked in a direction away from the Store & Lock. A block later, he removed the hooded shirt and his big white sneakers, tossing them into a trash barrel. He threw the .22 caliber pistol with the 3 chambered, ghetto silencer on the end, made from plastic water bottles, into the next dumpster. Making it easy for the police, who would certainly view the deli's security tape, and find only the evidence of one of the local black or Hispanic gang's guilt.

CHAPTER TWENTY-EIGHT
I LOVE A PARADE...

It was a problem of circular logic. Owing to Bill's national security position, the ride from LaGuardia for Janice and him was a mini-motorcade. Two Secret Service cars sandwiched an armor-plated Chevy Tahoe with flashing lights and two armed-to-the-teeth agents in the front. A New York City police car led the way. Bill pondered whether this was better than Janice and him just getting a cab and melting in with the thousands of others headed to the Big Apple. Didn't the flashing lights and sirens say "Aim here!" to any would-be bad guy?

Turning to Janice, he suddenly realized that all this security made her feel safer and therefore the argument in his head stopped. He placed his hand on her protruding belly as she sat in the half-rotated crescent moon curve a pregnant woman assumes when sitting. When he thought how the lights and agents also proclaimed "Stay away from my wife and kid," he took a deeper breath, relaxed a little, and watched the skyline of New York loom larger as the convoy raced through the unusually light early morning traffic of the Grand Central Parkway.

On the other side of the limo, Citi Field passed by, quiet in the morning light. The only barely noticeable activity was the small smattering of people and trucks along with a helicopter lashed down in the parking field.

∞§∞

Number 1 watched from the grip truck as the small cadre of cars with their flashing lights sped by. His walkie-talkie crackled. It was Number 4.

"Insurance has arrived."

Number 1 looked down at his copy of *Chemical Engineering Today* and the headline, "Hiccock to Address National Meeting in New York City." Beneath was the yellow-highlighted paragraph ending with "catch a show while we are there."

He turned and saw Number 8 checking the hydraulic line under the rear cowling of the craft. In the camera truck, the camera department was loading magazines. In a few hours, the *Caliphate* would begin. This one act would serve as a signal to all the cells, all the groups, all the freedom fighters to attack, overwhelm, and start the beginning of the end of the West's stranglehold on an entire culture. On a personal level, his brother's incarceration at the hands of the Infidels would be avenged. As he threw the magazine down on the table, a *Time* magazine from months before, with Bill on the cover, was right under it.

∞§∞

The Waldorf Astoria is an historic, world-class hotel on New York's Park Avenue. Kings, queens, and presidents have stayed in its opulent suites. To Bill's dad, the impressive part was that their room was one floor below the famed ballroom where Guy Lombardo ushered in every New Year for decades.

"It just wasn't New Year's until Guy Lombardo played 'Auld Lang Syne' at midnight," the elder Hiccock explained.

"Gee that's great, Pop, I've got my meeting now. You and Mom going to be okay here?"

"Very," he said as he poked at the overstuffed welcome basket, eyeing the chocolate goodies amidst the fruits, nuts, and jellybeans.

∞§∞

Janice was unpacking her dress for this afternoon and smoothing it out as Bill sat at his laptop and reviewed the top 50 e-mails forwarded by his staff. He quickly perused the headings and decided to go right to the SCIAD network. Only three messages in his in-box were from the Element ring.

One caught his eye with the heading, "Remo calculator – Q.E.D." What he found when he opened it was a program that was based on the data that Peter Remo's original "smuggled" *Harmonic Epsilon* manuscript furnished. It was the combined work of two nuclear physicists, three mathematicians, and two astronomers, who collaborated over the SCIAD network. Using GPS positioning and celestial charts, it calculated the nuclear cusps on the face of the Earth using the calculations and the formulas in the text of a book that purportedly got many people killed to protect its contents. The notation that accompanied this new software proudly boasted, "In 1968, the celestial and global data available was accurate to only eight decimal points. Today, thanks to shuttle flights, geosynchronous satellites, and the Hubble space telescope, we're able to reach out 24 places beyond the decimal point."

Just then, Cheryl knocked on his door. "Bill, your 10 o'clock is here."

Bill looked at his watch and pulled out his iPad. He synced the e-mails to it while he adjusted his tie. He then took the twenty steps into the meeting in the adjoining suite and toward the rest of his day, which would end up at the Brooks Atkinson Theater with his wife and parents tonight.

∞§∞

"They will be dispatched by myself and Number 9," Number 1 said to Number 8, referring to the two movie cops who just pulled up in their police cruiser.

Originally part of the TPF, the elite weapons and tactical patrol force of the old NYPD, today's movie cops are more like New York City's ambassadors to the film industry. In a good year, $3 billion dollars could be dropped into the city's economy by movie and TV production. The NYPD Movie Unit was the key interface between a massive operating city bureaucracy and the day-to-day running of the multi-billion dollar film business. Most of the time, they stopped traffic or helped control crowds, usually acting as the shepherds of the private security people the movie companies hired. Many of those hires were ex-cops or moonlighting cops. In fact, in many cop shows and cop films, retired and moonlighting cops made a bundle as extras or tech advisors. It was safe to say that in the relatively small group of movie artisans and craftsmen, everybody knew or heard of everyone else. That made it odd that out of this whole crew, the only person these two cops knew was the catering truck guy, Sammy.

Sammy was a new guy in the business, meaning he came around within the last 10 years. An Egyptian by birth, he started as a server for one of the biggest catering services in the business. He worked hard and opened his own business and now did very well supplying breakfast, lunch, dinner, and craft services to hungry film crews on the smaller films and shows across the city. Sammy also followed the first rule of the business: cops eat free.

"Officer Ralph and Officer Fernandez, good to see you. I got cheese croissants and hazelnut blend."

"Sounds good," Ralph said. "What's up for lunch?"

"Halaal food! Lamb, goat… you know!"

The Irish cop looked at the Puerto Rican cop and scrunched his face.

"The crew and the stars are out of Iran. This is what they eat," Sammy explained. Then he had a thought. "Wait, maybe I can find some roast beef and potatoes."

The cops smiled and Sammy got his assistant to take some food off his second truck going out to a small commercial crew shooting in Queens.

About mid-morning, the cops watched with little interest as the crew prepped for whatever they were going to shoot. Ralph looked at the permit. He saw the helicopter and some prop guns as wardrobe. The guns being wardrobe meant no gunplay and, therefore, they would not have to validate the licensee. New York law required that any gunplay, firing of blanks, or even brandishing a weapon was supervised by a licensed gunsmith or gun dealer. The cops would have to make sure his license was current and that no foul play or accidents could ensue. Also, they would call in to let the local precinct know to ignore any calls about gunshots or guns observed. At the bottom of the permit, Ralph noticed the production company had a Brooklyn address.

"Hey, didn't Sammy say these guys were from Iran?"

"Yeah, goat eaters."

"That's funny."

"It's probably a racist comment," Fernandez admitted.

"No, not the goat-eaters crack. The address here on the bottom of the permit… Let me check this out."

With little else to do, Ralph exited the car and set out looking for the producer.

∞§∞

Bill's secret, encrypted phone rang during his 11:30 meeting with the CEO of UniDyne Industries. "Excuse me; I'll have to take this in private."

He stepped into the outer room, closed the door, and answered.

"Bling," was the monosyllabic greeting.

"Bling brothers! How are you guys doing?"

"We're okay, sir. We are onto something, but the trail just split into two."

"Well, it's all moot now guys. In fact, I came up here in part to tell you guys it's over…to buy you dinner and let you get back to your lives."

"All the same, sir, it don't look over from here."

"What do you mean?"

"Not over the phone, sir."

"What do you need?"

"Is that Palumbo guy available?"

"When do you need him?"

"ASAP."

"I'll call you back."

Bill grabbed his regular phone.

∞§∞

"Well, he only said, 'Cheryl, cancel my meetings for the rest of the day,' then he left. He did say that I should tell you he'll meet up with you at the theater."

"You don't know where he went?" Janice asked.

"You know when he gets like that, you can't get anything out of him."

Janice took out her phone. She tried Bill. No answer.

"He doesn't want to be found," Janice said. Both women knew that this must be some security thing. Neither woman could conceive of Bill having a clandestine meet or tete-a-tete with a paramour. Although something in Janice's spine almost wished it was as simple as that. She knew if Bill disappeared, something big must be happening.

"Cheryl, could you try him again?"

∞§∞

Bill disabled his cell phone battery so that any GPS tracking data wouldn't give away his position, or that of Bridgestone and Ross, who he was meeting. As he exited his father's Cadillac, he approached two men sitting on the bench on the edge of the public park.

"Mr. Hiccock! We were expecting Palumbo." Bridge said.

"He was heading out to Europe. I turned him around, but he's at least four hours out. So I figured maybe I could help."

The two warriors looked at each other. Bill felt the need to intercede in his defense.

"Look guys, I've seen my share of action and I can handle myself pretty well if it comes to that. Now, what do we got?"

"Our movie producer, Rashani, is too clean. We've run him through a bunch of checks and double checks and couldn't even find a pissed off waiter that he stiffed. Too clean. Too neat."

"Look fellas, the nuke is accounted for. It's deep-sixed."

"That may be, sir, but what we're onto sure as hell lead us this far, and we're here because we were on the trail of the nuke."

"And...?" Bill asked, knowing that that fact alone could not form the basis of their case against the producer.

"Sheik Alzir El Benhan."

The name of the bio-terror mastermind and reason for the kidnapping of an ambassodor sent a shiver up Bill's spine. "Go on."

"Seems the movie mogul, Rashani, had a security guard who is an ex-chopper pilot for the Iranian Air Force. After we did a little digging, we found that the pilot came there" – Bridge hitched his head at the building across the street – "a few weeks back."

Hiccock could only imagine the trail of broken bones and ripped skin "a little digging" by these two might have caused. He looked across to the mosque on this quiet Jersey City street. "A little obvious, ain't it, using a mosque?"

"Just another benefit of the great American Suicide Pact, Mr. Hiccock," Ross said.

"No law enforcement agency could even surveil it now. Not with all the bleeding heart bullshit going on. But the subway boy who was released also came by this way. As far as we can tell, he's still in there."

"So why did you need Joe?"

"Ross did some investigating. Rashani's ex-pilot is working on a movie here in New York."

"But he's not working for Rashani; he's working for Alazir El-Benhan, who is posing as Rashani."

"You go to the head of the class, Mr. Hiccock."

"Been there, done that, got the egghead reputation to prove it. What's the plan?"

"Ross will stay here and bird-dog Rodney."

"Rodney?"

"Ali Rashid, also known as Rodney Albert, the guy who ran from the subway checkpoint. He's a loose cannon but he made his money as a freelancer in the L.A. indie movie biz, as an assistant cameraman."

"Movies again."

"Yeah. They'll be the death of Western culture."

"Let's go!" Hiccock said.

"Here. Know how?" Ross handed Bill a Sig Sauer .357. Bill popped the clip, checked the load, pulled back the slide, checked the chamber, released the slide gently, reseated the clip, and stuck the gun in his waistband.

"We'll take our car," Bridgestone said.

Bill tossed the keys of the car he drove to Ross. "It's my dad's."

"I'll be careful."

On the way, Bridgestone filled Bill in on the details. Hiccock started processing what he was learning from the pointy end of the stick that he pointed at the problem. His training as a scientist kicked in as he listened to data that seemed to contradict the commonly held belief that the suitcase nuke threat was over. Bill instinctively knew that the trail that brought B&R to this point could have been correctly on the scent of another nuke device. A wholly different one not connected to the one that blew up in the Persian Gulf.

The scientist caught himself in mid-thought. *It didn't blow up.* There was no detonation, just radioactive debris. Enough rads to be read as a spike by the satellites. But not a detonation.

He pulled out his cell phone and said, "It didn't blow up!"

"What didn't?" Bridge asked.

"Li, it's Bill. Have you done a high-resolution analysis of the Mahgra spike against the Persian Gulf spike? Could ja? Like now! Call me back A.S.A.P."

He killed the call, then redialed. "Peter, get over to Kronos right now. This thing may not be over. Call me when you get to Kronos'" He hung up.

"Tell me more, Sergeant."

As Bridgestone further explained the trail of events that brought them to New York, Hiccock realized they had bits and pieces of the puzzle but nothing hard, no evidence. Then Bill remembered that evidence was the purview of law enforcement and the kind of stuff you needed if you planned on going to trial. In this case, if there were a second loose nuke, there would be no trial. In fact, if they didn't follow these threads there might be no courthouse or enough people left to form a jury. The endgame here was not jurisprudence. The endgame was ending the game before, as the President put it, sudden death overtime.

In a moment of silence, Bill realized his deja vu was happening all over again. He had been here already. He had gone from being a paper-pushing bureaucrat into field operative before. He kept trying to tell himself it was just until Joey got back.

∞§∞

Number 1 looked at his watch and mentally went through the next steps: in two minutes, Number 3 would be on his way and executing his second diversion phase to take place in 33 minutes. In ten minutes, Number 4 would initiate the primary distraction and revenge for Number 1's brother. One hour from then, the package would be picked up, then five minutes later...

His mental checklist was interrupted when he saw one of the two cops that were chatting with the caterer approaching him.

"Mr. Rashani, Officer Ralph Chesney."

"Nice to meet you, Officer. Anything wrong?"

"Probably not, sir. But I need to see your original permit."

"May I ask why?"

"You could ask, but I don't need a reason."

"Very well." Number 1 picked up his walkie-talkie and called to his assistant director. "Please bring me the production book. I need the original permit."

Number 1 looked back to see the other officer still at the catering truck. "Officer Chesney, let's go to my camper. The A.D. will meet us there with the paperwork."

∞§∞

"Where did you get this?" Hiccock asked, looking over the filming permit.

"They are a matter of public record. You just go to the mayor's office and ask," Bridgestone said.

"Description of action to be filmed: 'Bita Asayesh, ace reporter, exits news helicopter, into boyfriend's arms, Crane up - End credits'." Bill looked at Bridgestone. "News helicopter."

"Yeah. Ya see where this could be going?" Bridgestone said.

∞§∞

Ross watched as the front door of the mosque opened and Rashid, a.k.a. Rodney, walked out carrying a suitcase. Although it was smaller than the nuke case they were looking for, it was suspicious enough for him to interdict. He approached Rodney as he walked towards the PATH train station, placing a call as he did so. At that moment, Bill and the sergeant were in the Holland Tunnel, so he got Bridge's voicemail instead.

"Bling. Rodney on the move with a case. Too small to be the bomb. I am going to stop him." He closed the phone and went right up to Rodney. "Hey, Mister, you got a light?"

"No, I don't smoke," Rodney said, never breaking his stride.

Ross pulled his gun, stuck it in Rodney's neck, and strong-armed him into an alleyway. "Where you headed, Rashid?"

Rodney was stunned that this man knew his real name. "I ... I was... Er..."

Rodney heard a pop as Ross' head exploded right in front of him. He heard footsteps running up to where he was. A split-second later, a man he'd seen at the mosque appeared with a sniper's rifle and scope attached to it.

"Go... Go! I will handle this."

"Who are you?"

"Number 1 had me stay here to make sure you weren't followed. Now go, Allah be with you! Here..." He tossed the still-shocked Rashid a handkerchief, then motioned his hand across his face.

Rashid wiped his face and pulled back the handkerchief to see red blood and gray matter. Then he puked.

∞§∞

As they were coming out of the Midtown Tunnel, Bridgestone proposed they go to the location and check out the copter. He motioned to the back seat. "Our rad detector is in the small case. If there's a nuke anywhere close, we got a good shot of picking it up."

Bill's phone rang.

"Li, wha'cha got?"

"Not even close, Bill"

"Best guess?"

"Radiological device, but no big plutonium signature.... Sorry I missed this before."

"We were all fooled by the false responsibility claim and...holy Shit!"

Bill grabbed his other cell and said as he dialed, "Janice, Mom, Pop."

∞§∞

"...pagers or beepers. Also the use of flash photography during this afternoon's performance is strictly prohibited..." was coming over the theater's public address as Janice obediently silenced her cell phone and slid it into her purse. She looked around one more time, but still saw no sign of Bill.

∞§∞

“What is it?” Bridge asked as he weaved in and out of traffic at 75 m.p.h.

“These guys duped us and the entire world, except for you and Ross. The message the NSA intercepted with Roosevelt and Mahgra was obviously a plant. The failed attack on the *TR* was just a dirty bomb suicide decoy. That and the premature Al Jazeera video were all part of a massive deception to get us to stop looking for the bomb and drop our guard.”

“Sun Tzu – all warfare is based on deception.”

Bill snapped his fingers as he remembered the reference. “Hence, when able to attack, we must seem unable.”

“I’m impressed, sir.”

“I studied Tzu when I played ball in college. Used many of his strategies.”

“Well, it seems the terrorists studied *The Art of War* before this game, sir.”

“Why couldn’t these guys have stuck to just reading the Koran.”

∞§∞

“Oh, I see now, it was only the photocopy that didn’t have the street address…” As Ralph turned to Rashani to explain the discrepancy, he felt a sharp pain in his chest. Number 1 then jerked the scarab up in strong pulls, ripping open Ralph’s ribcage. He finished off his work by slashing the policeman’s throat, leaving him to fall back onto the floor of the trailer.

Number 1 turned and nodded to Number 5, who was screwing a silencer onto his pistol. He stepped out of the trailer to summon the other officer, shedding his blood-splattered jacket along the way. He checked the side-view mirror of the lighting truck to be sure that he was clean.

"Officer? Officer Chesney would like you to join him in my trailer. There's seems to be a problem with the permit."

Sammy watched as the producer escorted the cop into the trailer. From this distance, he couldn't hear the dull pops the silenced weapon made. He did see the trailer rock once, but figured it was normal when people went to one side or another. He returned to dishing out the crew lunch.

∞§∞

"Take the BQE," Hiccock said. "I used to live here." Just then, Bridgestone's phone chimed, indicating that there was a voicemail. He retrieved the message as Bill watched his expressions. "Well?"

"Ross said Rodney was on the move with a case too small to be the nuke."

"Was he headed out of town or carrying something else?"

"We'll know soon. Ross was making a move on him. We must have been in the tunnel when he called. Anyway, you know the reason I asked for Palumbo was for cover, in case we had to deal with locals. Flashing an FBI card could keep a lot of nosy cops out of our business. I don't suppose you have any official looking I.D. on ya?"

"Well let's see." Bill opened his wallet and rifled through his I.D. cards. "Office of Homeland Security, no, National Security Agency, no, Defense Intelligence, nah, Central Intelligence, uh uh, Oh here we go, Federal Bureau of I. By the way, on this case I am the lead agency for all these agencies, so since they all are working for and reporting to me, I get to hold all the cards, so to speak."

"Cool!"

∞§∞

Customs Agent Hector DeNardo was scanning the last container of the current tier when the radiation monitor in his hand registered low-level contamination. He quickly got out his handheld scanner and waved it past the decal on the door. In an instant, the shipping history of the container was displayed on the device's four-inch display. He relaxed a bit when he saw it was from Teva Radiological Industries Ltd. Petah Tikva, Israel. Still he'd report it, after lunch.

CHAPTER TWENTY-NINE
D.O.A. IN JERSEY CITY

Sometimes Allah smiles on you and sometimes he's looking the other way. It was a fast shootout as the two Jersey City cops stopped and fought it out with the guy dragging the dead body down the alleyway. They happened upon him by accident while investigating a call on a gas leak. Since the dead guy with half his head missing had no I.D., the only thing they found was the set of car keys in his pocket. As other cops and investigators arrived, they pushed the button on the key ring. A half a block away, a Cadillac Seville beeped and its lights flashed. Three minutes later, the NCIC sent a flag to Homeland Security. As a major member of government, all Bill's friends and family were on a watch list. The inquiry tripped an alarm and the Secret Service detail assigned to Bill was signaled. They were embarrassed and professionally crushed that Bill had eluded them and wasn't in his suite. Furthermore, the one agent assigned to Janice and the Hiccocks almost gave his mom a heart attack when they rushed to the row in the theater and ascertained that the dead man on the street in Jersey City wasn't the registered owner of the Caddy, the senior Hiccock.

∞§∞

Bill's encrypted phone started to oscillate, the signal that indicated flash traffic. At the risk of exposing their location, he had to answer it.

"Mr. Hiccock, Brooke Burrell, sir. We've got a dead John Doe who had the keys to your father's car on him.

Do you know why your father's car would be in Jersey City?"

"Oh, dear god. How did he die?"

"Gunshot to the head, sir. Not pretty and the body had no I.D., sir."

"Agent, that man was an investigator for the White House operating under special orders from the President of the United States."

Bridgestone's hands gripped the wheel tighter as he overheard this end of the conversation. His partner and friend for the last four years was dead.

"Was a man named Rashid apprehended?"

"No sir. There was a shootout with Jersey City P.D. but the man who they killed was an R. Nadal. Who is this Rashid?"

"Rashid is a suspected terrorist on the loose with a suitcase device of some kind. He was the one stopped at the subway last week, so get an A.P.B. form NYPD. Ross was on his tail when he was... shot."

∞§∞

Number 8 started warming up the helicopter. The technicians and camera people started turning on lights and rolling the dolly up and down the specially made track that insured a smooth ride of the lens. The two stars, a little miffed that the first day of shooting was the big end scene, did the best they could to fill in the blanks in the less than helpful rehearsals they had been suffering through with some third A.D. They felt snubbed by the director, who only seemed interested in the logistics and effects.

∞§∞

The new floor construction assured that no one would discover him or what he was doing. There were still two weeks to go before the new Radiology Center was to be opened and the floor was empty. In its own room, the brand new nuclear medicine machine sat, partially crated, awaiting critical wiring to bring high voltage to its working parts. Slowly, Number 10 turned the knurled screws that held the expansion power supply access panel in place on the large, Israeli built, machine.

Later, no one at NYU Medical Center questioned the orderly pushing the clothes hamper into the elevator. Only the most astute observer would have questioned his pushing the button for the top floor when the laundry room was in the basement.

∞§∞

Bill jumped into crisis management mode. He had the White House switchboard conference his cell phone call with Agent Burrell with the DHS and the NSA. His orders were simple. Find Rodney, aka Ali Rashid, and find the case he was carrying. Get the N.Y.P.D. to release his mug shot from the subway arrest. Shut down all means of egress from the scene of the shooting. Widen the circle and stop and search everything that moves. Report to him immediately with any developments.

He hung up, breathed out, and started ticking off his mental checklist as Bridgestone took the exit to Citi Field. He was starting to second-guess his decision not to have added finding and securing his wife and parents in the call. He could order them into a basement or bunker of some kind. *But where?* New York City took down all the black-and-yellow-diamonded public shelter signs years ago. *Maybe a public school?* Maybe they still had stored water and food in the bomb shelter area. Wait, didn't Gracie Mansion have a bombproof safe room? How the hell could he get them up there? Why the hell didn't he check that before all this?

He then caught himself. Everybody believed the bomb was no longer a threat. That was the main reason to bring Janice along on this trip to hang with his parents. Except he brought them right to what was looking more and more like Ground Zero 2.

Bill then looked across at Bridgestone and his list dissolved. "Sergeant, I am sorry about Ross, he was..."

"Thank you, sir. Ross was good. The only way they could have got him was from up high and away."

"Sergeant, call me Bill from here on in."

"Thanks, Bill."

"How should we play this?"

"Question is, is the cat out of the bag?"

"If we play it like it isn't, we could be walking into a trap."

"If we come in guns blazing, we may force them to detonate."

"So what do you think, Sergeant?"

"They have to know that Ross is dead. They also have to know we got their shooter. That alone could move up their timeframe."

"So it's back to 'bomb, bomb, who's got the bomb.'"

"I'll just need 10 seconds to get a radiation reading on the chopper."

∞§∞

NJ Transit had a hit. A railroad cop lost a guy in the crowd who could be Rashid. The train had already pulled into Pennsylvania Station.

∞§∞

Number 1 used a disposable cell phone for the one and only time it would ever be used. "Number 4, don't miss your curtain."

Thankfully, Americans had a short memory, so no one was thinking that what happened in a theater in Moscow, only a few years back, could ever possibly happen to a theater in New York.

∞§∞

On the other end, Number 4 threw the phone under the wheel of a passing New York City bus. It flattened with a cracking sound swallowed up by the pre-matinee hubbub. The six doors of each of two ubiquitous stretch limos – in no way out of place in the theater district – sprang open and eight men exited from each, right in front of the Brooks Atkinson Theater. They all wore long bulky coats. Four of them separated into two teams of two each and spread to the stage door and load-in doors of the theater. Ten others walked right in. The two drivers followed, wheeling a case from the trunk. As the ushers and one security guard protested, each was shot in the face by suddenly raised guns with silencers. The men then just shut the doors behind them and one produced a chain, which they threaded through the panic bars of the main doors, thus sealing the patrons inside. The two who remained outside looked at one another and, upon a nod, lifted their machine guns out from under their coats.

Harold Benson had waited his whole life to see a Broadway play. So on the occasion of his 50th birthday, his wife Doris got two tickets from Decatur, Illinois to New York on Jet Blue, found an affordable Holiday Inn in midtown, and nabbed two tickets to the biggest show on Broadway. They had just finished his birthday dinner at Sardi's and were leaving. Cindy and Dan were running late and the traffic wasn't helping. Dan told the cabbie to pull over and that they would walk the next half-block to the theater.

Rimi Patel was walking with her grandson who had just scored big at the M&M store. His mother would be cross, but she was following the Grandmother's Oath, "First, spoil the child." They passed Vietnam vet Rufus Kincaid who sat in a wheelchair with his one and only leg and a sign explaining why he needed your change for him and other disabled homeless vets. Innocently, Rimi's grandson dropped three M&Ms into Rufus' cup.

When Harold started to falter, Doris instinctively grabbed him, thinking he was suffering from a heart attack. Then a bullet entered her and the searing pain made her collapse. Harold fell dead on top of her. The window on the cab that had just dropped them off shattered as the cabbie caught a round in his head and fell dead on the wheel, sounding the horn. The bullets spun around the man entering the cab and he slid down the rear panel of the car, streaking blood in his wake. His date was blown back into the cab taking three in the chest blossoming red bloodstains on her new dress for the evening.

Rufus heard the shots and immediately grabbed the little Indian boy and spun around his chair to shield him. Rimi didn't understand why the man grabbed her grandson, but started screaming. Her screams fell silent as she was hit with three rounds. Dozens of other people fell dead or wounded, turning 47th Street into the Great Red Way.

Edie Deagan was posing for a picture with his mount as two blondes from South Dakota had their boyfriends shoot the ubiquitous tourist shot in New York – the pretty girls smiling alongside the mounted policemen atop his "10-foot cop." The ripping of the machine pistols finally registered in his ear. He immediately kicked Atticus and let out the rein. The one-ton horse traversed the half-block from Broadway in eight seconds, during which time 10 people were hit. Eddie pulled his Glock and, like a cavalry trooper, started firing at full gallop at the gunman in the long coat spraying the street. His third and fourth shots found center mass on the shooter and he went down. A second shooter on the other side of the theater was too far away for him to get a good shot at while not hitting a pedestrian.

Atticus didn't hesitate when Eddie nudged him in closer to the shooter, yelling for everyone to get down and take cover. Two white-shield anti-crime cops who were looking out for scalpers and pickpockets had their guns drawn down and in front of them as they advanced one car at a time for cover towards the shooter. As soon as they felt they had a shot, they both swung onto the hood and trunk of a Town Car and pumped 30 shots into the shooter who went down screaming, "Jihad."

Eddie Deagan took on the role of lookout from his perch atop Atticus. He triggered his lapel-mounted radio. "MTS mounted to Central K. Shots fired, multiple gunmen IFO 256 West 47th Street. Repeat, multiple gunmen. Citizens down, many down." He scanned the street as the undercover cops kicked the dead shooter's gun from his body.

He saw a man in a wheelchair keel over as a young boy ran from behind him, then he realized it was Rufus, the vet he'd chased from spot to spot every day. Today, Rufus bought the spot he died in...a hero.

It went out as a Critical Response Call. Immediately, 75 patrol cars, almost one from each precinct in the city, headed toward the theater district. The rolling roadblock method they utilized, where the lead car blocks a crosstown street while the main body zooms by then takes up position in the rear, meant they cut a swath through the city at speeds as high as 60 m.p.h. They got there in less than 120 seconds from their recent post at the Museum of Natural History.

Eddie Deagan was down from his mount and, heard how the shooters were part of a group of men who went into the theater. He tried the doors, but they wouldn't open.

Of course, none of this happened without the news services being aware. News trucks and helicopters scrambled to the theater district.

For the terrorists, all was going according to plan.

∞§∞

A theater is acoustically a live-end/dead-end room. The live end, where the actors work, amplifies sound so that all their nuances of performance can be heard. The dead end, where the audience sits, is designed to muffle sound and absorb reverberation. So when the house manager came into the lobby to see what all the fuss was about, the shot that perforated her forehead didn't sound out more than 10 feet. The instant human reaction was also muffled, so the rest of the theater was not aware of what was happening in the rear of the house. In time, though, the screams became more numerous and, hence, louder and clearer.

From his perspective returning from the men's room, Phil Dunowsky, an off-duty corrections officer, gauged the situation and decided he could get the guy with the gun. He drew a bead on the guy who just shot the woman with the headset on. He was about to do it by the book and yell "Police, freeze," when he saw the thug point his gun at an old guy who witnessed the killing.

"You bastard. I'm going to shove that gun up your ass!" Mitchell Herzog, a veteran of the Korean War, blurted out. He was more angry than smart. He realized this when the hooligan with the gun turned it towards his face.

Phil fired three times and the bad guy fell. As he died a spasm-induced pull on the trigger fired the gun, just missing the old guy and shattering a sconce on the back wall of the theater. What Phil would never know was that there were more than just that guy in the theater. His world went unexpectedly black as another terrorist loosed a three-shot burst into his head from behind.

∞§∞

From their spot in the parking lot at Citi Field, 100 yards from the shooting set of the film, they began to see some activity.

"Let's roll," Bill said as his cell rang. "Yes, sir. Thank you, sir." He ended the call and said "Call Joey." to his voice-activated iPhone.

"Joey, the President has covered your agent Burrell under the same executive order as Bridgestone and Ross. Tell her she is free to use any means necessary."

"Roger that. Thanks, Bill. How's your end going?"

"I'm late for the theater and we are about to see if the movie guys are really making a bomb. Parking lot at Citi Field. Have NEST and extraction teams ready waiting for my order. If you don't hear from me in five minutes, come in blazing."

∞§∞

The inter-agency alarms, triggered by the possible sighting of Rashid, took 12 seconds to ripple through every cop, national guardsman, plainclothes and uniformed railroad security personnel throughout Pennsylvania Station. Within a minute, they thought they had a target located in the upper concourse next to the Amtrak waiting area. They didn't want to spook the guy until they had a clear shot and a chance to secure the case.

One of the FBI agents assigned to Penn made a chilling observation. The subject appeared to have radiation burns on his face and hands. This was confirmed when the subject passed within 10 feet of one of the radiation monitors and it reported, to the secure room deep within the station, that a low-level exposure had taken place. Two plainclothes officers, one dressed as a homeless person, the other as a Knicks fan, came up on either side of the target. They timed their approach just as the target was passing by a trashcan. In an instant, they grabbed him and, in one smooth move, wrestled the case away by breaking his wrist as he was going down. Then, like an NBA star, the "homeless guy" slam-dunked the case into the can. Fifty cops suddenly came out of nowhere, screaming for everyone to get away. The two plainclothes cops hustled the target out of the concourse.

From the side of the concourse, a forklift-type machine rolled out and towards the trashcan. The Kevlar and composite resin receptacles lined with blast absorbing bubble wrap like insulation, were located throughout the station and specially designed to direct a blast upward, not outward, to minimize collateral damage if a traditional bomb were planted in one, or, as in this case, placed there by police to limit damage. The forklift carried a two-ton cover cylinder of the same material as the can. It slid the cover over the can, sealing it under 4,000 lbs of weight. For good measure, the cop driving the lift pressed the forks down on the top, adding the weight of the machine to the downward force. In all, 32 seconds elapsed between the takedown of the target and the securing of the canister. Unfortunately, it took the rumors less than half that time to spread to the street.

CNN, being right upstairs and across the street from Penn Station, had the first scoop. Then it took all of three minutes and the word was out – worldwide. *Dirty bomb at Penn Station.* Every news organization was heading towards 34th Street and 7th Avenue, including at least 14 additional news copters who were not covering the Broadway theater hostage drama.

∞§∞

"Let me know if he talks." Bill slipped the phone into his pocket and turned to Bridgestone. "They're waiting for a robot x-ray of the bomb containment vessel to see what they're dealing with. Rashid ain't talking yet."

"Whose got 'em?"

"FBI AIC."

"Too bad. The agent will have to play by the book."

"*She'll* have to. The Agent-in-Charge is Brooke Burrell. Joey is heading to Headquarters. But you just gave me an idea."

Bill reopened his phone and pressed a speed dial key. "Get me the President."

∞§∞

Number 1 had just heard of the events at Penn.

Number 2 was concerned. "If it didn't go off, are we still going ahead?"

"Yes. Half of the news establishment is already at the theater. No detonation means there will be more reporters there, waiting for something to blow up so they can catch it on film. Yes, the threat of the bomb works better for us than the bomb itself! Let's go! Number 10 should be in position for transfer in five minutes."

∞§∞

"Roger that."

Agent Burrell couldn't believe her ears, but she trusted Joe and knew Bill. She hung up her phone, ordered all of the other agents out of the room, and told them to guard the door.

Rashid protested. “No woman. Only man! No woman!”

Brooke turned to a shackled Rashid. “Because women don’t have balls, Rashid? They are beneath you because they don’t have testicles? Well, we can fix that. That call was bad news, Rashid. The President of the United States just gave me permission to remove each one of your balls slowly and feed them to you.” She opened a knife that no self-respecting agent, let alone a woman, should carry. “So, soon we’ll be equals.”

Rashid stiffened.

∞§∞

Agent Warner turned immediately upon the first screams that echoed through the theater and instinctively grabbed Janice and headed for the exit. She was his primary concern due to her security clearance. Unfortunately, he was not responsible for the elder Hiccocks. Janice protested, but he overwhelmed her and got as far as the lower stage-right exit doors. They opened as two men, in long overcoats and brandishing machine guns appeared. Warner pushed Janice safely out of the line of fire and tapped two perfect kills in the foreheads of each intruder. As he reached down for Janice, she saw his chest explode as a fusillade of bullets ripped him from behind. He fell and didn’t move.

Number 4 grabbed Janice. “Your in-laws are dead unless you do everything we say.”

Janice was in shock, yet she noticed men in long coats placing sacks in doorways and stringing wires. Others were herding people at the back of the theater. The Hiccocks were being corralled up the aisle. To her, it was all like a dream in slow motion.

“Where is your husband?”

"He's not here. Why are you doing this?"

He slapped her. "Shut up. No questions." He then yelled to two others, "Find him. Try the lavatories."

∞§∞

"Hey pal, can I use the can?"

"Yes, it's by the white truck," Sammy said to Hiccock who hastened his step in the manner of a man responding to nature's call.

Bridgestone remained and chatted up the caterer. "Egyptian?"

"Yes. Been in America for 12 years now."

"Good business?"

"I have three trucks and do over 500 meals a day."

"It smells good."

"Try this." Sammy tore off a piece of flatbread and dragged it through some baba ghanoush. He handed this to Bridgestone with a napkin under it.

"Mmmmm, that's really good. Cumin?"

"Yes, and paprika and dill."

"That's really tasty. I can see why you are successful. What's going on here today?"

"First day of an Iranian film. They are shooting all the exteriors here in New York. Then they'll go back to Teheran and shoot the interiors. They should be here for a month. That's why the Halaal food."

"Who's the producer?"

"Rashani. Biggest producer in Iran."

"Which one is he?"

"Over there in the brown jacket by the helicopter."

Bridgestone looked and something clicked. Bill came over feigning relief, "Thanks, man. What are you guys shooting here?"

"He already told me. It's an Iranian film. Being made by that guy there, Rashani." Bridgestone turned back to the caterer. "Mind if we watch for a minute or two?"

"It's fine by me. If the A.D.s hassle you, just tell them you are with me, Sammy. Here take my card. I also do weddings, bar mitzvahs, graduations...."

Bridgestone turned and concealed a laugh. *Bar mitzvahs.*

"That's not Rashani," Bridgestone said to Hiccock as they walked towards the set.

"No, its Jahim El Benhan, Alzir's brother. His name was Dr. Brodenchy before he converted. He's a nuclear scientist, or was."

"No clicks from my counter. The bomb is not here."

They both watched as the "producer" boarded the helicopter. One of the A.D.s announced, "This is a camera rehearsal! Everybody clear the copter."

The blades turned and picked up speed.

"What do we do?"

Bridgestone grabbed a kid carrying a film magazine from one of the trucks. "What are they doing right now?"

"They're doing a test to see how the blades look on camera. If they go too fast we won't see them."

"So they're not taking off?"

"That thing? Nah, it don't fly, it's a prop. The action in this shot takes place after it has landed. The second unit will shoot a real helicopter landing from the air tomorrow."

Then, to everyone's surprise, the copter lifted off, tilted, and headed for Manhattan.

CHAPTER THIRTY
HAMMER OF GOD

"Come on," Bill said to Bridgestone. Bill ran to the cop car that was driven here by the now dead cops, got in, and drove over to Bridgestone's car. "Throw your shit in here. This will get us through."

The cop car fishtailed out of the parking lot and shuddered as Hiccock floored the accelerator up the ramp to the Whitestone Expressway. "Bridge, find the lights and sirens."

From the driver's side, Bill kept one eye on the copter, the other on the road. He took the BQE and jumped off at the LIE. Bridgestone was locked on the copter with his binoculars as they reached the peak of the rise of roadway right before the tunnel entrance. Hiccock took the exit for Van Dam Street in order to take the bridge rather than losing the visual as they went through the tunnel. They lost sight of the copter for a moment as they navigated the streets of this industrial part of Long Island City. Their red lights and sirens cleared the way for them to reach the bridge in record time. From the upper roadway, they re-acquired the copter as it hovered over a building on the edge of the river north of the bridge.

"What's he doing?" Bill asked as he swerved through one of the separators to take the single outside lane. "Looks like he's going to land on that white building.

"That's a hospital. It's an air med-evac landing pad."

"Holy shit!"

"What?"

"There's a flock of helicopters over that way and another over there!"

Bill looked left and saw what looked like a swarm of 20 or so helicopters circling and hovering over a part of midtown. To the right were another 15 or so. He flipped on the police radio. "Why didn't I think of turning this on before?"

There was a non-stop chain of radio reports and squelching. "Something big must have happened," Bridgestone said. "They are stepping all over their communications."

Through all the static and partial sentences, they gleaned that something was happening at Penn Station. A momentary clear allowed the words "NEST team" to jut out of the radio traffic. Both men instinctively knew the acronym: Nuclear Emergency Search Team. Bill then thought he heard "47th and 8th hostage situation." But it was quickly stepped on.

∞§∞

Joey Palumbo didn't wait to confirm the information before him. He dialed up Bill's cell. "Bill, Teva Radiological out of Israel had a Palestinian driver who met B&R's truck driver in the desert. He loaded the suitcase nuke into a nuclear MRI machine in a container. Like you thought, the machine was delivered before we clamped down, so they just inspected the container and verified a hot machine inside and then with a police escort passed all our detectors to ..."

"NYU Medical Center. I got it!"

Joey was speechless. Bill had hung up as Joey said, "How did you..."

∞§∞

The laundry hamper bumped and rumbled across the roof despite the efforts of the orderly not to disturb the case cushioned atop 10 dirty pillows and made snug by rolled-up heavy blankets on all sides. Once he landed, Number 1 ran to help him, ordering, "Lift; take the weight off the wheels to lessen the bumps."

Near the aircraft, they lifted the case, kicked over the hamper, and rested it on the hamper's side. Number 1 opened the case and methodically armed each part of the firing circuits in the exact sequence. The Russian legends and Cyrillic markings on the bomb, long since translated in his head, posed no challenge. Then he removed a lead separator, which kept the volatile nuclear isotopes relatively safe during transit. He dialed a timer to five minutes. Satisfied that this was done, he pulled a pin from a switch guard. There was no longer a physical obstruction in the way of the switch handle's path.

"For Allah, for my people, for my father and my sisters, and with my brother moving my hand, let the *Caliphate* begin."

He threw the last switch.

∞§∞

"The Ambassador to the U.N., her staff, Undersecretary of Commerce, and SCIAD." The head of the Secret Service read off the short list of administration assets in New York City to the President and his COS.

"Are they all safe and in secure environments?" The Chief of Staff asked.

The Ambassador is at the U.N. and has her detail. The Under Sec is now at the Fed Dep and secure. Quarterback, er, SCIAD and Mrs. Hiccock are presently unaccounted for."

"What does Bill's detail report?"

"Well, sir, I am sorry to say that Mr. Hiccock left the hotel without notifying his detail."

"He's a science nerd and he gave your top-notch agents the slip?"

"With all due respect, my men were essentially escorting him. We had no threats, no actionable intelligence. As you know, the weakest link in any protection plan is the protectee. If they don't play ball, short of physical restraint, there isn't much we can do. Unless the President orders us to close-cover the protectee as a national asset, then we remove the possibility of them exercising any discretion on the level of protection."

The COS waved him off. "Okay, okay. Don't quote me the manual chapter and verse."

"What about Mrs. Hiccock? I personally ordered protection for her. Can't we find her by calling them?"

"There's been some sort of hostage scenario occurring in New York. We're getting more intel now, but even the NYPD doesn't have a clear picture yet."

"First the radiological bomb in the station and now a hostage taking? What's the FBI think?" the President asked.

"They're just getting this also. We're talking the last 30 seconds, sir."

"Find the Hiccocks. I want quarter-hours on this. You brief me, Bob."

∞§∞

They were going up First Avenue when Bill's cell rang. "Agent Burell, have you found out anything?"

Bridgestone tried to glean the gist of the call.

"And you are pretty certain that this is golden? Okay, thanks and sorry you had to do that." Bill ended the phone call.

"What are we dealing with, Mr. Hiccock?"

"Agent Burrell learned that they do have the nuke and are planning on an airburst over midtown from the copter. You were right; the hospital was the cover for the radiological signature."

"How did the lady come to this knowledge?"

"She had to cut him a few times and threaten to take away his ability to procreate, but he ain't dead."

"We should buy her a drink if we survive this afternoon."

∞§∞

The Chief of Staff hurriedly entered the room. "Mr. President, Bill Hiccock on the line."

"Bill, where are you?"

Bill's voice filled the room from the speakerphone. "I'm in midtown Manhattan. Bridgestone and I are in hot pursuit of a news helicopter that may be the delivery method of the suitcase nuke."

"Another suitcase nuke? What makes you think that, Bill?"

"Could be the same one, sir. Dr. Quan Li confirmed the Persian Gulf spike was weaker than the refinery spike. The attack on our ship was intended to fail and appear like we sunk the suitcase nuke as well. It was just a low-level radiological device. Everything, including the seemingly premature announcement taking credit, was all deception. Thanks to your order covering her, Agent Burrell has derived intelligence to support that they have the loose nuke in the city and are planning an airburst."

"Airburst? How can they pull off an airburst?"

"Bridgestone's trail led to a movie company that rigged up a copter and we've just observed it landing at a hospital in Manhattan. They could be transferring the nuke now, sir."

"What do you need, Bill?"

"Opinions, sir. Do we shoot it down or do something else? I'm afraid we may only have a few minutes, if that much."

"Got it. Bill. I'm switching you to the Sitch Room. Ray and I will hustle down. Meanwhile, our military guys and nuke experts are there. Start without me."

The President put the phone on hold.

Ray picked up the other phone and ordered the call directed to the Situation Room, nine floors below. When he hung up, he asked the President, "Why did you choose not to tell him that his wife might be involved in the hostage scenario?"

"Do we know that for sure? He's the point man for this administration in what, God forbid, could turn out to be the greatest mass murder in history. I need him focused on saving millions. If we find out that she is in danger, we'll tell him what we know, but not rumors."

"Yes, sir. One last thing, sir."

"Yes."

"We don't know if the station bomb isn't a failed suitcase device. It may blow. I recommend you prepare for that possibility."

"How do you prepare for something like that?"

"Prayer?" Ray Reynolds said as he went off to put his staff and their minions on alert.

The President sat for a moment, the enormity of what could be going on settling in his mind. He looked at the picture of his daughter, Marie, on his desk. That nuke was still out there... the one they knew of. There could be more. He reached into his drawer and retrieved a folder. The breaking of the band that sealed the folder revealed in red letters across the face "Jesus Factor." Mitchell spent the next three minutes uninterrupted as he read what only one of his predecessors had even seen.

On the 69th parallel, in the Aleutian Islands, there was a DEW line early tracking station. In its four-foot, concrete-walled installation was a circa 1969 IBM Systems 360 – 65 computer. It was hooked up to two radio-telescope dishes located out on the frozen tundra. Their sole purpose was to track to within a meter the true distance to the sun from the Earth at every second of the day for every day in the 35 years since it went online. Two Air Force techs at the Defense Early Warning facility checked on it every eight hours. They didn't know why or for what reason they did this. The computer was hooked up to NORAD. There, at the North American Aerospace Defense Command, was a single unmanned console. The commander of the watch had sealed orders on how to operate the console if a call from the President ever came.

There was no need to authenticate the voice on the other end. The watch commander knew that this was the President's personal line to NORAD.

"Yes sir," he said crisply as he answered a phone that hadn't rung since the Cuban Missile Crisis of 1962.

"Commander of the watch, this is the Commander in Chief. Under National Command Authority, rule 10, I hereby authorize you to go to console 20-01 and place in these coordinates." Mitchell was reading from a hand-typed sheet within the folder. He then scanned a map and found America in quadrant A1. "A1. Repeat, Alpha 1."

"Copy and confirm coordinates. Alpha One, sir."

"Confirmed, watch commander."

The 42-year old colonel on watch broke the seal that held the plastic case over the old teletype-styled keyboard that was older than him. He opened his sealed orders, which still held the old name for NORAD, North American Air Defense Command, and followed directions.

In green dotted type on the round Multipurpose CRT in front of him was the simple computer query "Sector?: ___" He typed in A then 1. The keyboard actually clunked with each depression. A second later, a new line emerged.

It simply read, "Fair to 16:00 EST Rain From 16:01 to 4:32 EST."

He then dutifully read the "weather report" to the Commander in Chief.

The President wrote the information on his pad. He then called in his Nat Sec Advisor and formally initiated Archangel, a comprehensive, interagency directive that effectively put all the assets of government on what the military would call Def Con 1. Archangel specifically did not call for the military to change its defense condition. Against a domestic terrorism event, the military had little usefulness other than their traditional disaster roles. Archangel put the government on alert and put first responders on highest priority. It also authorized the release of N, B, and C countermeasures to be disseminated below the supervisory levels of federal and local response agencies in order to react more quickly to nuclear, biological, or chemical attacks in major urban areas. Archangel gave the government a prayer of a chance to stop or at least respond quickly enough to save some human life.

As he looked up at the TV in the Oval Office, he saw what millions of Americans were watching: the round edifice of Madison Square Garden rotating under the lens of the news helicopter circling above the Penn Station/Madison Square Garden complex, the thousands of flashing lights surrounding the Garden, and the thousands of flashing lights when the news channels cut to the other big story, the theater hostages.

It suddenly hit him. They created these preliminary events to get all of our first responders in one place, under the nuke. This would allow them to wipe out the city's essential services in one kiloton of fire and destruction.

He taped the folder as he murmured to himself, "God, don't let Hiccock be too late."

∞§∞

Peter entered Kronos' OEOB "office," which looked like a broom closet—which it had been since the Eisenhower Executive Office Building, nee Old Executive Office Building, was built adjacent the West Wing in 1877. In this case, though, the broom closet was stuffed with computers, racks, and plasma displays.

"Kronos, how are you man?" Peter said.

"I'm cool. What'cha got?"

"Do you have my copy of the book here?"

"Better than that; it's already scanned and searchable. All the formulas are inputted into our seven Crays across the SCIAD network."

Peter handed him a memory stick. "Here's what was in Ensiling's Viennese safety deposit box. It's a modifier to the aspect spectrum formulas."

As he spoke, Kronos called up those formula fragments.

"Now here's the tricky part. We have to move from eight-bit depth to 24-bit in order to achieve the same accuracy as..." Peter was speaking slowly so that he could impress the enormity of the task on Kronos.

"Done," Kronos said.

"Whoa, I guess with seven Crays lashed together, nothing is tricky."

"What's the range for F over the value of X?"

"Let's see; based on Ensiling's notes, F is 3.14 times 10 to the 23rd power..."

As they updated the programs with Ensiling's decoded formulas the two brainiacs bonded across mathematics that were four decades apart.

∞§∞

The gun smoke in the theater was causing the stage Fresnels to make cones of colored light. This made an eerie backdrop to the pandemonium in the audience. Janice had her arms wire-tied to a chair in the last row of the theater. A man was videotaping her as another wielded a scarab. He was speaking in half-English, half-Farsi. Janice knew he was threatening to cut her head off to whomever the tape was intended. The sheer terror of her predicament made her shiver, but she didn't bow. She resisted their attempts to manhandle her. That earned her a slap across the face. She snapped her face back immediately with a defiant look that needed no translation into Farsi. It was the only means of defiance she had left.

∞§∞

Hiccock almost hit his head as he slammed on the brakes to avoid a woman with a stroller who absentmindedly stepped out right in front of them.

"For Pete's sake!" Bridgestone snarled.

"That's it!"

"What's it?"

"Take the wheel," Hiccock said as he jumped out the driver door and around the front of the car to the passenger side. Bridgestone slid over and peered out the top of the windshield. He got a bead on the copter and peeled out before Bill had the door closed.

"White House signals, hold for Situation Room," the voice on the other end of Bill's phone announced.

"Tell the President I'll call him back."

That got an impressive look from Bridgestone.

Bill dumped the White House call and re-dialed. "Kronos… get Peter's book."

"You mean *Harmonic Epsilon*?"

"Yes. Put it up on the rings. I need this fast. Ready?"

"Got it; shoot!"

"The Jesus Factor. Where is New York City now and is there a cusp coming soon."

"Got it. Where are you?"

"New York. Chasing the suitcase."

"Are you out of your freakin' gourd?"

"What can I tell ya? Trouble is just my middle name."

"Where is New York now?" Bridgestone asked. "What does that mean?"

"What is New York's exact distance from the sun at this instant," Hiccock said.

Kronos came back over the speakerphone. "I got two Crays, strapped together at Dartmouth. We patched in Professor Quan Li and he is uploading an algorithm now."

"I thought you said one of the scientists on that original committee was the leader's brother, Dr. Brodenchy," Bridge said.

"Yes, and that was back in '68. But I am hoping for a two-cushion-shot here."

"Enlighten me."

"Back then, a computer could carry something to eight decimal points."

"You already lost me... Just give me the sit rep..."

"Huh? Oh, situational report. Well, I guess that abbreviation didn't save any time. We might be able to shoot the thing down without a detonation."

"How you going to pull that off? That's a suitcase nuke up there and they are not too stable. A little thing like hitting the ground at 300 or so miles per hour might just trigger the thing off."

"Jesus Factor, Bridge. We figured it out on a basketball."

Bridge slowly turned and looked at Bill with a screwed expression.

"There's a line in space, a cusp, and as the Earth goes through it, having large mass, one part is nuclear safe while the other is vulnerable. Then it all reverses cyclically. Depending on the position of a spot on Earth and the sun, you either can or can't have a nuclear explosion."

"I'll be dipped. Like how, on New year's Eve, it's already next year in Austrailia when the sun hasn't set in Times Square yet."

"Exact... Yes, that's exactly it. How come I didn't think of that?"

"We're running," Kronos reported over the speakerphone of the Blackberry.

"Peter Remo theorized about instantaneous values of Harmonic Epsilon. Kronos, can you run a time sweep and give me instantaneous values longitudinally? Also, can you give me an eight-place simulation as well."

"Peter's here and we already did that. Anything else?"

"Stand by; I am literally thinking on the run here."

Bridgestone had a light bulb moment. "Okay, so I think I got it now, the bad guys are working with old data from way back when and they obviously think it will go off. Meanwhile, you and the characters on the other end of the phone are checking to see if this thing maybe can't go off?"

"Exactly. Peter was involved in the early formulas and then worked with Ensiling on derivative instantaneous values of H33."

Bridgestone held up his hand to signal "I surrender."

Hiccock slowed it down, as much for him to work it through as to help Bridge. "What it comes down to is that the old equations just covered the U.S. in total, but New York is inside the footprint of America. It's at least 300 miles inside the Maine shoreline. Today, computers can carry a number out to 40,000 decimal places."

"160,000," Peter corrected over the phone."

"See, even better! Anyway, Brodenchy's calculations will tell him when the entire U.S., to Maine, is vulnerable to nuclear detonation before he fires. But Peter and Kronos, using Ensiling's new computations that Brodenchy couldn't get from Ensiling – or from his own brother, who we have in custody – can tell the exact second before that when New York turns destroyable. Prior to that, it should be safe to risk shooting him down."

Hiccock grabbed Bridgestone's sat-com phone from its clip on his belt and flipped it open. "Signals, this is SCIAD, I want a joint call to Sitch Room White House, military air command, and NEST."

"Stand by SCIAD. Voiceprint sampling now."

"William Hiccock, Special Advisor to POTUS." Bill spoke in an even tone, despite the frantic rush.

There were some beeps and a click. Both men strained to see the copter now disappearing and reappearing between the buildings of Manhattan.

"You drive; I'll watch it," Hiccock said with both phones in his hands and his head out the passenger window. "Go right on 34th...."

"I have a positive match. Your call is connected, SCIAD."

"General, do we have the ability to shoot down a helicopter over Manhattan right now?" Hiccock didn't know for sure, but assumed a general was somewhere on the line.

"Affirmative. We are two minutes into a CAP over Manhattan Island. Two F 15-E Strike Eagles out of Gabreski Air National Guard base on Long Island."

"Have them identify and lock on to a blue-and-white news helicopter right now flying directly over the Empire State building."

"Bill, this is the President. Are you targeting the press?"

"Sir, this is a stunt copter for a movie. Only one side is painted press. The other is all white. Maybe your pilots can confirm that. But do not fire, General, until I get the all clear."

"From who?" the General said with umbrage at the fact that there was someone else higher in the chain of command. Hiccock could tell from that response that it was probably the Chairman of the Joint Chiefs on the line.

"Peter, Kronos," Hiccock said and then talked into the other phone. "C'mon guys, I need to know now. There can't be much time left."

"Just a second more.... Got it. Okay, Cray Dartmouth says cusp in 40 seconds."

"Kronos, be very sure of your next answer. Which way is the cusp going?"

"Hold on. Okay, it's heading on a z axis through the ninth meridian..."

"Kronos! Is New York hot or not?"

∞§∞

The General's tone was one of seeming protest to the President. "Sir, this man is advocating a weapons-free rule of engagement over a major metropolitan area. Do you trust him?"

"He's trying to stop a nuke attack. He's never let me down before."

The Chief of Staff then interrupted and clarified, "Sir, the General needs to hear your order, sir."

The weight of this landed squarely on the President's shoulders.

"General, I order you to release weapons upon Mr. Hiccock's signal for you to do so."

"Duly noted. Thank you, Mr. President."

"CAP control, lock onto target but hold fire until my command."

∞§∞

Suddenly, a new voice came over Bill's phone; it was scratchy and carried a southern accent. "Cap Con this is

CAP One. I have acquired target. Confirmation it's our bird, a half-painted whirly."

"Now or never, Kronos," Bill urged into the other phone.

"Okay, Peter and I agree, at 160,000 decimal points New York gets hot in 30 seconds; at the Earth's 1000 mile per hour rotation and the angle of declination to the cusp line, the entire U.S. to Maine goes nuclear in 55 more seconds."

"So he thinks he can't detonate for 55 more seconds," Bridgestone said. Hiccock was amazed that Bridgestone just got the dangerous part of the idea – that you could preemptively strike with impunity.

They both looked up as the sound of the copter's rotors started to cavitate as it dug into the air in a maneuver to position the airburst in the most devastating position.

The sergeant looked at Hiccock and gave him a nod, setting his chin in the same way Bill's father did when he saw Bill halfheartedly daring to dive off the high board at Bronx Beach and Pool when he was 9. Bill survived the dive and went on to be a borough-wide swim team champ. If he were wrong, Bronx Beach and Pool and most of New York would be incinerated by his hand. But it was also a 100% certainty that Brodenchy didn't come all this way to bluff us. He will detonate.

"General, fire in 12 seconds."

∞§∞

Just then, the Chief of Staff was handed a note that read "Confirmation. Janice Hiccock held hostage in NYC theater. All agents in detail presumed dead."

He folded the note, running his fingertip along the new crease. *Hiccock and half of New York could be dead in a few seconds. I won't bother him with this news now.*

The General had looked up at the big, digital clock in the Situation Room when Hiccock gave the order to shoot in twelve. That was at 12 seconds on the timer, so he was waiting for 24 before he gave the final command.

Hiccock and Bridgestone had pulled over on 34th and 7th. Bill started flashing his F.B.I. I.D. as they made their way closer to Penn Station and Madison Square Garden directly above. They couldn't see the U.S. Air Force Strike Eagle circling its prey high above Manhattan, but the blue-and-white half-painted helicopter was right above them to the right. It hovered at about 300 feet above the sports arena.

"Is this going to work, sir?"

"The shot or the formula?"

"The shot's going to kill that bird, sir. That's a U.S. Air Force fact, I meant..."

∞§∞

It was Allah's will that one of Russia's precious devices—an instrument of the enemy of his family, invaders of his youth, and the drunken Cossacks who raped his sisters, killed his father, and forced him and his brother to become refugees—was transformed, in his hands, to the hammer of God. He was about to be the first of millions who would die in a burst of manmade sunlight. His death in the killing of so many Infidels would fulfill the prophecy, the Caliphate! It would be the supreme act of the Thousand Years War. His name would be hailed, studied, and prayed to in madrassas and mosques for a million-million years! He lifted his head to God, letting the prop wash from the copter cleanse his face in preparation for meeting Muhammad, when a white-hot yellow streak suddenly cracked across the skyline and bent in an arc towards the copter. As he saw the smoke flume racing towards his open door on the chopper, the thought in the younger Brodenchy's, a.k.a. Jahim El Benhan's a.k.a. Number 1's prodigious brain, which had conceived, executed, and was within seconds of accomplishing the greatest terrorist attack in history, was *How could anyone have found out?* He looked up into the sky and prayed and pleaded in Arabic with Allah, "I am your servant, your will be done. Allah Akbar!" He then awaited either the intervention of God or the face of God.

∞§∞

In the blink of an eye, the AIM-9 Sidewinder missile traveling at three times the speed of sound locked onto the heat plume from the copter's efforting engine. As the rocket swooped down and in, it aligned with the sun's reflection off the tinted Plexiglas window of the top floor of Two Penn Plaza, which confused the heat seeking infrared sensor that guided the 20.8-pound HE payload to a target. The missile adjusted and crackled past the copter and slammed into the hot sun glinting off the top floor of the Manhattan skyscraper. The Sidewinder was built to essentially pop a balloon, a pressured fuselage or delicate engine on a plane already going 500 plus M.P.H. Therefore as bombs go, 21 pounds of high explosives wasn't all that much. The building glass blew out and a small fire started. But because the building was right above Penn Station, evacuation alarms had sounded 20 minutes before, leaving no one on the top floor to be killed. Only minor cuts and scrapes befell those on the ground from the debris.

∞§∞

From the ground, Bridgestone and Hiccock saw the missile veer away.

"How much time left, Bill?"

"Twenty seconds."

Bridgestone turned and saw he was standing next to a Hercules cop in full battle array to his right. In one smooth move, he elbowed the officer in the throat and grabbed his M-16 as he fell. "Bill, protect me!" was all the Army Ranger said as he released the safety and trained the assault weapon at the copter, now 100 feet above the ground.

Bill pulled out his wallet and started waving his Homeland Security I.D. at other officers who were beginning to turn towards the "armed" man, "Hold your fire! Hold your fire! Homeland Security! This man is an agent! Hold your fire!"

∞§∞

Number 1 laughed and cried with joy as the explosion of the building snapped his eyes opened. Allah had swatted away the missile. Now nothing could stop them. In 20 seconds the "Allah Factor" would make New York hot for nuclear detonation. The delicate equation had been unknowingly calculated at Iran's Nuclear Research Facility under the guise of a theoretical celestial navigational problem. His joy was curtailed by the impact of bullets pummeling the cabin of the copter.

Bridgestone ignored the screaming of "freeze" by some of the cops pointing their guns at him and stayed on target, spraying the copter's body trying to hit the fuel tanks. Hiccock's protesting and waving his I.D. was the only hesitation that kept the cops conflicted and Bridgestone alive.

As Number 1 shielded his head from the bullets that perforated the skin and were ricocheting around the cabin of the copter, one of the bullets found the fuel line. The high-pressure hose burst and aerosoled Jet A fuel. A split second later, the next white-hot bullet that entered that area touched off the fumes and the rear half of the copter exploded. The explosion split the copter in two; the fiery body of the copter immediately began to counter-rotate in the opposite direction of the blades. This whirling dervish crashed on 30st Street into a 16-story building that was mostly rental space that musicians used for rehearsal. The plummeting copter had embedded itself five floors down, when the suitcase went off. Witnesses later would say that a secondary explosion shook the building and made the copter and everything else fall through six more floors. Twelve seconds later, the weight of all the debris from the top floors weakened the fifth floor, and the wreckage and the partially exploded suitcase settled in the basement.

NEST sensors and satellite sensors immediately lit up with a radiological impulse emanating from midtown Manhattan.

"Well?" The President asked.

"We're getting a plume, but that's more consistent with a radiological device," the Chairman reported. "I'm not getting any confirmation of detonation."

As soon as the copter exploded, Bridgestone dropped the weapon and put his hands on his head. Hiccock was now physically holding off cops.

∞§∞

"Is Hiccock still there?" Only static filled the room. "Is Hiccock still in one piece?"

The line cleared temporarily and the President thought he heard the human sounds of people, of Hiccock, dying. His mind raced to the thought of the two men in the street being immolated by radiation and not burning up, but burning out – outwards from within. Turning to ash as they screamed in agony. But the noise started clearing up and became easily discernable as laughter… and relief. Then a voice, Hiccock's, broke through.

∞§∞

"Sir, the bomb did not detonate; it did not fission. We're okay. Everyone is okay! Kronos, Peter, you guys hit it right on the numbers."

"Natra-friggin-lutley….. "

Bill turned to Bridgestone, "Natra-friggin-lutley, Bridge!"

"Roger friggin' that, Bill," he said as he kept his hands on his head hoping the cops heard that it was over.

"Bill, this is the President. Get out of that area. They are telling me the radiation is rising."

"We can help with the evac, sir."

"God damn it, Bill, we got people to handle that. Besides, there is something else. I'm sorry to tell you that Janice is being held hostage at a theater on 47th Street. We don't know any details yet, but we are assuming her detail is dead. It's a real shit-sandwich to hand to someone who just saved eight million people, but I'm sorry… truly I am, Bill… Bill?"

∞§∞

The rear view mirror sheared off at 45 m.p.h. as Bridgestone squeezed the squad car between a delivery truck and the wall of an office building as the siren wailed and the lights flashed on their way up to the theater.

"Why would they take a theater? And why now?"

The Chechins took a theater in Moscow. They've got a knack for it. They must have figured it was a strong diversion… or, maybe…

"Maybe what?"

"Maybe they were after you. You've ruined a couple of their last soirees."

"If they touch Janice, I am going to kill them. I will fly to wherever their families are and kill every one of them!"

"Whoa... where did that come from?"

"Burke Avenue. You got a problem with that?"

"No, but listen – when we get there, leave the ball-busting to me. You find and secure your wife."

"My mom and dad are with her."

"Shit. We'll just have to get all of them out."

"How we going to do this?"

"First, we'll have to get through our own guys."

CHAPTER THIRTY-ONE
SHOWTIME

The squad car careened around 47th and Fifth and into a wall of emergency vehicles.

Bill flashed his White House I.D. and they let the car through. Then they hit the FBI ring. An agent stopped them cold at 47th and 7th.

"Sir, you can't go further."

Hiccock fumbled trying to find his FBI I.D. but gave up. "Agent I am … fuck that, who's in charge?"

Special Agent Burrell, sir."

"Get her on your radio. Tell her Quarterback is here."

A moment later, the agent returned. "I am to send you on up, sir."

"Bridge, tell him what we need."

Hiccock made his way to the front line established by the police across from the theater. Brooke Burrell was there and she filled him in.

"Brooke, this is …. What's your first name, Bridge?"

"That's classified, sir,"

"No shit! Well then, Brooke this is Bridgestone. I want him to have full tactical control. He's my man and the President's."

"Full what? With all due respect, Hiccock, I'll have a HRT team inbound in seven minutes."

"My wife Janice is in there. She and the others may not have that long and Bridge can do things your guys can't."

"Is he Superman?"

"No, but he holds a higher form of Presidential Immunity than I got for you. But you'll have to forget that part. Besides, as the head of this joint operation," Bill pulled out his F.B.I. card, "my deputy director status outranks you. And thank you for getting the info from that dirtbag."

"That was you? Nice!" Bridgestone tipped his imaginary hat.

"Thanks. Okay, deputy director, what's the plan?"

"Whatever he says it is." Hiccock threw his thumb towards Bridgestone.

"Subway runs under here, so I need shaped charges and access to the adjacent basement. I'll need tac radios and weapons, stun grenades and five knives."

"Well, Rambo, I can do everything but the shaped charges, 'cause they're not here yet."

Bridge glanced away and saw the N.Y.F.D. Rescue One truck. An officer was unloading an acetylene tank in preparation for cutting through some metal gates.

Bill followed his stare. "I'm on it," Bill said, running over.

"Captain, I need...

"Lieutenant."

"Lieutenant, I need an acetylene tank. Right this second."

"You look familiar."

"The tank!"

The lieutenant ran to the rig and pulled an extra bottle of the gas. It weighed about 40 pounds and stood about two-and-a-half feet high. When he handed the tank to Bill, he snapped his fingers.

"I got it. You were the guy at the train station in Westchester when that building blew up... that woman under the rubble...then you got famous, all over TV and the maga..."

"If I get out of this alive, drinks are on me and we can reminisce. Gotta go."

Sardi's restaurant was famous but its basement was a mess. Bill, Bridge, and five SWAT guys put the green metal cylinder up against the wall between the restaurant and the theater. They listened, waiting for a train to pass under the building.

As the subway rumble approached, they took cover behind the tables and rolling bars that littered the basement. Bridge shot the acetylene bottle from across the room; the bullet hit dead center and dented the metal bottle; he then drew a bead and hit it in the exact same weakened spot and it exploded at the height of the rumbling sound.

In the theater, it was just heard as a slightly larger subway rumble, which, for the sake of the performances, the theater was built to filter out. The terrorists didn't suspect a thing.

The jagged hole in the wall opened to the back storage area behind the theater. There were many old props, sandbags, and lights stowed there. Bridge took the point and found the under-stage. He flipped down his night vision goggles. The trap doors and markings were all in phosphorescent paint and they glowed like neon.

He caught sight of a figure by the stairway holding a gun. The knife flew from his right hand and landed in the throat of the man, silencing him with a muffed gurgle. Bill saw the SWAT guys look at each other. This was not their way of engaging. They would be reviewed harshly for taking the life. But there would be no review for Bridgestone. He waved on the team and started up the stairs. They led to the wings of the theater's back stage. Bridge motioned for two of the SWAT cops to take position up on the catwalks above the stage. They silently found the ladders and scaled them in seconds. When they reached their perches, they drew a bead on the audience area and used their night vision sniper scopes to identify good guys from bad. They also radioed back to Bridge that the doors were chained and locked and that charges were wired across the span of the audience on makeshift cables attached to the balcony boxes at either side of the stage.

Bill went up the stairs and joined Bridge. In a soft whisper, Bridge said, "Is that your wife?" He pulled his head away from the sniper scope on his rifle and allowed Bill to peer through.

Bill's heart actually stopped beating and ice suddenly flowed through his bloodstream. He was turned inside out by the image of the man holding a knife to Janice's throat while another guy held a video camera up with a light shining on them. That was the good news for Bridge. That light killed the bad guys' night vision.

"Bill, make it for the first row then crawl up to the side where they are. I'll drop the knife guy when you pop up, then the camera guy. You grab Janice and dive under the seats for cover." He radioed two of the remaining SWAT guys to pick two targets each, clockwise, starting from the one at the exit door near the stage, and ordered them to go when Bill jumped up or if he was discovered. The cops up on the lighting catwalks had clear shots on the five bad guys in the back wearing the headscarves of the Caliphate.

He assigned the last SWAT cop to cut the wire on the string of explosives dangling over the audience. He had followed the detonator wire to the house right box where the line was attached. That trooper had to scale the back stage scaffolding and use a cast entrance from the loge. A quick learner, he went against his civil police training and coldly and without provocation strangled one of the terrorists who had been assigned that hallway to guard. He then took his position in the box and investigated the wires to make sure it was a simple two-wire open circuit and no tamper proofing was in play. When he reported that it looked like a simple cut and disarm, Bridge told Bill that it was all on him.

Bill waited until every terrorist he could see was looking the other way and then he scrambled across the lower part of the theater from the stage apron to the first row of seats. He stopped and listened to hear any sounds that would indicate if someone saw him. Over his radio, he heard Bridge.

"Good so far. Go slowly, Bill, I got my gun on the knife guy's temple. If he moves his hand, I pop him, so don't rush."

Bill shimmied to the end of the aisle. There were at least 12 rows that got wider and wider as the theater went back so that the end of each aisle was somewhat visually covered by the one ahead of it when you looked toward the stage from the rear. At the sixth row, a figure appeared at the exit door. At first, the young Jihadi from Jordan did a double take when he saw Bill just looking up at him from the floor. He then started to raise his gun and open his mouth. But from two different directions, muzzle silenced, bullets entered his forehead and he rotated back against the closed door and slumped to a sitting position, blood gushing from the blasted open back of his head. Bill froze again to see if anyone noticed that.

"Okay, you're clear; keep going."

One of the bad guys ran up to the guy holding the knife. He had a portable TV. He started talking in Arabic. On the TV was the news of the helicopter crash and the rumor that it had a radiological device of some kind on it.

The one with the knife then said something about Allah and started to say something else when his head exploded. His grip on Janice released. Bill shot up and ran toward her. The disconnected explosives fell harmlessly, like clothes on a broken line. A trooper started to open fire on two of the bad guys across the way. The cameraman went down next. The five at the back of the room all went down in one second. Out of nowhere, a screaming man in a headscarf came running in from the wings towards Bill and Janice. Bill fired from his rifle as he covered Janice and the guy caught two in the legs. He started to fall but kept firing as he fell. His bullets ripped into the seats around the Hiccocks as the stuffing flew. Two more hits entered the shooter's body as he was falling and he and the gun fell silenced.

Bridge was up and scanning now; he started yelling to the hostages, "Get down, Get down..."

They were already scrambling, flattening themselves out and trying to hide. Then he heard a scream. He wheeled around and one of the bearded henchmen had a woman in his grasp and a .45 automatic at her temple. The jittery Middle-Eastern man started to say something in Arabic, but Bridge fired and hit the gun, which in turn smashed into the guy's face. Immediately, blood started to come from the man's cheek and his hostage fell to the right. Bridge then hammered the gun into his head by successive shots sparking and clanging off the side of the pistol.

Bill grabbed Janice and got her to focus on him. "Are you all right? Did they hurt you? Are you okay, baby?" She nodded, shuddering, and then collapsed in his chest.

A scuffle broke out among the hostages. Bridgestone ran to the commotion to see an old guy wrestling with another man. The old guy was detaining him but the younger man socked him in the jaw trying to get free.

The older man yelled, "Shoot him. He's got a switch under his coat. He's one of them."

Bridge didn't have a clear shot. The old guy was still hanging on to the younger one, grabbing his arm. But then Bridge saw the button flash from under the guy's coat.

"Shoot 'em or he'll kill us all," the old guy yelled.

Bridgestone crooked his gun to one side and fired back at the two struggling on the ground. From that angle, the bullet went through the old guy's arm and into the chest of the younger one. Bridgestone knew he got him in the pump because the younger man died in an instant. His fingers never reached the plunger. The old guy grabbing at his wrist rolled out of the way in agony, a bloodstain now also blooming on his shirt by his waist.

"Pop!" Hiccock yelled, rushing to his father's side.

"We got him, right?" Hank Hiccock said, grimacing through the pain.

"Yeah, Pop. You got him. Don't move; help will be here soon."

Bending down to safety the detonator, Bridgestone commented, "Your father? I shot your father?"

"And I thought I liked you," Bill uttered as he moved to his mother. "You okay, Mom?"

"I've never been so scared in all my life."

He hugged her. "I am so sorry, Ma."

Hiccock's mom, unscathed, kissed him on the cheek. "For what, dear? You didn't start this." Then she rushed over to comfort her husband. "That was a dang fool thing you pulled, Hank. All these young men here and you had to fight these punks."

"Don't scold me in front of the fellas, will ya?" Then he looked up at his pride and joy and grabbed his bleeding arm. "Son, don't be mad at your friend; it was my lame-brain idea."

Bridge grabbed Bill's mother's scarf and made a tourniquet just above the hole in the septuagenarian's arm. He looked at Bill and said, "Sorry just don't seem to cut it, sir."

"Not so much," Bill said drily as he took over tightening the usher's flashlight that they were using as a turnbuckle.

"Except your dad was right. The dead guy could have killed us all with this." Bridgestone showed Bill the detonator cord, hard-wired to 100 pounds of plastique in a roll-around anvil equipment case.

Hank's mom grabbed his dad and kissed him square on the lips. "You saved us all. You are, and always were, my hero, Hanky."

"Icks-Nay on the Hanky-a."

The instant Bridgestone radioed "Site secured," the front doors flew off their hinges and were dragged on the end of a chain attached to an NYPD wrecker. Hundreds of SWAT, EMTs, and uniformed cops immediately swarmed in. Most tended to the hostages. Suits and gold braid followed. The suits were the crime scene investigation units, immediately photographing and seizing evidence. The gold braid was there to supervise and prepare reports to the commissioner and the Mayor. Two EMTs came to the elder Hiccock's aid. He tried to get up on his own but reluctantly accepted Bill's help as the EMTs joined in and immediately strung an IV and strapped him onto a gurney.

"Pop, you look like who did it and ran. Don't give these guys any guff, now."

Hank Hiccock looked at the EMTs. "Fellas, this is my son. He works for the President, telling him all about science. I thought it was a boring, cushy job. But, I'll tell you what, he damn sure makes it exciting."

Then Hiccock heard another EMT declare, "We got a pregnant lady here. I need her out of here and on the bus, stat."

He turned around to see Janice sitting upright, holding her belly. She had a sheepish grin. "My water broke!"

Half-crying, half-laughing, Bill came to her and hugged her until the wheelchair arrived. "When I saw that bastard holding the knife... I went nuts."

She cried on his shoulder as he held her tight. "You brought the cavalry in the nick of time." She kissed him as the EMT and Bill helped her into her wheelchair, the Med-tech making a point of Janice not worrying because he's delivered hundreds of babies in the back of the ambulance... and to keep taking deep breaths.

"Oh by the way, Mom and Dad, I was saving this for dinner, but that's kinda doubtful so here it goes. Janice and I are going to get remarried. Next week… if we're all out of the hospital by then."

"Couldn't you just have eloped and saved us all this commotion?" the elder Hiccock called as they rolled him out.

"It's about time, William," Bill's mother said as she walked behind Hank's stretcher.

Bill turned to Janice. "Well, Mrs. Hiccock, besides that how did you like the play…"

Bill's attempt at lightening the mood only got him a hug. "Bill, you saved me… us. You kept your promise to me."

"Honey, the guy who really helped all of us is right…" Bill looked around but there was no Bridgestone anywhere.

"He *is* a ghost…"

"Who is?"

"No one. Let's get you to the hospital. With Pop there too, it's going to be a busy night."

∞§∞

Somewhere in the middle of that busy night, while Hank Hiccock was restfully sleeping and being monitored by gadgets, gizmos, and Mrs. Hiccock in the chair alongside the bed, the younger Mrs. Hiccock was giving birth to the older's new grandson, Ross Bridgestone Hiccock.

∞§∞

In the aftermath of the helicopter crash, there was no attempt made to recover the copter, the device, nor the remains of any of the unfortunate souls who were killed in the building at the time. The entire building was sealed in 10 stories of alternating layers of concrete, lead, and sand. The foundation was also excavated and sealed in a similar method. The device and its deadly plutonium yoke was nestled in a concrete and lead egg, 50 feet thick on either side and 100 feet tall.

The entire midtown south area was decontaminated along with thirty thousand workers who got de-conned right at the scene by Homeland Security's mobile decontamination centers. Twenty-three tons of clothes were burned and six square blocks of drapes, furniture, and anything porous were trashed. Buildings were scrubbed down and air quality samples taken. Six months after the attack, the only reminder would be the cold concrete obelisk where the building used to be and a small plaque honoring the 18 people who died in the building during the first nuclear attack on American soil.

At the hospital two days after the birth, Bill received an unaddressed envelope left at the front desk.

In it was a simple note that read "For the kid's sake, it's Richard."

Bill went back inside Janice's hospital room to tell her, but she and little "Richard" Ross Hiccock were fast asleep, safe and peaceful. He had done his job for his country, his hometown, and for his little fledgling family. So with nothing left to do, Professor William Jennings Hiccock, possessing one of the most brilliant scientific minds in the country, just sat and, for what had to be the one-hundredth time in two days, marveled at the miracle before him.

AUTHOR'S NOTE:

This book is based in part on my actual experiences that are the basis to the Peter Remo character. I spent much of my life in dread that just the knowledge that the Jesus Factor existed, if broadcast to both the U.S.S.R. and America simultaneously, would instantly spark all-out war, because neither nation would hold its fire during a cusp that favored them.

In early 2007, I was able to spend some time with former President Bill Clinton. I asked him directly about the Jesus Factor and if anyone ever informed him that there were certain days when nuclear war was asymmetrical. His assurances that no one ever said that to him gave me the confidence to go forward with the writing of this book and let the Jesus Factor play its part in the fiction without my divulging any national secrets.

ACKNOWLEDGEMENTS

The contributions of the following people guided my fingers over the keyboard:

Colonel Michael T. Miklos, US Army, for not only the metal and gunpowder "hard points," but for embodying the modern warrior/patriot intellect, which so helped me imbue the characters with courage.

Ambassador Michael Skol
for his continued interest in my work and his priceless input on foreign affairs and diplomacy to assure a more believable
read.

Peter Kesselman, my partner in the Demiac 256, who was there with me in '68, for his insights and remembrances.

Len Watson who gave me the nod that I had a story here that should be pursued.

Anthony Lombardo, Retired First Grade Detective NYPD, for not only his knowledge but for allowing me to tap into his years of courageous service to the city.

My cousin, George Cannistraro, a brilliant writer in his own right, whose astute plot analysis really opened up the second half of this story.

Lia Matthow whose keen editorial sense and notes were the polish on this manuscript.

Monta, who is the joy of my life and believes in me even when I have my doubts.

To all the folks at NBC News, circa '68–'72, if you find yourself in the book or part of you in a character, it's because you helped shape the world for a 14-year old kid.

And Lou Aronica of The Fiction Studio, who deposited his three-decades-plus of publishing excellence, throughout this novel without ever leaving fingerprints.

And finally to you, the reader, because you have made it to the end of this book, thank you. Without you, I am writing to myself.

Dear Reader,

Look for more adventures of the Quarterback Operations Group in the third installment of my "thrillogy," entitled, *The God Particle.*

Book three, which was inspired by a brief encounter with a famous female writer while I was on a press promotion for book one, *The Eighth Day*, is more Brooke's book than anyone else's. It has more about her – her love life, her work life, her near loss of life, and finding a new life. Along the way we have modern-day pirates, real killer whales, sharks, Euro-disco, killer priests, foiled Pope assassinations, Class One religious relics, an old knights order kicking up dust, a dream weekend at Camp David, exploding Marine Ones, science and religion at each other's throats, kidnapping, master chess level strategy, the Large Hadron Collider at CERN, and the death of time itself. From the Indian Ocean, to Washington, to Paris, to the Sudanese desert, to the Cote d'Azur, to Geneva, it's quite a ride. The prologue and first chapter from *The God Particle* follows.

All three books are centered on my operating theory that what I write is science fact, fictionalized. As always, I rely on my history of having been in TV, worked for Congress, spent time in Washington and had some interaction with America's Armed Services and defense systems. Of course, my healthy respect for conspiracy theories, obscure science fact, and the insights into human behavior gleaned from decades as a film director all add up to the sum total of what I write.

I hope you like it. And remember my "trademarked, copyrighted, patent pending" logo line: "It's Only Fiction till it Happens!"

With deep appreciation for your readership,
Tom Avitabile
Tom@tomavitabile.com

Here are the opening pages from The God Particle*:*

Prologue

It wasn't really a lake, more like a croissant shaped, sudden contour of the river Rhone that disperses its undercurrent flow over such a wide area, that it flattens out into a calm, bay-like body. On the French end of the crescent, the quiescent waves are refocused into a flowing river once again. Its crisp, Alpine water resuming its seventeen-year destiny to empty into the Mediterranean. The shores of Lake Geneva are dotted with castles, chateaus, small villages and picture perfect walks that magically transport the common stroller into the regal past. All in all, a storybook setting that seemed the most unlikely origin point of the end of all existence on Earth, the solar system and the infinite universes beyond; the death of Time itself.

∞§∞

I. RUDE AWAKENING

Twang... Speeong... Pop... Grundle, she couldn't make out the noises through cottony ears. Like on an early school morning with her mother calling up to her room, *Brook... you'll be late for the bus*, and she didn't have the energy to open her eyes. *Ten more minutes, Mom.* She just wanted to lie there and catch a few more minutes of...

A distant cough rose from within her and upon inhaling, a knife like slice of acrid air made her choke again. Her right cheek was stinging. Kaarrack... the intensity of that next percussive punch popped her eyes open. They immediately started to burn. She focused on the world, the world around her; sideways, and on fire!

Before her mind could fathom the reality of the situation in which she had awakened, her instinct kicked in and she reared up, her palms scrapping against the same sandpaper rough surface that must have chewed into her cheek. Still disoriented, she sensed a blanket of intense heat enveloping her. As she tried to stand, her head spun and she fell back onto the skillet-hot, metal floor. *No, not a floor... a deck.* A fear welled up inside her that forced her brain to focus, to crystallize on the present. Without consciously deciding to do so, she was up and fighting a shifting equilibrium. *That's right, I was on a boat!*

Then a tongue of flame lashed out, the scorching tip causing her to recoil and topple over the side railing. She fell a few feet and smacked into the salty cold of the sea. The shock of the immersion, the sudden muting of all sound into a watery gauze and the radiating pain from the salt water digging into her scraped, raw cheek and hands, snapped her into another survival mode. She frog-legged back up to the surface. Gasping for her first breath, she broke the surface of the ink-black water, which was streaked with orangey glints reflecting off the wave tops. Using her arms proved painful, but she managed to turn herself in the water towards the heat and saw she was yards from a burning ship. Around her was fiery flotsam and debris. The main part of the vessel was gone, seemingly bitten off by a huge sea monster that took out the wheelhouse and most of the superstructure with one bite. *A bomb,* she thought as she spotted a chair cushion floating a few feet from her. Holding it beneath her chest and chin, she kicked her feet, creating more distance between her and the still exploding vessel. Another concussive thud was immediately followed by a flaming piece of wreckage that landed with a splash just ahead of her. She made her way around it.

Her head was sideways on the soggy, but buoyant, cushion. She had never been so exhausted, even on the survival course at Quantico, where pushing an agent to the physical limits for 3 days was the whole idea. Out of the corner of her eye, she saw something rip through the wave tops. She propelled herself upward to see if she could see it again. There were four of them. Four fins slicing through the water... *Sharks.* She turned; there were more of them, circling her and the wreckage. About 10-yards ahead of her, one breached the surface with its powerful jaws locked around the torso of a man. He screamed a blood-curdling scream. Its white underbelly flashed in the light of the flames as the creature smacked back down onto the surf bringing its prey beneath the waves. She heard the final scream of the man, gurgling as he was dragged below. Suddenly she was aware that the fins were closing in on her. She let the cushion go and keep turning in the water trying to see which one would close for an attack. A fin heading straight for her was hard to see, as it was just a thin line above the moon washed water coming at her. She braced herself; as the animal approached she punched down with all her might. She made contact with the nose of the killing machine and it flicked its tail and shimmied off, away from her. The punch cost her dearly. The pain in her arms almost knocked her out. There was another fin, about 20 yards out coming round and in. She wouldn't be able to muster that kind of punch again. She tried to position herself in the water to try and kick this one. Intellectually she knew this was a fight of attrition. She would not stop bleeding and they would not stop coming. She would be shark food as soon as her strength gave out or one blindsided her from the back or beneath. Then she saw it, to her right and 30 feet off-- a capsized Zodiac. She started to swim towards it, but her arms were like lead and the best she could do was thrash around. The shark was coming right at her now. In a panic she looked around and saw the cushion bobbing a few feet to her left; it killed her but she breast stroked over to it, then placed it under her chest again and kicked like the devil to make it to the upside down rubber craft before the shark intercepted her. She never worked so hard in her life. From the corner of her eye she saw the fin approaching as she was just feet from the boat, and safety. The shark was closing too fast. She abandoned the cushion and started long strokes; it felt like her arms were ripping out of their sockets. She was ready to give up and give in to the pain; instead she heard her brother Haley's voice, "Don't give up, Brooke. You can do it. Push harder! Come on Brooke, work through the pain." She yelled out of excruciating agony, "I can't Harley; it hurts so much!" She heard him insist. "You won't fail Brooke, you will make it. Don't give in." She screamed one more time and her hand touched the craft. She pulled herself up onto the slick bottom just as the shark struck. He took a huge bite out of the edge, a few inches from her dangling right foot. The impact threw her over the other side of the small boat. She went under and could see, in the dim moonlighted surface, the shark trying to rip the severed piece of the boat free as he wiggled his powerful frame to shake it loose. His small brain having not figured out yet that it wasn't flesh, but rubber. She scrambled back onto the boat one more time and centered herself and held on to the overturned prop off the outboard motor. Now she was the center of attention of at least 8 sharks circling her little island.

∞§∞

"Any word from Jakarta?" Agent Joey Palumbo asked as he entered the PEOC, putting his briefing file down on a nearby console.

"No, sir, just the satellite confirmation of the explosion and fire aboard the Vera Cruz," the satellite communications officer said.

"Air-sea rescue?"

"Scrambled from Diego Garcia but it's a long trip.'

"Why didn't we have assets in place closer?" Joey chided himself.

"What ever happened, sir, was unexpected," the satellite down link officer surmised.

"Is the vessel still afloat?" Palumbo asked as he surveyed the screens and console panels of the PEOC, the President's Emergency Operations Center, which was not the more famous situation room under the West Wing, but a converted, old World War II bunker, in the East Wing basement of the White House.

"All we know is that it stopped emanating the tracker signal... could be sunk or the tracker may have been discovered," a tech, manning a console, said.

Palumbo's lean frame hovered over the multi-purpose console, his face locked, with only the side-by-side movement of his square jaw as he chewed over his options. Bringing Brooke Burrell over from the F.B.I. had been his initiative; she was the best agent he'd seen. He wasn't going to lose her to the Indian Ocean on her first mission attached to "QuarterBack." His jaw then set and he reached for a blue phone, "White House signals... this is Half Back please voice print confirm... Halfback."

There was some switching sounds and then the voice of a female, "White House interconnect, state your emergency."

"I need to speak to CincPac immediately."

"Connecting"

A few seconds later, a squeezed voice shot out of the receiver after having been encoded, shot up 15 miles to a com sat, then bounced off a dish in Virginia, decoded and digitized and finally made analog to finish the trip on the oldest technology it would encounter-- the electro-magnetic receiver element of a Bell System phone, circa1966. "Commander-in-Chief Pacific Fleet Operations..."

"This is Joe Palumbo from special ops, White House, 'pea-ock.' Do you have any ships at or near 8 degrees 29 minutes north at 97 degrees 38 minutes east?"

∞§∞

The overturned Zodiac Brooke was clinging to was bobbing in the medium chop of sea south of Java. A body, floated face down right by her; she recognized a rifle strap slung across its back and tugged it over. When she flipped the body over, half the man's face was gone along with the center of his chest. A slick and blood red fish flipped and flapped out from behind the man's lung and squirted back into the water shedding its crimson covering and returning to its natural silver grey as it descended ahead of the red trail. She undid the sling and retrieved the AK-47. She then pushed off the body with her foot. Its new motion attracted two sharks that immediately descended on the body and tore it in two. Other sharks started thrashing around the blood slick now marking the spot. Using the butt of the rifle as an oar of sorts, she started paddling away from the sinking boat and hopefully the sharks. The upside down Zodiac presented so much drag that she wasn't getting very far, but at least she was drifting away. The weighted down end of the craft was where the overturned motor was. Its prop and small rudder pointing up gave her a foothold to steady herself against the pitching raft. She plopped her head down and told herself she'd rest a while then see if she could right the boat. As she attempted to relax, all the pain returned, reporting in from her hands, her face, her knee... *My knee?* She looked down. There was a gash across her knee spewing blood. With throbbing, bloodied hands, she ripped at the buttons of her blouse and removed it, then removed her bra. She wrapped the bra around her knee and cinched it with a square knot made out of the straps. The underwired cups snuggly contoured to her knee. She checked that it was secure and donned the blouse again. Being water logged, the back stayed bunched and twisted but it afforded her some protection against the sun, which was starting to boil off the fog to the east.

After an hour, she gathered her strength and, with her right foot wedged in the crook between the craft and the motor shaft, and her other foot high on the propeller, she tugged at the top of the boat trying to bend it back while at the same time, applying her weight to the prop for leverage. She started to yank and buck her body in an attempt to overcome her own weight holding it down. After three hearty attempts, her foot slipped and she slid down and crashed into the shaft. Had she been a man she would have seen stars; as it was it made her gasp and immediately shot her back to when she tried to learn to ride on her brother's bike. She scrambled back to her original prone position on the little rubber continent that she was the sole inhabitant of. She looked around and there were sharks still keeping pace. She realized she was leaving a blood trail as her bleeding was running off the side of the boat. She tightened the straps of the bra around her knee to stem the flow better. Then she splashed water to clean the surface of the boat and break the trail of crimson she was leaving in her wake. She aimed the riffle and took a bead on the closest fin drawn by the blood just washed overboard. When it got as near as she thought it would she dropped her sights and fired three shots into the body of the shark. It immediately thrashed and slapped in the water. The other sharks converged on the agitation and the new blood in the water and a feeding frenzy began. She drifted away from the school of sharks now busy devouring one of their own. She watched until she could no longer see the fins above the wave caps. Then she rested. She slept with her arm locked around the upright prop.

∞§∞

The *USS Nebraska*, Ship, Submersible Ballistic Nuclear or SSBN 739, an Ohio class submarine, was the second ship in the navy's history to bear that name. But its proud legacy in the silent service was now the province of her current Captain, Bret "Mush" Morton. Whose submariner Grandfather distinguished himself in major battle actions in these very waters during a stretch from 1942 to 1944, when, on a regular basis, ten boats would leave Pearl Harbor and only 4 would return. Those odds made that 24-month span in World War II equal to a century of patrol in submarine years.

In this "second century" of sub operations, the big boats, like Mush Morton's, were relegated to deterrence by guaranteeing the nuclear annihilation of any would-be aggressor. To insure that mission they needed to survive. In subs, that meant remaining undetected. Not so easy when you are prowling the ocean in something almost as long as a 56-story skyscraper is tall and 42 feet wide, containing the men, equipment, nuclear weapons and power plants to move the whole 18,000 metric-tons of the thing at a classified speed exceeding thirty-knots. So they ran extremely silent and they ran very deep. For that reason, Mush wasn't used to getting flash traffic in the middle of his 'hide and seek' peacetime patrols, and the order that he now held in his hands was as sketchy as they come. Simply stated and without the usual naval grammar, he was tasked to head for a map grid and look for anything unusual. That was it. No inkling of what he would or should be looking for. As far as he could remember, this would be the first time an SSBN was "looking for something" instead of trying not to be seen or heard by anything looking for it.

Back at fleet, the Rear Admiral, who was ComSubPac, was not sure either. All he had was a directive from the White House and some mission runner asking for assistance. But as the Commander Submarine Force Pacific, he was also part of the National Command Authority and this D.C. controller, code-named "Halfback," was invoking the highest level of NCA priority.

∞§∞

Brooke was alternately dipping herself over the side for heat relief and rolling on to the craft to ward off the chill from the Pacific. She had lost feeling in her toes; rubbing them helped get the circulation going somewhat. Dehydration and thirst were her big enemies now; she hadn't had anything to drink in 20 hours and had been baking in the sun for half that time. Her mouth was dry and cracked. As she learned in the rugged survival course, when she was qualifying to be an FBI agent, her last hope was to capture her urine and filter it through some cloth, like her shirt. She started unbuckling her pants when she heard a sound. A swoosh of air, about 500 yards off; something, maybe a whale had breeched the surface. It was hard for her to make out over the wave caps, which gave her brief glimpses of something in the water, a huge grey hulk. Her eyes were salt-burned and she squinted and rolled them wide open in an attempt to squeegee off the stinging salt, but she still couldn't focus. The she saw a glint; something metallic had reflected the sun's light. *A ship!* Brooke started yelling, but to her surprise, only a squeak came out of her parched throat. She grabbed the rifle, pointed it in the air and let out three shot bursts. Although deafening to her, from her low angle, the sound quickly attenuated across the wave crests, each robbing the sound of a bit of the acoustic power that the gun had generated. The few thousand waves between her and the boat had reduced the sound level to the point that, when it reached the conning tower of the *Nebraska*, it was little more than a burble masked by the wave splash against the hull.

After seeing no change in the direction or activity, in fact, seeing the hulk pulling away from her, she decided to try one last-ditch effort. She switched to semi-automatic, and tried something she hoped which would increase the effective range of the ubiquitous Russian weapon she had studied at Quantico. She emptied the entire clip as she shot upwards arcing the gun towards the hulk. The rifle couldn't hit the boat with a straight shot, but she hoped that by whipping the rifle and arcing the shots into the air, they would gain distance, like an artillery shell. The clip emptied in less than 6 seconds. And then there was silence. She was truly alone now and not able to signal them or any other craft.

∞§∞

Mush and his exec officer were manning the bridge when five distinct plinks turned the men around, using the binoculars they focused on the aft deck of the sub. Three dimples in the hull were highlighted as a bullet rolled around in one of them. "Sir, I think somebody just shot at us?"

"Bob, I believe you're right?" He then leaned into the voice-powered interphone. "Helm, come around one eighty, I want a fix on a point 500 yards off our stern and I want to be there 2 minutes ago."

"Aye, aye. Coming about, sir"

"Weps, I want the two fifty calibers manned, now? We might have pirates out here."

"Deck guns on the way, sir."

"Now who's got the balls to fire on a U.S. Navy warship?" Mush said as he scanned the stern and turned in the opposite direction of his turning boat, so that he kept his sights on the same patch of water that was rapidly coming around to his prow.

∞§∞

Brooke could see the boat turning now and she made out the conning tower jutting out of the water and its lookouts on the main mast. She tried to fight it, but a small cry welled up inside her. As the relief flowed from her chest in heaves and tears that washed the salt from her eyes, she thanked God. In a minute, she was checking herself; she reached around her back, arching her torso as she attempted to smooth out the crumpled back of her blouse.

∞§∞

"Is that what I think it is?" Mush said adjusting the focus of his binocs.

"It's been a long time, but not that long skipper. That... is a woman! A well built woman..."

Mush commanded into the interphone, "I want a recovery team on the deck now. Blankets, and alert sickbay. We got a survivor coming aboard."

From the front hatch on the foredeck of the *Nebraska* four men emerged with grappling poles, heaving lines and stretchers. Each man clipped his lifeline to the receded buckles on the edge of the decking, least they be inadvertently in need of rescue due to a rogue wave or flailing subject.

Chief Boatswain Murray couldn't believe what he was seeing, a woman in a wet, white blouse, clutching to an overturned Zodiac in the middle of the Pacific. *You couldn't make this stuff up.*

The Captain had made his way down to the bow where Mr. Murray was hanging off the edge reaching down to the woman. The other men stood gaping. She was a stunner and she was coming onboard in a transparent manner. Mush quickly stepped forward and covered her with a blanket and got her down onto the stretcher. She coughed out a "thank you." Then the other men snapped out of it and all helped get her below and into sickbay.

Mush looked up at the bridge; he shrugged his shoulders to his exec, who returned the shrug, both thinking the same thing, *How do we put this one in the log book*? Then he ordered, "Weps below. Clear the deck. I don't like being exposed like this. Pull the cork, Hank!"

Executive Officer Henry 'Hank' Evans hit the dive alarm and barked over the wailing horn, "Lookouts below! Clear the bridge." He waited for Mush to get below and watched the forward hatch wheel to turn, indicating it was water tight sealed, then he lowered himself into the bridge hatch yelling, "Dive. Dive. Dive."

∞§∞

"We got her!" Joey Palumbo blurted out as he barged into Bill Hiccock's White House office.

"Oh thank God, where was she?"

"Floating on a raft in the South Pacific about 3 miles from the sinking."

"She okay?"

"She's banged up and bruised but she is alive and we should know more after she gets some rest."

"We got lucky on this one, Joe"

"She's not the best of the best for nothing, Hic," Joey said as he left to make arrangements for her to be ferried back from Midway on a SAM flight direct to Andrews.

Hiccock sat back, his broad shoulders finding the wings of his too comfortable desk chair and breathed a sigh of relief. This, his first "op," almost bit the dust. Joey was right, Brooke Burrell had distinguished herself many times in her illustrious FBI career. Many times for Bill or something Bill was involved in. Bill glanced down at two platinum 5-point stars most people wrongly assumed were paperweights. This woman, Burrell, was a star in her own right. That's why he agreed to this whole cockamamie "ops" idea when Joey came up with it. The whole affair started out as a miscue by the modern day descendants of the Barbary Coast Pirates who plagued shipping lanes two hundred years earlier. Their new strategy was to board unsuspecting ships and usually just rip off what ever they could take from the crew's personal belongings and wallets, or what ever else was on board that they could fence on the open market. Occasionally there was bloodshed or a kidnapping but that brought shit loads of hell down upon them, so they dialed down their attacks to a level just below the point where any international effort to stop them could muster a counter force.

That was until they inadvertently took on a Maltese Freighter trying to navigate the straights of Gibraltar and stumbled onto an illegal shipment of nuclear material from the Uzbekistan arsenal, which was being siphoned off by a former Russian General with deep connections to the Moscow black market. The existence of the boat itself was a violation of 7 U.N. statuettes and 2 maritime laws. The hapless pirates catapulted a straightforward matter of piracy on the high seas into an international incident. Billions of dollars worth of American and NATO warships burned millions of gallons of fuel just hanging around the freighter. The most powerful military force on earth held impotent by the political realities of doing what the U.S. Navy was first commissioned to do by Jefferson in 1801: namely, seek out and kill pirates. So the strongest armada in the world and its allies just lumbered 200 yards from the rusting, floating violation, while their well-trained SEAL teams were specifically prohibited from donning so much as a bait knife.

The "crisis" was eventually resolved when a Russian destroyer sank the ship after an alleged rocket grenade attack from the freighter. Although every intelligence service in the world knew it was sunk to bury the evidence that would prove that Russia couldn't control its nuclear material. There it would have ended, except for something that came across Hiccock's SciAD network. A "compound" member of the network was approached to see if the Saudi company he worked for was interested in obtaining barium crucibles.

It was a suspicious request, in that it was an early chunk of nuke technology, more consistent with the Russian method of creating a bomb, as opposed to the American or Chinese, Indian or Pakistani. So Hiccock got operational authority to run a mission to acquire these crucibles to determine if, in fact, they were from the freighter and therefore prove the freighter was compromised prior to its sinking. If it were, it could be a golden chit to play in the international game of poker that the U.S. and other powers were enmeshed in. But for Hiccock it was pure defensive science; *Stop those things from getting into the wrong hands.*

For the delicate role of point person in this shady deal, Joey Palumbo, the former FBI Special Agent, now assigned to Hiccock's White House Quarterback group, tapped another FBI agent. One who had distinguished herself in many tight spots as an effective operator and one who was beyond reproach as to her loyalty and discretion. Her command of Farsi didn't hurt either.

Two very careful and elaborate backgrounds were established for Brooke, one as a high up arms merchant, Fiona Haran, who was masquerading as her *second* identity, Roan Perth, an insurance investigator. Brooke had to memorize the details of both identities to cover her real mission of getting the crucibles for America to study while blocking the bad guys from getting their hands on them. The "intermediaries" she was meeting with played along with her insurance identity, feeling confident and gracious enough to let Fiona have her little deception as Ms. Perth that they thought, she thought, she was putting over on them.

It was all going well until the op center lost her trail last Wednesday in a Maltese coastal town. Only to pick up her beacon, in the western edge of the Indian Ocean, an hour before what ever happened, happened.

∞§∞

Brooke awoke in a bunk looking up at the distinctive architecture of the riveted bulkhead above her. The room she was in smelled of metal, oil and men. She was on a ship. She felt her cheek and found a bandage covering it and a bandage covering the hand she used to inspect it. She looked down and saw she was wearing a blue pajama set. "U.S.S. *Nebraska*" was stenciled across the pocket over her right breast. She remembered her knee and lifted the covers and instinctively went to bend it and found it hard to move because it was wrapped in a Velcro bandage. There was a gentle whirring sound that came from everywhere. "*Power plant*" she thought. She became aware of the sound of a click every few seconds. She followed a tube up from her other arm to an I.V., the drip controlled by a machine which ticked as it released what ever they were mixing in it and pumping into her.

She pressed the call button she found next to her hand. A few seconds later, a blonde haired young man in an Ensign's uniform entered; she saw the medical staff insignia on his collar and judged him to be a "California surfer dude" turned Ship's Doctor or at least Pharmacist Mate.

"Good evening. I'm Ensign Howell and I run the sick bay. Are you in any pain?"

"No. But I am thirsty. Got any water around here?"

"Sure thing." The ice banged around the inside of the Styrofoam pitcher as he filled a plastic cup and brought it under her chin. She tried to hold it herself...

"Better let me help till you get those 'boxing gloves' off."

She drank and some dribbled; she used her bandaged hand as a napkin and dabbed her chin.

"How long have I been out?"

"About twelve hours. You were in pretty bad shape when they hauled you in."

"I need to speak to the Captain. I must make my report."

"He'll be here in a second; when you rang for me, I rang for him."

On cue, Mush Morton walked into the compartment. He was a big fellow with a full red beard that flouted regulations and soft eyes that were anything but regulation. His nose was well defined as was his scruffy jaw line and he wore his skipper's hat back on his head revealing a tuft of red. His uniform was loosely fitting, and yet despite all these non-regulation features, he still had the immediate effect of electrifying the room with command voltage as he entered.

"Happy with the accommodations? This, believe it or not, is a stateroom on a sub. Held in reserve for visiting brass. You seem like a pretty important V.I.P. so I figure it was appropriate. Need anything?"

"I need to make my report."

"Report to who?"

"Captain, can you excuse your man and close the door?"

"Sure. Mr. Howell, give us the room."

The door shut and Mush pulled up a chair alongside the bed.

"I am on a mission, or was, for the President of the United States. I was blown off a ship as I was negotiating to get back some critical material that was stolen."

"That explains the rerouting of a nuclear submarine on deep, deterrent patrol. My orders are to take you to Midway so the hospital can get a crack at you and from there you'll jump a Special Air Missions ride to D.C.. We'll make Midway by nightfall tomorrow."

"Can I radio my report? You do have secure uplink on this boat, don't you?"

"Yes, we have all the factory installed options on this model, like cup holders, 24-multiple reentry, Trident D5, strategic missiles, heated seats..."

Brooke gave a confused look. Maybe she was still too groggy for Mush's brand of humor.

"Lady, this is an Ohio class, fleet ballistic missile submarine, a stealth operating, floating launch pad. I assure you, we've got all the bells and whistles."

"Sorry Captain, I was a little out of it when you came to my rescue."

"Ma'am, who are you?"

"I guess we missed that part. Brooke Burrell, Special Agent FBI, attached to the Quarterback Group at the White House."

"Means nothing to me. Is it some super secret Presidential operations cluster?"

"Something like that."

"How did you wind up in a Kodiac?"

"What's a Kodiac?"

"It's what we call the Russian Zodiac styled boat you were clinging to."

"Russian!" It was starting to come back together for Brooke, "Captain... this entire boat might be in danger."

"More than usual?"

"I was on a Somali tanker, negotiating with an intermediary to an arms merchant when the world exploded."

"Tankers sometime combust, especially if the crew is untrained in siphoning off built up gases that collect in holding tanks and…"

"I remember now, just before the attack, a crewman ran in all agitated about something in the water… oh, what was it?"

"Well, we got surface radar, sonar and a few other gizmos so sensitive that we will know if a whale bumps into a minnow. So we should be safe."

"Whale! That was it! He said a whale had come up to the hull and then something about a mine… a limpert mine?"

"Limpet mine?"

"Yes, that's it."

The Captain reached over to the interphone on the bulkhead. "Con, this is the Captain. Take her up! Fast. Emergency blow. I want to run the surface all the way to Midway. And double the lookouts."

"What are we looking for, sir?"

"Whales, Mr. Sarin, whales."

"Wow. That was quick," Brooke said as a Klaxon sounded three times and a voice came over the P.A. "Secure for emergency blow."

"Better hold on here. We're headed for the roof," Mush said as he gently placed Brooke's hand on the railing of her bunk. The boat took on a deep angle and there was the sudden stomach wrenching feeling of the first drop of the rollercoaster only in reverse. Seeing Brooke's concern and uneasiness, Mush spoke in regularly measured tones as if this gut wrenching rapid assent was commonplace. "You got me with the limpet mines."

"What?" Brooke said, nervously looking around at the almost vertical stateroom as some things slid and collected in the corners.

"Nasty devices that frogmen attach to the side of an enemy's vessel and sink them. I don't know what's going on, but we can't see biologicals with our equipment, just the cavitations they leave in the water when they get spooked by us. But if there is a killer whale out there, armed with limpet mines, our only chance to see them coming is from the surface. In fact..." He reached for the interphone again. "Mr. Sarin, raise Diego-Garcia. Tell them we are on a special op for COMSUBPAC and request they scramble a TACAMO for round the clock air cover starting immediately. Compose the message, I'll be up to authorize it in a minute."

"Yes sir."

He switched off the box and turned to her; it struck him how good looking she was, not the frail, dainty features of a model but the kind of pretty that endures and gets better as they get older. "You can really see whales better from the air."

"Captain, I have to tell you, I am a little surprised you have reacted so strongly to my wild story. I mean, it sounded crazy to me as I was telling it to you."

"I have 155 souls on this ship, Miss Burrell; you make 156. We are also the fourth largest Nuclear Power on Earth, all by our lonesome. And we cost about a thousand billion dollars when you add up all the special equipment and Trident D5 warheads. So let's just say, erring on the side of caution is better than making a trillion dollar hole in the water."

Brooke took all that in, a warm feeling of safety wrapped around her for the first time since she started on this mission, "Thank you for saving me."

"I was just looking for the son of a gun who shot at my boat."

Brooke was about to say something silly like, "*guilty*" or "*I didn't know it was loaded*" but a sharp pain from her leg froze her brain.

Sensing her sudden discomfort, he unconsciously placed his hand on hers. "You want me to have Howell give you a shot or something?"

"No, it subsided, I need to have my wits about me to write my report." She looked into his eyes and saw genuine concern there. It made her wonder if he was a dad. Owing to her grogginess, she was about to ask him if he had kids, but he spoke before she did.

"I have to get to the con; just let us know if you need anything." He left and closed the door behind him.

I did shoot at his boat. To Brooke he suddenly went from "dad" to a teenager with a new car, preening and caring for it, sympathetically hurting with every ding and scratch. *Boys and their toys,* she thought. The last thing she focused on was her freshly laundered bra, on a hanger, under the overhead, as she started to glide off into a light slumber. It didn't last long...